To ...
with ...

Paul 4/6/02

The Mitzu Affair

By

Paul Mayer

ISBN: 0-7596-6266-5

This book is printed on acid free paper.

1stBooks - rev. 03/08/02

DEDICATION

This story is dedicated to my father whose sense of duty and honour and sense of humour helped me to survive thirty-one years as a professional soldier and enjoy most of it. He warned me however that when I accepted the "King's Shilling," I would also have to accept certain discomforts and inconveniences that go with it. Among these is getting shot once in a while. How right he was.

AN INTRODUCTION

In the eighteenth century, Von Clausewitz stated that war is an extension of politics. He added that the military figure is, in fact, the enforcer of the political aim, or in plain words, that the simple sailor, soldier or airman is the tool of the politician.

Throughout the ages, political leaders have wooed their military men, but mainly to place them in a position where they can easily be sacrificed if the over-extended arm of national policy is caught short or cut off.

Official communication between public servants is never easy, for it is governed by a series of principles of which security and interoffice procedures are the most common and by far the most abused.

It seems curious that it does not occur, even to many highly tuned minds, that the actual meaning of a text may be twisted by the blind or stupid application of the rules.

An extract from one government manual dealing with abbreviations states that the purpose of using these is to save time and space. However, it reminds the user that they should only be used when their meaning is unmistakable. The manual warns that misinterpretation could cause havoc. How true that is.

A government's Security Act tells us that an official document that contains information which may be of use to an enemy must be classified as Top Secret or Secret or Confidential or Restricted according to its content.

It also adds that prefixes such as Presidential or Prime Ministerial may be added when the subject matter warrants it.

The Mitzu Affair is surely an example worthy of study. It is an event that proves beyond any doubt that, given the chance, especially under the mantle of high security, the computer-like efficiency of the military mind when it is blended with the craftiness of the diplomat and the all-too-often-demonstrated stupidity of the politician, can and often will, screw up any situation.

The result is usually the same. The matter is quickly closed, the files are plunged into the depth of the national archives under the highest possible security classification and everyone in any way connected with the fiasco is dispatched to new, and often more responsible positions at other embassies. There, in fresh and greener fields, they can usually be relied upon, sooner or later, to build up a brand new crisis and revel again in the resultant confusion.

The situations described in this unlikely story are, I must admit completely imaginary and all of the characters are quite fictitious.

They do not represent any particular person living or dead. Of course, readers may recognize in some of the characters the saints or devils they have known or read about. Indeed, in some of them they may see traces or, signs of the famous or perhaps the notorious, or even some of the obnoxious.

That, naturally, is none of my concern. As for the state of Paguda; it really does not exist.

Paul Mayer

PROLOGUE

The British Prime Minister's country house.

Some twenty years after the Mitzu Affair.

It was one of those really lovely autumn evenings. Normally when she looked out of the study window at Chequers with its view of the manicured gardens and the broad field beyond, the Prime Minister experienced a feeling of contentment, that all was well with the realm and that all her problems would somehow be solved — but not so on this occasion!

She stood there gently tapping her glasses on the palm of her hand, her brow furrowed in deep thought. She turned to face Robert Ruall, her foreign secretary.

"Robert, this Mitzu business is an awful mess. How long ago did it take place?"

"Oh, I'm not quite sure, Prime Minister, about twenty years, maybe less."

The prime minister shook her head as she took her seat opposite him. "Goodness," she said, "not even during our party's administration. What kind of idiots did we have in Whitehall then? Who else knows about this, Robert?"

"No one else, Madame, the letter came directly from the Pagudan Embassy in Washington. They didn't route it through our embassy there. Even their embassy here is out of the picture."

"Are we going to have a problem Robert?"

"Hopefully not. As soon as the letter arrived, I contacted both embassies and asked them to do nothing until they heard from us."

"Excellent, Robert. As far as I can recall, the code name for this fiasco was Operation Feline. Now these damn fools want to reward us for our part in it. I can't understand this. Do you know how and why this operation took place?"

"I'll tell you what I know." Ruall paused as if searching for words. "It appears that some idiot of a staff officer at the Pentagon sent a truncated message about the island of Mitzu to one of their other bases in the Pacific. It contained a reference to RATS, the recognized abbreviation for rations in military lingo. A copy of the message was, as a matter of routine, copied to the Pagudan Embassy in Washington. Alas, the poor Pagudans, in their innocence, misinterpreted the terse message as a message of doom. Panic ensued and soon spread to the American Embassy in the Pagudan capital when they received a formal request for assistance in ridding Mitzu of its plague of rats. One thing led to another and there you have it!"

The prime minister chuckled. "Now I see it. The Americans couldn't get directly involved in a rescue mission because the Russians were bound to find out about their secret Mitzu base which they leased from the Pagudans. That's where we came into the picture!"

"You're right! Because there was so much tension at the time between the two super powers, Washington asked us to shoulder the job of killing the rats and cleaning up the island. No sooner had we agreed than we discovered we were to do the job with a horde of cats provided from American sources. The obvious misunderstandings were further complicated by the fact that Operation Feline was given a Presidential Top Secret classification, once that was done, no one could talk to anyone about it! What a farce!"

"My lord, Robert, if the truth about Mitzu came out we could be the laughing stock of the free world and you can imagine what a stink it would make in the States."

She stood up and began to walk about the room. "Are the files on the way up from the archives?" she asked.

"They should be here shortly."

The prime minister stopped as if a new idea had struck her. "You know, Robert, these Pagudans are well aware that any revival of the Mitzu affair will embarrass us."

"We are in a ticklish situation, Madame."

"I'll say! They are offering us six awards of the Most Exalted Order of the Golden Elephant to be given to the saviour of Mitzu, when they know perfectly well we don't want the Mitzu affair ever to be brought to light. Nor would the Americans care for publicity. I will get in touch with the president later to agree on a similar approach by both governments. No one would want this issue to be raised either in parliament or in congress. What the Americans did to hide their operational expenditures I'll never know. We had to cut aid to Paguda again to cover our overall deficiency."

The prime minister resettled herself in the deep chair facing the couch and began making notes.

"Doesn't it seem a trifle comical, Robert, that these self-styled democracies can put the bite on us, let alone the United States?"

"It does make one wonder," said Ruall.

"It certainly does and what's more I think it's about time..." She stopped as the door opened to admit an elderly secretary carrying two heavy bright red folders, each tied with a green cord. On the cover were the words *Mitzu*, followed by *Top Secret* and the initials, *PM.*

"Thank you Lily," said the prime minister with a smile as the secretary placed them on the table between them.

After the secretary's departure, Ruall eased himself forward on the couch and picked up a folder. He gave a low whistle, "My God, this is a PMTS!"

"Yes, Robert, and there is no way we can have it down-graded. This matter must stay closed."

"You mean we—?"

"Yes," she said, "I'm going to select six of our senior officials or people in the armed forces to receive the awards.

You'll be one of them. Then we'll give Paguda enough aid to shut them up."

Next morning at the Foreign Office, the defense minister and the minister of agriculture were waiting in Ruall's office. On arrival in the high-ceilinged, austerely furnished, paneled room, they had expected that Ruall's executive assistant would give them some inkling of the reason for this urgent summons. That keen young man, however, offered no explanation.

"Any idea what this is all about?" asked the defense minister.

"Not the slightest," replied his colleague. "I just hope to God no one has found some more bloody missiles on some other island."

"No, it can't be anything like that." George Barker shook his head. "I would have heard some rumour."

The agriculture minister was searching his mind for a clue. "I wonder if this is another one of these special aid programs. We seem to be helping everyone these days."

Aston Williams and George Barker were newcomers to the administration and indeed to public life. Before his election, Williams had spent many years as a professor of political science in a provincial university. Barker, on the other hand, had been an industrialist. Williams was in his early fifties, a tall, thin, bespectacled figure with a mop of curly hair. His trademark was a complete dedication to avoiding commitment in all forms of international palaver. He was a good diplomat.

In contrast, Barker was somewhat older, quite short, roundish and usually jovial. He was in every respect a self-made man whose directness in his daily dealings with the military services kept ambitious officers well in line.

Suddenly, Barker had an idea. "Do you suppose the Indians are in another mess with the Chinese in the Himalayas?" Williams looked aghast. "Surely it can't be that!" As he shuddered at the thought, the great oak door swung open and the foreign secretary entered. As if by agreed signal, both men rose to greet him.

Robert Ruall was an impressive man of precise military bearing. Prior to his entry into politics, while still in his early forties, he had been a most successful international banker. Now he was the prime minister's right-hand man, a position for which he was admirably suited. He was a man of hard and fast decisions. Ruall had few, if any, interests outside his job. It was he who had recommended Williams and Barker for their cabinet posts. He strode briskly to his desk and in his usual easy manner, waved the other men back to their seats.

"Sorry to have kept you waiting, but the prime minister would make no decision until we had all the facts straight." Ruall placed his weighty briefcase on the desk and sat down.

"Well now," he said. "This matter is related to a prime ministerial top secret event that occurred about twenty years ago."

"Twenty years ago?" exclaimed Barker. "But we…"

"Yes, exactly. In other words, this happened during another administration. But the prime minister and I spent some time studying the case and agreed we could not ignore the latest developments. By the way, is either of you acquainted with Operation Feline? Aston, are you?" Ruall glanced at the agricultural minister.

Williams thought for a moment, then shook his head. "Feline? No, I'm not. Maybe George is."

The defense minister hesitated. "Feline? Feline." He repeated, searching for a clue. Then he shook his bald head. "No, not me, never heard of it. Good God, what's it all about?"

"Well, I'm not surprised," said Ruall. "I'd better fill you in. Operation Feline, gentlemen, was an act of mercy that we carried out as a favour to our American friends. It cost this country plenty; and because it was given the highest possible security classification, not one word of it ever reached Parliament, the press or the public. What's more, it was a complete fiasco. Needless to say, our aid to Paguda, the country involved, was cut heavily. Personnel in any way connected with the affair were either sacked, moved around or dispersed, and every written evidence was placed in a PMTS file and buried in the archives. And there it stayed until yesterday when exhumed by the P.M.'s order."

"In the years since Feline ended, the Pagudan government has changed several times and aid to that country has been, well, I'd say, of a restricted nature. There have been several Pagudans requests but we've been able to let them linger. But now, I'm afraid, we have a new situation."

At this point Ruall stood up, unlocked his bulky briefcase and pulled out the two red files, each marked with the forbidding black letters PYMS and securely tied with green cord. He handed one to each of his bewildered colleagues. Then he sat down, leaned back in his chair and folded his arms.

"Operation Feline, gentlemen. It's all in there," he said with a slight smile." I want you to look through these files so that you will both be better acquainted with the act of benevolence which is going to earn each of you, and me too, and the three senior offices of the armed forces, the Most Exalted Order of the Golden Elephants of Paguda!"

"You're not serious?" said Williams.

"I wish I weren't," Ruall said bluntly. "No, I can assure you that I'm deadly serious."

Barker looked at the folder on his lap and shook his head. He mumbled several unprintable words.

"I know exactly what you are thinking, George." Ruall tried to sound sympathetic. "All I can say for now is that after you have read these files, you will see that, if only for reasons of national prestige, ours and that of our allies, the PMTS classification cannot be changed and the matter cannot be made public. You will also understand why great care must be taken to avoid leaks. Although the event took place under another government, the whole nation will be seen as prize idiots if the story ever gets out. Neither we, nor the opposition will be looking for publicity. In any case, there it is. Study it well. I have a meeting with the home secretary and I'll be back in about three hours."

The two ministers made no comment as the foreign secretary made his way to the door. It was some seconds before either of them spoke. As Ruall was about to close the door behind him, he heard Aston Williams' voice. Waited. "You know, George," Williams remarked, as the file fell open on his lap, "I have the damnedest feeling as if—as if—…"

"So have I, Aston," replied his friend. "So have I!"

Ruall smiled as he shut the door very gently behind him.

The prime minister, meanwhile had been giving the matter some thought. Perhaps it would be only fair to check with the Americans at this juncture.

Her attempts to reach the president bore no fruit. He was out jogging!

She did, however, get through to the secretary of state on the secure line.

"Mr. Secretary, sorry to bother you."

"That's quite alright, Prime Minister. What can I do for you?"

"It's this latest thing about Mitzu."

"Mitzu?" The American sounded surprised. "Did you say Mitzu?"

"Yes, Mitzu," she replied.

"I'm sorry, Prime Minister, you have me at a disadvantage. I don't know anyone or anything by that name."

"You don't?"

"No, I don't."

"But your president, surely he…"

"I'm quite sure the president, Madame, is of the same mind."

"Oh, I see."

"Anything else, Prime Minister?"

"No, thank you, no."

"I'm sorry that I can't help you, Prime Minister."

"That's alright, Mr. Secretary, but I must say I'm surprised that you haven't been briefed on the latest developments in the Mitzu affair. After all, your people initiated the whole mess. We merely became involved as a favour to your president. I suggest, Mr. Secretary that you check around. Operation Feline may cause us some embarrassment—and I do mean embarrassment. Your president should be made aware of this, believe me!"

The American was contemplating whether he should ask the prime minister to be more explicit when he heard the phone being slammed at the other end of the line.

"Damn that woman!" He looked at his senior aide. "Christ, that god damn female hung up on me. She can't do that to me!"

LATER OPINIONS

THE FIRST. After the Mitzu episode ended, a senior State Department official made this rather offensive remark. "Mitzu was an exercise in futility, totally bungled by the Limeys. Sad really, but ever since they lost their empire, they seem to have lost their touch for delicate diplomacy."

THE SECOND. Alas, someone in the Foggy Bottom palace leaked these remarks to the Foreign Office. The British response was as forthright as might be expected. "Mitzu!" Exclaims Sir Algernon Foggo-Finch. "Oh, yes. Some little island base in the Pacific they wanted to keep secret. The place was overrun with, ah...rats, or was it cats, or something provided by them. All very odd. Anyway, the Yanks should get full marks for that one. They really buggered it up. Too bad actually—normally they manage most situations quite well."

THE LAST. Perhaps the most interesting comment came from a former Pagudan official. At the mention of Mitzu, he chuckled and said "Of course. Our little island full of rats and all those lovely cats provided by our wonderful American friends! Thinking of the people involved, one is reminded of the early explorers. They were so adventurous, so ready to go anywhere. Yet most of the time, they never knew where they were going. When they got there they didn't know where they were or why. Finally, when they returned home, they could not explain where they had been or what they had accomplished. But you can't deny this—they were always ready for the next adventure!"

CHAPTER I

HOW IT ALL HAPPENED

Like most situations that throw the reasonably well-oiled machinery of government, diplomacy or management into a state of pandemonium, the events related to Mitzu resulted mainly from the super-initiative of a few highly trained idiots. But, no doubt about it, they did receive some assistance from others, less highly trained.

The whole affair started innocently enough. It all began in the bar of the Officers' Club at Bulabar Air Base where one of the regional United States Air Force headquarters in the Far East was located.

It was a Saturday night in late October and most of the usual traders in strong spirits, dining, and dancing had long since retired. Four of the older and more serious regulars, however, had entrenched themselves at one end of the long, highly polished counter where, over the hours and behind a steady array of filled glasses, their words became more garbled, eyes more glazed, and on occasion, their ideas and expressions wilder and cruder—much cruder, in fact, and much wilder than might be expected of gentlemen or senior officers of this type. In short, since tomorrow was the day of rest, Major General Walter Bellows, the base commander, and his three closest subordinates, all keen yes-men of the highest caliber, were slowly getting plastered.

For the past four hours, Max, the bar steward, had been surveying the scene warily. He was accustomed to this. But tonight there was something quite different about the atmosphere.

For one thing, the general was not his usual abusive self. The mean, sly look that Bellows usually wore, and which forecast danger to all who crossed or even approached his path, was not there. Instead, he looked weary and had that "to-hell-with-it-all" appearance. The bar steward decided something was wrong. The atmosphere was too tense, possibly even dangerous: it bore watching closely.

Even the conversation lacked interest. This bothered the bar steward. On other such occasions Max's quick ears were able to pick up all sorts of odd points of gossip about people at the base and quite often even a few new dirty stories. But not tonight. The general merely sat there and glared and drank. And drank. Occasionally, he would make some meaningless remark, in reply to which one or all of the other three would add some note of general agreement, such as "You're absolutely right, General," "You bet, General," or "Check, Skipper." The situation, Max decided, was not good.

For the past year, the bar steward had wondered at the harmony among these four men in particular, at their capacity for extraordinary late hours and strong drink, and at the obvious patience and kind dispositions of their respective wives, whom he rarely saw with their husbands—at the club, anyway. Max tried to recall just how long it had been since Mrs. Bellows had visited the club, but the general's loud, twangy voice broke into his meditation like a foghorn in the night.

"You know what I need?" said the general slowly, and with the slight slur of words normally associated with one who has had a bit too much. "I need a goddamn good week's leave in Hong Kong. That's what I need."

"Yes, sir, General, you sure do." agreed the bald officer on his right, then repeated, "You sure do."

"Yes, sir, I reckon I'll go for a week's holiday," continued the General, pointing his finger at the bald man, "and leave you bastards right here. That's what I'll do—let you see if you can run this goddamn place."

"Just say the word, General, and we'll fix it," put in Colonel Dixie Mason, his chief of staff.

General Bellows fixed Mason with a glassy stare and allowed his tongue to wander around his lips as if searching for crumbs after a meal. "Remember, Dixie, the last time we were there, eh? You remember, eh, you goddamn old cotton-picker?" The general burped loudly.

Colonel Dixie Mason said he did remember, and that started a series of sordid accounts of what had taken place during the general's and Dixie's last spot of rest and rehabilitation in Hong Kong. The session lasted until nearly four a.m., when the first light of dawn broke into the club barroom from the eastern sky. Max had heard most of these stories before, but the recounts always improved slightly each time in telling.

Later that morning Colonel Dixie Mason who, besides being chief of staff, was also the Bulabar Base senior operations officer, sent a short memo to his Flight Plans Section. They were to set in motion an exercise to carry out a test flight in which the base commander would participate personally. The Flight Plans Section logged it, gave it a number—Test Flight 255—and for good measure placed a security classification of top secret on it.

Test Flight 255, Colonel Mason decided, would carry Major General Bellows and a small select entourage from the Bulabar Air Base eastward over that delightful area recognized throughout the world as the neutral State of Paguda, up across the South China Sea, over the Philippines, to Hong Kong. There, in the lap of oriental and extravagant luxury known as the Peninsula Hotel, the general, accompanied by his aide, Captain Townes, who also happened to be the best of procurers, and a few other cronies would linger for six days of ecstasy. Everyone would have a wonderful time: each would do his Christmas shopping and be able, on his return, to pacify his indignant and thoroughly bored spouse with gifts and oriental adornments. Under normal circumstances it would have been a good idea.

But, as in all ventures, especially those carried out under the top secret heading and that involve long international journeys and the expenditure of government funds, one had to be extremely careful. The eyes and ears of the Treasury officials both at home and abroad were always quite sensitive. A jaunt of this sort would, if it were to escape adverse comment from the fiscal inspectors later, have to be planned with all the care to detail as though history itself depended upon it. The efficient Plans Section lost no time. It set its shoulder to the wheel, and by the following evening, Test Flight 255 had begun to take shape.

These things have always taken a considerable amount of coordination. Even to this day, the Air Force headquarters at the Pentagon takes a vital interest in the comings and goings of its detachments abroad and must always be consulted on a number of points. In this particular case, because it was to be a lengthy journey, a check had to be made of emergency landing fields en route, where the aircraft could take refuge in case of trouble and replenish its fuel and other supplies if the need arose.

An outline of the flight plan was therefore signaled to the Pentagon indicating all the usual items, such as time of departure and return, and the routes, planned altitudes, numbers and names of crew, type of in-flight tests to be made, and a list of the emergency landing fields along the flight path that the aircraft could contact if it ran into difficulties, such as severe storms.

The facts related to the request were thus presented, and only two things were demanded of the headquarters in return. First, final authority for the journey and, second a confirmation that the emergency landing grounds mentioned in the flight plan were, in fact, usable and that plenty of fuel and supplies were available at each place.

The answer to the first question was actually a foregone conclusion. General Bellows had signed the requisition himself. The go-ahead signal on the emergency landing ground and refueling and resupply stops, however, was quite another matter—one over which only one person had any control. That person was a newly promoted Air Force major named Horatio Bixon, and he occupied one of those unique positions at headquarters where he could make any one of the four—but only four—decisions clearly defined in his terms of reference without referring to anyone above him. He was what is known in security-conscious circles as a "special projects officer." Horatio Bixon was a hard-working officer. He was also a bit stupid.

At the Pentagon, Bixon was at the time the only officer in what was labeled the Special Locations Section. As such, he was in sole charge of a small, damp room in the basement. The door to this room had double locks; the filing cabinets therein had double locks, and so had the huge map case that covered one wall. It was these maps that showed the locations of all emergency airfields and emergency stores in every corner of the world—outside the Communist Bloc, that is. Bixon took great pride in keeping his oversized maps marked with military symbols that the staff college had impressed on his brain.

Horatio was a reasonably well-mannered young man, with all the usual good qualifications. His family had sent him to a fine military school, and from there he had followed on to the Air Force Academy. Finally, and quite lately, he had emerged from an institution of advanced military study the armed forces termed as the Staff College. It was on graduation that his instructors labeled him, to his father's bursting pride and to Horatio's everlasting doom, as "a serious, industrious officer with a good, sound knowledge of staff procedures, and plodding persistence for meticulous detail in his paperwork." It was not surprising, therefore, that eventually Major Bixon should find himself assigned to the highest headquarters in the land, where it was hoped his seriousness and industry and his knowledge of staff procedures would prove of value, but not bother anyone else too much.

Thus, the young major was plunged into the abysmal depths of an organization where the well-founded principles of clarity, brevity, judgment and decision are supposedly engraved on the heart of every incumbent. Inspired to receive promotion, Horatio let these words rest hopefully within him. Who could tell? He might someday be able to influence the course of history. All Horatio Bixon really needed was the spur to summon the initiative, to plod and to persist.

On a dull morning that heralded November, the official form of Test Flight 255's flight plan reached Bixon's desk. That was when the spur struck.

Bixon quickly observed that the flight plan had been processed through the proper Air Force authorities for clearance, as normally was required in such cases. Naturally, everyone in the Air Force sections through which it passed had placed on it a variety of stamps and signatures that indicated wholesale approval of the venture, despite its obvious aim. But all this was not quite enough; the Special Locations Section still had to signal clearance to Bulabar on the use of the emergency landing areas along the proposed route. Bixon was merely faced with a simple question to which he was asked to provide a simple answer. All the flight planners of the Far East Air Headquarters wanted to know was whether all emergency landing grounds between Bulabar and Hong Kong were in safe, usable condition and stocked with fuel and supplies. No more, no less. All Bixon had to do was to answer yes or no.

The positive approach, however, was not this rosy-faced young man's natural way of handling matters.

Having unlocked the map cabinet, Horatio checked his maps. Then he checked his records according to each location listed in the Far Eastern test flight plan. He confirmed that each of the landing grounds mentioned, together with their caches of emergency fuel and stores, was in a state of readiness. But, suddenly he noted a grave omission—no mention had been made by the flight planners of one particular place. Their list did not include the airstrip on the island of Mitzu. Horatio's reply therefore was presented in a manner he felt reflected the efficient staff officer at his best: serious, industrious, well-trained. His answer was indeed brief, but instead of stating that all locations mentioned were ready, including Mitzu, he wrote the following message:

TOPSEC. RE YOUR 255 PLAN.
WHY MITZU NOT INCLUDED YOUR FLIGHT PLAN?

That, thought he, would make those flyboys realize they had missed a vital point and that the all-seeing eye of headquarters had picked it up. As he signed the message, the thought did occur to Bixon that he might have sent back a message stating that all emergency landing areas were clear, well stocked with fuel and supplies, including Mitzu. Such a course of action would certainly have settled the matter once and for all. But Horatio was a well-trained individual. He prided himself on his knowledge of staff procedures. One thing at a time, only one, no more.

Some four hours later at Bulabar Air Base, the navigator of Test Flight 255 received Bixon's top secret reply. He scratched his head as he read Bixon's message. Of course, now he remembered Mitzu. He crossed the room to the large map where his eye took in the long stretch of sea between Paguda and the Philippines. In a few seconds he saw it, an almost invisible speck on the huge, colored chart. He circled it with a black grease pencil, then returned to his desk where he made out another message—this time directly to the Special Locations Section, demanding information about the facilities on Mitzu. The message read:

FROM AIR BULABAR
TO SPECLOC SEC
TOP SECRET
REGRET OMISSION MITZU — REQUEST STATUS
ALL FACILITIES MITZU

The navigator signed the message, stamped the words SECURE-CODE on it, placed it in his out-basket and rang for his clerk.

The clerk, Corporal Lewis, answered the summons with his usual speed and cheery attitude.

"Hi sir, I'll take the Mitzu message if it's ready."

"It's there in the basket," replied the captain. "By the way, what's the name of that idiot who runs the Special Locations at headquarters?"

"Bixon, Captain, he's not a flyer. You know he's just a PPP, you know sir, a Pentagon paper pusher."

"Wonder why the hell he didn't just tell us the Mitzu situation was clear, instead of sending this stupid message."

"I guess he must be a staff officer, sir."

"Yeah, I guess that accounts for it. Once they graduate from that staff school, they go nuts for procedures."

Corporal Lewis picked up the message and left.

CHAPTER II

Mitzu is an island; it is very small—a minute piece of almost barren land about one and a half miles long, and a quarter that distance in width. It has belonged to the ancient Far Eastern State of Paguda since time immemorial, and it lies basking in almost never-ending sunshine some four hundred miles off the Pagudan mainland to the east. To some people its value might seem doubtful. Yet, it does have one: it lies in direct line from Paguda to the Philippines, and it has a single long plateau that serves admirably as an emergency airfield. During the war, the Japanese held it, and clear evidence of their tenure still exists among the population.

Shortly after the war, when clouds of conflict again began to gather over a tired world, the United States government decided to establish a number of special locations that could be used as emergency landing areas and resupply points, as well as weather stations. Thus, Mitzu was leased from the Pagudans in return for a massive aid program. Mitzu's actual existence therefore was then classified as top secret-plus. It was never to be discussed, except between a very few most senior Pagudans and American officials, and was never to be mentioned on paper or in radio traffic except in an emergency.

The inhabitants of Mitzu consisted of some four hundred souls of rather mixed ancestry whose main aim in life appeared to be the avoidance of any sort of labor other than copulation, fishing and pearl diving, and they were a happy group. They did very little, thought very little, and cared much less. It is doubtful if anyone, even the United States, the U.N. or any of the international banks could have ever encouraged them in any other direction.

The Pagudan government sent out a ship loaded with purchasable supplies twice a year to coincide with the date of the meager payment the Defense department made the natives for whatever work they may have done on the airfield, and of course, to collect taxes—usually in the form of select pearls that the natives harvested in remarkable quantity from the shallow, clear lagoon on the north side of the island. The actual amount of money the American government paid the natives was not large; and, because of the timely arrival of the Pagudan government ships with supplies of colored cloth, shiny pots and pans, cheap toys and other attractive items (and, of course, the tax collectors), the token coinage was never very long in the natives' hands.

The emergency strip maintained on Mitzu was one of a chain of such secret installations throughout the southeast Pacific. The military establishment on Mitzu consisted of four noncommissioned Signal Corps personnel who rotated every two years. They kept the island's children well supplied with gum and candy and employed anyone who was willing to put in a few hours' work on the airstrip surface.

From the metal Quonset hut that rested on the slight rise at the eastern end of the island's plateau and in which the four Signal Corps men worked and lived, the signalers checked and reported the local weather in code to a weather ship some four hundred and fifty miles away. They did this twice a day but remained ready to answer any calls for help from the aircraft in need of an emergency landing area, provided, of course, that the aircraft knew the proper code word. The weather station on Mitzu was under strict instructions not to communicate with the outside world unless it was a matter of life and death.

There was, however, one regular contact. Every three months a lone aircraft came in, off loaded boxes of supplies and mail, picked up all the outdated supplies, outgoing mail and any requests for special supplies and then departed. It was rarely on the ground for more than two hours, and the only person the crew ever saw was Staff Sergeant Morton. Such was the security surrounding Mitzu.

Even Bulabar Air Base, some four hundred miles away, did not exchange traffic with Mitzu. The Bulabar Base sent out coded information twice a day that the Mitzu signalers merely listened to and logged. Naturally Bulabar did send in the one plane every three months with supplies, food and fuel for the Signal Corps generators, but that was the only contact the signalers had with the outside world. To the world in general and especially to any potential enemies of the U.S.A., Mitzu did not exist.

The four Signal Corps men took turns at housekeeping and, of course, watching the natives when the latter could be induced to rake or roll the airstrip and keep the place generally tidy. The signalmen also provided, by their presence alone, a guard of sorts for the foliage-covered cement mound near the shack, which all and sundry referred to as the Hush-hush.

The Hush-hush lay in a wire-enclosed area about one hundred yards square. It was an old Japanese pillbox complete with weapon slits and a heavy steel door. A security fence of rusty barbed wire surrounded it, and to this day the fence is still adorned with faded signs in English and Pagudan that state the property belongs to the Defense Department. The words *restricted and danger* are quite prominent on each sign and, curiously enough, are still respected by the population. The place still is, as it has been for the past thirty-odd years, the airstrip's storage vault for emergency supplies.

The actual contents of the Hush-hush were known only to the Senior Signal Corps man at the station. Four times a year, coinciding with the visit of the supply plane, Staff Sergeant Morton unlocked the steel door and disappeared inside. It was up to him to determine the state and the date of each of the sealed boxes of supplies and emergency rations. He then filled out and signed form E55016-2, placed it on the clipboard attached to the door and retained the copy for headquarters, together with a list of replacement supplies. He removed all the outdated or damaged boxes, stacked them outside, and locked the door.

The next contact flight took the report and the outdated boxes away, and eventually these were replaced by the next incoming shipment. Every three months, Morton received the special code word and repeated the process. Needless to say, the only person who could send out that special code word was Horatio Bixon.

When the latest message from the navigator of Test Flight 255 arrived with the inquiry about Mitzu, Horatio Bixon was preoccupied with what is commonly called a skin book. He acknowledged the deposit of the message in his in basket by his clerk with merely the raising of one eyebrow and a sly smile. It was almost quitting time, and he never did feel overly energetic at this period of the day. His better instinct, however, told him he should at least look at it. He reached for the message, and as he read it, a tremendous feeling of satisfaction swept over him. So, the flyboys at Bulabar had realized their mistake. Well, that should teach those sloppy guys a lesson. Bixon switched on his intercom set and buzzed the outer office, where his clerk Dooley sat looking through another skin book, the one Major Bixon had discarded last week.

"Dooley?" Horatio leaned toward the squawk box on his desk.

"Sir?" Dooley, his only clerk, sounded far away, as usual, and somewhat disinterested.

"Dooley, prepare a wire for me direct to Far East Air Force at Bulabar in reply to this one-er-number 4711."

"Yes, Major."

"Tell them Mitzu is okay for all conditions, and don't forget the classification. It's top secret."

"Right away, Major, sir."

Bixon switched off and returned his gaze to the luscious curves on the centerfold page of his magazine. He whistled quietly. Boy, wouldn't that be something if his wife Heidi looked like that. The thought almost made his knees buckle.

Some ten minutes later, Horatio put down his book, took his feet off the desk and stood up to stretch his somewhat chubby frame. He then slid aside the grilled opening in the wall between the two offices and inserted his hand. When he withdrew it, holding the slip of pink message paper, he walked to his wall map and held the message up to study it. He read it aloud slowly.

> CONCERNS MITZU STOP AIRSTRIP OK STOP ASSISTANCE APPROXIMATELY TWO HUNDRED NATIVES AND FOUR SIGNAL CORPS WEATHERMEN STOP RATIONS PLENTIFUL STOP.

Bixon returned to his desk and again switched on the squawk box.

"Dooley," he yelled angrily.

"Yes, sir?" Dooley sounded cagey this time.

"Dooley, for Pete's sake, how many times over do I have to tell you about the way to write a message for overseas units. Dooley, damn it, are you there?"

"Yes, sir, I'm here, Major."

"Now, look—no, better still, damn it, come in here." The major cursed his clerk silently, then muttered, "These slow-witted civil servants—why does one have to put up with them."

Dooley was a tall, thin, pale-faced youth with a tiny hairline mustache he stroked, brushed and otherwise groomed incessantly. He gave one the appearance of a tidy and efficient floorwalker at Woolworth's, one in constant need of a quart of blood. His hands twitched and his face bore the lingering smirk of the young civil servant who knows he cannot be fired no matter how incompetent he is. There was little love—or, for that matter, respect—between the youth and the major who greeted him with a superior, icy stare.

"Oh, there you are, Dooley. Now, look here, messages that are going to important headquarters overseas must be kept short. How often must I impress that on you? We must maintain a high standard of staff procedures. You know that, dammit."

"Yes, sir. I'm sorry, sir."

"Okay, now, I'm going to rewrite this one properly, but I want you to note the way these messages should be written.

They must be kept short, sharp, definite, to the point. Understand?"

"Yes, Major."

"Now, don't forget it again. Accuracy, brevity and clarity are the keynotes. Understand? And do not use the full word when there is a proper abbreviation for it. For instance, you know very well that the word rations has a definite authorized abbreviation, which is rat. Now, don't you? Man, let's be professional about all this."

"Yes, sir."

"And why use the word *assistant*—ten letters-when you have the world *help*—only four letters. Do you see? And *weathermen*—why not *met*-men? Good Lord, man what's wrong with you?"

Dooley made no retort as he disappeared into his own office.

It took Bixon another fifteen minutes to produce the final message. Then he stood up, burped loudly, circled the desk twice as he read it, and finally pressed the buzzer again to summon his clerk's attention.

"Sir?" Dooley's voice sounded nervous this time.

"Listen to this, Dooley, carefully. Dooley, are you listening?"

"Yes, Major."

Bixon cleared his throat and read: "Concerns Mitzu stop strip and pol OK stop rats abound stop help natives and met-men stop."

There was a marked silence during which Bixon stared at the squawk box as if waiting for some comment from his subordinate.

"Did you hear that, Dooley?" he asked testily.

"Yes, Major. I heard it. I sure did."

"Do you realize that I have cut out eighteen syllables?"

"Yes, Major."

"And do you realize that in doing so I have saved over twenty-five percent of the coding and decoding time?"

"Yes, sir, but don't you think."

"No buts, Dooley. Accuracy, brevity, clarity. Just remember those three. And don't forget, when we do have authorized abbreviations, we must use them. Understand? Now, get it out fast."

"Yes, Major, I'll do that, right away.

Bixon crossed the room, opened the message window and pushed the paper through the opening. He then returned to his desk, sat down, and picked up the telephone to call his wife Heidi. He was, as usual, hungry and wanted to find out what they were having for dinner. He hoped it might be goulash or spaghetti and meatballs.

Whatever other shortcomings Archie Dooley, the clerk in the outer office may have had, complete lack of common sense was not one of them. He also had a certain youthful vision. And while perhaps some of his hopes and ambitions were well beyond his capabilities, nevertheless, they were there.

Dooley studied the message for a moment, and it occurred to him that somehow the tone of it did not exactly sound right. Anyway he retyped it on the proper pink form, stamped it top secret and took it in for his major's signature. As he laid it on the latter's desk, he ventured to speak.

"Major, sir."

"Yes, what is it now, Dooley?"

"It's about this message, sir."

"This message, Dooley? What about it? I suppose you figure there's something wrong with it?"

"Well, yes, sir. It doesn't sound quite right."

"Look here, young fellow," snapped Bixon, "what the devil do you mean? That message is a perfectly straightforward message. It gives all the essential elements of information required." Bixon signed it with a flourish.

"Yes, major."

"Here, take it and see that it gets away—now."

"Okay, if you say so," Dooley said quietly as he picked up the message and retreated to his own room.

But, something was wrong, and it bothered him. He reached for a reference manual. There it was, just as he thought: Mitzu belonged to Paguda. He pressed the buzzer to get his superior's attention.

"Well, what is it now, Dooley?" The major's voice indicated both annoyance and sarcasm. "I suppose there's something else wrong with that message?"

"Sorry, Major, but I think there is one other point about the message—"

"Haven't you sent the damn thing off yet?"

"Mitzu, sir, belongs to Paguda, sir."

"So, it belongs to Paguda. So what?"

"Well, sir."

"Yes, yes, of course it belongs to Paguda. Do you think I'm stupid? But, what about it? It's top secret, isn't it?"

"I know that, sir, but shouldn't we send a copy of this message to the State Department? What I mean is, sir, the regulations say that any message concerning a foreign country should be referred to."

Bixon was getting madder, but he tried to calm himself. "Yes, yes, of course we must. Very good thing you remembered. Thanks." Smart bastard, he thought as he switched off the intercom system.

The clerk typed an additional copy of the message for the State Department, classified it, placed it in a double envelope and sealed it and put it beside the original addressed to Bulabar. After all, even with the smallest of foreign islands, one could not ignore the demands of protocol.

CHAPTER III

On the following morning, a Saturday, the event that had been set in motion first by the contemplated test flight from Bulabar, then by a reference to an insignificant speck in the Southwest Pacific Ocean, progressed one step further toward the possibility of unpredictable crisis. The extra copy of Bixon's message to the Far East Air Force found its way to the State Department.

It arrived on the Southeast Asia Section desk by the hand of a special messenger from the Pentagon. There it was duly logged, stamped and signed for by a youthful, bespectacled product of Harvard—and other select exclusive places of learning on the eastern shores—who reposed somewhat uncomfortably behind a small desk sign that read "DUTY OFFICER".

Mr. Claude Osser Bruck III was only twenty-four. He hailed from Boston, and he had just completed his second month as a foreign service officer at the lowest starting grade. He was a thin, terribly serious young man who was dedicated to his chosen career only because his mother had always told him his father would have probably become an ambassador had he not been thrown from a spirited horse during one of his foreign tours. Mrs. Bruck, of course, never mentioned the fact that her dear husband had been completely plastered at the time. However, she had spared no opportunity to advance her son's cause, even to a point of having recently deposited herself in his small apartment in Washington where she could, as she said to him repeatedly, insure he got the proper food, met all the right people—and did not get married. She spared no pains to point out to Claude whenever she got an opportunity that the capital was full of wily young women waiting for the chance to trap any promising young diplomat.

Claude listened to his mother's opinions of everything and everybody by the hour. He discussed all his problems with her.

She was his champion. And in her ambitious advice, he imagined he saw promises of great things in store for him. But, today, here he was, the duty officer of the Southeast Asian Section of the State Department. It was Saturday, he was alone, and facing him was a top secret telegram that certainly looked as though it might require some sort of urgent decision. He read the wire over and over, then he dialed his mother's number. There was no reply, and he remembered that his mother was out shopping. Claude Bruck's eyes took on a misty hue as he replaced the telephone. He felt the rolling waves of nausea breaking over him. His heart pounded and he stared past the paper in his hand up to the bare, high ceiling, as if searching for some sign of celestial help. Not that he thought for even a moment that he could tell his mother anything about the contents of a classified message, but if only he could have heard her voice it certainly would have steadied him. Claude Bruck III was suddenly very lonely. He placed his head between his hands and tried to think of what to do. Finally, taking the telephone off the cradle slowly, he gave a sigh of utter desolation and began to dial the home number of his section chief. He just hoped Mr. Ryder had not already departed on his week's leave.

An age seemed to pass before he got an answer. Luckily it was Mr. Ryder who answered, and he did not sound at all agreeable. For one thing, it was Mr. Ryder's first day of leave, his golfing day, and he had made up his mind he was not going to miss it.

"Yes, Ryder here. Who is it? Oh yes, you, Bruck. Well, what is it man? Don't you realize I'm on leave now? I thought I left orders I was not to be bothered."

"It's a telegram sir. I thought that..."

"Yes, well, who is it from?"

"It's from the Pentagon, sir, to the Far East Air Force, and it's about an island, and..."

"Well, read it, man, read it. Let's not dilly-dally, damn it all. What's the matter with you, Bruck?"

"Yes, sir, but I can't, sir. It's—er—too—it's too classified. It's—er—it's top secret."

Ryder was becoming exasperated. "Well, hell, you can at least tell me what it's about—in guarded terms, of course, —or why the hell did you call me?" Ryder could hear his wife Leila leaning on the car horn outside.

"It's about an island, sir. It's about—I can't say the name sir."

"Yes, but what is it about? What do you want to know? Hurry up, or I'm going to be late for my game, damn it."

"Apparently, sir," said Bruck, "the island is full of rats and the natives are in need of help. At least that's what is implied here."

"Yes, yes. Wait a moment, Bruck." Ryder placed his hand over the receiver. "Leila," he shouted, "for Pete's sake, quit that goddamn noise."

"Yes?" the shrill voice came back.

"For god sakes, woman, will you cut out that bloody honking. I'm on the telephone. It's the office calling, so cut it out!" he shouted the last words.

"Okay, but we're going to be late then," came back Mrs. Ryder's high-pitched reply.

Ryder removed his hand from the telephone. "Bruck, are you still there?"

"Yes, sir, I'm here."

"Now, let's get this straight. This is a copy of a message from Defense Headquarters to one of their overseas headquarters, and it deals with an island, its name starts with M, right?"

"Yes, sir," said Claude nervously. "That's right, sir."

"All right, then, my boy, you don't need to worry your head. Defense always sends us a copy when the subject deals with a foreign country. That's all. No need for you to take any action. Although—wait a minute—it might be a good idea to send a copy of it by special messenger over to the Pagudan Embassy. Yes, it would, I know the Air Force has some special weather station there, and if the island is by chance being plagued with rats, of course, they would be the ones to let us know first. Yes, that's it. Obviously, that's what has happened. It's all quite clear to me. So you just get a copy of this over to their embassy. That's all. And, look, Bruck, I won't be available again until this evening. Golf, you know. Besides, don't forget, I'll be on leave for a week. So you just go ahead, young man, and sail the ship, okay? Bye."

Ryder looked at his watch as he hung up. Hell, he was going to be late. He heard Leila sound the horn again as he picked up his golf bag and hurried out to the car, cursing audibly.

On the way to the club, Ryder quietly damned all duty officers and all Pagudans. Yet, in a way, he felt sorry for Bruck. For a moment he wondered whether he should have thanked his subordinate—to encourage him. But, no, it was against Ryder's policy to thank anyone below his own rank. Besides, it might easily have been worse; he might even have had to return to the office for a crisis conference. He pondered this latest business of rats on such a location. It would probably involve some extra work when he got back to the office, as Paguda had a high priority when it came to aid. Oh, well. Then, as he turned into the club grounds, Ryder wondered if rats on Mitzu really mattered and, if so, why?

Every day between the hours of three and five in the afternoon, like all good Pagudans everywhere, Mr. Chu Tu Liu, the newly appointed ambassador plenipotentiary and extraordinary to the United States of America, took his siesta. Mr. Liu enjoyed his two hours of quiet slumber. Not only did it settle his five-or-six-course, richly spiced lunch, it also helped to soothe his invariably ruffled nerves. Mr. Liu's appointment to his present position was not in any way due to his ability as a diplomat or negotiator. He had, until last year, been one of Paguda's biggest dealers in opium and, for a number of years, had run some of the best opium dens in the country. But, as luck would have it, his competitor was the grand chief's uncle's wife, who had long been trying to ease Mr. Liu out of business in the capital. It was she who persuaded the grand chief to ease the situation for her by assigning Mr. Liu as ambassador to Washington. In the six months since Mr. Liu's departure from Paguda, this lady had taken over all of Liu's business in the capital and was thus enjoying freedom from any competition.

When, at a little after three-thirty, the third secretary of the Pagudan Embassy pressed the buzzer to signal his entrance into his master's restful domain, he must surely have realized he would be somewhat less than welcome.

Ambassador Liu was at the time stretched out and fast asleep on the red velvet couch by the French windows, across which the long, heavy, red curtains had been drawn. At the first sounds of intrusion, Mr. Liu merely grunted, settled himself more comfortably against the cushion and pulled the bulky wool rug over his face. When he heard the door start to open, however, Mr. Liu cast off the cover, swung his short legs to the floor and sat up, stretching his hands above his bald head as he yawned. To the anxious third secretary, he seemed belligerent.

"Mr. Ambassador," said the secretary through the half open door, "excuse me, sir."

Mr. Liu looked at him with unconcealed irritation. "Well, don't stand there like an ogling idiot, come in. Do you by any chance realize what time it is?"

The secretary closed the door behind him and stood there, bowing slightly. "I know, Excellency," he said, "but this telegram has just arrived." He held out the piece of paper as if it were slightly contaminated, then added, "It seems to be most important. It's about Mitzu."

Ambassador Liu rose to his feet slowly. He yawned again and then bent down to pick up the large tabby cat that apparently did not mind, in spite of the fact that it, too, was performing its own stretch and yawn routine. Mr. Liu stroked the contented animal and began to pace the carpeted floor.

"Well, go on, read it," he directed.

The secretary ventured another pace forward into the room, bowed, took a deep breath, and recited the contents of the wire slowly: "Concerns Mitzu stop Mitzu strip and pol OK stop rats abound stop help natives and met-men stop."

"Is that all? Who sent it?"

"That is all, Excellency. It is the copy of a message from the Pentagon—from the Defense Department, which has a small communications station on the airfield at Mitzu—to their Air Force Headquarters at Bulabar, sir—sent to us for information."

"I see." Mr. Liu drew the curtains apart with his free hand, then turned back to the other man. "Let me see it." He dropped the cat to the floor, moved with a waddling motion toward his assistant and grabbed the paper out of his subordinate's hand. The representative of Paguda read the words out slowly first, and then read them again even more slowly, then looked up.

"Do you realize the vast importance of this?" Liu asked his rather bewildered assistant. The third secretary merely shook his head. "Ah, I see you do not. Rats, my friend, rats—doesn't that mean something to you?"

"Oh, yes, Excellency, rats—now I see," said the docile assistant. "And they abound it says, sir. Our poor people, what will they do?"

The Pagudan ambassador placed himself in front of the large window and gazed at the expanse of city buildings below him. From where he stood, he could actually see the Capitol and the cluster of government buildings. He thought for a moment, then his words came out almost as a soliloquy.

"Rats. This situation may be bad for Mitzu. Yes, for Mitzu it is very bad. But for our country as a whole, no, it could be extremely favorable. Oh, indeed, yes, it could. Our friends here in America have been very good to us. I mean, to warn us of this plague of rats. It could become a disaster—bubonic plague even. Yet this report gives us an unparalleled opportunity to demand assistance—special aid to combat this—er—plague. Furthermore, because we are a neutral state and our lease of the island to them is very secret and very essential to them, I am quite sure they will give us anything we ask for. It could not have come at a better time. Now, we must not get overeager or excited about this. We must, however, insure that no word of this gets out to other foreign representatives or agencies—at least, not yet. This is a matter for Paguda and the American government alone. Now, let me think."

He made a complete tour of the large room as he contemplated his course of action. Then, having set himself again in front of the window, he spoke very slowly.

"All right, first, do not mention a word of this to anyone else here. Now, I want you to take down this message, so sit down. It's going for eyes only to our state secretary in Paguda. Here it is:

> "PENTAGON REPORTS PLAGUE OF RATS ON MITZU ISLAND STOP MATTER HERE TREATED ON TOP SECRET BASIS STOP ADMINISTRATION HERE WISHES TO MAINTAIN SECURITY DUE TO POSSIBILITY BUBONIC PLAGUE AND CONTINUED USE OF AIRFIELD ON MITZU STOP SUGGEST YOU MAKE FORMAL REQUEST TO AMBASSADOR WILSON FOR ALL POSSIBLE AID TO DEAL WITH PLAGUE STOP IF AID REFUSED THEN FEEL WE MIGHT TURN TO ARTOVSKI AND SEE WHAT HIS REACTION IS STOP WILL DROP HINT HERE THAT WE PREFER WESTERN AID BUT ARE PREPARED TO ACCEPT AID FROM EAST BLOC SHOULD SITUATION SO DEMAND STOP AM SURE ANY REQUEST TO WILSON WILL RECEIVE QUICK CONSIDERATION AND WILL BE HONORED HERE END OF MESSAGE."

"Now, that's it. You get that off at once, and when I see their state secretary tonight at the Yugoslav reception, I'll see what I can do to lay the groundwork."

The third secretary rose, bowed very low twice and made his exit quietly, whereupon the Pagudan ambassador lit one of his dark brown cigarettes and turned once more to view the city.

"Rats," he muttered.

He felt a movement by his leg and looked down to see the cat observing him. He bent over to pat his back. Then, after a moment's further thought, he butted his cigarette and returned to lie on the couch. He pulled the rug over himself and shut his eyes. As he fell asleep, one comforting thought passed through his mind—thank God he would not be in Paguda when the wire he had just dictated arrived.

CHAPTER IV

Paguda is not a large country, but its position as a buffer state of loudly and frequently declared neutrality, with certain periodic Western leanings, makes it most desirable that the United States government do everything possible to maintain a friendly relationship. They are doing this but sometimes its difficult to explain the expense involved.

For this reason, but often to a point of severe strain, the United States has maintained in Paguda a very large mission of aid attached to an oversized embassy and a series of other less important agencies scattered about the land to insure that the Pagudans get whatever assistance they think they need. The population as a whole has always been generally appreciative of anything being done for them, providing they can see it, feel it or eat it. To the Pagudan army, navy and air force, all of which are still trained mainly by the remnants of an army that once belonged to a great colonial empire, the American Military Assistance Group offers technical assistance, and the embassy's military attachés keep an eye on the more ambitious officers to see that they don't start plotting to overthrow the present regime.

The actual government of Paguda is itself a rather loose affair, run by a self-appointed president for life, the Grand Chief Sultopan, who presides over a cabinet composed of relatives, and wealthy cronies, the grand chief's wife, known as the Sultopana, and the grand chief's mother. The grand chief's uncle and a variety of other lesser relatives are usually also involved in the overall process. On the whole, one could say it is not a bad government—not too corrupt. Yet it would surely be stretching the point to say that honesty is one of its common virtues.

Like all small oriental states that have any pride in their history and whose location is of recognized strategic value, Paguda's attitude is obviously based on the fact that both East and West will continue to woo it and hand out unlimited aid as long as either side believes it might succeed in winning over the country in the long run. In any case, the United States government's efforts are considered worthwhile, for neither of the American legislative houses seems to object to the lavish appropriations set aside each year as aid to Paguda.

Paguda's international relations have always worked like a seesaw. The American aid program built a hundred-mile stretch of highway for them, then the East Bloc retaliated with a new hospital. An East Bloc donation of some road maintenance equipment might have been countered by an American gift of a few prize bulls, or perhaps a whole experimental farm. The scale of popularity, in Sultopan's book, of either side, East or West, was generally judged by the size of its gifts. Often, after some members of the Pagudan government returned from a trip to one of the more advanced areas of civilization, they immediately reported their findings to the grand chief, and the American ambassador was faced with a demand for something special that the visitor had seen during his tour. Rumor has it that one particular official who had toured the United States became obsessed with what he considered a novel form of capital punishment and even asked for an electric chair to be installed at a new prison in Western Paguda. Alas, this was one request that had to be refused, mainly because, as the U.S. State Department put it, these items were in rather short supply at home. Besides, there were other considerations associated with this request; such a gift would also have involved the building of a new prison and a new power plant, among other things. Subsequently it was discovered that the request was made with these latter aims in view.

Thus, one might really consider diplomatic and trade relations with Paguda something of an endless game. A Pagudan official would first find an excuse to be invited to the United States. During the visit, he would be shown as much as it was felt he could or would understand. But invariably during this process, the visitor would see many things of which he had not the slightest knowledge. Sure enough, on his return to Paguda and after having reported to the grand chief, he would gather about him a number of government colleagues to whom he would relate the story of his visit abroad and with whom he would then draw up large lists of items to be demanded in the form of aid. These requests, curiously enough, would often be for things that by themselves mattered little, but that usually required a great number of other things to make them work.

A few years ago one such request had been for a new waterworks for the upper regions of Paguda's most northern province where, incidentally, there was no water. There never had been any water. Unfortunately for the U.S. Mission of Aid, this particular request was somehow approved in Washington. When the vast mass of waterworks equipment arrived at the port of Paguda, someone at the Embassy gave the matter a second thought and raised the point that in order to install a water plant, one really should choose a place where there was at least some sign of water. Despite this mental effort, the problem grew overnight. First to arrive were the well-drilling equipment and the crews to operate it. But before the well-drilling rigs could start to drill, another major requirement came to light: A road was needed over which the equipment could be moved to the site of the proposed water plant.

Having gone this far, the Mission of Aid was forced to oblige; in due course, huge numbers of road construction machines appeared, together with operating personnel. Luckily the public's ears never did hear the outcome of this matter. Suffice it to say that, after the road was built, the government of Paguda changed its mind. Why? The answer was simple. A brand new set of Pagudan ruins was suddenly discovered embedded in the steaming jungle within two miles of the road terminal. Needless to say, the question of the waterworks never came up again. The new road was put to good use by the masses of tourists going to visit the new ruins, and thus the tourist business in that part of Paguda was revived to booming proportions. The grand chief was delighted, but the American ambassador and the chief of the aid mission were recalled home and sent to Latin America to negotiate things of less material value.

The one member of the embassy actually responsible for this latest and rather expensive error, however, was transferred to a post in central Africa where, despite his unexplained promotion, he is being carefully watched and not permitted to dabble in any aid matters.

Paguda's ruling class, made up of no more than a dozen families, is all connected to the grand chief by marriage.

In this manner, it makes for a close and happy organization, and the mounting daily returns from the tourist silver and silk shops, the dance halls, the opium dens and the Pagudan servicemen's whorehouses and other places of amusement, are channeled in the right and proper direction.

Foreigners, apart from the few fabulously wealthy plantation owners who naturally pay heavy taxes, are never allowed to conduct business on any long-term basis. They are permitted to start a business; but, if after a few years the enterprise flourishes, the Pagudan government is allowed to buy into the business with the idea of eventually taking it over. It is, all in all, a gainful arrangement for the Pagudans.

Despite these national peculiarities, Paguda could be considered a relatively happy land. And while it does cost the United States and other gullible nations many millions of dollars to maintain this state of eternal bliss, no one has ever really complained about it. It actually becomes more apparent as the years pass, especially in the United States, that everyone from the president down has agreed on one thing: Paguda must not ever be allowed to take on even the slightest pink tinge.

The American embassy at Paguda, the small, smelly but tidy capital of Paguda, has always been a hive of earnest activity. It was one of these places where the flight—from panic to confusion—and back to panic—prevailed frequently. Recently it was discovered that a large shipment of cement had disappeared. It had been used by several officials to build five villas for themselves.

The villas were confiscated by the court. The officials concerned were reprimanded by the grandchief. An official apology was sent to Washington, the source of aid, and thus the matter was settled. Payment for the fifty thousand bags of cement was naturally never mentioned, not even by the United States Senate committees. However, there was one consoling note; the villas were quickly put to good use. They were rented to one of the East Bloc embassies at quite a fabulous sum. That settled the matter for good and, from all accounts, the grand chief's wife the Sultopana proved to be a popular landlady.

It can be appreciated then that the American ambassador in Paguda was indeed a man of many worries and problems. On this particular day he was, to say the least, perplexed. He was brooding somewhat helplessly over the latest Pagudan demand for aid. This one was for a thousand Yamaha motorcycles with sirens.

Mr. Bartholomew Westfield Wilson was not a professional diplomat. He was what is commonly known as a political appointee. He was in his mid-fifties and short of stature and rather thin, but very happily married to a delightful hare-brained lady whom he lovingly referred to as Mama, and to whom he confided most of his thoughts but few of his worries. In contrast to her husband's hundred and twenty two pounds spread over a lithe five-foot-five frame, Mrs. Wilson, some four years his senior, was nearly six feet-two inches tall and, when at home on her chicken ranch, sat on her favorite Palomino at a neat one hundred seventy-five pounds. They were a devoted couple, but nevertheless nonprofessionals in the hard and costly business of national representation. Mr. Wilson had received his appointment directly from the president two years ago and had thus been urged to leave his successful import-export business for the good of public service. It could be said quite honestly that he was making a tremendous effort, often against equally tremendous odds.

These odds took a variety of forms. At present there was his new economics assistant who would have to be spoken to very soon—gently, of course, but reminded of his responsibilities as a representative of his country.

This gentlemen had a wife whose activities with several members of the Pagudan Cabinet were becoming much too obvious. Then there was that secondary secretary, Mr. White, whose reporting of recent events was becoming so verbose and so meaningless, despite the brilliance of his English, that even Ambassador Wilson could not make out what White was trying to say. Besides this, there appeared to be a constant verbal battle between his military attaché and his chief administrator. This had recently reached a boiling point, and the latest complaint from the latter about being called a four-letter word would certainly require delicate handling. He could not have one member of his embassy staff calling the other a shit and useless tit; although, as Mrs. Wilson had stated when she heard about it, the colonel did have a point and wasn't too far out in his judgment.

The ambassador was not actually unhappy in his present post, but on occasions such as these, Mr. Wilson longed for home and the relatively carefree life of ordinary business. Sense of responsibility and duty were, however, words that had real meaning in Ambassador Wilson's life, so he remained in Paguda without complaint, awaited events and tried to keep the Pagudans happy in accordance with the rather unclear, yet elaborate, directive he had brought with him.

So far, he had done his job well. The Pagudans liked him, and his popularity with other diplomats in the small city was obvious whenever the select group assembled for business or pleasure. But he had his share of problems. Today's huge demand for the thousand motorcycles was the prize at the moment, but Mr. Wilson was aware that the next demand could be equally frightening.

Mr. Wilson went over to his file cabinet and extracted a green folder. He then returned to his desk and began to review the requests for aid over the past four years.

The first one puzzled him: four fully equipped veterinary vehicles for a mobile veterinary clinic. Strange, thought Wilson, there isn't a single vet in Paguda. He noticed that request had been approved by Washington. The second item was equally strange; it was for twenty-four commercial washing machines. That was approved too. The next fourteen requests were reasonable, but the last two were quite shocking; one was for twelve full sets of musical instruments for the Pagudan Royal School of Music. Of course the school existed only for a month after the instruments arrived. Then it was suddenly closed. It was still closed.

The last item was for two hundred thousand "rubber goods". Condoms? Good Lord. Mr. Wilson saw this request had also been approved-approved over his objections. He closed the folder and tossed it aside.

"What the hell," he muttered, "what's the use."

CHAPTER V

It was on this particular day, too, at exactly eleven o'clock just as Mr. Heng, the Pagudan state secretary, was telephoning his wife to tell her that her brother was to be given command of the Royal Pagudan Mounted Police, a new motorcycle police battalion that Grand Chief Sultopan had promised to organize (if the state secretary got the motorcycles from the United States), that an excited assistant rushed in with a message. The state secretary took the paper and read it over placidly as he continued his conversation with his excited spouse. Suddenly his face took on an ashen hue, and without further ado he hung up. He placed a hand flat on the desk on either side of the message and stared at it. One word escaped him.

"Mitzu," he whispered.

"Mitzu," said his assistant, "and rats."

"Rats?" said the state secretary in astonishment.

"Rats," repeated the younger official.

"Summon the cabinet at once," said the state secretary, nearly choking on the words.

"Immediately, sir," said his assistant and vanished.

It took just thirty minutes to gather together the only four members of the Cabinet who happened to be in town. The minister of agriculture was the first to arrive, closely followed by the defense minister. They were both quite excited and were asking the state secretary the cause of their hasty summons when the minister for internal security and the minister of finance appeared. Both of these men seemed more than a little annoyed by the quick call to duty.

"Well, what is it this time?" asked the minister of finance in disgust. "I was just about to leave for the coast. I'm a busy man, you know—just can't waste time."

"And I can't stay long," added the minister for internal security. "I'm due to leave in an hour for Bangkok."

"Neither can I," said the minister of defense. "I have two inspections this morning."

"I'm supposed to be at the weekly rice producers conference in fifteen minutes," remarked the minister of agriculture.

"This won't take long, my friends," the state secretary assured them. He waited until they were seated, then strode to the center of the floor brandishing a piece of paper.

"This has just arrived," he announced. The others looked slightly interested. Then he continued, "Mitzu is full of rats."

"Rats?" said the minister for defense quietly. "Not rats, surely?"

"Yes, thousands of them." The state secretary looked rather sad.

"Does that mean plague on Mitzu?" asked the minister for internal security. "If we have a ship available, I will send it at once to check this report, or is that necessary?"

"Quite unnecessary," replied the state secretary. "Our friends the Americans have already confirmed there are rats on Mitzu. That's enough for us."

"Rats!" exclaimed the minister for agriculture. "Wait a minute. Personally, gentlemen, I think this is wonderful. It's just what we need."

"Wonderful?" the minister for finance was surprised. "How can you say that? Mitzu is our island, our people. This is dreadful, and you think it's wonderful? You must be out of your mind."

"Yes, yes, I know," said the minister for agriculture, "but that's exactly what I said, this time it's wonderful. I think our State Secretary knows what I mean. Gentlemen, this news places us in a very good position to acquire additional assistance from our friends. Think of it. Mitzu, while it is only a small island and really of no importance to us except for a small pearl industry, does nevertheless represent something to the Americans. The Americans want to keep the weather station there and they do not wish to let the airfield fall into other hands. So our position is, as you can see, extremely good. Particularly so, as we were not the ones to report the initial matter of the rats being there. It was they who called it to our attention. Now, as I see it, the way is clear for us to ask for unlimited aid, or at least for them to increase what they are now giving us."

"Yes, I agree, you have a point," said the state secretary, "but just what form do you think this aid should take, apart from asking them to send a team of exterminators there?"

"I will explain." The minister for agriculture rose slowly and took up his position behind the large desk. "First of all, we ask that all persons on the island—naturally, with all their belongings—be removed to the mainland here at once. But as we have no proper accommodations for them, we ask for it in the form of these small prefabricated houses they have erected for their own people. We shall need added quarantine facilities to keep these people apart from the rest of the population for at least six months."

He paused to let his words sink in. "We shall need medical supplies, furniture, blankets and bedding and food. Then, while we attend to the needs of the refugees here in Paguda, we can ask them to go ahead and deal with the rats on the island. The danger of the plague must be pressed home to them. And if they wish to burn the entire island—well, let them. After it is all over, we shall of course want to rehabilitate the islanders, for, obviously, if we do not do so, we can explain that we face vast loss of revenue in taxes from the pearl industry there. So, as our friends will want the weather station and airfield reestablished, we naturally want the population re-established and in nice, clean prefabricated homes owned by our government. As I see it, it's quite simple."

"You mean brand new homes?" asked the state secretary.

"Exactly," said the minister for finance, "new homes, new fishing boats, new nets, fishing tackle, new drying sheds for their fish supply, a medical center in case of-well, in case anyone gets sick later."

"And," said the minister for internal security with new enthusiasm, "with a new community, perhaps a police station and even a radio station, or even a new hook-up to us here." The ex-policeman rubbed his hands in anticipation.

"As you can see," explained the minister for agriculture, "the possibilities are quite immense. Now one thing, above all, this matter must be kept absolutely secret. Just between ourselves, Mr. Wilson, and the Mission of Aid. Not one word will be divulged to any other foreign government unless the state secretary or I say so. And we will only do this if our American friends do not appear willing to cooperate. Personally, I think they will." He chuckled then added "Of course they will."

The secretary of state smiled, and he too rubbed his hands together as he spoke.

"My dear colleague, this is quite a masterpiece, an absolute masterpiece. I take it you will tell the grand chief when he returns to the capital tonight."

"Yes," said the minister for agriculture, "I will. But, for the present, the grand chief and we five are the only ones who will have anything to do with this matter. When it is over and Mitzu has been cleared up and repopulated, we can then decide how to re-allocate the aid and absorb it—well, you know what I mean."

He looked around the room and saw from their satisfied smiles that the other men knew exactly what he meant.

The four men were about to depart when the secretary of state let go his parting shot.

"One final thing, gentlemen. Not one word of this to the minister of tourism. He has a brother in Washington. Don't trust him."

"Wait a minute," said the minister for internal security, "it's all very well to say that, but that's not going to be easy. He gets back tonight from Bangkok with the Sultopana. He's bound to get wind of this."

"No, he won't," said the secretary of state with a grin. "He arrives back at half-past eight, and I will arrange it so that by ten o'clock he will be on the way to Indonesia for a tourist convention."

"Good," said defense. "He'll love Djakarta."

"Excellent," added the minister for finance. "Bali is delightful too. But wait a moment, he's just been to a tourist convention in Bangkok. I didn't know there was another one in Djakarta."

"Well, actually there isn't," said the secretary of state. "But he doesn't know that. In any case, don't worry about it. I'll call our representative in Djakarta and tell him to make sure our minister of tourism is kept busy for the next ten days or so. That should do it."

"Very good," said the minister for agriculture, "very good indeed. That should certainly do it."

"I take it," said the minister for finance, "that you, as secretary of state, will handle it from here."

"Yes," replied Mr. Heng. "As senior Cabinet member I will go to see Mr. Wilson and present our problem at once. I will leave as soon as the proper request for aid is typed. I shall feel better if the request can be presented in the manner required by protocol."

The minister for agriculture beamed "Of course, it would be better."

"Naturally." This last word came out as a well-timed chorus from the other three men, who then bowed and left the state secretary's office. This formality, not always practiced between oriental colleagues on home ground, denoted to the state secretary and to the minister of agriculture that, for the moment anyway, they were being held in deep respect and that the pickings of this latest plan appeared, in prospect, better than usual.

The state secretary then telephoned the Embassy of the United States and made an appointment with Ambassador Wilson that afternoon.

Having notified Ambassador Wilson that the Pagudan secretary of state was due within the hour, Miss Loffatt, his lanky, bespectacled girl Friday, warned the sergeant of the

Marine guard at the front door. The sergeant there looked outside to insure that there was a parking space for the expected official car, then told the local employee who was washing the lobby floor to get out and take his equipment and labors elsewhere. The floor washer had barely picked up his mops and pail when suddenly the door flew open. The state secretary of Paguda was through it, past the outer Marine guard, into the inner hall and halfway into the elevator before the Marine sergeant quite realized the blur of activity was man-made. He rushed to the hall, managed a weak salute as the lower half of the Pagudan senior cabinet official disappeared up the elevator shaft, and then returned to his desk to signal Miss Loffatt. There was no doubt about it, Mr. Heng—if indeed it was State Secretary Heng—was in one hell of a hurry.

The Pagudan state secretary flew into the outer office of the Ambassador's suite, past the three bewildered secretaries and was almost at Miss Loffatt's desk and still going before she realized it. When she saw that Mr. Heng had no intention of being swerved from his path to the Ambassador's door, she pressed the warning bell. It was the least she could do in the face of impending panic. Then, as she saw the state secretary disappear into Mr. Wilson's office, she took what is commonly known at all better organized embassy offices as crash-alert-crisis action. She called all the first and second secretaries, the military attaché, the chief officers in the Mission of Aid, gave each the ambassador's compliments and told them to stand by for a crisis conference within the hour. Having thus prepared the embassy staff, she resumed her knitting.

Miss Loffatt noted proudly that not even Mr. Heng's abrupt entrance had caused her to miss a stitch in the socks she was making for that cute looking new third secretary whose glance she had caught quite often recently.

Just as Mr. Wilson's warning bell sounded, the door burst open and Mr. Heng seemed to fling himself in just at the time the ambassador was about to take his mid-morning tranquilizer. Both men looked at each other in silence for a moment.

"Mr. Ambassador," said Mr. Heng, "good day. I have a most—"

"Excuse me one moment," said Wilson as he swallowed his pill and drained the glass of water. He felt he was going to need this one.

"Now, my dear Mr. Heng, to what do I owe the pleasure of this visit?" He rose, circled the desk and extended his hand to the Pagudan state secretary.

"Excellency, a most important matter," said Heng. "I think I will sit down..."

"Do, please," Wilson could see that the Pagudan, who appeared harassed in even the calmest of situations, was certainly not in good shape today.

"If it is about the motorcycles..." ventured Wilson hopefully.

"What motorcycles?" asked the Pagudan state secretary with a blank look.

Wilson quickly saw he was not on the right track. Mr. Heng produced a large manila envelope, extracted from it a single sheet of heavy paper and handed it to the other man.

Wilson returned to his desk, sat down and began to read. His eyebrows twitched noticeably. The restless Mr. Heng got up again and began to pace the floor, just as he had rehearsed it mentally on his way to the Embassy. He felt he must give Mr. Wilson an impression of great urgency.

"Rats?" The ambassador forced himself to hide the faintest smile.

"Yes, Excellency, the report comes from a most reliable source. The situation there is very urgent. Plague is possible."

"I'm sure it is," said Wilson. "But rats? How?"

"We do not know, Excellency, but there are thousands of them," wailed Mr. Heng, "spreading plague and disaster."

"Yes. I mean, quite likely," said Mr. Wilson.

"This is a black day for Paguda," proclaimed the state secretary.

Wilson read the cable again, slowly and aloud this time. "From Ambassador Extraordinary to Secretary of State Paguda-urgent-stop-We have received a report that rats are overrunning island of Mitzu-stop-Immediate help requested-stop-Airstrip reported in good condition-stop-In view of probable outbreak bubonic plague request you ask Mission of Aid to provide all possible help to evacuate island now and initiate program to exterminate rodents-stop-Understand this end such a request will be honored-stop."

Wilson put the cable down and looked up at the other man inquiringly.

"That is the official translation, sir." Mr. Heng said hastily. "We have only just received it."

"This would appear serious," said Wilson. "Yes, indeed-quite serious."

"Disastrous," said the Pagudan.

"Yes, yes, I guess it is. Indeed, it could be… disastrous."

"You will do something, of course, Excellency. You notice the last sentence about the request being honored?"

"Of course, Mr. Heng, but what sort of assistance have you in mind?"

"We must have immediate aid, Excellency, to prevent the spread of plague."

"You mean to exterminate the rats?"

"Of course—exterminate the rodents and evacuate the island at once, or I should say, evacuate the island first."

"I see. You will, of course, formalize your request for this aid. What I mean is…" Mr. Heng reached into an inner pocket. "I have it here, Excellency." He handed Wilson another large white envelope. He paused while the ambassador opened it, read it, and scanned the long list of demands attached.

"What will you do?" asked the state secretary.

"Do? Well..." This is a stupid question, thought Wilson. How in the hell would he know what to do? "I'll call in my experts for an immediate conference, of course. Don't fear, we will act quickly." It was as good an answer as he could think of.

"Thank you, Mr. Ambassador. We Pagudans are most grateful. Thank you." He reached over to shake Mr. Wilson's hand. Then he waddled toward the door, mopping his face with a rather dirty handkerchief.

It had not even occurred to Ambassador Wilson to rise and open the door for Mr. Heng. He sat still, his eyes glued to the list of aid items contained in the Pagudan request, a list that covered four-and-a-half closely typed pages. He just could not believe his eyes—and all this in addition to one thousand motorcycles.

Mr. Wilson was still at his desk holding his head between his hands when Miss Loffatt's next signal on the warning bell announced the arrival of the other embassy officials for the ambassador's crisis conference.

After a brief exchange of normal greetings, the nine visitors sat themselves down and waited in silent anticipation. Behind the ambassador, Miss Loffatt also waited, pencil poised and beaming a benevolent smile for Mr. Stark, the cute new third secretary, for whom she found herself developing a rather strange fascination. She was glancing at his foot, trying to guess the size of Mr. Stark's socks, when Mr. Wilson coughed his signal for attention.

"Well," the ambassador began, "we appear to have a brand new crisis on our hands. This." He held up a paper.

His subordinates had a fair idea this would be another fantastic request for aid. A few half-spoken exclamations intermingled with what sounded like any one of the better known four-letter words floated unnoticed toward Wilson.

"You are, I assume, acquainted in one way or another with the fact that the island of Mitzu belongs to Paguda," said the ambassador. "I have a report here that states a plague is rampant on the island. I also have here an official request from the Pagudan government for assistance—first, to carry out an immediate evacuation of the island's population, and then to arrange for the extermination of the rats, and the eventual rehabilitation of the island. There is, so I am told, some danger of plague—bubonic possibly." He let the words float out and sink in before he continued. Wilson felt that the word bubonic might liven the interests of his usually dull and disinterested audience. It didn't even seem to register. Mr. Wilson was not surprised. It generally took quite a shock to make any of his staff come alive and take interest this late in the day.

"Now," he went on, "in the light of these reports I feel we must do something—and quickly. Obviously the evacuation of the island comes first. Then we must determine the best method of dealing with the rats. So, I want some ideas. There are about four hundred Pagudans and four of our own servicemen on Mitzu. It's not going to be easy because these people will want to bring all their personal belongings with them. Another thing to remember is this: if the plague is possible, we must get the people off in a hurry. That means a sea task. All right, since this whole thing indicates a great deal of organization and the use of ships is involved, I think perhaps Colonel Johnson might give us his views."

Colonel Leonard P. Johnson was the large, lazy, blue jowled military naval and air attaché. It could be said with absolute accuracy that Johnson's hatred for work was considerable. The service attaché did, however, have his good points. He had a good wartime record as a bomber pilot, he was an excellent person at a party and his capacity for liquor and riotous fun was enormous. But then, so was his ability to delegate. And usually he could find some less fortunate and less senior soul to whom he could pass any actual labor, either manual or mental. This whole situation smelled of work. Colonel Johnson's brain therefore was working at top speed with one aim—to avoid any actual participation.

"Sir," he said, "we are, I greatly regret to report, not in a very good position to do much about evacuation from here. The Pagudan Navy has no ships available now, not one. Not now, that is."

"No ships? Oh, for God's sake. But didn't we give them four just two months ago?" The ambassador was more worried than annoyed.

"Yes, sir, we did give them four ships," said Johnson, "but one of the frigates is in for hull repairs, and it won't be ready for six weeks. The other is waiting for a new propeller from the manufacturers in England. The gunboat lacks a captain and first officer, both of whom were arrested last week and are awaiting court-martial for selling ship's rations, and the minesweeper, well, it ran aground last Friday night on the south reef. Our own nearest vessels are at our own naval base at Singabar, sir. I would like to suggest we have Naval Defense Headquarters signal the naval base there and ask that they take this on."

The ambassador cast him a look of disbelief. "All right then, what about the three cargo aircrafts we gave them, where are they?"

Colonel Johnson did not look at all happy. "Same thing with the aircraft, sir, none is in working order. Besides, you know, under our regulations covering the station at Mitzu, no aircraft are ever allowed in that area."

"No aircraft and all four ships out of action, eh? That's not very good publicity for our training cadres, now is it? Oh, all right, draft a message for me to the Department, give them the whole general picture here. Tell them there are no ships or aircraft available here. There is no need to go into the details. Ask them to request the Navy at Singabar to provide ships to evacuate some four hundred-odd persons, plus their personal effects, from Mitzu to the Pagudan mainland. Make it urgent, and let's hope to God they won't charge it against our financial allotment. You might make that a final point in the wire. Anyway, you go ahead."

Johnson jumped to his feet, saluted and hastened his exit gratefully. Thank God he would not have to go to Mitzu himself.

"Now, Mr. White." Wilson turned to his second secretary, who was at this time next in the chain of command due to the deputy chief of mission's absence on home leave. "So much for the evacuation. You had better insure that the Pagudans have enough accommodations, medical supplies to look after the evacuees, etc." The ambassador raised his voice sharply. "Mr. White, did you get that?"

"Oh yes, sir, I got it."

Alfonzo J. White, a man with the sallow countenance of an overworked undertaker, looked anything but happy, for despite his answer, all he was really thinking of was his own home leave that was due to start in four days.

"Yes, sir," White repeated, "I have it, sir, but I wonder if perhaps Mr. Wentworth here might not be the man best able to offer us some expert advice on this, so we might suggest it to the department."

Silas Wentworth was the current acting head of MOA, the Mission of Aid. He was tall and very thin and his slow drawl marked him as a Texan. Mr. Wilson was not too sure about Silas Wentworth, who seemed to spend much too much time out of his office and far too much time out of the country on so-called aid liaison duties. It was one of these recent trips that had aroused Wilson's suspicions when he learned through a reliable source that Mr. Wentworth and the wife of the director of the Pagudan Central Bank had shared a suite at the Peninsular Hotel in Hong Kong.

"Well, Wentworth, what about it?" The ambassador sounded irritated.

"There are several ways to exterminate rats, sir," Wentworth began to explain, "but they are all very costly. But then this sort of thing is always expensive. I recall once in Texas—"

"All right, Wentworth," said the ambassador, "but what are they?"

"Well, first of all, sir, there's poison. We could poison the rats, or we could ask the Department of Defense to use gas on them."

"Both very expensive," said White, wondering at the same time why he didn't keep his mouth shut and thus not get too involved.

"True," said Wentworth, "and of course it would go against our budget if we had to arrange a poison program—and, you know we don't have much money left this year. On the other hand if we passed it over to the Defense Department, we would arrange for it to be billed against them, and anyway, they probably would be glad of the chance to try out some of their stuff—poison or gas or something."

"That seems like a pretty sound idea," agreed the ambassador. "We will certainly suggest it."

"Now, mind you," continued Wentworth, "Treasury might agree to let us have more funds for this, but they probably would want to deduct it from our next year's budget. That's why I suggest we pass it to Defense and ask them to handle it. Really, sir, they're the best people for this one."

"That's good, very good." The ambassador nodded. "Any other ideas? Anyone?" He looked at each of the others in turn.

Mr. Stark, the embassy's dapper new third secretary, now claimed attention by raising his hand. Being a recent arrival, he had not had much chance to say anything at the last two staff meetings, but today Charles Quentin Stark felt the time had come to make a point for himself.

"What about cats, sir?" Stark's words came out quickly.

"Cats!" said Wilson. "Did you say cats?"

"Yes, sir, cats. Several years ago the same sort of thing happened on an island off Japan and they brought in a lot of cats. It proved quite successful according to the records. They even produced a report on it."

"Oh, I see," said Wilson unhappily, thinking the fellow must be mad. "Well, I suppose it's a thought. We can certainly mention that as an alternative." He rose from the table. "All right, then, here it is. The attaché and you, White, will look after the whole project. You and Johnson draft the message to the Department as soon as you can. Give them the whole background and make a few suggestions—poison or gas, or cats—for that matter, suggest that Defense may want to experiment with some form of gas. As a matter of fact, I am of the opinion that it may be a good idea to suggest the whole program, evacuation and extermination, be given to the Pentagon. Yes, let's put it that way. Remember, anything to do with Mitzu is a very special matter. Top secret. So be careful."

"Very good sir," said White.

The meeting ended there.

As the last of the embassy staff left the office, Miss Loffatt handed Wilson another glass of water and his second tranquilizer. He looked at the pill, raised an eyebrow to his secretary, swallowed it and drank gratefully.

"Will that be all, sir?" asked Miss Loffatt.

"Yes, thanks," he replied. The ambassador turned to look out the window. "By the way, that wasn't such a bad idea of Mr. Stark's. Cats, I mean. Mind you, I can't quite see how cats would handle a serious situation like this, but—" Mr. Wilson looked around and realized he had been talking to himself.

The nimble Miss Loffatt had already made her exit and was back at her knitting. She looked at the one completed sock and decided at a glance that it must be made a bit longer for Mr. Stark's foot.

"Who are you knitting those for," asked Ethel, the junior secretary.

"These?" Miss Loffatt, "Oh, I was thinking of giving them to the new third secretary. He has holes in the heels of his socks and his wife isn't here yet—besides, I think he's cute."

"Cute! Oh for God's sake, Loffie, the little bastard tried to make me two nights ago. He's got more hands than an octopus."

"Maybe he's lonely," said Miss Loffatt. "Besides, he's such a little man."

"Lonely, my eye. It's those little ones you gotta watch. They're the horny ones. I'm telling you, so you watch out."

"Oh, Ethel, you worry too much. You suspect everyone."

"Okay, don't say I didn't warn you. Stark will take a jump at you first chance he gets."

CHAPTER VI

Surprisingly enough, Colonel Johnson and Mr. White had the draft of the message to the State Department on Ambassador Wilson's desk within the hour.

Mr. Wilson had Miss Loffatt read it to him, and he made several minor amendments.

"What do you think, Miss Loffatt? About the cats, I mean?"

"Well, it's certainly a novel idea, sir, and cheap. So novel and so cheap in fact, I doubt whether anyone in Washington will take it seriously."

"Funny," said Mr. Wilson, his voice tired. "That's just what I think, the whole thing is so simple. They'll probably throw it out and propose some huge scheme, costing thousands, and then charge it to us here."

"Oh, surely not, sir," Miss Loffatt quietly trying to sound supportive, yet sympathetic.

"Oh, I don't know. If I were on the receiving end of this message, I'd be inclined to think the ambassador and, in fact, the whole embassy staff in Paguda had gone mad. Well, now honestly, wouldn't you?"

"We could send a follow-up message, sir."

"A follow-up?" The ambassador was curious.

"Yes, sir. In fact, you could emphasize the renewal of our lease of Mitzu and ask them to pass the mission on to the U.N. or a neutral nation—something like that—for humanitarian reasons."

The ambassador looked at his secretary for some seconds, mulling her words over in his mind. "You know, Miss Loffatt, you make a lot of sense. We'll do it. Let me read that message again."

From: EMB PAGUDA
To: STATE
TOPSEC - CONCERNS MITZU STOP HENG BROUGHT IN OFFICIAL NOTE TODAY ADVISING RATS FORCING EVACUATION OF MITZU ISLAND STOP DANGER OF BUBONIC PLAGUE STOP REQUEST NAVY ASSIST FOR EVACUATION FOUR HUNDRED NATIVES PLUS FOUR OUR MEN FROM MITZU STATION STOP SUGGEST PROGRAM OF RAT EXTERMINATION BE UNDERTAKEN IMMEDIATELY STOP SIMILAR SITUATION ON JAPANESE ISLAND SOME YEARS AGO HANDLED SUCCESSFULLY BY USING CATS STOP THIS METHOD RECOMMENDED AS CHEAPEST AND SAFEST STOP CONSIDER ANY WIDELY PUBLICIZED PROGRAM MAY RESULT IN ADVERSE CRITICISM STOP REQUEST YOUR VIEWS AND DECISIONS ALL POSSIBLE SPEED WILSON

That was the first message. The second followed within an hour.

From: EMB PAGUDA
To: STATE
TOPSEC - CONCERNS MITZU IN VIEW OF DELICATE SITUATION REGARDING OUR PRESENCE THERE RENEWAL OF LEASE AND USSR ATTITUDES STOP WOULD IT BE POSSIBLE TO PASS THIS MITZU PROJECT OF EVACUATION EXTERMINATION ETC AS MERCY MISSION TO U.N. OR NEUTRAL NATIONS ON HUMANITARIAN GROUNDS STOP WE COULD COOPERATE HOWEVER BY ARRANGING ADMINISTRATIVE MEDICAL FACILITIES FOR REFUGEES STOP ADVISE WILSON

Armed with these two messages, John Bosk, the American secretary of state, having called General Jason Howell the chairman of the Joint Chiefs of Staff and Tom DeLong the national security advisor, wasted no time in asking for a meeting with the president.

"Sounds pretty serious," said the president, putting down his glasses. "Is this that serious?"

"No doubt about it, sir," replied John Bosk. "Would you like to take it from here, General?"

The chairman of the Joint Chiefs cleared his throat. "I've just had my office contact the Special Locations Section for a status report on the rats. Their reply should be here soon. And as the secretary of state and the national security advisor suggested, I have put a presidential top secret classification on this matter and informed our base on Bulabar and Singabar that Mitzu is closed to all traffic until further notice, and there is to be no communication to or from Mitzu unless it is a matter of life and death. That also applies to our weather ships in the area. Here, Mr. President, is a copy of the message we sent out."

The president took the message and read it out loud. "Concerns Mitzu-considering temporary evacuation all personnel from island stop all facilities on Mitzu closed till further notice stop repeat no further communication with Mitzu permitted stop you will be advised stop this matter is PTS stop end of message."

"But you don't say why," said the president. "Shouldn't we say something about the rats?"

"We don't consider it advisable, sir," said the national security advisor. "As you know, the Mitzu signal station is a most secret installation and for use only in emergencies. It cannot come on the air except in absolute emergency. As far as any of these bases in the various regions is concerned, their existence is never discussed if we can avoid it. These stations, like Mitzu, do not even come on the air unless it is a matter of life and death, or they are requested to do so by flashing them an emergency code word."

"Yes, yes," said the president. "I see."

"I agree with the general, sir," said the national security advisor. "Giving any hint might be harmful at this time."

"Okay, I don't need to be convinced. But now what comes next?"

"You have the gist of Wilson's suggestion, sir," said the secretary of state, pointing to the shorter message the president had placed under a paperweight on the edge of his desk.

"Yes, and I must say I like it." The president walked around the desk to the long windows and gazed outside toward the garden for a few seconds before he continued. "Wilson is absolutely right. We cannot get involved in anything in that area right at this time, what with the disarmament conference coming up next month. If we start moving ships and aircraft around the Pacific, it won't go unnoticed and it could throw a monkey wrench into our negotiations in Geneva. I wonder."

"What do you have in mind, sir," asked the state secretary.

"Well," replied the president, "we can't ask the U.N., or someone will accuse us of interference in the internal affairs of Paguda. Besides, if we ask them, someone is bound to make an issue out of it, and the Soviets are bound to raise the roof when they find out we've had a signal station on Mitzu for the past few years. I suppose we could ask one of our allies, but I don't know—only two of our allies, Britain and Canada, know about Mitzu."

"Do you think, sir," said the general, "the British might take this on for us? Or even the Canadians?"

"The British are the people I was thinking about, you know. I think the British might do it, particularly if we offer to help them."

"It's an idea, sir." The general sounded enthusiastic.

"What do you think Tom?" The president looked toward his national security advisor.

"They might. It won't hurt to ask them," the advisor replied.

"Okay, then—may as well try it now."

The president settled himself at his desk, picked up the red-and-white phone and, having paused for a few seconds to look thoughtfully at the instrument, pressed down hard on the buzzer.

A few seconds passed before the green light on the telephone cradle lit up to indicate the scrambler was on.

"Hello? Hello. Yes, Prime Minister, how's the weather there? Rain and cold, eh? Well, no, everything is fine here. Look, Prime Minister, we have a bit of a problem facing us here, and we need your help. Yes, quite serious. No, no. No more missiles. No, nothing like that—thank God. It's about Paguda. Paguda. Yes, that's it. What? Yes, that's it. I know you haven't any representative there, but we have. Yes. His name is Wilson, yes. Anyway, I'd like to send John Bosk over to see you. Yes, today. In fact he can be there in about eight hours. Yes, please, we'd appreciate it, and, by the way, we've put a PTS on this one. Yes, the same as your PMTS—it's got to be, I'm afraid. You'll understand when you hear it all from Bosk. Okay, Prime Minister, 'bye-and thanks. We'll be in touch."

The president winked at his state secretary as he replaced the phone. "The prime minister says he'll see what he can do. He has to put it up to the Cabinet."

The three other men looked at him as he put his forefinger to his lips, pointed to the still-visible green light, and picked up the phone again.

"Hello, who is this? Look, I don't know how you got on this line-oh, it's you, honey. How did you get on this line? You what? Look, Valerie, honey, I don't care if you are the president's wife. This is none of your business. No, you have no business listening in on this line. You'll what? Don't be funny. Now be a good girl and put the phone down, and please don't do this again. Yes, you are embarrassing me, cut it out."

The president replaced the instrument slowly and shook his head. "What do you know, she thinks she's entitled to-Good God, General, let's make that line secure from now on. Bloody women. Give 'em an inch and—oh, hell, what's the use."

"I'll get on to it right away. The general looked a trifle embarrassed.

"I'll leave as soon as possible, sir," Bosk said.

"Do you want me to go with you?" asked the general.

"No, I can handle this, but we'd better have a talk before I go. I don't believe the British have any ships in that area, and we may have to loan them some. We can do that."

"Oh, yes," said the president. "Do you think we should pass on this business of the cats to them? It's a cheap method, certainly. It may appeal to them."

"No reason we shouldn't, sir," replied Bosk. "I did check it out with the research people, and they tell me that not only is it true, but it worked very well—for the Japanese."

"Did the Japanese produce a report on it?"

"Yes, sir, they did. I'm taking several copies of it with me to leave with the British prime minister and I'll see you get a copy before I leave."

"By the way, General, didn't you say the Special Locations Section would give us an updated sitrep on this rat plague?"

"I've asked them for one," the general replied.

"Good. Now, let's think for awhile about security. For the moment, I don't want the press in on this in any way, nor do we want Congress to get any word of it. Can we fix that?" The chief executive's tone made it clear that he was worried. Besides he hated the speaker's guts.

"I think we can, the PTS classification should deter even the defense secretary." Clearly, the secretary of state was not one of Mr. Horace Kleffen's admirers.

"I'm keeping the need-to-know list to a minimum," added the general.

"What do you think, Tom?" The president glanced at his national security advisor.

"Mr. President, I think, as long as we keep the media off the scent of this, we're safe. But, if they ever get a whiff of this, it will be trouble with a capital T."

"You're right, Tom, let's pray we can avoid that. Now, any other thoughts on this?"

It was just after lunch when Horatio Bixon received the call from Major Bonwell, aide to the chairman of the Joint Chiefs.

"Hello, Bixon here," he chirped.

"Oh, Bixon, this is Major Bonwell, aide to the chairman of the Joint Chiefs. My general wants a special report from your office. You should get his message by hand messenger within the next few minutes. The information requested is for the president, so hurry up with it and be very careful. Note the classification."

"For the president?" said Bixon, "Well, well."

"Yes, Bixon. This is an emergency, top priority, get it?" said the major impatiently.

"Yes, yes, I get it."

"And don't forget, it's a PTS."

"What? A PTS. Holy cow—a PTS."

"Yes, Bixon, and hurry it up." The major hung up.

Bixon was still staring at the phone when Dooley entered with the message.

"This just came in, sir, and the messenger says he is to wait for the reply."

Bixon tore open the envelope hurriedly. It read:

FROM CJS
TO SPEC LOC SEC
PTS BY HAND
CONCERNS MITZU-CONFIRM STATUS OF RATS-URGENT

"Don't go, Dooley, I'll have this ready for you in a minute." Bixon reached for his message pad and began to write with a trembling hand. It was the first PTS he'd ever seen.

TO CJCS
FROM SPEC LOC SEC
PTS BY HAND
CONCERNS MITZU. CONFIRM REPORT RATS. THREE THOUSAND-PLUS ESTIMATED.

Bixon read the message over once. Good, it was clear. It was brief and gave the information requested. He signed it, placed it in an envelope and handed it to Dooley. Dooley placed it in another larger envelope and sealed it.

"Okay to go, sir?" asked Dooley.

"Yes, Dooley, okay to go."

Bosk and the general were on their way to the door when it opened. The president's secretary came in and held out an envelope to the senior soldier.

"This just came from the Special Locations Section, sir."

"Thanks," said the general. He took it from her and she left.

He broke the red seals on the envelope and extracted a single sheet of paper, which he studied. "There we are, Mr. President. There's our confirmation."

The president had just read Bixon's message. "Three thousand-plus rats. Good heavens, that's awful. Well, that does it. I'd like a copy of that Japanese report on their operation as soon as possible."

"I'll have one made and sent over to you, sir," Said the general.

"You know, our man in Paguda is right. The president's eyebrows seemed to form a single shaggy line as he looked at the two others, "We cannot take unilateral action on this one—not after all the row we got into over that Caribbean affair. I'll speak to Ambassador Berger later."

"Berger?" said the state secretary. "Surely you don't want the U.N. in on this, sir?"

"No, we don't, but I do think our man Berger at the U.N. should know about it so that if anything leaks out he can tell the secretary general what has happened and explain why we're asking our friends to help us."

"Yes, I know, sir—but do you honestly believe the British will agree to play along? They have no one in Paguda." The state secretary sounded dubious.

"Yes, that's true, but it's the only thing we can do now. You get a message to our ambassador there before you leave. You can give him all the details later, and you can tell their prime minister we can even provide the ships and aircraft on loan. By that, I mean they can take over our ships and sail them under their own flag for whatever period is necessary. Bulabar can provide any transport they need, and as far as communications are concerned, they can—well, General, what about the communications required for this? mean, I don't know much about military matters."

"Very simple, sir," answered the general. "We'll establish a link between their defense headquarters and our bases at Singabar and Bulabar via their foreign office to State here. Once the actual operation has started, the ships can communicate directly with Singabar, who will pass to me directly, with copies to State. And, of course, their chief of defense staff and I can always get together quickly if necessary."

"Sounds fine. Well, you get going. Keep me informed, John."

"Yes, sir, you can be sure of that," replied Bosk.

"And one more thing, John," added the president. "Give them anything they want. They're really doing us a big favor. As a matter of fact, we should be able to give them some help without arousing suspicion."

"Yes, Mr. President, there are a number of ways we can help. First, I doubt if they can find enough cats for this operation. Well, we can get some for them. And the general tells me he can open up one of the old camps as a concentration area for them."

"Is that correct, General?" asked the president.

"Yes, sir," he replied. "Actually, I have one in mind—Camp Billings in Mississippi. I'd suggest, if you agree, that I have my chief of procurement take on the matter of finding the cats and an officer who has been on Mitzu to supervise the whole project from this end. And he can if needs be, arrange for the RAF crews to take over whatever transport aircraft they need at Tenpost Air Base near Billings. We'll assemble the cats at Camp Billings and move them by road to Tenpost Air Base. We can have aircraft there with RAF markings that the RAF crews can take over for the trip to Bulabar, and ships ready at Singabar for the Royal Navy to take over. Then, when its all over, the British merely return the aircraft to Tenpost and the ships to Singabar. It's really not too difficult. I hope you understand, sir." The chairman had obviously done his homework. "If you agree, I'll start the ball rolling on this right away."

The president replied thoughtfully. "By the way General, when does our noble defense secretary get back from Korea?"

"Not till tomorrow night, Mr. Secretary."

"I take it you will brief him as soon as he arrives?"

"Yes, sir, I'll do that," answered the chairman.

"What do you think, John, about the British?" asked the president. "I mean, can we trust them with this?"

"Well, sir, I'm pretty sure we can and I can get the British to agree if we are prepared to help them to that extent. After all, their part in this is merely one of transportation. I doubt if anyone can give them a black mark for that, on that basis. I'd say let's go for it and hope they'll do it."

"All right, John, we'll go for it. It's up to you to convince their prime minister. And remember, it's not going to cost them a dime. We can even agree to covering the cost of pay and allowances for their crews, but keep that only as a final point if they need more convincing."

"I'll keep that in mind, sir," said the secretary of state. "Goodbye, Mr. President."

"Goodbye, John. Good luck, and don't stay away too long."

John Bosk lit his cigar, raised his eyes to the ceiling and puffed slowly. From the other side of the desk, the British prime minister regarded the American statesman with a puzzled look.

"John, surely you don't really mean cats?" humanitarian reasons., "I know, but—"

"You do understand," continued Bosk, "we're not in any position to make a move in that part of the world at this time. We have too much to lose. But your people—and the Canadians in particular—with your reputation as peacekeepers and for helping underdeveloped countries without any idea of territorial or other gain—well, you can do it. If by chance it should become known, your efforts can be passed off as a fantastic mission of mercy. No one would dream of accusing you of any underhanded or veiled intentions. You'll be doing us all a good turn—one, in fact, that could be carefully publicized after the event—and do your nation immense good."

"Yes," said the prime minister, "I see your point—I do see it."

"Well then, sir," continued Bosk, "let me tell you what part we can play to help in this. First, all our services in the Far East and our embassy and staff in Paguda will be at the disposal of your Commonwealth forces. Naturally, we would have to tell the Pagudans quietly that you've agreed to help them out and explain why we can't do it ourselves. You can rely absolutely on our representative there. Wilson will be instructed to make all the arrangements needed to support whatever you do. Furthermore, you can use all our facilities at the Bulabar and Singabar bases and, in fact, anywhere you have to operate, without any cost to you whatsoever. Besides this, if you need anything—and I mean aircraft, ships, anything—the president tells me to inform you that it will be provided, again at no cost. Just use it and give it back to us when it's all over. But, of course, we must insist that whatever we lend you must carry no sign of our ownership. That way, no one can point the finger in our direction. The movements of your ships or aircraft can be explained more easily. I hope you agree."

"Yes, yes, that's true enough," said the prime minister. "If we do it, it should pass without comment. In any case, we can always pass it off as either a training or a goodwill mission. There should be no problems as I see it. But quite honestly, it's the idea of using cats that I just can't quite get into my mind. Its a bit—odd."

"But why, Prime Minister? This is an operation of mercy. The only reason you can't publicize it is because of our presence on Mitzu. And, besides, we don't want to cause panic in the region. You surely understand that. We'd do it like a shot if it weren't for the disarmament conference. You know yourself you'd be the first ones to raise an eyebrow if it became known that our ships and aircraft were milling around Paguda, or Mitzu for that matter, particularly when you're trying to support our disarmament policies. I'm sure you understand that methods such as gas or poison or shooting are out. You cannot employ any of these methods in that area, not now."

There was a long silence before the prime minister spoke. "You're right. Of course I'll have to consult the cabinet, and if for any reason we can't do it, we'll ask Canada."

"Good, and thanks," said Bosk. "You'll never regret this. How long do you think it might take for your people to decide on this?"

"I don't know," replied the prime minister. "I don't know yet whether we have enough cats for this sort of thing. I mean, if we go on this, we'll need, what, a thousand or more? I can't say. In any case, I'll get on to this right away."

"That's something you don't have to worry about, Prime Minister. We're going to find the cats for you and concentrate them at a special camp. Our SPCA people hold about four thousand, and I hear the Canadian SPCA has another seven hundred. We're also finding one or two officers who know the Mitzu area to go along and observe and help supervise the operation on the island."

"That's very good of you," said the prime minister. "I'll get our people together as soon as I can. I suggest you call me in about four hours. But, wait a minute—I made a call to your president; I think it's coming through now."

The buzzer sounded and the prime minister picked up the phone, "Hello Mr. President...I beg your pardon. Yes Madame, I want to speak to the President. Oh, he's not in...I see...what's that? I see, you are...in the Oval office...but Madame, oh, you can give him a message? Well Madame, please tell the president that I'll call back later. Good day Madame". He practically threw the instrument down on its cradle. "Good God, I've never heard anything like it. What's the matter with her?"

"Who or what was that all about?"

"That, John, was Valerie, your president's beloved. She proudly announced that she was in the Oval office and would take any message for the president. I find that a trifle strange and a bit dangerous, if I may say so."

"Damn that woman. I thought we made it clear to her that she is not ever to use that particular phone and that she has nothing to do with this matter. I'll take this up when I get back."

"I hope you will, John. I gather she feels she is quite capable of making any decisions relating to anything connected with the president. I find that very odd. You'll have to change that."

"Like hell she is! She'd like to run the whole government. I promise you, I'll see that this matter is settled. Just because he makes her the chairman of some committee, she's acting like a goddamn empress. Don't worry, Prime Minister, I'll fix it, even if it costs me my job. And I have an idea she'd like that, too."

There were only five members of the Cabinet in town to answer the prime minister's call to duty. Luckily, the foreign secretary was among them, as were the ministers of labor and trade and transport, and the chancellor of the exchequer; but the defense minister was not available, and the war office apparently did not see fit to send anyone in his place.

The prime minister's request to them was both short and a trifle confusing. To get quick results, he first told them the

American president had asked the British to undertake a special and secret mission of mercy; and, because of the forthcoming disarmament conference and of the existence of several secret installations in certain strategic areas, he personally recommended the British do whatever was possible to help. The prime minister explained that he had been approached personally by the president and had just had a long discussion on the subject with State Secretary Bosk. If the Cabinet would agree to British participation, the prime minister predicted that, in due course, the image of all Britons throughout the world would be raised to immeasurable heights. Furthermore, if the Cabinet approved, the matter would be handled under the highest security classification. Naturally, he did not mention how the operation was to be accomplished.

Somehow, the five members of the British Cabinet did not appear too interested. The prime minister quite understood. He looked at his pocket watch and saw it was approaching the lunch hour.

"Well, gentlemen," he said. "I realize most of you have to get to your clubs for lunch so I suggest we adjourn until three, perhaps." He looked around the table, saw the three o'clock deadline was not at all welcome, then added, "Very well then, lets make it four-thirty, and, as the defense minister is away, I want the chief of defense staff here. Don't worry about tea, I'll have some here for you."

Without a word, the five Cabinet members rose and made for the door.

They gathered again at four-thirty, and this time Field Marshal Sir Ronald Jones, the chief of defense staff, was with them.

The prime minister looked serious. "Now, gentlemen, let's get on with this." He then presented them with the facts related to the president's request, making no mention of cats.

"Prime Minister," Sir Ronald said, "while I believe that in the interest of humanity we-er-should be-er-eager to assist our American allies, I must remind you this operation would require the services of some four hundred members of the Royal Navy and Royal Air Force. That may interfere with our participation in the NATO exercise due to start in five weeks. Apart from that, we have no one available in the three services who has had any experience on Mitzu or in Paguda."

"I know all that, Field Marshal," the prime minister said with some annoyance. "But I think all our learned colleagues here are aware this is a top-priority task we must undertake."

"Hear, hear," said the foreign secretary. He leaned over to whisper to the prime minister. "Are you going to mention about the cats?"

The prime minister shook his head. "Not on your life. If I do, they'll never agree. You can tell them after, certainly not now."

"Who, the Cabinet?" asked the foreign secretary.

"No, no, not the Cabinet. The field marshal."

Meanwhile the conversation around the conference table was becoming noisy. Both the chancellor of the exchequer and the minister of labor were in heated argument over something.

"Just a moment, gentlemen," the prime minister broke in. "Let's have a little order here. I haven't finished yet."

The murmurs and mutterings subsided.

"Field Marshal, I have already told the president we will do this for them if we possibly can. I hope the Cabinet members will agree with me."

The foreign secretary made a motion that the government undertake this mission of mercy. Before the vote could be taken, the prime minister's red-and-white phone rang indicating a call from Washington.

"Hello, Mr. President, I was hoping to hear from you again. Yes, as a matter of fact we're discussing it now. Yes, I understand. No, we'll use our own aircraft. It will be good training for the crews. Where? Oh, Tenpost Air Base. Near where? Oh, Camp Billings. Oh, yes. They will be assembled by your people at this camp—under whom? Some officers who have been on Mitzu. To observe and report on how the operation progresses. That's very good. Fine. Yes, I have it. And—oh, the ships. No, again, thanks for the offer, but we will use our own ships and aircraft too. They'll sail from Hong Kong to Singabar. What's that? You will pay all the costs? No, Mr. President, thanks again, but we will handle our own costs. Your offer is certainly generous. Very good, Mr. President, I'll go back to my Cabinet. Yes, I'll be in touch. Goodbye."

He hung up the phone. "Gentlemen, you heard most of that. They even agree to pay the whole shot so it won't cost us a penny. But I declined that. If they were to pay for the whole thing, eventually we would get no credit for this, so we'll pay our own way using our own ships and aircraft. That way it won't appear that we're doing this just because they asked us. Now, Foreign Secretary, what about that motion?"

The motion was repeated. "Her majesty's government should accept the tasks outlined in the relief of Mitzu." It was carried unanimously, although the chief of defense staff had doubts as he held up his hand in agreement.

"Has anyone any questions?" asked the prime minister.

"Yes, Prime Minister. What about the NATO exercise?" asked the chief of defense staff.

"What about it? Field Marshal, are you telling me you are not wholly agreed with us in this?"

"No, Prime Minister, not at all. If that is the order, you may be sure we will abide by it." The field marshal's face was redder than usual. Perhaps it was his blood pressure building up. On his retirement in four months he had been promised a life peerage by the prime minister. He did not want to lose that.

"Here, gentlemen," said the prime minister quietly, "we have an order. And, remember, this is a prime ministerial top secret. Conduct yourselves accordingly. Thank you.

The five members of the British cabinet gathered their papers and began to leave the room.

The field marshal was picking up his own papers when the foreign secretary tapped him on the arm.

"By the way, Ronnie, our Foreign Office Liaison chap, Albert Rollins, will be reporting to you later. He has all the facts and will give you the prime minister's notes on the direction he wants this thing to take—and, oh, yes, don't forget to brief your minister."

"I'll see to that," said Jones. "Thanks."

At the War Office, Field Marshal Sir Ronald Jones was just signing some overdue reports when the chiefs of the three armed services entered.

"Have a seat, please. I'll be with you in a moment," he said and, without looking up, added, "I have a real dilly for you."

Admiral Sir Hugo Stagg, General Lucius Topps, and Air Marshal Douglas Burrows took their places around the small conference table.

"Right," said Jones, rising from his desk and going over to seat himself at the head of the table. "Bloody hell, chaps, I'm damned if I know where to start. By the way, do any of you know where this place Paguda is?"

"Paguda?" Admiral Sir Hugo Stagg looked puzzled.

"Oh, Paguda," General Lucius Topps said hopefully. "Oh yes, yes, of course. It's—ah—it's, well, it's somewhere near Borneo, isn't it?"

"Oh, no, no. My dear chaps, it's between Thailand and Hong Kong." Douglas Burrows sounded confident.

The field marshal smiled. "It's easy to see you chaps are not up on your geography. Paguda is actually between Thailand and the Philippines. Anyway. Paguda has an island called Mitzu some four or five hundred miles off its east coast. Now, here's the gen as I see it. First, Mitzu is under secret lease to the United States. It's one of a group of very secret airfields and weather stations in their Pacific strategic layout. The Soviets do not know about it. Anyway, Mitzu has been reported overrun by a plague of rats, and something has to be done about it. The Americans want us to clean up the place after evacuating the population, of course, and make it habitable again. They wanted to loan us whatever ships and aircraft we needed to do the job and even agreed to pay us for the troops we use. But, thank God, the prime minister wouldn't accept that bit of charity. So, we'll use the RAF and the Royal Navy. This fellow Rollins is coming over from the Foreign Office to brief us further on this. So, we'd better wait until we hear what he has to say. Oh, by the way, I have to leave this afternoon for Rome, so maybe you, Lucius, could coordinate this in my absence. All right with you, Hugo?"

Admiral Stagg indicated his approval by waving his pipe. "All right with you, Douglas?"

"Fine with me," the air marshal agreed. "Lucius can have it."

"Well, Lucius, the sooner you hear from this Foreign Office chap, Rollins, the better. Apparently there's some urgency on this. As I said, I'm off to Rome and Ankara in an hour and won't be back for ten days. By the way, don't let the prime minister push you around—or the defense minister, for that matter. We service people are not too high in their estimation. The defense minister wasn't at the meeting, so you'll have to make sure the secretary of the defense council—what's his name, Captain Dalkye—briefs him when he turns up. I've made a heap of notes for you, and Rollins will no doubt fill you in."

The field marshal rose, collected his papers, tossed a file folder toward the chief of Army staff and started for the door. "There you are," he said, "it's all there. Can't say I like it too much, but there it is."

"I say, Ronnie," said the admiral, "isn't there something rather odd about all this? I mean, you don't think the Yanks are…"

The field marshal turned at the doorway. "Something odd? My dear chap, I haven't the slightest idea. But anyway, over to you chaps, over to you—see you in two weeks." With that remark, he walked out.

Shortly before he left London that night, John Bosk called at his own embassy.

The duty officer thought it was a bit peculiar when the state secretary asked him to place an overseas call through to the director general of the SPCA in Washington. Mr. Bosk took the call in the ambassador's office.

After the state secretary's departure, the same duty officer wondered whether he should have attempted to return the somewhat mischievous wink the senior statesman had given him as he passed toward the outer door.

In an hour Bosk was in the Concorde on his way to New York. Six hours later he was in his office in the State Department. After an hour's cat-nap, he showered, put on a clean shirt and departed to meet the president. "Ah, there you are, John," said the President. "How did it go? So they're going to do it. God bless them."

"They'll do it, sir," said John Bosk.

"With cats? I bet the prime minister wasn't too keen on it."

"Yes, sir, with the cats, and they insist on paying their own way. But then, you know that from your talk with the Prime Minister. No way were they going to let us pay."

"What about the cats?"

"We'll have plenty within a few days. The prime minister balked at first when I told him about the cats, and that was a condition of their acceptance—that we find and concentrate the cats and the officers to handle them and supervise the operations on Mitzu. So, I've asked the military people to make some arrangements to find as many cats as they can, and I've also spoken to old Admiral Lyman, the director of the SPCA, and asked him to cooperate with whomever the military puts in charge."

"We'd better be very careful about who is selected to be in charge of the concentrating of the animals. You know what I mean. There will be hell to pay if he happens to be one of these publicity seekers. When you find out who it is, let me know. How will the cats reach that camp from the SPCA compounds?

The president seemed to be getting worried.

"I imagine the military will probably have to use helicopters from the compound areas to the camp, and I hope they do it at night so as not to arouse suspicion."

"Oh good. That's sound thinking," said the president. "That's about it for now?"

"Yes, sir. By the way, I had General Howell send a personal message to the commanders at Bulabar and Singabar. Told them the British are doing us a special favor on Mitzu and they are both authorized to cooperate directly with their military services through my department on the matter. That is to say, the British services will establish communication with Bulabar and Singabar through my department. We made it clear that any request for assistance is to be met without question. No one except Bulabar, however, is permitted to make any contact with Mitzu, and then only on my orders. The prime minister quite understands the importance of all this, and he has given it the same security classification we have—a PMTS."

"Excellent," said the president. "I'm glad he understands our retention of the Mitzu strip could be important to both our countries if anything big happens in that area."

"I'm sure he does, sir," said Bosk.

"By the way, how did his military people react when they heard about the use of cats?"

"I don't know, Mr. President. He hadn't told them when I left. He was keeping that till the last."

"He's a smart man," said the president. "That's the way I'd have played it—tell it to them later. Yes, sir, he's a smart man. When this thing is over, I think we should give their CDS and his service chiefs some sort of recognition-perhaps a Distinguished Service Medal—and we ought dream up something special for their prime minister. Think about that will you? We'll owe them one, besides you never know, it might get me an honorary knighthood, Valerie would really love that."

"It well might, Mr. President." Said Bosk. "No problems rewarding their military people but for the prime minister, I wonder if we can do that without informing congress. I suggest that we wait until well after the whole business is over and then present the whole matter of awards to congress. That way no-one can complain."

"I see your point." The president said. Anyway, think about the others and our military people too. I mean, they'll deserve something."

"Yes, Mr. President, I'll do that."

"You know, John, I wish we had someone more reliable at Defense. I worry about that. The only reason I gave Kleffen the job in the first place was because of his—well, his generosity toward the party. Frankly, I was hoping he'd screw up before too long, and I could get him out, make him an ambassador to someplace. I know his wife would go for that. So would he."

"Well, Mr. President, I'm quite sure the chairman of the Joint Chiefs and I can ease your worries by arranging some—well—some trips for Mr. Kleffen."

"Not bad, John, not bad at all. You have my blessing. But don't forget, if you get the opportunity of mentioning to our friend, the prime minister...well, about the honorary knighthood, if you get him alone some time I'd be grateful. Its the one thing that would really please Val."

CHAPTER VII

"No, no, definitely not," said the Prime Minister. "No publicity. It's out of the question, completely out of the question."

"But," pleaded Rodney Boswell, the foreign secretary, "surely it would do no harm. After the operation, I mean, to let the word out that we've just completed a mission of mercy. After all, it could mean a Nobel Prize for someone, for you perhaps. And, another thing, the fact that we are now using our own ships and aircraft and have refused the president's offer to cover all our costs, means that we British, as a nation, are rallying to the assistance of these poor people. When all this is over, the Yanks won't be able to claim all the credit they would have if we had let them pay us off. Declining their offer was a very sound move. It will make good reading—in the future, of course."

"In the future, yes, but not now, Rodney. I'm sorry, we cannot take a chance on any leaks. By the way, why wasn't the defense minister at my meeting? I don't think the blighter likes me."

"Oh, it's some anniversary of his, sir, said the foreign secretary. "I gather he had some personal business to attend to. The field marshal has been instructed to make sure the defense minister is briefed on the matter as soon as possible. I'll have a word with him too."

"Now," said the prime minister, "as I already told you, the Americans want us to try the same simple formula the Japanese used some years ago in similar circumstances, and I agree with them. All they did was round up a few hundred cats, evacuate the population by ships to a nearby area, put the cats on the island for a few days, then went back with some sanitation experts to clean up the place so the people could be rehabilitated. That's really all we've been asked to do by our friends. So as far as I'm concerned, it's sort of a special aid program your office should be able to take on. The principal reason we don't want any publicity is that, first, there's always a chance of people panicking about bubonic plague. Second, we don't want the public to think we're doing something just because the Americans ask us. We must maintain, especially now, an attitude of neutrality. We are not involved in finding the cats, the Americans are doing that. They're even setting up a place to concentrate them and finding some people to handle them. Of course, we shall have to have someone to sanitize the place after the cats have done their work."

The foreign secretary was shaking his head.

"Now what, Rodney, what is bothering you?"

"Well, we haven't mentioned the matter of cats to the field marshal yet. He may not like it. He may even balk at the idea. Nick Farr, the defense minister, I know will be difficult."

"Oh don't worry, Rodney. I'll write out a directive for Rollins to take to them both. The field Marshal and Nick Farr both know that if they give me any trouble on this, their chances of a life peerage when they retire will vanish."

The foreign secretary looked uneasy. "You mean—"

"Exactly, my dear Rodney, you and I must not let these bloody service chaps or that clot of a defense minister give us any nonsense. If we had mentioned cats in the first place, I doubt whether the others in the Cabinet would have bought it. No, let's leave the mention of cats until the very last. In fact, and for the record, this is just a special form of aid."

The Foreign Secretary smiled faintly, then scratched the lobe of one ear thoughtfully. "You're quite right. This is a form of aid. But, although my office can certainly handle it, don't you think it would be a good idea to turn over the management of this whole operation to Defense? After all, they're the people who will provide the air and sea transport, and we'll have to ask their engineers and medical specialists to sanitize the island."

"I see your point," said the prime minister, "and actually I agree. You arrange it with them and be sure to give them my notes and my consent, and you can keep me informed periodically on progress. You know, Rodney, I'm getting a bit fed up with the defense minister. He's always off on some silly inspection. As a matter of fact, I rather think we shall have to start laying down some hard and fast rules for our ministers. They spend far too much time away from their desks. The home secretary is the worst offender and the minister of trade isn't much better. They all love to gad about. No bloody wonder we don't get things done. But, to get back to our operation. I do agree we should hand it over to Defense. But, make no bones about it, they must keep me and the Foreign Office informed at each step."

"Certainly, sir, I'll get the word to the defense minister at once. Oh, one more thing. Do I understand their president actually offered to cover all costs—ships, aircraft and manpower?"

"That is correct," said the prime minister. "They offered to pay for everything. They must really be up a tree on this one." The prime minister looked at his watch. He saw he only had twenty minutes before the car arrived to take him to the airport. Thank God, he thought, for these next ten days in the sun in Bermuda.

Besides, this was as good a time as any to get out of the country.

When Rodney Roswell returned to his office, he found a caller from the American embassy waiting for him. It was Tom Fash, one of the senior ministers. They shook hands.

"Well, Tom, what can we do for you?

"I've just been given a copy of a cable to pass on to you." Fash handed it to the other man. "Our secretary of state apparently forgot to send one to your prime minister, but our president called him and warned him about it. As you can see, it's from our defense department to our Far East bases. We've already confirmed there are rats on Mitzu, and we've closed the airfield facilities till further notice. Then we sent this. By the way, only the ambassador and I are aware of all this."

The foreign secretary took the paper over to his desk, sat down, adjusted his glasses, and began to read:

FROM CJCS
TO BULABAR
SINGABAR
STATE (FOR EMBASSY PAGUDA AND UK FOREIGN OFFICE) PRESIDENTIAL TOPSEC FOR COMMANDERS EYES ONLY

PARA 1 MITZU AIRFIELD CLOSE UNTIL FURTHER NOTICE TO ALL, REPEAT ALL TRAFFIC.

PARA 2 ISLAND WILL BE EVACUATED TEMPORARILY BY ROYAL NAVY OF ALL REPEAT ALL PERSONNEL. MOVE BY SEA TO PAGUDA WHERE SPECIAL ARRANGEMENTS HAVE BEEN MADE BY EMBASSY.

PARA 3 IN DUE COURSE AFTER CERTAIN CLASSIFIED TRIALS HAVE BEEN CARRIED OUT BY BRITISH GOVERNMENT FORCES ON MITZU, POPULATION WILL BE REPATRIATED

PARA 4 YOU WILL BE CONTACTED BY BRITISH DEFENSE AUTHORITIES THROUGH STATE DEPARTMENT FOR REQUIREMENTS. THEY HAVE BEEN NOTIFIED AND YOU ARE HEREBY AUTHORIZED TO LOAN WHATEVER NEEDED WITHOUT COST OR RESTRICTIONS. BRITISH SERVICES WILL ADVISE ETA

PARA 5 WITH REGARDS TO ROYAL AIR FORCE MOVEMENT TO ALABAMA FROM TENPOST. YOU WILL BE ADVISED ETA'S, FUEL REQUIREMENT, MAINTENANCE ETC.

PARA 6 SPECIAL BULABAR: YOU WILL CONTINUE TO BE SOLE CONTACT WITH MITZU IN ACCORDANCE WITH EXISTING POLICY NO. 5-8-199-008. BUT NO REPEAT NO CONTACT IS TO BE MADE UNTIL AUTHORIZED BY THIS OFFICE.

PARA 7 ALL COSTS WILL BE REFERRED TO FISCAL CODE 007-415-02.

PARA 8 THIS PTS OPERATION WILL BE CONSIDERED TERMINATED ONLY ON RECEIPT OF CODE WORD FINAL COUNT FROM ME.

"Well," said the foreign secretary, "that appears to be a well thought-out document."

"Thank you, sir," said the visitor quietly. They shook hands again, and Fash departed.

At Bulabar Air Base, General Bellows was just making up his Hong Kong shopping list when Colonel Mason handed him the message. The general read it, initialed it, and handed it back to his chief of staff.

"Good God! What's all this about? This means the Hong Kong Trip is off? Oh, hell." The general was obviously not happy.

"I guess so, sir, at least for now. Must be something big coming up. I hope you don't want me to question it."

The general looked at him sharply. "Hell no. Question a PTS, Dixie? You think I'm crazy? No, sir, I'm quite content here. No, if the president says Mitzu is closed, that's it. No questions."

Okay, sir. No questions," agreed the colonel.

"And," added the General firmly, "no discussion about it around here either."

"Check, general, and no discussion," repeated Mason.

As he reached the door, he heard a chuckle, "Say, Dixie, what the hell do you think is going on?"

Colonel Mason looked at his superior for a moment before he answered. "Beats me, General, probably some clever son of a bitch in Congress has discovered we're on Mitzu and is plugging for the headlines."

"You may be right, Dixie. We sure have some dillies. Those bastards would do anything to get votes. Did you hear about the congressman who was caught by his wife laying one of his aides on his desk?"

"Yes, I did, but I heard he made amends by laying his wife on the steps of the Capitol."

The general burst out laughing as Mason made his exit.

When Mason entered his office, he found Major Carr, the G4 and Captain Townes, the commander's aide waiting.

"What's up Colonel?" the major asked.

"What's up? The Hong Kong trip is off. So Test Flight 255 is on hold and you two had better get busy and cancel all the reservations and whatever other arrangements were made."

"Oh my God." exclaimed the aide. "Why? don't you realize we've got all the women—."

"OK captain, stop right there. I'm telling you it's off."

"May we know why colonel?" Carr asked.

Dixie Mason leaned forward and spoke in almost a whisper. "Do either by any chance know what PTS means?"

Major Carr jumped to his feet as Captain Townes blurted out two words “Jesus Christ” followed by “PTS, holy cow.”

“Dammit man,” Mason said angrilly. “keep it down.”

Now both men were on their feet. “OK sir, we get it. We’ll get onto it right away. Mind you sir,” Townes said almost apologetically, “we may have trouble getting the same gals. These were, well, these were special, real different.”

With a smile of understanding on his face, the colonel said, “Sorry about this gentlemen. You do what has to be done. But both of you, remember, it’s PTS and not a word to anyone else about any of this. Now you have to move on it.”

As the two officers left, Colonel Mason was wondering what on earth Townes meant by real different.

CHAPTER VIII

The three Far East experts of the British Foreign Office had been summoned hastily by their chief to consider a matter of utmost urgency. By the time they reached the conference room, each of them had examined the folder of documents related to Mitzu and Paguda, and they had all apparently come to the same conclusion. This appeared to be a tricky job, and they were anything but happy about it. It all smelled of work and a ruined weekend.

"Well," said the foreign secretary, "now you have it all. Mitzu is full of rats—bubonic plague may be imminent. The only hope, as I see it, of our American allies hanging on to this important airstrip that is a vital link in their strategic strike-force communications, is to help clean the place up as soon as possible. The prime minister wants the place evacuated, the rats destroyed, and the island cleaned up and made habitable again. The population and the signalers on the weather station must be re-established as quickly as possible. They've asked us to help, and we've agreed. The matter is to be considered PMTS."

"A PMTS? My God." Exclaimed Tim Jones from Far East Political Section A. "This is terrible. It will surely bugger up the week-end. What the hell am I going to tell my in-laws?"

"Oh dear Lord." Hal Innis from Section B was not happy. "We'll be working round the clock for a month."

"We're not equipped in any way to do this, sir." Said Bob Ritchie, the Far East Economics expert. "We're already overloaded with four other reports that have to be prepared for some parliamentary committee. We..."

"My dear chaps, I don't think you understand." the foreign secretary explained. "You are not actually doing it. We are merely assembling all the facts to pass on to Defense, and that is exactly what you three have to do. Damnit gentlemen, don't you get it? Just prepare the facts. That's all you have to do. Here is the folder containing the prime minister's direction on the matter. Get on with it."

The foreign secretary handed it to Tim Jones. "Please don't let us waste any time. We must put the defense people into the picture. We must get to it. Remember, the prime minister wants us to use cats." Then he left.

For a moment there was dead silence.

"Just a minute, what in hell are we worrying about." said Jones of section A. "Defense are the ones who will do the actual work. Aren't they?"

"You mean we're really expecting Defense to take it on?" asked Ritchie the economist.

"Of course, the prime minister has confirmed that."

Hal Innis from political section B was clearly not convinced." Oh, I don't know, all this has a funny smell to it."

"You really think Defense will accept it?" Ritchie the economist asked.

"Well, they might if..." Innis shook his head.

"I'm pretty sure of one thing," said Tim Jones "that they'll never accept it if cats are mentioned."

"You don't think so?" Bob Ritchie now was sounding uncertain.

"Dammit man, would you? They're not that stupid." Jones did not have a high opinion of the military and his generosity on this occasion surprised the other two.

"No, I guess not, but how about Rollins throwing it in after they accept. About the cats I mean." Hal Innis said.

"Well now," Bob Ritchie appeared interested. "That, my dear colleagues, is not bad, not bad at all."

The decision was reached without any further discussion. An hour later they called in Mr. Rollins, the Foreign Office chief liaison officer with the Department of Defense, briefed him completely and told him to prepare an official request to that department, bring it back for the foreign secretary's signature and then take it personally to Defense.

The inter-departmental memorandum gave a brief background of the matter and requested in the most loquacious terms that the Defense Department be prepared to undertake the evacuation of Mitzu in the interest of humanity and implement a plan to make the island habitable again. The letter did not, however, make any mention at all of the method to be employed. In any case, it made no mention of cats.

Mr. Rollins was lucky that day. After only five phone calls, he secured an appointment with Captain Staunton P. Dalkye, the executive secretary of the Defense Council.

Captain Dalkye, a lanky, retired naval officer, was a man whose position in the hierarchy of departmental control should never be underestimated. He, in fact was a key figure, the one link between the working servicemen and the politically or otherwise appointed senior public servants in the Defense Department. He was the gentleman whose task it was to inform the defense minister on all matters such as the situation on Mitzu. When he had given his master all the facts and received the ministerial blessing, then and only then would the members of the Defense Council be summoned to the conference table.

On this particular day, however, a deviation from the normal course was necessary. For one thing, the defense minister was out buying his wife an anniversary gift. Nor did Captain Dalkye fare any better when he sought the associate minister. That gentleman was also out, buying an anniversary gift for his cousin, the defense minister's wife. Undisturbed by these mishaps, Captain Dalkye therefore took the line of least resistance. He called a conference of the Defense Council anyway and penciled a reminder in his calendar to inform the defense minister later.

When Mr. Rollins arrived at Room 8439 in the vast complex of a firetrap that housed the War Office, he found a startling array of rank awaiting him. He was, to say the least, a trifle surprised. However, Captain Dalkye, that tall parson-like figure, explained to them, in view of the nature of the request tabled in the letter from the Foreign Office, that he had felt it necessary to call the Defense Council to give the matter immediate consideration.

Rollins was then introduced to the others. He met General Lucius Topps, the chief of Army staff, tall, distinguished and badly in need of a haircut, and Admiral Sir Hugo Stagg, top man in the Royal Navy and a typical red-faced sea dog, who, they said, even in peacetime, was a fire-eater. It was rumored that he chewed up the ends of at least two pipes every day. The air marshal went by the name of Douglas Burrows. He was short, fat, and sported the largest and most untidy mustache Rollins had ever seen. Fourth man in the room was Captain Proud, a lean, freckle-faced armored corps officer. He was Topps' personal aide. On first appearance, it seemed to Rollins that none of the three senior officers was feeling too friendly. Vaguely, he wondered why.

"Well, Rollins," said Topps, "the field marshal tells us you people have a little problem."

"You have received our official request, sir?" asked Rollins pleasantly.

"Yes," said the general, waved a piece of paper. "We have it here. Interesting, very interesting, as a matter of fact. I take it we are all cleared to go ahead, Dalkye? I mean, it's all cleared at the front office?"

"The defense minister was out," replied Dalkye. "As a matter of fact, so was the associate minister. I'll inform them later. I called the conference because, well, while we're not giving Paguda any aid at this time, request for this particular assistance has come from Washington and it has been accepted by Cabinet. I'll tell Mr. Farr as soon as we're through here."

"That's fine," said Topps, "but what I mean is, have we got the clearance to go ahead on this from the Cabinet?"

"Oh, yes, of course we have. I got that from Mr. Rollins. Right, Rollins?"

"Yes," said the liaison officer, "we have it direct from the prime minister himself."

"Good, then," Topps said, "we can get on with it. Now I take it that since the chief of defense staff is away, you gentlemen won't object to my chairing this session?"

"You go ahead," said the admiral, "Douglas and I are all ears."

The general cleared his throat. "Well, gentlemen, here is the story as I have it. An island called Mitzu lies here." He pointed at the large map on the sliding panel and finally to a speck in the South China Sea. "It belongs to the State of Paguda. Its value lies in its airstrip on lease at present to our American friends, and there are four signalmen doing weather watch duties on it, plus about four hundred natives. A report has been received that the island is being overrun by rats. Normally, the Americans would handle this themselves, but because of the disarmament conference at Geneva, they cannot get involved in the area at this time. They do not want to rock the boat. The task for us is not too difficult. Evacuating the population from the island, killing off the rats and doing a methodical cleanup of the place so the islanders can return. We can use the American bases at Bulabar and Singabar as staging areas, and we have complete authority to deal with the American base commanders through the State Department. Are you with me so far?"

Topps looked at Stagg and Burrows. Both waved their hands in confirmation. The general continued. "Good. Well now, the problem as I see it is really quite simple. We ask the Foreign Office to arrange with Paguda to lease the island to us for a series of training exercises. This will provide a cover in case anyone at the UN gets curious—you know."

"Sounds very good to me," the admiral said.

"Me too," agreed Burrows.

"It should be a jolly good show," the admiral added, "and it will give my sailors an interesting trip to the Far East."

"Yes. Burrows grinned. "I just might go along on this one myself—haven't been in that part of the world for a while. Might be fun, eh, Hugo? Besides, we can work in a visit to your chaps in Hong Kong after it's over."

"Anyway," Topps went on, "it's going to be a very stimulating little project. I don't think the Foreign Office will have any trouble in arranging the lease for us. So, once that's done, we can decide the extent to which each of the services will participate. Just off the cuff, I can see several possibilities. We might consider the use of gas or poison, or some of the Navy's lighter guns could provide low level air burst. For that matter, the Air Force could drop some of our old antipersonnel mines. This would tend to scare the rats and drive them into the sea, which I hear is full of sharks. That should settle it. I doubt whether anyone cares how we do it as long as we get rid of the rats. Then, after that, there will be a job for our engineers and the medical unit. It could be a bit of an adventure for all of us. I'm really getting quite keen on it. One other thought does come to me. We might conceivably work on some sort of combined operation."

Rollins, whose face had taken on an ashen color, and Dalkye exchanged worried glances. Rollins shook his head and turned to Dalkye and whispered. "These men must be mad. They're all crazy. What are they talking about?"

General Topps turned to Rollins. "Now, Rollins, about the lease. Can we leave that to you to arrange? Say for about eight weeks? That should give us time enough to clean the place up."

"It might take even longer if we damage the area," said the admiral.

"You're right, Hugo. What do you think, Douglas?

Douglas Burrows shrugged. "Better be on the safe side. I'd ask for another two weeks."

"All right, Rollins, I think we'd best play it safe. Ask for a ten weeks' lease of the island. Rollins, damn it, did you get that?"

"Yes, General, I heard what you said, but—"

"Now, now, Rollins, no buts, just get on with it. And quickly!" The General barked out the last words in obvious annoyance.

Rollins became aware that something was very wrong. He leaned over to whisper to Dalkye and grabbed his arm.

"General, sir," Rollins said, surprised at the demanding tone of his own voice.

"Yes, Rollins. What is it now? You people are always trying to boggle us up."

"I'm sorry general but Captain Dalkye and I have to excuse ourselves for a short while. We have to check on a very important point with the foreign secretary. We'll use the phone in the outer office if we may. We won't be long."

"Oh, very well. Go ahead. But please do not waste any more time. We must get on with this."

Luckily the foreign secretary was in. He almost exploded when Rollins reported what Topps had suggested. "What?" he exclaimed. "Lease the island? The man must have gone around the bend. Have you given him the prime minister's directive yet?"

"No, sir," replied Rollins, "I never had a chance. He started off talking about a lease of the island for some training exercises and then suggested using poison or gas, and even letting the Navy and the Air Force attack the place. I felt I should warn you at once that this whole thing is getting out of hand."

"You did the right thing, Rollins, but you get back in there and—by the way, is Dalkye with you?"

"Yes, sir, he's right here beside me."

"Good. As I said, go back there, give them the Prime Minister's directive and do not accept any arguments from Topps. And tell Dalkye, as secretary to the joint chiefs, he will report to the prime minister immediately after the meeting on whatever decisions are made. Whatever you do, make it clear to them there can be no lease of the island to us for any reason. They must follow the prime minister's instructions to the letter, and that is that. Get going and good luck."

"Very well, sir. I'll do my best. I'll—"

"One more thing," the foreign secretary interrupted, "let me have a word with Dalkye."

"He wants you, Captain." Rollins handed the phone over to Dalkye.

"Yes, sir, Dalkye here." For the next minute as he listened to the foreign secretary's voice, Dalkye's face underwent a series of color changes. And, finally, when he replaced the phone, he shook his head and muttered, "Good God."

"Well," said Rollins, "you heard the man. We go back, we give them the prime minister's directive, and you have to tell them the prime minister wants a report from you on what they decide."

"Yes, of course," Dalkye replied shakily. He clearly was not happy at the prospect.

"Right. Let's go back into the lion's den." Rollins sounded quite confident as he turned toward the door.

As Rollins opened the door to the conference room, he heard the air marshal's loud voice. "Quite frankly, Lucius, I don't see your gas or poison program either, or Hugo's shelling. My Air Force can do the whole thing using loads of old anti-personnel mines. By the way, did anyone think of asking the Marines to this meeting?"

At this point, Dalkye interrupted hastily. "I did not invite them for one good reason. You surely must understand that movement of any kind by the Marines is likely to draw attention. After all, once we start to move our international troubleshooters, it would be picked up and we would be in trouble. I hope you agree."

Admiral Stagg's temper got the better of him. "Huh, troubleshooters? And where the hell is there trouble for them to shoot at? Good God, are you trying to be funny Captain?" Sir Hugo Stagg did not like the commandant of the Royal Marines and never made any bones about it. Topps turned to the others. "Now, let's get on with it. We're wasting valuable time, even now these rats must be breeding and multiplying and spreading plague all over the place."

"Somehow, I don't like it," complained the admiral. "I just don't like it. This whole thing smells."

"All right," the air marshal said, "You don't like it. Well, I don't like it either, but since we've been asked to do it, the RAF is ready to take it on."

Rollins raised his hand and waved the prime minister's directive in Topps' direction. Topps pointed his finger toward Rollins and said angrily, "you must wait a minute. I'll get to you later."

"I think, gentlemen," Dalkye said quietly, "you should listen to what Mr. Rollins has to say. I believe what he has in his hand will have a most important bearing on all this."

Dalkye's new audacity surprised Rollins, who realized his own courage was in for a severe test.

"Please, gentlemen, this has gone far enough." Rollins said nervously. "I have just spoken to the foreign secretary. He told me to remind you the island of Mitzu does not—repeat, not—belong to us and no poison or gas or shelling or bombing will be permitted. And, there is no question of any lease. Absolutely none."

"So it doesn't belong to us," Air Marshall Burrows said sarcastically. "Well, so what? It's still full of bloody rats."

"Yes," added General Topps, "not much use to Paguda or anyone when it's overrun by rodents. Besides, what does the foreign secretary know about dealing with rats? He's a bloody civilian. Knows bugger-all about it."

"Hell," said the air marshal, "isn't that what you asked us to do?"

"Well, I'm sorry, gentlemen. This directive will give you all the information you need to act on."

"But hell, man, that's just what we are going to do, but we intend to do it our way, and that's it," Topps said firmly.

"Sorry, gentlemen, but I can tell you the prime minister would never agree to destroying the island and any publicity about Mitzu will result in very bad reaction throughout the world. We might even start a war."

"Look, Rollins, surely the prime minister can arrange for a lease as a cover for the operation. That makes sense, damn it."

"It certainly does make sense, and any reasonable chap should see that," the air marshal added.

"We have leased small islands before," the general said slowly, as if to convince the others. "In this case, we go in, kill the rats, clean up the place, then the Yanks can have it back, and no one will be any the wiser."

Rollins held up the hand with the prime minister's directive and waved the paper. "Look, gentlemen. Here is what the prime minister wants. The prime minister has discussed this matter with the president of the United States, and they have come up with a very special plan that I—"

General Topps put both hands on top of his head in exasperation as he raised his voice to drown out Rollins. "If the prime minister is worried about security, he need not be. We have a classification of PMTS on it. Great guns, Rollins! What do we have to say to convince you that we are capable of doing this?"

"All right, General," Rollins said loudly, "we cannot—in view of our present policy on world disarmament-take a chance on creating a brand new world crisis. We cannot use gas or poison or high explosives on an island that belongs to a neutral sovereign state. As I have been trying to tell you, here is a detailed directive from the prime minister. If what you are suggesting occurred, we and our allies would most certainly be branded as aggressors by the other side and by the U.N. My God gentlemen, do we want another war?"

In the silence that followed, Rollins mopped his moist brow and took a deep breath before he continued. He waved the paper in his hand once more. "Here is the directive, General. It spells out exactly what you are to do and how you are to do it."

Rollins placed the paper on the table in front of Topps. General Topps looked at the sheet before him and was muttering something when the phone at his elbow rang.

"Topps here. Oh, Prime Minister, yes, sir, it has just been handed to me by Mr. Rollins. I was just about to study it. Yes, sir, we are going to discuss it now and—oh. Certainly, Prime Minister. I'll make sure Captain Dalkye has all the facts so he can brief you."

He no sooner replaced the phone when it rang again. "Damn," he muttered as he picked it up. "Topps here. The foreign secretary? Yes. No, he's not interrupting anything, thanks. Ah, Mister Secretary. Yes, sir, I have it in front of me now. We are taking it on immediately. Of course, we all appreciate the security angle. I have that well in hand. Yes, Rollins has been very helpful. And very cooperative. Yes, sir, I trust you'll see fit to extend his present tour with defense. Quite, sir. Yes, he did. He explained it all very clearly. Of course. Yes, absolutely, sir. You think Rollins and I should go over there as soon as possible? Yes, we'll do just that as soon as our plans are firm. Very well, thank you. Bye." Topps was smiling as he hung up the instrument.

"Good news or bad?" asked the admiral.

"Very good, actually," replied General Topps. "That's a bloody change," remarked Burrows. "Well, what do you know, Rollins, it seems you and I are destined to visit the good old USA. We'll leave as soon as we can tie this up."

"What about the directive, General?" Rollins said in a demanding voice.

"Ah yes, of course, the directive. Well now, let's see." Topps picked up the paper and glanced at it. "Look at this. Hardly legible. Why can't these damn politicians learn to write? Ever see such a scribble?" He held up the paper and laughed.

"Almost as bad as my doctor. He can't write either," observed the admiral.

"Well, my dear colleagues. I shall now take a few moments to study this magnum opus from the prime minister, which I feel is going to tell all of us old sweats how to do our job."

"Oh my God," muttered the admiral, then added, "not again."

"Amen, said Topps.

"Oh, shit." Added the air marshal.

"Steady old boy," the admiral warned with a chuckle, "you're on dangerous ground if you are referring to our beloved prime minister. Might cost you that life peerage when you retire."

There was a distinct warning cough from Topps, who was studying the prime minister's directive as he stroked the back of his overgrown hair. Admiral Stagg, with a loud crunch, bit off the end of his first pipe for the day, and Air Marshal Burrows tugged at his unruly tobacco-stained mustache. Dalkye gazed upward absently, as if calling for help from some unseen saint on the ceiling. He was secretly wishing he could have found some excuse to be elsewhere when the rather shaky voice of the aide to the chief of army staff made itself heard.

"General, sir?" Captain Proud said carefully, "I—"

"Yes, Proud, what is it? And hurry up, we're wasting time."

"Yes, sir. Last year I read in a magazine—"

"You what?" The Admiral's words came out in the form of a nasty snarl.

"I have an idea, sir," said the junior officer. "It might help."

"An idea?" Topps looked about the room as if calling for support. "An idea. Well, why didn't you say so? Let's have it, man, by all means, and quickly."

"It's about a plague of rats, sir. The Japanese had one several years ago on one of their small islands, and they—"

A smile of satisfaction seemed to spread over Mr. Rollins' face as he interrupted. "That was just what I was about to mention, General. It's exactly what I've been trying to tell you."

"Oh, you were?" said Topps testily. "Well all right, tell us now and hurry up about it."

Rollins swallowed nervously. "Yes. Actually, about eighteen years ago, the Japanese encountered the same problem, and they solved it with cats. The prime minister likes the idea and accepts it. In fact, it's what he wants. The prime minister wants us to use cats."

"What?" Burrows yelled the word. "Did you say cats?" The room suddenly became very silent.

"Do you really mean cats?" asked the horrified admiral. "Cats. By God, you do mean cats. General, I'm getting out of here. This chap is batty. Mad as a hatter, just like most of those foreign office jokers."

Rollins looked around at the others meekly, but with an inner sense of victory.

"Dalkye" Topps swung around to face the unhappy man "surely this fellow has gone mad. He's round the bend. What is this all about?"

"Well," answered Dalkye. "I can't say really, except that the prime minister's decision is to carry out this project with the minimum of expense and, he accepted the suggestion of using cats as it is very economical. Besides, the President has promised to produce all the cats we need for this operation. Our services will evacuate the island, take the cats to Mitzu, and then clean up the place and make it habitable again after the cats have destroyed all the rats. Something like that."

"Good God Rollins, is this what you had in mind?" said Topps. The chief of Army Staff was clearly astonished.

"Well, yes General, as a matter of fact, it is exactly what the prime minister wants. I'm sorry about it, sir, but the prime minister discussed it with the foreign secretary and he gave me this directive." Rollins pointed to the paper. "All of this is right there gentlemen."

"I'll be damned." Topps appeared more surprised than annoyed. "Cats," he repeated the word in a tone of complete disbelief. I never thought that I'd ever hear the likes of this. Never. You're all crazy."

Suddenly General Topps began to laugh. Then, the air marshal began to laugh. "This seems to let me out," he cried happily and started to rise.

"On the contrary, sir." Rollins' composure had somehow returned. "The prime minister wants this done with all possible speed, and the Air Force has a large part to play in this. He wants the same plan followed as the Japanese did when they had this problem. I have all the prime minister's notes here on the Japanese enterprise. And, as a matter of fact, this is a complete dossier on the Japanese operation. Here it is."

He handed the folder to Topps, who, after turning over a page or two, began to read aloud. "Evacuation of population by sea by a naval force, after which a force of cats provided by the U.S. government would be flown by the RAF to a nearby base where they would be transferred to ships of the Royal Navy, which would take them in landing craft to the island. I just don't believe it. I've a damn good mind to resign."

By this time Rollins had reached the door. "I think that's about all the help I can give you, gentlemen," he said quietly. "Incidentally, apart from you here, only a few people—the prime minister, the foreign secretary and I—know about this. Good day, gentlemen."

No one attempted to stop Rollins or said a word as he made his exit.

Once outside the room, Rollins propped himself against the wall. He felt faint, and it was a full minute before he began his journey back to the Foreign Office.

On the way Rollins was rather pleased with himself.

After all, it was not every day that anyone could get all three services to cooperate. The operation, he was sure, could now proceed and, if anything went wrong, well, that was up to Defense.

"Well, Albert, how did it go?" asked the foreign secretary.

"Oh, not too bad sir," replied Rollins.

"Did you mention about the cats?"

"Yes, sir, I did."

"I'll bet they blew a fuse on that one."

"I rather imagine they did, sir. Frankly, I didn't stay to find out. I just handed them the prime minister's notes and his directive."

"Smart fellow, not to get caught up in the backwash. Oh, well, we'll soon find out, won't we?"

"Yes, sir," said Rollins. "I'm sure we will."

CHAPTER IX

For a few moments after Rollins had departed, an atmosphere of tenseness hung over the room. General Topps looked out the window and scratched his hair where it fell over his shirt collar. He seemed lost for words. Admiral Stagg leaned back in his chair, snorted, and puffed his smelly pipe. Air marshal Burrows, having carefully completed the last delicate fold of a paper aircraft, held it up with one hand while the other gently stroked his whiskers. Dalkye merely stared at the floor. Proud, as usual, sat by waiting for the string of curses and general abuse that invariably fell upon him on all such occasions of crisis. At the idea of cats, even he managed a sly smile. Suddenly the general turned.

"You know," he began, then his gave fell on his luckless aide and he stopped. "*You,* Proud, what's so damned funny?"

Proud practically sat at attention and in doing so almost overturned his chair. "Funny, sir? Oh, nothing funny, sir. I was just thinking. I was—sorry, sir."

"Well, don't think, and wipe that silly damn grin off your face."

Finally, Admiral Stagg removed his pipe long enough to spit out one word. "Cats! No bloody wonder the Americans fluffed it off on us."

"Yes, Hugo," said the air marshal. "Cats—and it's my Air Force that has to arrange a lift for the brutes. Hell, we'll all be laughed right out of our jobs when this gets out."

"You should worry," said the red-faced admiral. "So you have to airlift them. Well, my Navy has to carry out an amphibious operation with them. I can see the headlines now. What bright clot got us into this one?"

"There will be no headlines," said the general curtly, "of that you can be sure. Anyway, chaps, we have our orders."

"You don't honestly imagine you can keep this out of the papers, do you?" said the air marshal.

"Yes," said Topps, "I do. This is now a prime ministerial top secret project, thank God, and it will stay that way until it is declassified by the prime minister himself. Public Relations will be briefed by me personally. There will be no releases concerning this and no answers to any queries from the press. We shall just deny everything. Everyone concerned will receive a direct order from the top through me to the effect that not one single word of this must leak out. Proud, tell the chief of Public Information—what's his name, Downey—tell Downey I want to see him after I return from the American Embassy."

Captain Proud catapulted out of his seat, thankful for the chance to leave the room. "Right away, sir," and he was gone.

Dalkye began to make notes.

"Now, Dalkye," Topps turned to face him. "Let's get everything straight for the record so that you will be able to brief the minister of defense. Correct me if I get off the track. The island of Mitzu is being overrun with rats. There is a danger of bubonic plague. The government of Paguda has formally asked for help through their ambassador to the U.S.A. The Americans have passed it to us. The Foreign Office, after consultation with the prime minister, has passed a formal request to us in the Defense Department to take on the whole project on a prime ministerial top secret basis. Am I right?"

"That is absolutely correct, sir," said Dalkye as he scribbled on his pad. "I shall take notes for the defense minister on your decisions as you go along."

The general sat down and looked through the folder before him for several minutes. When he finally spoke, his voice took on a sterner tone. "Okay then, here it is: First, you, Douglas, you'll have to put the necessary RAF crews on standby to be ready to leave for Tenpost Air Base in the U.S. Once there, the RAF will pick up the cargo of cats and deliver it to Bulabar. Bulabar will then arrange to move the cargo by road to Singabar where your sailors, Hugo, will take over, using whatever ships you need for the final transfer to Mitzu. Actually, both the Navy's and the RAF's parts are quite limited. Just collect the cargo at Tenpost and fly it to Bulabar. From Bulabar, Douglas, you can bring your chaps home. As a matter of fact, on the way back, I see no reason why all of your people can't stop off in Hong Kong and have a good week's leave. Is that all right with you both?"

"Sounds good to me," said the air marshal.

"Fine with me," said the admiral. "I say, Douglas, we can both go and meet our chaps there. Might be fun."

"Now," Topps said, "As I understand it, General Howell is going to nominate someone to coordinate the concentration of the animals and he's going to find some officers who have some knowledge of Mitzu to land with the cats and keep track of the whole operation on Mitzu." The general paused to study his notes, then he went on. "I hope, since this is a PMTS, we can get the cargo into Bulabar at night so it can be transferred by road to Singabar and loaded on your ships, Hugo, all before daylight. That is quite essential. You will both have to impress on all your people here of the great importance for complete security. Any leakage will be dealt with ruthlessly. Understand? Impress on them this is a PMTS and you'd better be sure they know what it is."

"Got it," the admiral and Burrows nodded. Both men were hastily scribbling notes.

"The operation," Topps continued, "will be known as Operation Feline. I will brief Rollins myself on how we intend to carry it out, and my operations office will control the timings of departure from Tenpost Base. The Americans will loan us two officers and some NCO's to go with the animals to Mitzu. I did mention that, didn't I? They will not necessarily go ashore but will observe and report progress back to the headquarters ship. I imagine if we can give the cats two to four days on the island, we'll have time enough to have a special medical unit ready to fly into Mitzu with the usual equipment to disinfect the island, bury the rats and generally make the island habitable again. I will brief the CO of this unit myself prior to departure."

"What about the evacuation of Mitzu before all this?" asked the admiral quietly, with a sly smile.

"I'm coming to that," replied the General, who had actually forgotten about it. "Douglas, you arrange to get a message to the weather station on Mitzu if you can, through Bulabar. They must tell the people on the place to be packed and ready to evacuate the island by sea on short notice. You, Hugo, be sure your ships are large enough to take off the entire population of Mitzu, about four hundred with all their goods, and deliver them to Paguda, where the U.S. State Department will have made arrangements for them. You'd better brief your ship crews very carefully on this. Now, one last thing. I estimate it will take about six days for the Americans to get the cats concentrated at Camp Billings, so let's work on that basis. Today is November the fourth. The gathering up of cats is the only thing that will take time. Let's set a tentative date—November sixteenth or seventeenth will be D-day, or the day it is decided to move the cats out of Camp Billings to Bulabar. Damned if I know how many cats we'll need. We'll let the Yanks worry about that. Rollins said a thousand or more."

At this point the door opened, and Captain Proud reentered. General Topps looked at him inquiringly. "Yes, Proud?"

"It's all set, General," he said. "The Public Information officer will be in your office waiting for you."

"Good," said the general. "Take this folder, Proud want you to give this matter careful study in case I've missed anything, and remember this is a PMTS matter." He handed the aide the papers.

"Right, General," said Proud. "I'll get onto it at once." The captain withdrew.

The general turned to Dalkye. "Now, Dalkye, have you got all that?"

"Yes, General," Dalkye replied. "I have it all here."

He tapped his notebook.

"Then we can leave it to you to brief the prime minister and defense minister without delay. By the way, where the devil does Mr. Farr keep himself? I have a number of items for his consideration, and I can never find the blighter. Is he sick or what?"

"I have the same trouble with the little bastard," said the admiral. "Whenever I call, he's away on some jaunt to NATO or at his tailor or at his club. I simply can't understand why the prime minister ever gave him this job. The chap is a total misfit in this business. Never around when he's needed. Probably has a popsy somewhere he has to keep happy."

"Never around when there's any work to do either," said the air marshal who had little use for Mr. Farr.

"I believe you're right on that," said the general. "Anyway, he's the minister and I guess we have to put up with him. But you be careful, Dalkye, when you brief him, make him realize this is a PMTS matter. Otherwise, he'll have all his friends at his club in on it."

"Yes, sir, I will. But I wonder-do you think I'd better also tell the associate minister of defense?"

"No, Dalkye, I do not," Topps said firmly. "I suggest we tell only the minister, and let's hope he understands that because this is a PMTS order, only those who need to know will be told—and that does not include his relatives." He turned to the Navy and Air Force chiefs. "This also applies to your people, so don't forget that each message you send must begin and end with PMTS. In that way, we should be fairly secure."

Burrows did not appear overly happy. "This is not going to be workable," he said. "My pilots will have to know, so will the crews and the men who load the crates, and your sailors, unless we can keep all the cats quiet. If we can't?"

"Oh, but you can," said the admiral. "Before they leave Billings, surely they could be given some sort of tranquilizer. What I mean is, they often do it to large animals, don't they? Injections or something. Surely our medical people can come up with something."

"Wonderful idea." General Topps looked pleased. "Now we're thinking. Make a note of it, Douglas."

"Well," said the unhappy air marshal. "If you say so."

"By the way," added the general, "I think I might just dash over to Washington to meet the chap who is collecting the cats and the officers who are going to Mitzu. I'm going over to see the U.S. attaché now. See you later."

Operation Feline now began to take shape. Admiral Stagg personally drafted the message to his opposite number at the Singabar Naval Base. He informed the admiral there that four ships of the Royal Navy would arrive there within the next few days to pick up a special cargo that would be delivered by road from Bulabar Air Base. Three of the ships would then clear Singabar before eighteen November, proceed to Paguda where they would lay over until ordered to proceed to Mitzu to evacuate the population to Paguda. The fourth ship, carrying the special cargo and equipped with six small assault landing craft, would leave Singabar a day or so later and proceed directly to Mitzu to offload its cargo. The captain of this vessel would be given sealed orders to be opened when the ship was well clear of Singabar waters. The last paragraph informed the American admiral that the Royal Navy convoy commander would be Captain Oliver Jacques-Orville, DSO, DSC, RN, a veteran of the Atlantic campaign. The message ended with the usual letters, PMTS.

Air Marshal Burrows had his staff select six of the best transport crews, and he briefed them himself. "Gentlemen, this is a PMTS operation. You will very shortly be leaving for Tenpost Air Base in the United States, where you will pick up a rather strange cargo and deliver it to Bulabar Air Base in the western Pacific. While your cargo may seem a bit odd, I assure you that you will be engaged in an operation of vast importance." Burrows paused to allow the words to sink in, then he continued. "After your cargo has been offloaded, you will remain at Bulabar until the Royal Navy has completed its part of this operation from Singabar Naval Base. When it's all over, and that should be by the twenty-fifth of November, the chief of Defense Staff has agreed that you may proceed to return home via a ten-day stopover in Hong Kong. Oh, one last thing. Just remember this is a PMTS operation for us and a presidential top secret one for our American friends. Security must be absolutely tight."

With that last remark, the air crews were dismissed. As they left, it was evident from their mumblings that they were not overjoyed, although one was heard to say, "Hey, what about that! Ten days in Hong Kong, and just before Christmas too."

That was that, decided Air Marshal Burrows. Now all he had to do was wait for the chief of Army Staff to say when. Thank God, he thought, his task was not any heavier or more involved. Ten days in Hong Kong with Stagg should make up for it.

As General Topps sat in his car on his way back to his own office after his visit to the American military attaché, he mulled over what had taken place in the American's office.

He had started off by asking Colonel Sullivan whether he was aware of Operation Feline. He was somewhat surprised when the colonel bounced out of his seat, opened the door to the hall and looked out in both directions. He then closed the door bolted it and crossed the room to close another door. He then returned to his desk.

"My God, General, Feline, that's a presidential top secret," he said. "How do you know about it? We only heard about it thirty minutes ago."

The general smiled. "Oh, we know about it. Don't you?"

"No, General. I don't even know what it's about. The ambassador called me in a few minutes ago and told me there was an operation, code name Feline, being planned, that it was a PTS and to be sure any messages related to it were not seen by anyone else, only he will deal with them. So, that's all I know. It's only the second PTS I've ever seen. How come you know about it?"

"Oh, that's really quite simple," Topps replied. "You see, we're doing it. As a matter of fact, we put the Feline tag on it, and our prime minister called your president. I shall be going to Washington tomorrow to discuss it with your General Howell. I'll see about filling you in when I return or ask the foreign secretary to brief your ambassador."

"Thanks, General. I appreciate that. You really startled me when you mentioned Feline."

"Sorry about that."

Since the poor chap didn't seem to have a clue about it, Topps thought it best to say no more.

Once back in the War Office, Topps headed straight for the Operations Center. He had made up his mind that the one man to direct all the intricacies of Feline was his operations chief, Major-General David Ruthers. When he entered the center however, he was surprised to find Ruthers there but he was certainly not attired for active duty. General Ruthers was in civilian clothes with overcoat, bowler hat, gloves and umbrella.

"Hello David, off somewhere?" Hoping he was wrong.

"Good day General. Yes I am. Just came in to get my travel papers. Off to Europe. On furlough, you remember?"

Ruthers sounded much too happy. It upset Topps to see any of his officers this happy.

"Oh yes. Of course I do. Well, I just thought I'd wish you a happy holiday. Have a good time David.

"Thanks General." The rather surprised Ruthers took his chief's hand and left hurriedly.

As Ruthers left, Topps felt a bit awkward.

"Anything I can do for you Sir?" The female behind the typewriter asked.

"No thank you sergeant. "I'll see the general when he gets back."

Topps was muttering to himself as he swung into his own office where a scholarly and bespectacled colonel awaited him. This was Downey, the chief of Public Information. He had about him the nervous air of an expectant father, a usual state for those gentlemen whose task was not only to keep the armed services mistakes off the front pages but to inform the public whenever the soldier, sailor or airman does something creditable. Providing of course, it did not remind the taxpayer too much of what was being done with his defense pound.

"Ah, Downey! There you are." This hearty greeting alone immediately put the visitor on the alert. This, Downey told himself, was bound to be something nasty.

"Good day, General," he said quietly. "You have something for me."

"Yes, have a chair," replied Topps, settling himself behind his desk.

Downey took his seat opposite Topps, who looked at him sternly.

"Downey, what do the words prime ministerial top secret mean to you?" Topps smiled as he spoke, for he reveled in bullying his nervous subordinate. The words hit the other man hard, just as he hoped. The Public Information officer, whose motto (which he repeated to everyone he met) was "breathe confidence," looked as if his aorta had suddenly plugged up, his face turning a dull white.

"Well?" said Topps, "Tell me, do you?"

"Prime ministerial top secret!" exclaimed Downey.

"Why, General, it's—we've only had one of those in the past twenty years. You mean it's another Cuba?"

"No, no, Downey, not another Cuba. But, anyway, I see at least you know what this phrase implies."

"Oh, yes, General, I see it." The color was gradually coming back to Downey's face.

"This one," Topps said, "is about Mitzu, and it's a very hot one."

"Mitzu, sir?" Downey's geography was clearly not up to date.

"Yes. It's a small island in the Pacific. Oh, I should start by mentioning Paguda. You see, Mitzu belongs to Paguda. We are about to undertake a special project concerning this island. Now, as from this moment, you know nothing about Mitzu or Paguda or anything concerning either the island or the country. If anyone asks you any questions, you know nothing, understand? Nothing."

"Yes, General, but what if—"

"But nothing," said the General sternly. "This is a PMTS."

"Very well, General. I was only thinking that—"

"So, Downey," Topps interrupted, pointing a finger at the already distressed officer, "don't ask anyone about Paguda, don't think anything about Paguda, no speculation, not one word. It is being dealt with by us in cooperation with the Foreign Office on a need-to-know basis only under the prime minister's personal order. Is that quite clear?"

"Yes, perfectly clear, sir." Answered Downey, wishing he had never heard of Paguda, or of the prime ministerial top secret, for that matter.

"All right. I rely upon you to insure that not one word of this is leaked to anyone, Downey. That's all. Oh, by the way, I shall be leaving for a short visit to the Pentagon tonight, but I'll be back in three days."

Downey left the Chief's office a bewildered man. How in hell, he wondered, was he to insure that not one word of a matter about which he knew nothing leaked out. He speculated briefly whether or not it might be a good time to retire and go back to teaching school in MacIntosh Corners, his hometown on the northwestern coast of Scotland.

General Topps and Mr. Rollins were waiting for the chairman of the Joint Chiefs in the warmth of the latter's office at the Pentagon. Topps hoped this meeting would not last too long. He was tired, having only arrived at Andrews Air Force Base an hour before.

"By the way Rollins, have they got you at the Mayflower too?" He asked.

"No, sir. I'm staying with George Weyland, the first secretary. He has a home in Foggy Bottom. The foreign secretary asked me to have a word with him about one of our people here—bit of a scandal, I'm afraid."

"Not serious I hope," said the general. "I mean, he's not going around coveting some other bloke's oxen or asses or wives-or is he?"

"Something like that, sir. Perhaps you know him, Roger Waterfield?"

"Good Lord," exclaimed the general. "Old Roger! Oh my, my. Yes, of course I know him. We were at Eton together and he was in my regiment during the Korean affair. Damned good officer, clever chap. Speaks about four languages, but, hell, he must be nearly sixty. Surely he's past the old stud stage by now. Is he married?"

"No, sir. He was divorced about twelve years ago. A rather messy affair."

"Oh, well, then, can't blame the poor chap for a little hunting on the side now, can you? I wouldn't take it too seriously if I were you, unless of course, there's something odd about it."

"Well, as a matter of fact, sir, there is something a bit out of place. Roger has been reported, as our American friends put it, shacking up with the wife of a Korean diplomat, and also the wife of a Finnish military attaché. The foreign secretary didn't mind the Korean really, but he thinks the Finnish lady is a bit-well—a bit too near Moscow, if you know what I mean, and he wants me to tell him. I don't relish the idea, but I'm afraid I have to do it."

"Yes." agreed the general. "I suppose you do. Well be sure to give him my best when you see him." As he rose he waved his hand at the array of photos. "Quite a rogues gallery. I probably know a few of them."

Topps and Rollins were looking at the photos of the previous chairmen of the joint chiefs which lined one wall when General Jason Howell entered.

The British general had always had great admiration for this remarkable man, tall, always well tanned and with the build of an athlete. Everything about Howell spelt out the complete soldier who, like Topps, had been many times wounded in combat.

"Well, well, Lucius," the chairman of the American Joint Chiefs of Staff hailed him. The two generals shook hands.

"This is Mr. Rollins, General. He's the Foreign Office liaison man for Feline. I thought he should come over and meet the chaps who are going to be directly involved in this."

"Good idea," said General Howell. "But let's all have a seat. Would either of you like a cup of coffee?"

Both Englishmen shook their heads.

"Okay," Howell went on. "I've been thinking about some of the people who will have to be involved in this operation. One of them is our chief of procurement. Name of Jansen. I think he'll be the ideal man for this. He's away today but I've asked his deputy to leave a message on his desk to report to me as soon as he returns. Now, if you're ready Lucius. Fill me in on how things have progressed at your end."

Topps was delving into is briefcase when the door opened and one of the joint chief's aides entered and handed Howell a message.

"Ah good." He said after glancing at it. "Mr. Rollins, if you will accompany this officer he will introduce you to our two liaison officers with the state department who are going to be involved in this business."

"Excellent." Topps said. "That's a good idea Albert but don't stay away too long because General Howell may have some questions for you."

"Very good sir."

As soon as Rollins and the aide had gone, Topps spread his planning notes on his lap. "Well now, let's see. By the way,

Jason, has the secretary of state heard anything from your president or prime minister on our plan for this?" Topps asked.

Howell shook his head. "If he has he's not passed it on to me but...I'm not surprised. This whole thing about Mitzu has our president scared silly. As an economist he has little knowledge of or interest in military affairs. He doesn't consider us military people near his own level of ability or intelligence. I imagine you have the same problem with your politicians in the UK."

"Alas yes." Said the British general. "I guess that's the way things were meant to be. We are the eternal servants. Damned if I can figure out why anyway." He passed Howell several papers. "Look it over Jason, I'd appreciate your opinion."

Meanwhile, back at the War Office in London, an event had taken place that had a distinct bearing on Operation Feline.

The student of world history will no doubt realize that often a most insignificant occurrence can change the triumphal march forward into a retreat in disorder, or turn a well-planned event into the proverbial snafu. In the eight minutes it took for Captain Dalkye to go from the conference room back to his own office, where he intended to inform the prime minister and the defense minister of the latest development on Operation Feline, it happened.

Miss Sophie Weisbaum had left the canteen laden with three cups of coffee, two melted cheese sandwiches and two pieces of banana cream pie. She made her way slowly up the cold stone stairs. Once on the main floor, however, her confidence of footing returned and with her eyes focused on the whipped cream topping on the pie, she swung and bounced her way along the corridor toward her boss's office. Colonel Hoggings loved his coffee, his melted cheese sandwich and his banana cream pie. This mid-morning repast, so he said, made his day. Sophie turned the last corner at the same time as Captain Dalkye. The crash of two human bodies as they hit the floor, the curses, the loud expressions of apology broke the normal silence and resounded down the hall. When Colonel Hoggings opened his door to investigate, he saw Miss Weisbaum sitting on the floor looking very much like a centerpiece at a rather disorganized smorgasbord table. The coffee and cream-bespattered figure with blood on his face, who flew past him in an advanced state of agitation and muttering unmentionable words, he did not recognize at all.

Captain Dalkye stopped at his office long enough to wipe the gore from his bleeding nose and to collect his coat and hat. His secretary was not available, so he left her a note. It read, "Have to go home—bad cold."

By the time he reached his house he had sneezed eight times and the bump on his head was throbbing severely. He undressed, put his soiled clothes in the laundry basket and had a shower. In the shower he sneezed again four times. That and his aching head was a clear signal to the captain that he'd better take precautions.

When his wife returned from her daily shopping, she found him in bed with an ice-bag on his head and a heating pad on his chest.

Of course, it had not occurred to Captain Dalkye that the notes on Operation Feline he had prepared for the prime minister and the minister of defense were still in the pocket of his discarded jacket. To be perfectly honest, at that time, he could not have cared less.

CHAPTER X

If complexity is one of the main characteristics of the United States Department of Defense, then versatility must certainly be another.

Over the years, the Department has enrolled and trained men, horses, mules, dogs, sea lions, dolphins and pigeons—and, of course, it has also produced individuals who are classed as staff officers. In the Defense Department, General Robert Wallace Jansen, or Fireball Jansen, as he was known, was the one person responsible for procurement of personnel and everything that goes with them to enable an army to live, to move and to fight. Actually, as the man in charge of Special Projects Logistic Support, he was the right man for the job. He was, for all his two hundred and thirty pounds spread over a five-feet-six-inch frame, the Army's workhorse. If anything got done, it was generally Jansen who did it. "Yes, sir. You ask it, we got it, and we deliver it anytime, anyplace," was his motto, and he lived up to it.

It was true: One had but to ask, and whatever was required would be on the way to the right place at the right time and in the specified quantity without delay. The general had long felt sure his name would be one the country would remember. That was before Operation Feline.

When Jansen reported to General Howell's office, laden with his folios of facts and figures, he was in his usual cheery mood. He nodded cockily to his chief, to the longhaired uniformed figure of General Topps, and the odd-looking civilian standing by the window. General Howell introduced them with a wave of his hand.

"General Jansen, meet General Topps, the British Chief of Army Staff, and Mr. Rollins, the British Foreign Office senior liaison officer."

The three men exchanged greetings, and Rollins winced visibly when Jansen grabbed his hand in an overly strong squeeze.

"Well, gentlemen," said General Howell. "Jansen is the man who is going to find your cats for you."

Normally, Robert Wallace Jansen was not one to be easily shaken. But for one moment it seemed to him the world had stopped. Jansen was not quite sure if his ears had caught the right word. For a moment he had been ready to give Topps and Rollins his stock greeting: "Yes, sir, you ask it..." But he stopped himself just in time. As he sorted out his papers, General Jansen had, for the first time in his distinguished career, a feeling of impending doom. He wondered if his chief really had said *cats*.

Within the next half hour, however, while Topps looked at his carefully manicured hands and while Rollins sat in the deep leather chair gazing at the ceiling, Robert Wallace Jansen was given the details and provisions of Operation Feline by General Howell. He made several pages of notes but kept his eyes down to prevent the other men from seeing the look of sadness and distress in them.

Despite his shortness of stature, General Jansen was, above all, a man of immense pride. While his new assignment jolted him severely, he did not show a single sign of discomfort or emotion. He finished his notes on the security aspects and personnel requirements, and when he reached the door to go, his exit line was characteristic of the reputation he had gained. "Okay, gentlemen," he said, "cats you need, cats you get and," he added, "no publicity. I'll start the ball rolling at once."

General Jansen was as good as his word. Within the hour, a presidential top secret message had been prepared, and now Jansen gazed at the words he had written.

PERSONAL FOR COMMANDER'S EYES ONLY.
PRESIDENTIAL TOP SECRET. THIS IS AN URGENT REQUIREMENT. ALL CATS YOUR AREA TO BE SHIPPED TO CAMP BILLINGS ALL POSSIBLE SPEED. NO PUBLICITY THIS MATTER EXCEPT ON CJCS. PERSONAL ORDER - PTS - ACKNOWLEDGE.

It was, Jansen decided, a clear, concise message. He was pleased with it. Now it only remained to select the addresses, get the message encoded and dispatched. There were, he surmised, two main sources of cats: the larger service establishments and the SPCA compounds. But, Jansen reflected, any approach to the SPCA and to the bases would have to be carefully considered if security was to be maintained.

Eventually, after an exhaustive inspection of the services location list, he selected the six largest army camps within a radius of 500 miles from Camp Billings, plus a smaller assortment of Air Force bases. In any case, the recipients, who were to be the senior officers at each establishment, would have only to note the first three words of the message to be spurred into instant action. While all the messages were identical in content, each was addressed to one individual commander. Thus, none of the recipients would know who else had received it. This, Jansen felt, would further insure security.

Insofar as Camp Billings was concerned, Jansen knew that General Howell had already sent the officer in charge a PTS telegram ordering Billings to take action 4-10-2, which, in lay terms, meant to reopen the camp. Colonel Byron Slate, the commander of Camp Billings, would know what to do.

There did remain the matter of the SPCA. Jansen pondered the matter. Would the president of that organization cooperate? When he looked at the SPCA brochure that listed its officials, he felt much better. As luck would have it, he noted that four of the ten directors were retired generals or admirals, and the president was none other than Admiral Lynden Lyman.

He had little trouble in securing an immediate appointment with his old comrade.

As he left his office to meet with Lyman, he handed the written message in the usual secure double envelope to his secretary.

"This is presidential top secret," he told her. "Get it down to signals, get a copy to the defense secretary's office by hand, and address each copy to only the single addressee by name."

The secretary nodded her head and Jansen left.

His meeting with the retired admiral was more successful than he had hoped. The old sailor glanced at the three words Jansen had written on the slip of paper and had placed before him. Then, with a smile, he handed the paper back to Jansen. It was clear that Admiral Lyman knew what those words implied.

"What can I do for you? By the way, has this visit something to do with General Howell's call?" he asked.

"Yes. I need cats, all you've got," replied Jansen.

"When?" asked Lyman.

"Soonest."

"Where?"

"Camp Billings," said Jansen. "For a very special and humanitarian project—and they must be taken there by road transport, if possible by night."

"I may have trouble explaining this to the other directors, said the admiral. "What the devil shall I tell them?"

"You can always give them the PTS treatment," Jansen said hopefully. "After all, that amounts to a no-question order from the top, and since most of those directors were in the service, they'll understand it. You may have to explain PTS to the others."

"Yes, I can try that, but don't forget that not all of these men are on the government's side. There could be a leak and some questions raised in Congress."

"We'll have to chance it, Admiral," said Jansen emphatically. "This is urgent."

"All right. Cats to Camp Billings it is then. I can have some on the way by this evening."

Jansen took the older man's hand and shook it warmly. "Thank you, sir. You have just rendered me a great personal service. He picked up his hat and was about to walk away when Lyman stopped him short with a question.

"By the way, do we get them back?"

"Get what back, sir?" asked Jansen.

"The cats we're going to give you, of course. Well, do we?"

"Oh, well, I..." It suddenly occurred to Jansen that no one had actually said what was to be done with the cats after the operation was completed. He put his hat on carefully before he answered. "Well, no, sir, I'm afraid not. But mind you, these cats are going to receive the best of treatment. And one thing you can be sure of; every single one of them will end up in a good home." He edged nearer the door, hoping the admiral would not pursue the matter further.

"You know Fireball, you're really doing us a big favor."

"That's all the better then." said Jansen.

"Yes." Lyman explained "I did a survey only last week. We have some twenty-three compounds all within a three day drive from Billings. Once I give your people what they have, I'll have reason to accept animals from some of the overcrowded northern centers. So really, we don't have a thing to worry about."

"That's encouraging, I was worried you might not have enough for us." Jansen moved towards the door.

"Nonsense Fireball, you will get all you need and by the way, give my regards to Mrs. Jansen."

As the door closed behind the general, the admiral drew a folder from his desk drawer. "Cats to Camp Billings. Well, well." Now he had to decide what would be the best way of telling the managers of these compounds that they were to ship all cats to Camp Billings. It had to be done with great care. Perhaps a short personal and confidential letter to each resident manager would be the answer. After a few seconds, he decided that was the course to follow; registered and special delivery.

That would certainly produce the result required. Having made this important decision, Lyman rang for his secretary. He would have to help her run the duplicating machine. Ah, well, he thought, recalling with boyish relish that the last time he had seen Miss Langley turning the handle on the ancient duplicator her bosom had bounced up and down in a most delightful manner.

"Ah, there you are, my dear," he said as the buxom Miss Langley made her entrance. "We have a little job to do, you and I."

Miss Langley blushed, beamed, and settled herself in a chair with pad and pencil—ever ready to go to work.

When Jansen returned to his office, his secretary informed him General Howell the Chairman Joint Chiefs had been trying to contact him. He lost no time in calling the general, who sounded a bit cagey on the telephone.

"Oh, that you, Bob? Good. Look, the secretary of defense is back from Korea and wants to see you. Apparently, he got a copy of your message a few minutes ago, and he just about hit the ceiling—started to ask me a lot of damned stupid questions. I told him that as a presidential top secret matter I could not discuss it over the phone and referred him to you. So you'd better get down to his office right away and tell him as much as you can about it. I understand my executive secretary Dalkye was supposed to brief him, but I understand our bright boy must be ill because he went home early. I'd have done it myself but, honestly, I can't stand talking to that idiot. In any case, you're the key man in this, okay?"

"Okay, sir," Jansen replied gloomily. "I'll see him right away."

"Good man. I'll leave it to you then." The Chairman hung up.

Mr. Horace Cuthbert Kleffen III, the secretary for defense, was in his usual foul mood when Jansen arrived. He greeted the general as he did all service officers, with a curt, pompous greeting and never the offer of even a chair, let alone a welcoming hand.

"Well, well, Jansen. Very good of you to come," he remarked with obvious sarcasm.

As Jansen approached the large, well littered desk, holding the manila envelope that contained the top secret details of Operation Feline, Kleffen waved a pink message form at him. They presented a curious picture, these two. Jansen, the essence of a fit, professional perfectionist despite his short, stout stature, and Kleffen, equally professional, but uncouth, untidy and flabby.

"This arrived on my desk," the secretary said with obvious arrogance. He waved the paper high above his head.

"I know, sir," replied Jansen. "I sent it to you, sir."

"Very decent of you, Jansen, considering it's a PTS." The fat, flabby face deepened in color and his jowls twitched from the lobes of his ears to the tip of his treble chin. "Now, suppose you tell me what in the hell is going on—or do you know?"

"Operation Feline, sir," Jansen said. "The State Department has made a request to our British allies to help clear up a plague of rats on the island of Mitzu, on which we have the lease for one of the secret weather stations and an emergency airfield. The president decided to ask the British to do it, and they agreed to take it on. General Topps, the acting chief of the Defense Staff, has already had a conference in London with the heads of the British Armed Services. And they've formulated a plan for the evacuation of the population to the Pagudan Mainland, the destruction of rats by placing several hundred cats on the island for a few days, following which a special Sanitation Unit from the Royal Engineers and their Medical Corps will clean up the place so the inhabitants can return."

"Very interesting, but why wasn't I informed earlier?" the irritated secretary demanded.

"Because Sir, you were in Korea and the president decided..."

"All right, all right general. Go on. Tell me the rest of the comedy."

"The Royal Navy and Royal Air Force agreed to their part of the plan, and I've been given the job of finding and concentrating the cats for this operation. It's all really quite simple, and at the moment the entire operation is under tight control and all under a PTS security coverage. We've asked certain army and air bases and the SPCA to provide some of the cats we need. After a period of concentration at Camp Billings, which the Chairman ordered reopened, the cats and their handlers will be flown to the U.S. airbase at Bulabar by Royal Air Force planes. From Bulabar they will go to Singabar U.S. Naval Base by road, where they will be transferred to ships manned by the Royal Navy for the journey to Mitzu. In Paguda, the State Department is handling the medical and other aid needed for the evacuees. That's about it, sir."

"That's about it?" said the sour-faced defense secretary. "Oh, so we're going to spend a few hundred thousand of the taxpayer's dollars flying cats around the world, and all you can say is, 'that's about it.' Who, may I ask, suggested the services should perform this farce? I suppose the State Department just foisted it on us, and we, like a bunch of idiots, agreed to it? What's it going to cost us? Just a million or two? You tell me."

"It's not going to cost us anything for the air transport or use of the ships. At first, the president told the British we'd handle all costs, but they declined that offer. They're paying their own way on this."

"Yes, that's fine," said the anxious defense secretary, "but what about our cost of this at home? You tell me, how much is that going to run?"

"That, sir," replied Jansen, "is hard to say at this time. There will be some cost involved in reopening Camp Billings and the pay and allowances for the two officers who accompany the shipment. Apart from that, well, I don't think it will amount to much."

"You don't, eh? Well, I want this accounted for, you understand? Every cent, from start to finish. Every cent, you hear me? I want a full report."

"Yes, sir," Jansen said. "I'm sorry, sir, but as I understand it, the matter was discussed by our own secretary of state with the British prime minister, and, in fact, it initially came as a personal request from the president to the British."

"Oh—it—well, all right, fine," Kleffen said. "But then, if it was the president's decision, why wasn't I told by the Chairman Joint Chiefs? Why do I have to learn all this from a copy of a wire and from you?"

Jansen let the last remark fly over him.

"Well, sir, first of all you were not here, and that's why the Chairman, General Howell, asked me to brief you, as I am handling the matter."

"I suppose you expect to keep all this out of the papers. If so, tell me how?"

"Sir," Jansen said, exasperated, "this is a PMTS matter for the British—a PTS for us. General Topps in London has told his public information people this, and they will stand by that decision. Believe me, sir, we and the British have a reasonably efficient organization. You can be sure of complete security."

"Yes, but what do I say if this is brought up by some fool in the opposition? You tell me, eh? Am I going to be the scapegoat? Am I to be left holding the bag?"

The stupid son of a bitch, thought Jansen, but held his temper. "Sir, being a PTS matter, sir, you can always make a statement to that effect. After all, members of both houses are well aware of the implication of the words. So is the press, for that matter. As for direct liaison, sir, I can always brief you-daily, if you wish it."

"Yes," said Kleffen, "yes, I suppose you can. Well, see that you do. By the way, does the assistant secretary know anything about this?"

"No, sir, he does not. Being a PTS, it is preferable to keep this matter very close, on a need-to-know basis, I should say."

"I see. Just who does know?"

"Apart from the president, there's the secretary of state, the Chairman Joint Chiefs of Staff, the national security advisor, the British Defense Council, and—oh yes, a Mr. Rollins, the Foreign Office liaison officer and, of course, our ambassador in Paguda. Pagudan representatives in Washington know of the general situation but none of the details. They know we are providing some sort of special aid on a PTS basis. The actual details of using cats are not being divulged to any of the camps or bases concerned, not even Camp Billings, Bulabar or Singabar, or even the people who handle the cats, until they leave for Mitzu.

"These will merely follow whatever orders are given them. The Pentagon has already ordered their bases to cooperate with the British, so we are cleared for action. However, everyone has been informed this is a PTS matter."

"Well, you apparently have more faith in this than I do. I hope to God you're right." Pompous man, he paused for effect. "For your sake, General."

"I would suggest, sir, that I brief you daily starting tomorrow—on the highlights that is. No need to go into all details. If you'd care to select a time of day, I can be available at any time."

This suggestion did not make the overfed incumbent of the top defense post feel any better. If he were fully in the picture, the secretary of state, or even the president, might start to call him at some ungodly hour. He was not quite sure he wanted this. Still, it was defense money that was being spent, an expense for which no one had planned, an expense for which he as defense secretary might be called on to explain to one of those damned Senate committees. No, he decided, the less he knew of this, the better. Actually, under the guise of the PTS classification, he could say that in the interests of national security he had ordered Jansen to handle it and to refer to him only in case of emergency. Knowing the Chairman, he felt quite sure Howell would not want to approach him if he could avoid it. Then, if anything went wrong it would be up to Chairman Howell and Jansen. They would have to explain it.

"General," said Kleffen, "in view of the speed in which the Chairman of Joint Chiefs and you may have to make decisions, I think it best for you two to take complete charge of this operation. I'll ask for a briefing when I feel it timely. In that way, your—er flexibility of action will not be hampered. I'll call you from time to time to get up to date on it. Yes, that's what I'll do."

"Very well, sir," said Jansen, sensing that the fat man was already searching for a scapegoat, he was glad to close the door and get away.

The Secretary of Defense was one of those whose vast wealth had bolstered party funds to such an extent that his political appointment to high government position had long been a foregone conclusion. Naturally, because he knew nothing about the Navy, Army, Air Force, or the Marines, the defense slot was an obvious choice for him. The president had felt he would not be biased and that his reputation as a tight-money man and as a determined pacifist was needed in this business. The president had hoped that neither the press nor the public would ask too many questions about Kleffen's appointment. They knew that it was based on his donations to the party.

The president repeatedly reassured himself and his closest advisors that he had done the right thing. But over the last six months some of Kleffen's activities in and out of the Pentagon had caused several senior officials and some cabinet ministers to complain directly to the president about Kleffen and his suitability in the defense slot.

The president, ever aware of Kleffen's contributions, continued to reassure himself but to a point lately where even he was not sure of what.

After Jansen's departure, Kleffen sat staring at the mass of papers scattered on his desk. Then, for some reason, he slammed his hand hard down on the desk top.

"I'll show them," he muttered. "I'll show those bastards."

He got up and paced the floor. Why, he asked himself, had the Chairman Joint Chiefs not briefed him personally? Why the devil did he, the secretary of defense, have to find these things out for himself? He wondered whether it might not be a good idea to discuss General Jansen's suitability as the man in charge of Special Projects Logistics with the president sometime soon. Damn them anyway. Damn all generals. A cabinet minister can't have a mere general trying to run the whole department. Next thing he knew, that fellow Howell would be telling him how to manage the Pentagon. He would show them just who gave the orders around here. Besides, he recalled sourly, at the last National guard Ball, Jansen was one person who had not asked Gladys Kleffen for a dance. That alone had upset his life at home for almost a month.

He recalled his wife's remark at the ball: "Horace, doesn't that man know you're in charge of the Defense Department?"

"I think so, dear."

"Doesn't he realize," she said, "you are the one person hand-picked by the president to oversee the defense of our country?"

"I think so, dear."

"Well then, surely you should remind him of your position. Who does he think he is? Just another…"

"I think so, dear."

CHAPTER XI

The reactions of the recipients to General Jansen's PTS message were mixed. Some read it with surprise, some with horror, some didn't believe it and several miscalculated its meaning.

Within the next twelve hours, at least half of the addressees had replied that they would fulfill the instructions contained in the PTS message, while the other half reported that an assortment of the feline species was already on its way to Camp Billings. How the cats were gathered was not explained, but in the days following, administrative officers at some of the larger camps received irate letters in which camp wives set forth their complaints. The contents of the letters ran pretty much the same: the family pet cat had been let out to perform its natural functions prior to the family's retiring and had disappeared. It had not returned. In one particular instance, a Mrs. Walter Wells stated that she herself had seen two strangers lurking in the shadows with a large sack into which a hapless animal had been lured.

At Camp Stunger, the commandant called in his senior military police officer.

"Major," he announced after closing the door, "I have a job of the highest importance for you; I know you can do it."

"Thank you, sir," replied the major with that certain keen look of anticipation that always pleases a superior. "Just give me the order."

The commandant waved a paper. "I have here a PTS message. Do you realize what that means?"

"PTS, sir?" The major appeared baffled. "Something to do with physical training, sir?"

"No, no, a presidential top secret, my boy—the highest security classification possible. I doubt whether any more than six people in the whole country know about this—and you are one of them."

If this was calculated to make the major feel proud of the fact, he did not show it. He merely moved his tongue around his cheek and waited for his superior to be more explicit.

"Now, Major, how many cats do you figure we have in camp at this time?"

"Cats, sir?" said the major. "There are none in this camp, sir."

"None—but that's impossible, of course we have."

"No, sir. The last one I know of was Mrs. Harkowitch—you remember her, sir—last year. And even she wasn't doing it for money. She was lonely while her husband was away."

"No, no, Major. You don't understand. I do not mean anything like that. I mean cats, real cats, cats that meow."

A relieved look came to the major's face. "Oh—cats, sir. Well, now, let's see. I can't give you any figure on cats. Dogs, yes, because they're registered in camp, but cats? I could make a rough guess based on the number of families. What I mean is, Colonel, if we can establish the number of families that have a dog, we can cross them off because usually people with dogs don't have cats. Then we can take the remainder and estimate a percentage. We could even—"

"Oh, damn it, Major," said the irate commandant, "I'm not interested in any percentage. All I want you to do is produce as many cats as you can for me by tomorrow morning. Your men will crate the cats, and I want you to deliver them personally to Camp Billings. As a matter of fact, I want the cats caught, crated, and out of camp before dawn tomorrow."

"But, sir," said the major, "the cats in this camp all belong to someone. There are no loose cats just running about. I mean, we'll have to ask the owners, surely, for permission to take them."

The commandant brought his hand down on the desk angrily. "Major, the wire I have here is a PTS. It amounts to no less than a direct order from the president himself, from your commander-in-chief, and let me make this quite clear, Major, if my commander-in-chief wants all the cats or dogs in camp collected and sent to him at the White House, he will get them. Now, is that quite clear? I want action and I want it now."

"Yes, Colonel, but—"

"No buts, please. I have now passed on the order to you, Major. Your mission is to collect, crate, and take all the cats you can find to Camp Billings." The commander pointed a finger as if to make the point final. "You are to be on your way by dawn tomorrow. You have, as I see it, exactly sixteen hours in which to do it. Now I reckon you'd better get started—and remember, this is a presidential top secret assignment."

The major found it difficult to concentrate as he drove back to his office, so much so that he went right through one stop sign and had his jeep's number taken by an angry lady outside the commissariat. But it mattered little; he had a mission to perform, and he lost no time.

Having assembled the entire military police platoon of sixteen men assigned to the camp in his small office, the major explained to the group the purpose of the meeting. He gave it to them straight: All available cats were needed for a secret mission. It was their job to go out to the married quarters area after dark and pick up every cat they could find. Strong cardboard or wooden boxes were to be gathered from the camp groceteria. Once captured, the animals would be placed in a box and loaded onto a truck. The hunt would commence at 2000 hours and would end an hour after midnight. This would give the men five hours. Upon termination of the hunt, the vehicles would be covered by heavy tarpaulins and be prepared to leave the camp by a back route. The major himself would remain in his office during the operation and receive reports from his men in coded phrases over the camp police radio set. He set the goal for the night's work at fifty cats.

They managed to snare forty-one of the creatures, but not without some bites and scratches.

There was one particular miscalculation when an overeager corporal pounced on an unwary animal that was busily engaged with the contents of an overturned garbage can. Alas, he realized his mistake too late. The garbage eater was furry, it was black and white, and in the moonlit darkness it did look like a cat. Corporal Blincow withdrew hastily from the engagement but was forced to walk the two-odd miles back to the MP compound, carrying with him the odor of his error.

The major, while he was not elated by the evening's catch, did not complain. He had done his best. At a little after four in the semi-gloom that precedes the dawn, he led his two vehicles full of cats toward Camp Billings.

At the School of Military Engineering, the message arrived shortly after three in the morning. Lieutenant Brown, the keen young duty officer only five months out of the Academy, opened the outer envelope given to him by his orderly, still half asleep. He saw the inner envelope with the letters PTS on it and unsealed it with trembling hands. In his training at the Academy, they had told him about security classifications. He recalled how his instructor had listed them—restricted, confidential, secret, top secret. Finally, in almost a whisper, the instructor had uttered the three words "Presidential top secret." He recalled the words with a slight shudder. "Short of a global nuclear war, none of you," the instructor had explained, "will probably ever see one of those. If you do, watch out—but, there, you now have the full list anyway."

Lieutenant Brown shook his head as the drowsiness left him and brought him to a stupefied state of awareness. Having read the message over and over and being unable to reach any decision as to what exactly should be done, he picked up the phone and called Colonel Platters, the officer in command of the school.

After what seemed an age, his superior answered. "Yes?" Colonel Platters sounded sleepy.

"Oh, Colonel, duty officer here, sir."

"All right, what the hell is it at this time of night?"

"A message, sir—a PTS message."

"A what?" said the colonel. "Are you nuts?"

"No, Colonel. It's a PTS—really."

"What about?"

"It's about cats, sir."

"Cats? What about them?"

"They want us to send all available cats as soon as possible to some place called Camp Billings, sir."

"To Billings, eh?" There was a pause, but Colonel Platters was a man of action. He wasted no time. "Okay, Brown, you get the engineer projects officer up out of bed at once; tell him to get those forty-odd cat tractors we have sitting there in the compound loaded onto flat cars or transports by seven this morning. He knows what to do. If he seems in any doubt at all, just tell him I said it's a PTS, okay?"

"Yes, sir," Brown said. "You bet, sir, right away, sir."

"Good man, and thanks, Brown." Platters hung up and settled back in the bed.

By mid-morning, as Colonel Platters tried to extricate himself from the deep sand trap halfway to the fourth green of the camp golf course, he heard the chugging of a train as it passed along the north edge of the camp. Looking up briefly, he saw the train carrying his forty-two new Caterpillar tractors to Camp Billings disappear behind the woods. He wondered why someone couldn't invent some method of lessening the noise of trains.

There were other examples of misinterpretation. On his way home after a particularly hectic evening at the Officer's Club, the colonel in charge of the Edgewater Air Force Base decided to look in on the base duty officer, just in case anything of importance had happened.

Normally, the colonel did not veer from his homeward path, but this evening just as he was about to leave the club, he had made the mistake of calling his wife, Lena, and informing her he would be home in a few minutes and was, as he put it, "loaded for bear." Lena, who could not be termed a good-tempered woman, had been asleep since ten o'clock. Naturally, when the phone rang at just after three and she heard the drunken voice of her spouse announce, "I'll be home in five minutes, honey, and I'm loaded for bear," she knew full well what was on his mind. Her retort had taken the wind out of the colonel's sails.

"Oh! So you'll be here in five minutes, eh, and you're loaded for bear?" she replied. "Well, listen to me, you liquored-up old goat, you just go look for your goddamned bears some other place, and don't you dare wake me up again."

The sound of the phone being slammed down still rung in his ears. He wondered, as he entered his outer office, how in hell he had ever managed to stay married for so long to that foghorn.

"Good evening, Colonel," the duty officer said. "Glad you called in, sir." He held out an envelope as he spoke.

"What the hell is it?" said the bleary-eyed colonel.

"It's a PTS, Colonel," said the duty officer. "First one I've ever seen, as a matter of fact."

"A PTS?" asked the colonel. He accepted the envelope and stared glassily at the seals. "Holy smoke," he muttered. "It is a PTS."

"Yes, sir."

"What did you say?"

"I said yes, sir—sir."

"A PTS. Oh my God. Look, I'll take it into my office. Get me a cup—no, make that two cups of black coffee."

"Yes, sir," the duty officer replied as the colonel disappeared into his office.

"Cats?" murmured the colonel as he fell into a chair. "Cats from an Air Force Base. Someone must be nuts." He re-read the message aloud this time. Suddenly his face lit up. "Cats," he repeated half aloud. Then it dawned on him, "Cats. Oh, for God's sake, the Catalinas. Flying boats—those goddamn old PBYs."

It had to be that. After all, the signal was not even addressed to anyone else. He placed a phone call to his base supply officer, Mullins, who, despite the early hour, sounded quite cheery.

"Harry? Look, don't ask any questions. We have a really fastball here, a PTS. How many of the old Catalina flying boats have we got here on the training equipment slate?"

"Cats?" said Mullins. "We have five, maybe six, counting the one in the workshop hangar. They're all okay—I mean they fly. Did you say PTS, Colonel?"

"Yes, I did. Are you sure they're all airworthy? I mean, can they go as far as Camp Billings?"

"Oh sure, Colonel. They can go that far. Colonel, is this really a PTS?"

"Yes, Harry, it is. Now look," said the colonel. "I guess you know Camp Billings. It's about two hundred miles south of here in the swamps. You remember, it was a camp for dames during the war, a training area, I guess."

"Yes, sure, I remember, that's where I met Janet."

"Oh? Now, listen, these cats are to be flown to Billings as soon as possible. Now, Harry, this is a PTS, you understand, a maximum security job, so make sure the crews know it too. This must be something pretty important. They'll take the planes to Billings and remain there with them until we get further orders from the Pentagon."

"Wait a minute, Colonel," Mullins said slowly, "let me get this straight. The five old training cats we have here are to be flown to Camp Billings. But does Billings have a seaplane landing area?"

"What? How the hell do I know. This came from God himself, so it must have. Just get cracking on it." He glanced at his watch. "It's nearly four o'clock now. I want those planes on the way by ten, okay?"

"Okay, sir, on the way by ten," Mullins said.

The colonel felt better already. He allowed himself a smile of satisfaction. He had been forced to keep those flying dishpans for the last six years on his equipment establishment for training of his ground crews. Now, with them gone, he could surely place a bid on the budget estimates for some newer models. Vaguely, he wondered if Camp Billings did have a seaplane base. Hell, it must have. A PTS signal didn't ask you to send flying boats to a place where they could not land. Obviously, Billings had a lake or some other such water landing facilities. He decided he'd better send the CO at Billings a message giving him a time of arrival of the aircraft.

It took him ten minutes to handwrite a signal and give it to the duty officer for dispatch. It took him a further ten minutes to drink the two cups of coffee and to summon up enough courage to continue his journey home.

Casual events in other parts of the country added to this snowball of errors. Captain Dan Fox was on duty at the Webster Hood Service Hospital. He was seated at his colonel's desk playing solitaire, waiting for a ward call, when his eye caught the note scribbled on his commanding officer's date pad. Captain Fox quickly realized "feline" was not a word the director of medical services used under normal conditions, but it was the second and third words—"vaccine" and "Billings"—that aroused his interest. Separately, the three words meant nothing, but together the words "Feline," "Vaccine," and "Billings" were quite enough of a clue for the disgruntled young doctor. Camp Billings, he recalled, had once been a large training camp for women, but for a number of years it had been on dormant status. Now, however, it obviously was going to be reopened. Not only that, it looked as if the camp was again to be filled with females. He pondered the matter. Why shouldn't he go to see the medical personnel officer at the replacement office—see what the chances were of getting a quick transfer to Billings. Ye Gods! he thought, what an assignment that would be—doctor to a few hundred females. After further consideration and a further look to insure his privacy, he unlocked a file cabinet and found the Medical Corps register. Yes, there was a doctor at Camp

Billings, but he had been there for nearly three years. That meant he might well be ready for transfer. Captain Fox decided this must be investigated.

Next morning, Fox covered some half mile of corridor in short order to present himself at the hospital commandant's office, where, having requested an urgent interview, he was ushered in to see Major Brooks, the officer in charge of Medical Administration and Assignments. Captain Fox's reason for his request for transfer to Camp Billings was, so he stated, based on his desire to be near his seventy-nine-year-old mother in her declining years. The major said little, but he was quite moved by the captain's touching request. The transfer was granted, and it was to take effect at once. Actually, Major Brooks was extremely pleased, for the past two months he had been wondering who to send to this insect-, rodent- and reptile-infested area in the midwestern marshes. Now out of a clear sky, Lord be praised, he had a volunteer.

And so it happened that almost overnight, Camp Billings went through a severe shock treatment. That, perhaps, is the simplest way of saying the machinery of military management was working at its usually efficient level.

As the London rain spattered against his office window, General Topps gazed at his cigarette thoughtfully. He looked at Sir Hugo Stagg and Douglas Burrows before he lit up, then took a long draw on it.

"I wonder how Jansen is getting along with his collection of cats?"

The air marshal chuckled. "My dear Lucius, these Americans are all keen go-go types; they've probably got five thousand by now."

"Maybe ten thousand," suggested the admiral, "and your Air Force has to airlift the bloody things, and my Navy has to—oh, dear Lord, I should have heeded my mother's advice and gone into the church."

"I should have heeded mine too, she wanted me to be a stockbroker and make money."

"Funny you two should bring that up," said the general. "Mine wanted me to be a ballet dancer."

"You don't say, Lucius, she really wanted you to be a ballet dancer?" The air marshal laughed. "And yours, Hugo, wanted you in the church? That's damned funny."

"Don't laugh, old boy," Sir Hugo chided, "remember, I'm Catholic and going into the church for us—well, you know what that means. No ladies, no fun, no—well, you know. Pretty dull, eh?"

"Oh, I don't know," said the general. "Who knows, you might have become Pope, the first British one in—well, hundreds of years. Think of that, Hugo. Pope Hugo the First!"

"Stow it, old chap. All I can think of now is Her Majesty's Royal Navy being used to launch an invasion with cats—hundreds of bloody cats."

"Thousands, old boy, thousands," added the air marshal.

General Lucius Topps managed a weak laugh. The other two men were strangely silent. "I doubt if we'll need that many."

"Bloody awful weather," said the admiral. "I wonder what the weather is like on Mitzu?"

"Probably hot as hell," said the general. "Don't you think so, Douglas?"

This question caught the air marshal off guard. Douglas Burrows' thoughts were far away in Hong Kong. Actually, he was wondering whether he could persuade his naval colleague to accompany him to Macao for a couple of nights on the town. "Sorry, Lucius, what did you say—or was it you, Hugo?"

"I didn't say anything," replied the admiral. Actually, I was thinking the church might not have been too bad—regular life, good hours, all that sort of thing."

The air marshal raised his eyebrows. "Yes, I suppose so." At the same time he decided that Hugo Stagg was really not the type of companion with whom he could investigate and share the delights of Macao. At least, not the types of delights that Douglas Burrows had in mind.

CHAPTER XII

At his office of Special Projects Logistic, General Jansen was still faced with one problem of some magnitude. He had to find two officers to send on the mission to Mitzu, someone to actually take command of Operation Feline, to assume responsibility for the cats and to see the whole project through to a successful conclusion, and someone to represent him on the operation. As he had made a few notes on the matter, it became clear to the general that whoever was to be in charge had to be a person who not only liked cats but preferably one who knew something about Mitzu, or at least had some knowledge of or experience in the Orient. Above all else, Jansen decided, it had to be someone who knew how to take orders, who would ask few questions, and most important, someone who would keep his mouth shut. In addition, whoever was selected must not be the type who might be stupid enough to complain to his local congressman about the peculiar assignment after it was all over.

There must be no chance that the security under which the operation was being conducted might be prejudiced. The Chairman Joint Chiefs had made it quite clear, if for only one good reason: that until the project was over and done with, the American taxpayer must be given no inkling that hard-gained Defense Department funds were being used to gather cats all over the country, no matter what the reason. Not that combating a plague of rats was not an excellent cause, it certainly was, but in these uncertain times, one could not expect the average man on the street to understand the implications of such a venture, at least not at this early stage. No, the general told himself, he must see to it personally that not one word about the operation leaked out.

On the other hand, when it was all over, and Mitzu was once again habitable, the president might agree to make some sort of a release. Jansen could almost see the headlines relating how his government was ever quick to appreciate the dangers of a bubonic plague, had rendered a service to the free world without fuss and in a most practical and economical manner. Jansen tried to imagine the headlines-Paguda, a poor little country needing urgent aid and his country, the champions of democracy, hearing the appeal, rallying all its resources and rushing to assist. It was quite possible that he, Robert Wallace Jansen, would be named as the man who had made it all possible. It gave him a tremendous feeling of satisfaction. He even cast a quick glance at his left breast to see where he might fit in the appropriate medal-perhaps even three medals. There was bound to be at least one from Paguda and probably another from his own government and certainly one from the British.

The general's mind toyed briefly with the prospects of the eventual publicity. He wondered whether he should put down a few notes for the press.

Then General Jansen's thoughts released the fantasies, and once again he had to face reality. He still had to find two officers to send to Mitzu.

Suddenly, the notion struck him, Personnel Statistical Records should be able to provide an answer. Jansen reached for the phone.

Some twenty minutes later, a thin freckle-faced young female clerk was standing by the information computers in the Personnel Statistics machine records office. As she waited, she watched the multitude of dials and gauges while the monstrous contraption clickety-clacked away, indicating it was digesting the essential facts that had been fed into it. She was awed by what was commonly referred to in the department as automated management.

This fascinating process, recently installed by the new administration to save man hours, mental stress, and to promote efficiency, was performing a function that at one time represented the individual brains and efforts of two hundred and four people. The fact that this modern marvel had thrown all those people out of work was barely remembered and certainly not to be discussed. After all, this was progress in its finest sense. But to ease the burden of these newly unemployed, the president had promised to provide funds to retrain them all as lifeguards, firemen or miners in Alaska and even chicken pluckers, badly needed in some states.

Suddenly, the dials stopped, the monster sputtered, and a small white card meticulously punctured by unseen hands dropped into the tray. The young lady carried the card to her bureau chief, who barely glanced at it. He placed it in a red envelope, stamped it with the imposing words "TOP SECRET," and then placed it in a second envelope. This he tossed with a seemingly careless gesture into his out basket. He then reached into the lower desk drawer and produced a copy of the Wall Street Journal, which he carefully folded and placed into the inner pocket of his jacket. Then he stood up. The rumbling noises emerging from his lower bowel and a hurried glance at the office clock were signs enough. As he made his way to his unofficial reading room, it occurred to him that nature called with amazing regularity.

The president was expecting John Bosk and General Howell when his private phone rang. It was his brother.

"Look, Robby, I'm very busy, what is it?"

The president looked at his watch as he listened.

"What? Sorry Robby. That's not possible. No, I can't do that. You cannot have Camp David for a party with Helga, and certainly not on Tuesday night. Dammit, Robby, that's the night Valerie is away with her committee in New Orleans and Helga knows she has to be here. I arranged that with her two weeks ago. Now, here's what I can do. My boat is down at the Marina. You can have it for four days on the Potomac. Look, I can give you four good prospects too. First, if I were you, I'd try Jenny; she's a good lay any time. Now Marianne is a real active one, but her mother is staying with her. I doubt if she's open for business now. Lola's good too, if she's back from Nassau with her senator. And lastly, you might try Wanda; about half the

House has tried her at one time or another, but she's good company for a night. What? No, Robby, that's the best I can do. If you get Jenny, give her my best." He hung up, at the same time wishing he could get Robby to go back South and start looking for a job. Even the interns around the White House were getting tired of Robby's bum-patting and other obnoxious habits, all of which Valerie thought were rather amusing.

As he sat there stroking his forehead and silently cursing his younger brother, his warning buzzer sounded.

His Secretary of State and General Howell had arrived.

After the visitors were seated the president rose and began to walk back and forth behind his desk as if contemplating his next move.

"Is there anything wrong sir?" Bosk asked.

"Oh no." he replied. "I called you because I want to establish clearly how many people actually are in the know about this operation. How about your people, John?"

"Well, sir, at this time in the State Department, besides myself and my executive assistant, there are Mr. Ryder and his assistant, Ambassador Wilson, and that's it. Five of us. How about you, General?"

"I've kept this whole thing pretty close," replied the Chairman Joint Chiefs. "There's myself, my aide and General Jansen, who are fully in the picture. The Chiefs of Staff of the Army, Air Force and Chief of Naval Operations have only been told by me that the British are carrying out a PTS exercise on our behalf, and that they will not be required to participate in any way except to okay the orders I give them with regard to cooperation and to carry out those orders without question. And, of course, the defense secretary."

"Very good, General. That's exactly what I want," said the chief executive. "So I take it you <u>have</u> briefed the defense secretary. What was his reaction?"

"General Jansen briefed him yesterday, sir, and I regret to say that the secretary gave him rather a bad time, began to ask a lot of questions. But, Mr. Kleffen backed off somewhat when

Jansen told him you, Mr. President, had placed a PTS classification on the matter and he would be briefed on a daily basis by Jansen."

The President scratched his head and leaned back in his chair. "You know, John, I think we should find some way of getting our friend Kleffen out of the way for a couple of weeks or so. He's a bit of a publicity seeker. I'm not happy about his close relationship with some of the press, especially Dan Samson. I'd rather have him out of the country while this is going on. Any ideas?"

The state secretary shook his head. "He's only just come back from Korea, sir."

"General, what about it? Any suggestions?"

Howell was consulting his note pad. "There are two possibilities, Mr. President. One, over in NATO where we have invited Prince Philip to be a guest at one of our airborne exercises. He could be there to represent you."

The president clapped his hands. "Why not!" he exclaimed. "He could have his picture taken with royalty. That's a great idea. But, there's only one drawback. There could be a number of reasons why Philip might have to change his plans. What then?"

"Well, sir, I have another and, I think, even better idea. We are just starting a series of cold-weather exercises at our Arctic Training Base north of Fairbanks in Alaska. You, sir, could tell him you had intended to go up there for a few days, but you cannot make it, and ask him to go and represent you."

The president chuckled. "Hey, I think that's the best yet. Let's go for that one." He pressed his buzzer.

"Yes, Mr. President." It was Duff Patty, the White House Chief of Staff.

"Duff, please put a call through to the secretary of defense."

"Anything else, Mr. President?" inquired the Chairman.

"No, thank you gentlemen, I think that's about all for now. Thanks very much."

Just after his visitors left, the president's phone rang. "Yes, Duff? You did? Good, when is he coming? But why was he going to Nova Scotia? What—fishing? Well, you'd better inform him that I want to see him as soon as possible. And, Duff, when he does go, make sure he doesn't use government aircraft like he did for that last trip to the Cayman Islands. By the way, was he taking his wife? He wasn't? Then who? Oh, yes, I know her; I hear almost everyone—oh, well, forget it. Bye for now."

General Jansen and General Howell were in the latter's office discussing the progress of Operation Feline. Jansen was all smiles as he displayed a list of the replies he had received in answer to the request for cats.

"Amazing," said Howell. "Absolutely amazing. I would not have bet a dollar on getting more than a few dozen cats from all the services. You have certainly done well."

"I must say, General, I'm a bit surprised myself," said Jansen, "but as you can see, forty-one from Camp Stunger, a hundred and twenty-nine from camps in Texas, eight hundred forty from SPCA, and even five from the Edgewater Air Base. Oh, yes." He held up a paper. Here's forty-two from the School of Engineering. So far, a total of eleven hundred eighty-four."

"Excellent," said Howell. "How many still to hear from on this?"

"Well, if the present total is an indication, we'll probably get over fifteen hundred when the other addresses reply. I've told the commander at Camp Billings to start his carpenters building a couple of hundred crates."

"Good." Howell nodded. "Now, Bob, there's only one thing I still worry about—security. I think we'd better decide on one thing: the only file on Operation Feline will be kept by you. Will you insure that as soon as the cats leave Billings, all copies of wires, in fact, any copies of any papers that refer to Feline held by anyone, *except you,* are shredded? I feel this will be the wisest course to follow. We keep a complete set and burn the rest."

"You can be sure I will do just that," said Jansen. "And I'll make sure Rollins gets the word to the British and the people at the State Department work on a similar basis."

"Now," said Howell, "who have you got to command the project—on Mitzu, that is? I take it you have found a suitable officer for it, or maybe two."

"Oh, yes," replied Jansen hopefully. "Oh, yes. I do have a good man. As a matter of fact, we should have his card up here from statistics in a minute or so."

General Howell stood up and began to pace the floor, stopping periodically to scratch behind his right ear. "You know, Bob," he said, "while I don't think there's much chance of a leak of information from our services, I do wonder about some of the people over at State. They're a gabby bunch, and so is the defense secretary too, for that matter. They're liable to get panicky. What's the answer to that?"

Jansen looked up from the folder he was studying. "Simple enough. Don't tell the bastards anything unless you have to. What they don't know, they can't talk about, at least that's my theory."

"Yes, I suppose so," said Howell, "but what about our laughing boy of a secretary. He's got a mouth as big as a platypus and loves to yap. My Lord, I can't stand the slob. I don't think he can stand me either. By the way, the president is going to send him off on a special mission to Alaska for a few days to get him out of the way."

"That's the best news I've heard today, but I don't think you need to worry about him," said Jansen. "When I briefed him, I informed him the SPCA had agreed not to breathe a word about sending cats to us, providing we in the Defense and State Departments kept our mouths shut. On the other hand, I warned him, if we or the State Department people say a word about it, Admiral Lyman said he would spill the story to the papers in full."

"Oh, good God, did he really say that? The SPCA, I mean? Did they…"

"Of course not. Admiral Lyman knows the matter is PTS, but I didn't tell that to the Defense Secretary. So, knowing him and the way he feels about guarding his position, I think we're safe. As a matter of fact, he told me today, just as I was leaving, he only wished to be briefed when we thought it necessary and, as I see it, that won't be too often."

At that moment, Major Bonwell, Howell's aide, entered. He passed an envelope to his boss and then left hurriedly, almost tripping as he reached the door.

Jansen laughed. "That young man doesn't waste much time moving around."

"Oh, Bonwell? He knows if he hangs too long, I'll find something else for him to do." He then withdrew the small white perforated card from the inner red envelope and inspected it.

"George Gilly? Gilly?" Howell looked puzzled. "You know Lieutenant Gilly?"

"George Gilly?" Jansen paused to ponder the name. "Well, well, well, of all people, good old George. Oh, I tell you, we have a good man. A good officer, and he knows Mitzu—he served there. Retired now, but still a first-class man, good brain, keen, a real doer, old George."

"That's our boy then," said Howell. "Wherever he is, you'd better get him assigned here for special duty for an indefinite period as fast as you can. We can't waste time now, and make sure he's well briefed. And, Bob, promote him to captain. I hope to God he's healthy."

"I'll put a call in to him right away," said Jansen as he made for the door. "You say you don't know him?"

"George Gilly?" The Chairman Joint Chief shook his head. "Never heard of him. Where is he now and what's he doing?"

Jansen slipped the folder from one hand to the other and delved into his jacket pocket.

"Let's see," he repled as he looked over the machine records card. "He runs a garage now at Mooneyville Junction."

"Oh, good, good, excellent, Bob."

"See you later, General," said Jansen. Once out in the corridor, General Jansen gazed at the card again. This time he spoke the words aloud. "George Gilly? Who the hell is George Gilly, and where the hell is Mooneyville Junction?"

CHAPTER XIII

In any small town or village, curiosity, while it may not be classed among the virtues, is nevertheless an essential part of community life. Mooneyville Junction, in Missouri, where George Gilly lived and worked, was no exception. Everyone there made it his or her business to find out as much as possible about everyone else. Some people were more successful than others in this sphere, depending, of course, on who were one's friends, enemies or other connections. The mayor of this haven, for instance, who was also the local undertaker, enjoyed by far the greatest influence in local intelligence, not through his profession, naturally, but rather through his twin fifty-two-year-old spinster sisters, who were the sole custodians of the village telephone switchboard and the post office, and also through his older brother Judd who ran the telegraph office at the railroad station.

The Misses MacKay were regular whirlwinds of activity, and no one had ever been quite able to explain how they managed to handle all phone calls day or night without assistance and also run the post office, but this is just what they had been doing for the last twenty-eight years. Whenever one of the twins got sick or was otherwise indisposed, the other merely carried on alone. It was a formidable combination. In this manner, it could safely be said that the entire media or internal communications in Mooneyville Junction was pretty much a closed shop, which Munro MacKay, the mayor, and his kin had long since decided must be guarded well against any intrusion.

The population of the place, 709 in all, was a tightly knit group. They lacked little in the ways of normal life circulating around a better-than-average farming area. There was the railway depot with its two side tracks, the watering point and telegraph facility. A small grain elevator stood by conveniently. Then there were the eight stores, a school, the doctor's office, the bank, the garage and filling station, Munro MacKay's funeral parlor, and the little church. Last, but by no means least, there was the community hall, an edifice of vast importance since it doubled on two nights each week as a movie theater. The Mooneyville Junction Clarion which appeared every two weeks from the mayor's duplicating machine was the sole source of local information. The twin sisters and brother Judd however had long ago learned that it was their duty to pass on to their younger brother anything they learned.

It was here in Mooneyville Junction that George Gilly had been born and raised, and so had Julie, his wife. George now ran the garage and filling station and, what is more, he owned them, having purchased the centrally located site with his service benefits when he returned from Korea and extended duties in other parts of the Far East, including Mitzu. Business in these last four years had been extraordinarily good. George and Julie had added a small apartment over the garage and even purchased the well treed lot behind the service station with a view to erecting their own house. As garages went, it was reasonably well equipped, and a sufficient number of vehicles and tractors could be found in the surrounding area to provide an adequate living for the Gillys and Tom, an older, odd-jobs man, who now worked for George.

On the morning when General Jansen placed his call to Mooneyville Junction, George was away. He and three hunting friends had left early to try to bag a few of the ducks that literally infested the marshes to the south. Jansen's secretary did however get through long enough to start the ball of speculation rolling. Miss MacKay, the elder by some eight minutes, was at her usual post when the light flashed to indicate an incoming call.

"Hello, this is the Mooneyville Junction exchange," the lady chirped in her high soprano tone.

"Hello," said the Pentagon operator. "Mooneyville Junction? We have a call for a Mr. George Gilly from the Department of Defense. Can you locate him for us please? We need to contact him as soon as possible."

For a moment the overwhelming excitement and anticipation almost toppled Miss MacKay from her seat. "Did you say for Mr. George Gilly?" she asked.

"Yes," said the operator. "From the Department of Defense."

Miss MacKay was, luckily enough, able to provide a fast answer. "I'm sorry, operator," she said, "but Mr. George Gilly is out of town for the day and is not expected to return until late tonight. Would you care to leave a number where he can call you when he returns?" asked Miss MacKay.

While waiting for the answer, the elder Miss MacKay beckoned to her sister. Even from her postal desk at the far end of the room, the younger sister had managed to catch the note of elation in her twin's tone of voice.

"Who is it?" she asked.

"A call for George from the Pentagon, from the Department of defense."

"What? From the Capital? Oh!"

"Yes. Shhhh. Yes, operator?"

"Would you please have Mr.—I beg your pardon, Lieutenant George Gilly call General Jansen's office in the Department of Defense as soon as he returns? The number is Teakwood 842-2206, extension 2718."

"Indeed I will. Thank you." Miss MacKay's hand was shaking as she disconnected the lines. "Well," she said breathlessly. "What do you know about that? Our George, and a general calling for him. Wants him to call back right away. Isn't that something?" The other lady giggled.

"And what's more, the message is for Lieutenant George Gilly. I must tell Munro at once." She gathered her rabbit's fur jacket and made for the door.

Munro MacKay was listening to the radio news when his sister entered. The fat, jovial forty-eight-year-old mayor and undertaker lay back in his easy chair. He was in shirtsleeves, having just completed fitting old Abe Burke into a three hundred dollar coffin. He was also enjoying a glass of his wife's blueberry wine. This obvious note of delinquency did not escape his sister; she fixed her brother with a long, suspicious look.

"Munro, are you alone?" she asked.

"I guess so," he replied. "Gladys is out shopping. Why?" He noticed her staring at the glass he held, and he blushed like a naughty schoolboy."

She laid her bag on the table and seated herself opposite him. "Munro, I have the most exciting news for you. It's about George Gilly."

"Oh, George? What's he done?" said the mayor.

His sister placed a hand on his arm and her voice fell to a whisper. "It's not what he's done, Munro, but what he's going to do. A half-hour ago there was a call for him from a general in the Defense Department."

Munro MacKay was not normally easily stirred, but this brought his feet to the floor. This was news, this was something.

"George Gilly? From a general? Oh, it couldn't be, not George."

"Oh, but it is, and what's more, they referred to him as Lieutenant Gilly. Now what do you think of that?"

The mayor moved quickly, first to the door leading to the kitchen where he listened for a while, then over to the bottom of the stairs, where he repeated the sentinel-like pause.

"Why, Munro, what's the matter?" asked Miss MacKay. "Are you all right?"

"Shhh, not so loud." The mayor was now peeking out through the window curtains. Then, having satisfied himself that no one was approaching the house, he turned back to his older sister. "Now, Maria, not one word of this to anyone. Funny, but I always had a feeling George was something more than he seemed. Now I think I know. You'll understand what I mean when you hear my speech tonight at the annual church turkey dinner. But even then, don't say one word, not a word to anyone."

"Of course. I won't, and I'll warn Nora too."

"Yes, yes, do that," said Munro. "Now, please go back. We don't want to arouse any suspicion. You'd better warn Judd at the telegraph office, too."

"All right, Munro, I will. See you tonight."

Neither the duties of mayor nor town undertaker received much attention from Munro MacKay for the rest of the afternoon. He sat glued to the radio listening to the latest variety of news reports. One of these was particularly suitable to the mayor's mood and to his thoughts, for it recounted how in Moscow, the Soviet premier had made the most violent and threatening speech of his career. According to the commentator, that very day Mr. Kutchevski had, in a few well chosen phrases, branded everyone in the Western alliance a warmonger and declared that if the West did not get out of Germany, Korea, Cyprus, the Middle East, and countless other lesser places, he would smite the West a staggering blow. Reactions to the threat were, according to the radio announcer, ones of determination. The British and Canadian prime ministers had called a special meeting of their cabinets. The U.N. was summoning the Security Council to consider an accusation by Paguda's Grand Chief Sultapan against five of the neighboring nations, and the president of France announced he was considering reforming two extra regiments of the Foreign Legion to be used as peace-keeping troops by the U.N.

All in all, it was most invigorating, and the mayor of Mooneyville Junction just sat there and lapped it up. But Munro MacKay was also thinking. Why shouldn't he, too, make a special speech tonight at the church turkey dinner, a speech to stir up the emotions of the community, to arouse his listeners and to prepare them for the trials and tribulations that might lie ahead. He could even inject a hint on the possible recall to duty of George Gilly. Yes, this certainly seemed the course to follow. It was too good an opportunity to miss.

Mayor MacKay was an avid reader of newspapers and he had a better-than-average imagination, a quality that stood him well later that afternoon when he began to write his speech. His original intention had been to give his audience his usual half-hour of jokes, reminiscences, garnished with a bit of election propaganda. But not this time. The world had changed, and whatever it was that George Gilly was about to do would no doubt change Mooneyville Junction. Fiery words dripped off the major's pen as he prepared his elaborate epistle.

At the annual church social and turkey dinner that evening before some hundred and fifty of Mooneyville Junction's most prominent citizens, Munro MacKay made his speech. The contents of this dramatic blurb rivalled anything that even the government's public information office might have dreamed up. Its title alone was calculated to make his listeners sit up and take notice—and some did. He called it, *Duty Above All.*

Monologues, even among the classics, rarely last more than fifteen minutes; Mayor MacKay's speech lasted well over an hour.

Having first covered world history with the broad brush of the uninformed, Munro proceeded to denounce Russia, Red China and Cuba. He denounced each member of each country's ruling body by name and went on to say that if the Red leaders persisted in their threats, true patriots, like the people of Mooneyville Junction, would not stand idly by. This raised a rather weak cheer from the far tables, and it was on this note of encouragement that the mayor decided to offer his choicest morsel of news. Like the actor he and Gladys had watched on TV last Sunday night, he mopped his brow and looked slowly around the hall. The resultant silence on the Mayor's part was enough to quiet the rattle of conversation and cause his fellow diners to look up to see what was going on. Munro therefore lowered his voice and made his final point.

"And," he concluded slowly, "I know of one man, and he is here—yes, right here in Mooneyville Junction, in our own very midst to whom this country is going to turn in its hour of need. In fact, I learned just today that he has already been called. One thing I am sure of, and that is, when he is assigned his duty, he will do it with honor and bring credit to us, his fellow citizens of Mooneyville Junction."

Applause, led mainly by Mrs. MacKay, grew and echoed through the crowded banquet hall. Munro felt he had scored heavily. He decided he had said enough.

After the dinner, while the ladies cleared away dishes and generally prepared the hall for the square dance to follow, the mayor enjoyed the spotlight. His friends gathered about him, either shaking his hand or slapping him on the back.

"Great speech, Munro," exclaimed Dr. Sloan. "Great! You certainly have a way with words."

"Come on, Munro, tell us. What's all this call to duty business about," demanded Silas Jenks, the general store manager.

"Yes, Munro, who is it? Anyone I know?" asked Tom MacIntosh, the manager of the grain elevator.

Mr. Martin, the banker, was particularly curious. He leaned toward the mayor's ear and whispered, "If it's something that could benefit our little city, Mr. Mayor, it might also result in some profit for the first people who know."

The mayor was a trifle surprised. "Oh, yes, I suppose so. I'll keep that in mind," he said, wondering just how anyone could profit from George's recall to the service. Then he felt someone tapping his shoulder.

"Oh, Reverend Black." The mayor turned and beamed at him.

"Mr. Mayor," said the good reverend, "your speech has given our citizens new hope, new horizons. I congratulate you, I really do."

The mayor was about to murmur his thanks, but four or five other men clustering about him began to grab his hand and to express their curiosity.

"Sorry, gentlemen," replied the mayor, "I can't say another word. Later perhaps, but not now. National security, you know.

Mustn't let out anything now. All in good time, be assured of that."

On the way home in the car, Munro could feel his wife's inquisitiveness as she eyed him.

"Munro MacKay, you sly old dog," she said quietly, "you've been holding out on me."

"Yes, my dear," said Munro, grinning. "I have a heavy duty to bear. One of our local boys has been sent for by the government—a very special assignment. We shall know who it is shortly."

When they arrived at the house, Gladys made her cup of hot chocolate and prepared for bed. The mayor, however, had another heavy duty, that of embalming the late Amos Jackman, and Amos weighed over two hundred and sixty pounds—alive, that was. While Munro did not relish the job, it had to be done. Anyway, once he got started, the mayor never really minded. He could always rehearse his next speech to Amos.

As he labored, he could not keep his mind off George Gilly. He wondered if old George had been with the CIA. He remembered reading about one man who had retired from the CIA and had been recalled for some special mission. Someone had referred to the man as a "sleeper." Maybe George was a sleeper, probably a specialist of some sort, being ordered to carry out a secret sortie into Communist territory. Munro MacKay felt a surge of excitement. His mind toyed with the prospects of George's return; the story of his mission would no doubt eventually come out, and he could well become a real hero.

On the other hand, supposing George disappeared or was killed—killed while on special duty for his country. Well, that might not be so bad. The government might be very generous in—well, there would be embalming, a really classy container, maybe with brass handles and a grave with a magnificent headstone, and all of it at government expense. The possibilities were endless. Then he mused on the preferred burial plot. It must be high up. Mayor MacKay tried to remember who owned the plots around the big oak tree that overlooked the town cemetery. That would be the obvious spot for George Gilly, and with a hero to bury, surely the Defense Department would not haggle about the price.

Billy Swenton owned the cemetery; it occurred to the mayor that the sooner he saw Billy the better. Billy was one person he could trust, and together—well, it could be something very worthwhile.

Yet, the idea of George Gilly's demise must not be taken for granted. What if he returned safe and sound? What if the citizens of Mooneyville Junction started to think of George Gilly as the man they wanted to replace Munro MacKay? No, the mayor decided; he must not think of that. A dead George Gilly would be much better for all concerned.

CHAPTER XIV

Early next morning, the elder Miss MacKay telephoned George Gilly. Julie explained that her husband had not returned until three AM. He was still asleep, and she didn't want to disturb him. Nevertheless, the older lady told Julie that George was required to call a General Jansen at Defense Headquarters in Washington D.C. as soon as possible. This puzzled Julie; she wondered for a moment whether she should wake up her husband but decided against it. George must get his sleep. Besides, he was sure to wake up for lunch.

Shortly before noon, George Gilly did wake up. As usual, he made his way into the kitchen, found Julie had his lunch ready and gave her the usual light kiss as she leaned over to put his well filled plate before him.

"Hello, sugar," he said, "thanks for letting me sleep. Much business out there today, I wonder?" He nodded toward the window.

"I guess not," she replied. "Haven't heard a word from old Tom anyway. By the way, how were the ducks yesterday, or didn't you get any?"

"Oh, we got enough. Matter of fact, I got eight. They're hanging out on the back stairway—not very big. Some of the others had better luck. But it was fun and not too cold."

"Eight! Oh well, better that nothing," said Julie. "I'll dress them and put them in the freezer. We might even have one next Sunday, if you'd like that."

"Good idea," said George. He began to eat. They had been sitting opposite each other in the pink and white dining nook for some time before Julie handed him the slip of paper. George looked at it, frowned, then took another mouthful of scrambled egg.

"General Jansen—a general?" he mumbled. "What for, I wonder?"

"What could it be about, honey?" his wife asked. "Or can you say?"

"Darned if I know. A general? I don't know any generals, but I'll call him back as soon as I finish lunch. Say, how'd the church turkey dinner go last night?"

"I didn't get to it. I had so much else to do, I just didn't go." Then she added as an afterthought, "Are you mad at me for not going?"

"No," replied George, "I sure don't blame you." He reached over and gently patted his wife's arm. She looked up and smiled.

Julie was glad that news of the phone call had not upset her husband. Not that George Gilly ever got too upset. Actually, in their five and a half years of marriage, she couldn't recall ever seeing her husband really worried about anything. As she watched him finish his lunch, she let her mind wander over the past. She had been just twenty-three and George five years older when he returned from Korea and the Far East. Their first meeting was at the Valentine dance, and from that time on, neither had cast a single glance toward anyone else. When wedding bells rang for Julie and George that fall, it was Mr. Martin, the banker, who had given her away. Yes, Julie had told herself, they had been really wonderful years, and George was a wonderful man.

"Oh!" She almost choked on the word as she jumped up form the table and rushed toward the stove. "Oh, George," she cried, "my rolls. Oh, darn it."

"Burning, I guess," observed her husband with a wry smile as he downed the last of his coffee.

As Julie extricated the smoking baking pan from the hot oven, George pushed away his empty plate and rose from the table.

"Well," he muttered, "I'd better get that call in. General Jansen, eh?"

Jansen's secretary informed George that the general was only across the hall and if Lieutenant Gilly would hold the line she would try to get the general on the phone. As George waited, he cradled the phone between his head and shoulder and began to dismantle a carburetor, wondering as he did so what the devil he had done to deserve a call from the Defense Department and especially from a man who he had read recently was the chief of Special Projects Logistics. Surely to God they did not want him back in the Army. He tried to remember whether any other of the young men in the area had been reinducted, but he couldn't recall having read of any. He let his mind wander across the past years.

George was just twenty when he volunteered for the service in the Korea War in 1950. He had stayed in the Army for eight years. They had been eight good years, during which he had not only enjoyed himself but had been able to save quite a lot of money. At the time of his call into the service, George was working as a mechanic at the garage he now owned. He was a good one too-good with anything in the way of motors and engines. Mechanics to him came as second nature and he was never happier than when he had something to tinker with, take apart or put together. But George Gilly was also a good learner, even as a soldier.

And so it happened on one hot day at Camp Benton, when his class instructor, who was explaining the more intricate workings of the transmission of a truck, was called away, George Gilly took over the class. To young Gilly, even the most delicate function of any type of machine raised in him a peculiar form of curious excitement. The mysteries of combustion, of gears, of voltage regulators were his field, and he felt at home with them. So much so, that before he realized what was happening, Private Gilly found himself sent off to a special school, from which he emerged four months later as Second Lieutenant Gilly of the Army Transportation Corps. From the school, it was but a short step to Korea and the police action war, which, alas, was soon to be forgotten. Funny too, thought George, people forget so easily. He remembered reading how it had cost something like a hundred thousand-odd men killed, missing and wounded.

When the fighting in Korea ended in July 1953, George was given a new assignment. He was sent by sea from Pusan to work with a maintenance unit located on the tiny island of Mitzu. His job there was to supervise the maintenance of the heavy equipment being used to construct a new emergency airfield recently acquired, so he was told, by a secret treaty with Paguda. That was George's first experience with Mitzu, the Pagudans and the hush-hush. It was to last for three tours for a total of five years.

George made many friends overseas, especially during his tour on Mitzu. He had learned Pagudan in a passable sense, and when he came home, he had a considerable amount of money. Actually, twice he had asked politely to be considered for repatriation, and twice his superiors informed him he could not be spared. Eventually the size of George's unit was reduced, the landing strip with its weather station was turned over to the Signal Corps and in the summer of 1958, the Army decided the services of Lieutenant Gilly were no longer needed. So, George returned quietly to his home in Mooneyville Junction. He bought the garage from his previous employer, met Julie, got married, and that was that. Now he had a home, a pretty, loving wife, a good promising business and one thousand six hundred and forty-one dollars in the Mooneyville Junction State Bank. No bad, really, he thought, not bad at all—then the voice at the other end of the line spoke.

"Hello, is this Lieutenant George Gilly?"

"Yes, this is George Gilly," replied George quietly.

"Lieutenant Gilly, I have your party coming on the line—General Jansen at the Defense Headquarters. One moment, please, Lieutenant."

General Jansen, as always, came to the point quickly. George was to be recalled to active duty at once. If he still had his uniform, he was to wear it. It was imperative that the lieutenant report to the Pentagon within forty-eight hours, and he was not to discuss the matter of his return to duty with anyone. The general explained he could say no more over the phone. He terminated the conversation by telling George there would be a first-class train ticket for him at the station office next morning to take him to St. Louis and a plane ticket would be available at the United desk at the airport. George's part in the entire conversation was somewhat restricted; it consisted of three "Yes, sirs," and two "Very good, sirs."

One can never be quite sure how these things happen, but the next morning when George, uncomfortable but resplendent in his old but rather tight uniform, arrived at the Mooneyville Junction station with Julie, Mayor MacKay was there. So was the mayor's wife, a sizeable jabbering crowd, the school band, and all five members of the Mooneyville Junction Town Council. To the blaring tune of *Hail the Conquering hero,* the Gillys were led to a hastily prepared platform bedecked with flags, where everyone seemed to be shaking hands with everyone else. Then the mayor held up his hand and made another of his speeches. Munro MacKay told the assembled gathering that in a world crisis the country had recalled one of Mooneyville's most distinguished sons to special duty. It was obvious, he said, that Lieutenant George Gilly, hero of the Pacific War, had been chosen to help stem the Red tide and that the fate of the free world may be hanging in the balance. Amid the applause, he turned and spoke to George.

"George, my boy, you need never look over your shoulder or worry. We will safeguard your little home and your business, and when you return we shall all be here to welcome you with open arms. We are proud of you, George, my boy, you are a real patriot." The three cheers he asked for from the noisy crowd were not particularly enthusiastic.

The applause was drowned by the ever-ambitious school band that, despite the fact that the trombone was off-key, struggled through the National Anthem. George was quite overcome, and even Julie shed a tear, while Mayor Munro MacKay quietly but deliberately contemplated the possibilities of a full-scale military funeral, all paid for by the government.

Then the train whistle blew. George shook hands all around, kissed Julie hurriedly and gave her his bank book. And, as the train pulled out, the band struck up a medley of military marches. The trombone was still off-key, but somehow the shrill whistle of the train seemed to fill in quite well for it.

CHAPTER XV

Mr. Ryder, of the Far Eastern Section in the U.S. State Department, never did get his week's leave. He was called back to his desk on Tuesday to keep an eye on Operation Feline, which, as the state secretary explained to him, was PTS and was to be carried out by the British on Mitzu as a favor to the United States Government.

He noted that the file was completely up to date. All the PTS details of discussions between the president and the state secretary, the national security advisor and the Chairman Joint Chiefs were there, thus providing him with a running account of all events in progress. He noticed Mr. Bruck's minutes to the effect that the copy of the original message from Special Locations Section to Bulabar concerning Mitzu had been sent over to the Pagudan ambassador by hand. He saw the copies of the two messages from Ambassador Wilson at Paguda to State. These, he noted, had been referred to the state secretary personally, who, in turn, had passed copies to the British Foreign Secretary for their Defense Department's action. There was another message from the state secretary to the U.S. Embassy at Paguda, authorizing Mr. Wilson, on behalf of the state secretary, to provide whatever medical and administrative aid was needed for the population of Mitzu when it reached Paguda.

Ryder also noted with satisfaction that the state secretary had initialed each folio in the floater, thus placing official blessing on all that had taken place to date. For a moment he wondered why other ministers had not seen the files. Suddenly, the explanation was clear. On the front page of the file was a paragraph in the state secretary's own handwriting. It read:

As this matter is PTS and therefore on a "need-to-know" basis, no reference to it will be made to any other member of the Cabinet unless he is directly involved and is in the country. Should it be necessary to involve any other official, he will be briefed personally by me. As far as Operation Feline is concerned, all decisions concerning Paguda, Mitzu, and the British Government participation, will be referred to me.

The bold but unintelligible signature and state secretary's personal stamp made it the final executive order.

Ryder called young Mr. Bruck in and asked him whether he had seen the state secretary's order. Bruck said he had. Ryder then asked him if he understood the PTS aspect of it. Bruck said he did. There was no more to do but place his own initials and stamp on each page. He did this, then threw the files into his pending basket. After all, Paguda was not the only country in the Far East with a hungry look; and, besides, the whole thing was now safely in the hands of the British. What a wonderful thing it was, thought Ryder, to have such good allies. He wondered whether, when all this was over, he might not expect an assignment to London. Maybe he should ask for it.

When the order to close Mitzu was received by General Bellows at Bulabar Air Base, he realized he had to forget any idea of his Hong Kong holiday. The classification of PTS made it clear that something important was about to happen.

"By the way, Dixie," he said to his chief of staff, "make sure all preparations for test-flight 255 are cancelled."

"Sorry about that, sir," said Colonel Mason. "It probably means no shopping trip for a while, but there you are—I wish we knew more about what's going on."

"So do I," said the general, "but that's it. Apparently something big is coming up."

Some twenty minutes later, Mason brought in the PMTS message from the British Chief of Defense Staff. And while the general still could not make head nor tail of what was going on, he did at least understand that a most secret cargo was being airlifted by the Royal Air Force from somewhere on the mainland to Bulabar and that he had to provide road vehicles to transport that cargo to Singabar.

"We'd better call a conference, Colonel," said Bellows after he'd read the British message. "I'll have to impress the importance of this to our senior staff. We can't afford any slip-up on a PTS matter, or someone will have my balls."

He acted accordingly, reminding the members of his staff that the operation was presidential top secret. These words alone, he felt, would be enough to dampen any further curiosity. But just to be sure, he said, "And if any of you spill your guts on this, *I'll* have *your* balls."

Further north, at the Singabar Naval Base, when he got the British message, the admiral there followed the same procedures as his air colleague. He called his chief of operations immediately.

"John, something's brewing, and it must be something really big. The redcoats are coming. We'd better get ready for them." He passed the message to the operations chief.

"Okay, Admiral, I'll call a meeting."

"Yes, John, good idea, but just the senior officers."

Like all the admiral's conferences, it was short and made all the more effective when, in closing, he said, "Gentlemen, this matter is presidential top secret. Govern yourselves accordingly. And let me warn you, if anyone here screws up on this, I'll have his balls."

Meanwhile, on Mitzu, the four signalmen were seated around the table gazing at a single slip of paper. It was the message to close down and evacuate Mitzu that Pope had just decoded. They were certainly perplexed and more than a little worried.

"I just don't get it," said Staff Sergeant Morton. "I just don't get it at all. What the hell is happening? Why are they closing us down and evacuating the island?"

"Well," said Jackson, "it's clear enough, Staff. It says this airstrip is closed to all traffic and the Royal Navy is going to evacuate the island. But it doesn't say what to do with all the equipment, except to secure it, whatever the hell that means. What the hell are the Brits up to? Maybe we're giving it to them."

"We'd better check back," said Watowski, the youngest and fattest of the four. "We can't just lock up the place and go. What about the hush-hush? And why the Royal Navy—where the hell is our own navy?"

"But why are we to be taken off?" said Pope. "After they send us a message asking to confirm the airstrip is on and there are supplies here—something's crazy. Maybe somebody goofed?"

Morton shook his head. "Well, the message didn't say anything about the hush-hush. All it says here is presidential top secret. Prepare to evacuate the island. You will be advised of timings. Royal Navy will move all persons and belongings from Mitzu to mainland Paguda. Senior service person will secure all equipment and inform local headman of these plans. By the way, did you ask Yung Bhop to come over?"

"Yes, I did," said Jackson. 'He's coming right away."

"Maybe they just decided to cut out this station," said Watowski. "Or maybe, as you say, the limeys are going to take it over? As far as I'm concerned they can have it."

"No," Morton said, "that can't be it. It can't. If it was, we'd be packing up all this junk and taking it with us or we'd be told to transfer the stuff to the British. Besides, the whole island population wouldn't be moving too."

"You're right, Staff, that can't be it," said Pope. "It's got to be something more serious. But hell, there's been nothing on the radio—I mean, no news to give us any idea that anything is wrong. Too bad we only have the one contact with the outside or we could try to get some answers. They may tell us yet. I mean, we may get another message."

"Not a goddamned chance," said Jackson. "If it's a PTS, the brass will never tell us."

"I doubt it too," said Morton. "Especially since it's a presidential top secret message. Besides, with the outdated equipment we have here, we're damned lucky to have even one connection with the outside world—and don't forget, no one is supposed to know we're here anyway."

"You don't suppose there's a war or something like that started?" asked Watowski. "Maybe they think the Commies are going to drop one of their super bombs here?"

"How the bejesus can I tell? There could be," said Morton.

The door of the shack opened and the four men turned to greet Yung Bhop, the local headman and spokesman for the islanders. He was very old, very thin, and moved slowly but with great dignity.

"Hi, Yung," said Jackson. "Come on in."

"Mr. Morton, is it true that we must leave here?"

"I guess it is, Yung," replied Morton, "at least that's what the message says."

"But why? My people wish to be told."

"Sorry, Yung, but I can't tell you. All I know is that we got this damn signal. It says here we're all to leave the island. The Royal Navy will be here in a few days to take us all to the mainland."

"But that is very far," said Yung slowly. "My people will not be happy in Paguda. They fear they will be heavily taxed there."

"Like I said, Yung, I'm sorry, but we have orders from our government. The whole population of the island must be taken off with all their belongings. You'd better gather your people and tell them to prepare to leave. That's all I know."

"Is it perhaps another terrible war?" said the native chief.

"Maybe, but I can't say. But you know we aren't in a good position to ask questions from here. Don't worry, Yung, soon we'll get another message telling us when the ships will be here. We're all sorry, Yung, but please try to understand. We have to obey orders. You just go and tell your people to start packing their belongings—be a good guy, please."

"We'll tell you more as soon as we get the information," added Pope.

"Very well, then. Thank you, Mr. Morton." The wrinkled old headman of Mitzu turned and began his walk back to the settlement.

The staff sergeant rose from the table to get himself a drink of water. "You know, it doesn't necessarily mean they've started a war already, but it could be that they think one is going to start, so they're taking precautions. Doesn't that make sense?" Morton somehow didn't feel at all sure of his statement.

"Could be, sounds reasonable," said Watowski.

Morton came back to his seat. "Look at it this way," he said. "We're here to pass on weather reports when we're asked to. We're not allowed to go on the air ourselves except in a matter of life or death. Other than that, we get our nuts in the wringer. So what do we do? You tell me."

"Hell, Staff," said Jackson, who had produced the book of departmental orders for the weather station, "we'll all be court-martialed if we break in on the air except for an SOS—it says so here. Listen to it: 'It is imperative that no effort to communicate with Bulabar or with any other station or ship or aircraft will be made except where it can be construed to be a matter of life and death.'"

The staff sergeant, a veteran of over twenty years' service, scratched his balding head. "Yes, I know. Look, we can't do a thing except carry out the orders we've been given. If the government wants to move us from Mitzu to West Berlin and take the whole population of Mitzu there too, then that's what they'll do. Don't ask me why and don't ask each other why. We've got our orders and that's it. Besides, remember this is PTS."

"Sure, sure," said Watowski, "but what about all this goddamn equipment we've signed for. It's all on our charge, ain't it? That's a lot of dough tied up in it and its our dough."

"Yes, I know," Morton said, "but they don't say a thing about taking it with us. All it says here is secure it—lock it up in the hush-hush. I guess that's what they mean. After all, who in hell can steal it if there's no one left here on the island?"

"So, what now?" asked Jackson, who had risen to get some cigarettes. "Just when I was getting used to the place. Let's start packing everything we can in the security lockers. We can remove essential parts of equipment later."

"Yes, but when will we close down operations?" asked Pope nervously.

Morton considered the query. "Can't say for sure, but my guess is that during the next twenty-four hours they'll tell us when the ships will be here and when to close down the station."

"Maybe," suggested Jackson hopefully, "we'll open up again in Paguda, or maybe they'll send us home. Whatever they do, it certainly can't be worse than being in this place."

"Leave me in Paguda with the MAAG and the PX and I'll be satisfied," said Watowski, rising. "Besides, I could stand some of that better class, slant-eyed stuff too. There sure isn't much of that available here."

"You know, Watty," Morton said seriously, "some day when you die they'll open up your head, and I have a good idea what they'll find."

Pope and Jackson laughed.

Watowski looked out of the half-opened door. "No kidding, Korea wasn't half bad," he said. "There, every evening a batch of sexy-sexies would appear walking around the compound perimeter with a government blanket over their arms. You could take your pick. Me, I'm all for the mainland—besides, it's safer there."

"The way it looks now," said Pope, "we're all for the mainland or home."

The staff sergeant stood up and stretched. "All right, fellows," he said with quiet authority, "let's start the packing. Personal kit first. Arms and ammunition we can leave in the cases and carry it out with us. Leave two footlockers free for the essential equipment. Jackson, you and I will start to dismantle the transmitter as soon as we get the order."

"Roger, Sergeant," replied Jackson.

"Say," Pope said, as if he had a brilliant idea, "Wonder if Paguda is another hardship post. I mean, I wonder if the allowances are the same as here."

"I have been told," replied Morton "that Paguda is the asshole of the world."

The others looked at him. "That's what they say," he added. Suddenly Pope burst out laughing.

"Go on, Sarge, you're kidding," said Watowski.

"Sure, he's kidding," said Jackson.

"Say you're kidding, Staff."

But the good staff sergeant said no more. However, he was inwardly enjoying a good laugh as he left the hut.

"I think he was kidding," said Pope.

"I guess so. Paguda can't be that bad, surely." Watowski did not sound convincing.

"If we've got an embassy there and an AID office, there must be a bunch of white secretaries around," Jackson said hopefully.

"Yeah, but—" Pope began when Jackson interrupted him.

"But you know damn well those bastards from the MAAG there will have all the available stuff locked in with them. I tell you, fellers, I'd rather go home and find me a nice virgin who—"

"Boy," Watowski said, "are you dreaming. Not me, I don't want to get married, I want to have some fun first—in Paguda or wherever."

The staff sergeant had reappeared at the door. "I think wherever might be a lot safer than Paguda, Wattie. They tell me that for what one gets in Paguda, it'll take the medical people fifty years to find a cure."

"Staff, you're a real goddamn killjoy," said Jackson.

"No, I'm not. After twenty years, I still believe I can have a real party at home if I keep it in my pants while I'm away."

The three other men looked at him as if lost for words. It was Jackson who spoke first.

"You mean you've never sported around, Staff?"

"Old Mr. Clean himself," said Pope.

"Better Mr. Clean now," said Morton solemnly, "than Mr. Sorry later."

"I guess you have a point, Staff," said Pope.

"Yeah, he's got a point," said Watowski, "and he keeps it in his pants. Staff, I think you're trying to make screwing unpopular."

"Fellows, we've got things to do," Mortin said, his tone changing.

No offense, Staff," said Watowski. "I didn't mean it."

"Well, as I said, we got things to do, and I mean it." The staff sergeant turned on his heel and left the three signalmen exchanging puzzled glances.

CHAPTER XVI

In Paguda itself, events related to Mitzu had brought about one significant change. Ambassador Wilson, having been summoned to Bangkok for a conference on aid policies and other essential matters, had just turned over his representative duties to Bill White, his first secretary. Mr. White, a delicate individual at the best of times, decided somewhat hastily to succumb to a renewed bout of malaria. As a result, White was quietly evacuated to the Philippines where he could receive proper treatment in the mountains around Bagio and cool his anger over the forced postponement of his home leave. This left Mr. Wilson little choice. Notification was, therefore, sent to the capital by priority signal that due to these varied and unfortunate circumstances, there was no one else in the Embassy but the new third secretary. He would assume the duties of acting chargé d'affaires for the short intervening period.

Under ordinary conditions, this could have been classed as an unhappy choice. With Operation Feline in the offing, the choice would prove to be not only unhappy but expensive and disastrous. Alas, some unenlightened individual in the State Department signaled agreement to Mr. Stark's temporary acting appointment as chargé d'affaires.

Mr. Charles Quentin Stark had arrived at the Pagudan post from Paris. A dapper, ineffective egotist with an unconcealed urge to bask in any sort of personal glory, his unheralded move from the lively French capital was the result of a number of highly indiscreet adventures with a variety of ladies, most of whom were unluckily associated with the diplomatic service of other countries. To his ever-loving and gullible wife, however, he had offered, as always, the simplest of explanations—the ladies in question had pursued him and pressed their attentions to such an extent that he must, purely on the point of honor, leave Paris. She believed him; she always did. He did not mention that at least two other members of the diplomatic corps had threatened to shoot him.

Ordinarily, this pint-sized Casanova might have been expelled from the foreign service, but not Charles Quentin Stark. With a senator for a father and an uncle in Congress, he was quick to appreciate the situation and to act. When it became clear that events were about to catch up with him and several of his lovely associates were about to create a scandal, he had dispatched letters to a sufficient number of influential relatives to guarantee his transfer and escape from the French capital. The arrival of this self-styled sexpot in Paguda was thus quietly unnoticed.

Now, he was acting chargé d'affaires, the sole senior representative of his country in Paguda. Here at last, he thought to himself, was the opportunity to make his name.

It was a bright sunny morning, and Charles Quentin Stark, having inspected his impeccably groomed appearance in the hall mirror and having leaned forward to pass a perfectly manicured hand across the wisp of moustache, turned to the door held open by his white-clad houseboy. Then, with a final pat on his receding hairline and an adjustment to his pince-nez, he sallied forth at a brisk step toward the embassy. As he tripped lightly along the boulevard, his mind wandered about the limitless realm of his imagination. Here were new worlds to conquer, greener fields to cultivate and a brand new bevy of ladies to observe and possibly pay court to in due time. He halted momentarily, produced his gold cigarette case and with infinite care extracted one of his perfumed specials. Then with equal care and with the timing of a professional actor, he flicked his lighter.

When Mr. Stark reached the embassy door, he was politely saluted and informed by the Marine guard on duty that Mr. Heng, the Pagudan state secretary, was expected shortly. To the new chargé, this was exciting news; he lost no time in depositing himself in the ambassador's office, an act made easy for him due to Miss Loffatt's traditional early visit to the powder room. By the time she returned to her desk, Mr. Stark was comfortably settled in the ambassadorial chair surveying his newly acquired domain with great satisfaction. He pressed the buzzer to call her.

"Ah, Miss Loffatt, my dear," he said, "how utterly delightful you look this morning. Such a becoming dress—lovely, very lovely. Turn around, my dear, and let me admire it."

The ambassador's secretary was no novice; she was quick to sense danger and therefore took no notice of his request. She cast Stark a suspicious look that increased in its intensity as he rose and placed a chair for her. Moreover, as she sat murmuring her thanks, Miss Loffatt felt the new third secretary's hand brush lightly against her arm and then across her bosom where it seemed to pause.

"Comfortable, my dear?" Charles Stark fairly blew the whispered words into Miss Loffatt's ear, then drew back as she turned her head away meaningfully.

The man must be mad, she thought, little realizing the agile Mr. Stark was beginning what he proudly boasted to himself was his power play that, curiously enough, had seldom failed to produce the required result—in Paris, anyway.

"Ah, my dear," said the little man, seating himself, "I understand that Mr. Heng, the state secretary of Paguda, is coming in to see me this morning. Pray have him come in as soon as he arrives. Have you any idea what it is about, Miss Loffatt?"

"He didn't say, Mr. Stark, but in my cabinet I do have the file Mr. White was working on. It must be on this new aid program." With that explanation she got up and left the room to return a few moments later. She placed the hefty folder before him.

Stark opened it rapidly with the air of one who is in complete control of the situation, and as he did so, he whistled a few bars of Friml's *Indian Love Call.* "Ah, a PTS matter—how very interesting."

After only the barest glance at the top page, Stark looked up at Miss Loffatt, who was now sitting well away from him.

"I think I have the problem, my dear. You may send in Mr. Heng as soon as he arrives—oh, one more thing, Miss Loffatt. Please remember, my door is always open to my staff. Anytime you have anything you want to discuss or any little problem on your mind, please do not hesitate. The morale of those under me is always my foremost concern."

The longer he spoke, the more convinced she was that the third secretary was not only quite mad, but a prize idiot as well.

At just that moment the ambassador's warning bell sounded to signal the arrival of the Pagudan state secretary.

Miss Loffatt moved to the door. "That is Mr. Heng's arrival. I'll show him in."

As he waited for his visitor, Mr. Stark's eyes scanned the listings of the items stored in the mission of aids warehouse. It excited him to realize that he alone was in a position to distribute whatever he wished from this vast supply of stores. It was then that with a light knock on the door, Miss Loffatt ushered in Mr. Heng.

"Ah, Mr. Heng, how delightful of you to visit us."

"Good day, excellency." Mr. Heng bowed deeply. "I hope I am not disturbing you but this whole disaster on Mitzu is very worrying." Mr. Heng then began to pace the carpeted floor.

"Not at all, Mr. Heng. I am here solely to assist you and your people. Would you care to sit down and rest?"

Mr. Heng did not respond; he kept on slowly pacing the length of the office, stopping occasionally to wipe his face with a dirty red handkerchief. Mr. Stark remained behind the ambassador's desk.

Finally, Mr. Heng stopped his march across the room and stopped in front of Mr. Stark. "Now, I think I must rest," he said.

"Would you like a glass of water?" The third secretary asked, pushing the tray with glass and bottle across the desk.

"Yes, I think so." replied Mr. Heng pouring himself a drink. "Now, I am ready to hear what you have for us."

Mr. Stark was now looking at the warehouse lists.

"Ah, now for the main items. We have ready for erecting, twenty-six of the prefabricated houses, with enough beds, bedding, blankets, utility furniture, kitchen items and other household necessities. We have three complete hospital tents, one complete army kitchen, two tons of mixed medical supplies, five tons of tinned food, three tons of fine rice, eight cases of vaccines and a half ton of baby food. That is the initial list of main items. The other three pages, I see, contain most of the things that are to be found in our AID holding warehouses here. We can deal with them later. Now, Mr. Heng, what about your own government's contribution to this-to this-to the effort?"

The Pagudan official, having reached the limit of his exercise over the carpeted floor, seated himself and sighed heavily. "Paguda, Excellency, will have twelve doctors and fifteen local nurses on hand to assist in the hospital, but we must, of course, erect the houses and the tents as soon as possible. When do you think we might begin to put them up? Or I should ask, when may we expected to take delivery of these things?"

"Well," said Stark, "I see no reason to delay the matter. I think we may be able to arrange to do it today."

"Excellency, you are very kind. You can be sure we Pagudans will not forget this great and generous gesture. But, there is one more thing I would request. Would your Excellency consider providing me with one or two technicians from your people with the MAAG to supervise the erection of these new houses and tents?" Mr. Heng leaned across the desk with the expression of a faithful dog begging for its food. Mr. Stark quickly agreed and made a note of it.

No doubt about it, Charles Quentin Stark was enjoying himself beyond his wildest dreams. He had just been addressed as Excellency three times in as many minutes. This, he decided, was the way things should have been all along. Mrs. Stark would be thrilled when he told her.

The results of Mr. Stark's enthusiastic generosity were soon made manifest. An hour later when Mr. Heng left the Embassy, he had in his possession the clearly signed and sealed authority for the Government of Paguda to draw from AID's warehouses in Paguda practically every item the Mission of Aid had on hand. Not only did Mr. Stark authorize the release of the things listed by the Pagudans, the chargé himself threw in, for good measure, many other items, assuring himself glibly that it all fell within the instructions outlined by his government. After all, he was the man in charge; he was the representative on the spot.

No, he told himself, the State Department would have to understand sooner or later that when Charles Quentin Stark was at the helm, things would get done.

For some time after Mr. Heng's departure, Stark reflected on the manner in which he had handled the visit. It was true that Mr. Wentworth, the chief of the MOAP, should have been the one to undersign the aid document; but after all, when he had phoned the MOAP[1] office, he had been told Wentworth was out of town on a field trip and wouldn't be back in Paguda for four days—so despite a gesture of disapproval from Miss Loffatt, he had signed. After all, things as important as this could not wait until tomorrow. They had to be done now. If aid was needed it must be given when it was needed.

Stark wondered whether he had displayed the proper amount of flourish and dramatic timing when he had applied his signature to the document. With deliberate and bold strokes, Stark signed his name several times on the blank pad of paper before him. By the time he had completed his sixth effort he was sure the Pagudan state secretary must have been duly impressed. But why, wondered Stark, had Miss Loffatt left so hurriedly?

The bare fact that he had, by the stroke of a pen, just given away well over a half million dollars' worth of supplies in aid to Paguda bothered the chargé not the least. On the contrary, he merely revelled in the sheer delight of self-exaltation. That he had also donated from the goodness of his heart almost another three hundred thousand dollars worth of goods over and above

---

[1] Mission of Aid Paguda

the amount authorized by his own government apparently did not even occur to him. If it did, Mr. Stark must have dismissed it as a trivial and totally unimportant point.

But one thing did bother Mr. Stark: Miss Loffatt had suddenly walked out of the office almost in a huff while Heng was still there. Why had she done that? Could it be she was unwell?

Actually, the ambassador's secretary was not only quite well, she was also extremely angry. At one stage, before Mr. Stark signed the aid clearance papers, Miss Loffatt had felt it her duty to place a note before him expressing an opinion on the items included by Mr. Stark, since it was quite clear the evacuees from Mitzu would find little use for two pianos and, among other things, fourteen high powered outboard motors.

However, when Charles Quentin Stark exclaimed, "Miss Loffatt, please!" and then turned to the Pagudan State Secretary and compounded the offense by adding, "I'm sorry, Excellency, but being merely a member of the staff and not as highly trained as we senior diplomats, Miss Loffatt is only trying to be helpful."

That did it.

"To hell with you," she muttered as she walked quietly out of the office. Miss Loffatt stopped by her desk long enough to pick up her bag and a few odds and ends, and having tossed Mr. Stark's half-finished sock into the waste basket, she told her assistant to take over.

On his return to his own office, a very contented Mr. Heng reported in person to Sultopan, the Pagudan grand chef. His mission, declared Mr. Heng, had been most successful, but he warned the Sultopan that the cloak of secrecy had been insisted upon by their benefactors and he had agreed to it. Sultopan agreed and promised he would hold a conference later that day, and he would issue a formal warning to all the others concerned about the security of the matter.

“When will the work of erection commence?” asked Sultopan.

“As soon as we draw this list of stores from their warehouses,” replied Mr. Heng, waving the release papers.

“Excellent. But, where are the buildings to be put up? Have you chosen a location—and what about the tents?”

“I have suggested, Your Highness, that back of the State Park grounds near the harbor will be an ideal place with the medical tents behind them. You recall, sir, it is the acreage we confiscated from the French chemical company last year.”

“Of course,” said Sultopan, “a wise choice.”

“Yes, I believe so, sir. Especially so as we can later rent the bungalows later to some of the diplomatic missions for their staff members.

“Do you think,” suggested His Highness, “that in view of the event we might strike a special medal?”

“It would be most applicable, Highness. But the question of cost and availability of the gold or silver arises, sir.

“Oh, surely our benefactors might be approached to grant us a small loan of the precious metals required. What do you think?”

“I fear not, Your Highness. They have already extended us most generous aid in this matter. We could of course try. Mr. Stark does appear to be an easy man to persuade, much easier than Mr. Wilson. But...”

“Yes, go on,” said the chubby-faced Pagudan ruler.

“Well, sir, we could sell the marine equipment—the fourteen outboard motors—to some of the plantations upcountry. Being on the river they would, I know, welcome them. Also, there are some pianos, and even two or three of the prefabricated houses would fetch a good price. We could raise some extra funds ourselves very quickly in this way.”

Sultopan shrugged. “Well, see what you can do. And, by the way, I do think we could show our appreciation by giving a buffet party for the officers of the evacuation fleet when it passes through on the way to Mitzu.”

"Yes, of course, Highness," said Heng, "but what do you think we could tell the other diplomatic missions when they see the houses and tents being erected and the hospital people about? There are bound to be questions."

"We shall inform them," said Sultopan "that the ships of certain allies are taking part in a goodwill visit and that the activity related to the new houses, the hospital tents and the medical supplies are part of a health exercise to benefit the poor. That should be enough, surely."

"Yes, sir," said Mr. Heng doubtfully.

"As a matter of fact, I want you to have the invitations prepared for the buffet. Include all diplomatic missions. You can make it a royal command. Yes, do that. That will insure attendance. Send them off when you know the ships will be in the harbor here."

"Yes, Highness," said Mr. Heng, bowing his way toward the door. "Will that be all, sir?"

"One more thing," said the fat and exalted Sultopan, who had remained seated cross-legged on a large cushion throughout the discussion. "When does ambassador Wilson return?"

"In four days, sir."

"I see. Then I want those houses and tents up in three days. Get the Army to do it."

"It will be done, sir," Mr. Heng said, and, with a series of extra low bows, began to withdraw.

"Oh, by the way—as you leave, will you please send in my son. He is waiting in the hall."

"Certainly, Highness," said Mr. Heng as he made a final bow and prepared to back away from his ruler.

"Oh, I almost forgot to ask you. The minister of finance mentioned to me something about the ships belonging to the British Royal Navy—is that true?"

"Yes, Highness. The Americans considered it better not to arouse suspicion by movement of any of their forces at present and wisely asked the British Government if they would take on this mission of mercy. They have agreed to do so, with their

Royal Navy and the Royal Air Force, to evacuate the island and to clean up the plague of rats."

"I see. The grand chef nodded. "I see. But can the British be relied upon to maintain the security of this matter?"

"I believe so, sir," said the state secretary. "In any case, they are not involved in any of the matters of aid related to the Mitzu plague. They are only doing the evacuation and the clean-up later. Our ambassador in Washington informs me the Americans have told him very little about this except that the British are also working under a complete security blanket and will continue to do so until the mission is completed."

"Good, good, very satisfactory. Excellent. Don't forget to ask my son to come in."

"He will be told, Highness." The state secretary bowed low again; moved backward to the door and vanished.

The Sultopan rose to pace the floor. As he did so, he looked at the three letters he had extracted from his pocket. Mitzu was one problem, but, certainly, here in these three epistles was another. They were, in fact, letters of respectful complaint from three families he knew well.

Each letter presented him with the same problem: What, inquired the writers, was to be done about the child expected within a matter of weeks by the eldest daughter of each family? Would the Sultopan agree to compensate the individual family—or would he perhaps agree to his 17-year-old son marrying the young lady concerned? The grand chef smiled sickly. The fact that he had produced such a virile offspring did not console him at all.

But, in considering the facts of the case as he gazed at the skyline of the Pagudan capital, he realized that there might be a solution.

All three families were wealthy; one especially so. It owned four large plantations each with its own cannery. A marriage into such might prove a sound investment with vast possibilities.

As for the other two families, ambassadorial appointments might well be the answer. He must remember to give it more consideration. As the door opened to admit his erring offspring, he realized that for the moment anyway he had an urgent family matter to try to solve.

CHAPTER XVII

George Gilly arrived at the Washington National Airport just after eight o'clock. He was looking around him when he felt a hand touch his shoulder. Turning, he saw a short pudgy-faced army captain about his own age with hand outstretched.

The man smiled. "You're George Gilly, I guess?"

"Yes, I'm George Gilly." George took the hand, wondering if he should salute.

"Great," said the captain, "I'm your official welcoming committee, Tom Drewer. Got all your baggage?"

"Oh, sure, I just brought the one bag."

"Good. Then let's go. You just follow me." George wondered why all the hurry as his guide set a quick pace toward the street.

A five-minute cab ride later, they alighted outside an untidy sprawling grey mess of a building, on top of which flew three flags. Drewer led the way up the steps and then for what seemed to be half a mile, along a badly lighted and rather smelly corridor. Eventually, the journey came to an end in front of a huge green door on which was attached a brass plate, indicating this was the office of the Chief of Special Projects Logistics. This was General Jansen's official abode.

Drewer obviously knew his way about the place. George wondered if perhaps Drewer was the general's aide. Drewer looked like an aide—very neat and dapper, he gave out the appearance of a toy soldier just removed from its box.

George tried to recall if he had ever met any other aides, but his line of thought was shattered by a bull-like bellow from the inner office.

"Drewer, where the hell have you been? Have you got Gilly?"

Drewer led George toward the voice and after passing a miniskirted female stenographer who was obviously having difficulty with her manicure set and a sergeant reading *Playboy*, they were in General Jansen's inner sanctum.

It was a large air-conditioned room, its walls plastered with maps and colored charts, a clear indication of the tenant's addiction to statistics. The sparse government furniture gave it an austere look.

General Jansen seemed to bounce across the floor toward them, hand outstretched.

"Lieutenant Gilly, by all that's holy, am I ever glad to see you, my boy." The general kept pumping George's hand as he steered him toward a chair.

George managed a weak, rather sloppy salute, then removed his hat.

"Sit down, my boy, sit down. Cigar?" Jansen offered a large silver box to which George shook his head. "Ah, a nonsmoker, eh? Good man. A young man can't smoke and keep fit. Now, let's get right down to business. You sit down too, Drewer."

The aide picked a corner chair as Jansen paced to and fro in front of the window.

"Lieutenant," said Jansen, "have you any idea at all why we have sent for you? Have you any idea why you are here?"

"No, General," said George. "I have not."

"Lieutenant—" Jansen stopped and turned to gaze intently at first at his visitor, then at his aide. "Didn't you tell him anything, Drewer?"

"No sir, not a thing," replied Drewer. "I thought that—"

"So, Gilly, you have no idea at all why we wanted you?"

"No, sir." George was getting a trifle worried now. "Not the slightest."

"Ever heard of Mitzu, Lieutenant?" asked the General quickly. "It's an island."

"Mitzu? Why, yes, sir, I was there for a while after Korea," replied George Gilly. "I think it belongs to Paguda."

"So you speak the language?"

"Pagudan, sir? Well, a bit, sir. I mean, passable."

"Good, now, I'll tell you the full story. By the way, Lieutenant, there is one question I must ask you before I start. Do you like cats?"

"Cats, sir? Oh, I like all animals. I have a dog."

"I asked you if you liked cats, Lieutenant."

"Well, sir, there are cats and—well, cats."

Drewer fidgeted uncomfortably in his chair. He had a feeling this fellow Gilly was going to be difficult.

Jansen was not the sort of person to be sidetracked. "Now, do you by chance own a cat, Lieutenant?"

"No, sir, but I do have a dog and some rabbits. I used to have a cat once, but—"

Drewer coughed to draw George's attention, for he could see that his general's face was growing redder than usual.

"I see. Then you don't have a cat?" said the general.

"No, sir, I do not. I don't mind cats, though," replied George starting to feel a bit wary. "I really don't, sir."

"Gilly." The general had turned now to face the lieutenant, and he spoke the name quietly and with just the proper amount of dramatic accent. "We have a problem, a very grave problem on Mitzu, and the government, ours that is, feels that you are the one man who can help us." He paused to let the words sink in before he went on. "Now, here it is. A short time ago the State Department informed us the island of Mitzu was being overrun by rats, any of which could carry bubonic plague. Now, apart from the American signalmen on Mitzu, there are about four hundred Pagudans; you probably know a good many of them. As you well understand, Mitzu has an airstrip and is one of our emergency airfields and supply points, so that makes it all the more important. Now, our problem, then, is to safeguard the island; so we intend to have the Navy evacuate the inhabitants back to the mainland of Paguda and then land a force of cats on the island to deal with the rats. And that is where you come into the picture. I hope you follow me, Lieutenant?"

"George's eyes had been growing larger with each of the general's words. At the last sentence they nearly popped out.

"Do you understand, Lieutenant?" Jansen said. "Cats to take on the rats, eh?"

"Yes, sir," George mumbled slowly. "That is, I think I do. But what do I have to do?"

"I'm coming to that. Now, due to financial restrictions, we could not use some of the more modern ways of extermination, such as poison or gas. So we have decided, on the president's order, to assemble a huge force of cats, probably up to two thousand or more, at Camp Billings. There we will feed them for a couple of days, then prepare them for their battle against the rats on Mitzu by restricting their food. The cats will be crated, taken by road to Tenpost Air Base and then flown to Bulabar Air Base by the British Royal Air Force. From Bulabar they go on to Singabar by road. At Singabar they will be transferred to a special Royal Navy ship carrying landing craft for the final leg of the journey to Mitzu. Your job, Lieutenant, is to supervise the concentration of the cats and the airlift and see that they are landed at the right place—on Mitzu, that is. You will be in sole command of this operation. Naturally, we will give you any assistance you—er—may require."

The general paused to light a cigar before continuing. "Now, once the landings have been carried out, you and your assistants will observe and report the progress of the operation directly to me—through the Royal Navy, who will provide whatever communications equipment you may need. Now do you get it?"

George hoped he did not look as baffled as he felt.

"Yes, sir," he answered slowly. "I guess so, sir."

"Good man, I knew you would," said the general. "One final word. You must never forget this is a presidential top-secret assignment. Therefore, not one word of it must get out. The number of people who know about Feline—that's what we have named the operation—is very restricted. It must be left that way. Until the operation is completed, we must maintain complete security. Now, I want to work fast. You have exactly ten days to get the animals ready. Get it?"

"Yes, sir," replied George, thinking of Julie and his garage.

"Good luck, my boy. And, oh yes, I have good news for you, you are promoted to captain as of today, so get that rank up right away. Now, Drewer, you take him to see Administration for whatever has to be done and see he gets his identity card and papers and pay fixed up—and to the QM stores for whatever extra clothing he needs. You'll need a new uniform too. I've Okayed this already. The QM is expecting you."

Drewer and Gilly stood up; the latter saluted rather uncertainly and hurried to the door. Drewer was about to follow but Jansen called him back.

"Oh, Drewer, have you given any thought to the selection of an officer to assist Gilly in this operation?"

"No, sir, not yet, sir, but I wondered if—" He was about to suggest the delegation of this particular task to someone else on the general's staff.

"Well, don't worry about it," the general said. "I've already made the decision. You will be my personal liaison officer on this operation. You will be the executive officer for Gilly."

"Me, sir? But, sir, what about—"

"What about what? My dear boy, you are the obvious choice. No, I insist. So you two get down to Billings and let's get the ball rolling. Drewer, what's the matter with you?"

"Nothing, sir, just—what I was going to suggest, sir, was someone to replace me here, sir, to assist you, sir."

"That's very thoughtful of you, Drewer," replied Jansen, "but I've already selected your successor. He'll be here tomorrow."

Drewer managed a foolish grin, then he too saluted and left.

Camp Billings is not what might ever be termed a paradise of any sort. It is a small compact camp, and its most recent use was during the last war, as an indoctrination center for servicewomen who were destined to go to the Pacific, had the A–Bomb not forced the final issue. As such, it was an ideal spot. In summer, it had all the flies, swamp snakes and other discomforts one normally associated with the tropics. For the past several years, however, the camp had been used only for the National Guard training exercises and, thus, was listed semi-dormant. It had a commandant, a couple of administrative staff sergeants and two clerks, a small Engineer's Corps maintenance staff, a medical officer, a nurse, and a few casual laborers.

The camp staff was kept just big enough to handle the usual weekend training exercises by National Guard units, although in some past years, it had been expanded temporarily to cater to Boy Scout Jamborees, a Girl Scouts Summer Camp and several month-long training periods for the Special Forces.

Since the arrival, however, of the heavy manila envelope that contained the first instructions concerning Operation feline, things had begun to move. Obviously, the camp was in for a rapid change. First, an elderly veterinary officer and four veterinary assistants from the National Experimental Farms moved into camp without notice, and the commandant had been authorized to increase his labor forces by eighteen men. Then four huge cases of special animal vaccine had just been delivered by express package.

Colonel Stewart Slate was a tubby, yet medically fit, neurotic bachelor of fifty-odd years whose only claim to military fame was mainly due to his graduation from the Academy and to an overbearing and influential mother who had assured his safety throughout his service by seeing that his assignments were to non-danger areas and that his climb up the rank ladder progressed, despite the fact that he was a confirmed alcoholic.

Colonel Stewart Slate was, in fact, what the British refer to as a slacker, a person who, when faced with a dirty job or one in which he may be injured, decides it's not his cup of tea. His answer invariably was "Let the other chap do it." Slackers are dangerous; they are selfish, and you dare not trust them because they will let you down every time, at least that's what President Teddy Roosevelt said. Yet, in one sense, the colonel's continual state of inebriation stood him well, in that he was unable to interfere with the superbly capable Staff Sergeant Bill Jones, who ran the camp in a most efficient manner. On this particular day, however, Staff Sergeant Jones was not happy. For one thing, the colonel was quite sober—this in itself was a bad sign.

Yet, it could be stated honestly that Colonel Slate's sobriety was due entirely to the instructions he had received from the headquarters concerning Operation Feline. First had come the PTS letter by hand from the Chairman Joint Chiefs of Staff telling him to take immediate action to reopen the camp for an indefinite period in order to handle a presidential top-secret assignment. Next arrived the copy of General Jansen's directive to one of the other camps ordering all cats to be sent to Billings. That in itself was really enough to sober up any man.

The camp commandant was not regarded too highly for his initiative. Actually, he felt lost even thinking of the deluge of organizational detail that now threatened him. His camp was suddenly to become a haven for hordes of cats, quite the severest blow he had ever had. The colonel was baffled. He hated cats; in fact, he hated animals of any kind. Thank God the whole scheme was a PTS, at least he would be spared any publicity. Slate shuddered at the mere thought of the howling brutes. He suddenly wished he had a proper staff of officers so he could call a meeting. If ever there was a time to delegate authority, this was obviously it.

Slate felt sure his blood pressure was rising; his head ached. It had begun first thing yesterday morning when he had received, by rail, forty-two Caterpillar tractors from the Engineering School. Later in the day, five seaplanes had flown in to land on Billings Lake, which was the best fishing area for miles around, and now hordes of cats were about to descend on him.

Suddenly the colonel caught a glimmer of light amongst his jumbled thoughts. An increase in personnel—why? Tractors—why? Seaplanes—why? Could it be that Billings was to become a combined camp for the three services? That could be it. A tri-service camp—well, well—that could be a horse of a different color. The very idea encouraged him. After all, he was senior enough for the promotion to brigadier general to command the camp. No, it might not be so bad after all. The thought occurred to him that the sooner he wrote to his mother, the better.

One thing, however, did please the colonel. His small bar situated in the largest hut, which normally doubled as a camp club, was doing absolutely a roaring business. All of the fifteen Air Force officers and crewmen who brought in the seaplanes were imbibing supernatural quantities of beer. Colonel Slate wondered how long they might stay. When they reported in to his orderly room, the officer in charge merely stated that he had been ordered to bring in the seaplanes and wait for further instructions from his headquarters.

It became even more of a puzzle to Slate when, shortly after the morning coffee break, he met two strange officers outside the club. Captain Gilly handed the colonel a letter form General Jansen that Slate read ponderously. Slate then beckoned them to follow him to his office. He lost no time in calling Staff Sergeant Jones to sit in on the meeting.

"At last, I am beginning to see some light," said Slate. "I see it now, you two officers are here to supervise the arrival and concentration of the cats."

"Yes, sir. Just as the letter states," said Drewer.

"Oh and I gather from the general's letter the overall impression we are to give is that these animals are being gathered together for some special vaccine experiments by one of our research groups—is that it? They will be crated here and dispatched by road to Tenpost Air Base on a given date—is that right?"

"Exactly, sir," said Captain Gilly.

"How long do you expect them to be here, gentlemen, or do you know?"

"That depends, Colonel, on how fast they come in. We expect well over 1,700 in all, counting the ones from SPCA," explained Drewer, consulting his small notebook.

"Do we have a count yet, Sergeant Jones?"

"Yes, Colonel," said the sergeant. "Right now we have nine hundred eighty-two, and that does not count the eighteen new mothers with an average of four kittens each."

"Hmm." The colonel frowned. "Well, all we can do is wait, I suppose."

"Shall I get the laborers on to building the crates, sir?" asked the staff sergeant.

"Yes, yes, do that, Jones, please, at once. And you will please arrange a meeting of all the various camp supervisors for two p.m. today in this office, the vets, the doctor, the superintendent of the laborers, etc. I want them all here."

The staff sergeant nodded, made a note, and suddenly looked up. "But, sir, this is a PTS. What will you tell them?" He inquired quietly.

"Oh yes, yes, you're right. What do I tell them, eh, Gilly? You, Drewer? You two are in charge of this. What do we tell them?" Colonel Slate was uneasy and beginning to feel thirsty.

Drewer looked at Gilly as he spoke up. "I think, Colonel, you just tell them a presidential top secret and special research program has been started near here or near Tenpost Air Base, and that the cats are needed for vaccine research. Captain Gilly and I will supervise the crating and feeding. I take it that cat food has arrived?"

"It has, sir," said the efficient staff sergeant. "Two tons of it."

"All right, then, sir," continued Drewer. "when all the cats are here, then we inform General Jansen. Apart from that, we feed them well for a few days, but we don't start restricting their food to make them hungry until we're ready to leave here. General Jansen will tell us when to go. The aircraft at Tenpost Air Base should be all ready for us. Tenpost will send vehicles for the cats when we give the word, and that's about it, sir."

"You mean," said the now worried commandant, "that this is all Billings is being opened up for—for this—for Operation Feline? I mean, I thought perhaps since the tractors and planes arrived that, well, that something else was coming up. Are you sure?"

"*That,* we can't say, sir," said Gilly with a shrug, "but my guess is that, what with planes and all those tractors here, there must be more to it than our operation. don't you think so, Drewer?"

Drewer somehow didn't think so, but said he did anyway. The sigh of relief and the look of sheer expectancy on the colonel's face indicated to Drewer that he had said the right thing.

That afternoon, Gilly and Drewer settled themselves into fairly comfortable quarters in the old camp hospital, the regular officers quarters being somewhat overcrowded with members of the seaplane crews, many of whom appeared to be quite drunk already.

For the rest of that evening and throughout the next three days, cats of all shapes, colors and sizes continued to pour into Camp Billings. Drivers of the vehicles that transported the animals were naturally somewhat curious. However, Colonel Slate had provided a ready solution. After each driver had delivered his furry, and usually noisy load, he was ushered into the commandant's office where the colonel greeted him, gave him a cup of coffee, and then quietly explained that a special vaccine research program was taking place and that naturally it was a most secret project. The military drivers understood it well enough. Some of the civilian drivers from the SPCA at first raised a few questions, but the mention of Admiral Lyman's name and one or two references to the fact that the admiral had personally given his blessing to the matter satisfied any doubters.

On the fifth day at Camp Billings, however, a sense of uncertainty again came over the dangerously sober commandant. His mind was muddled.

The camp resounded to the meowing of some sixteen hundred-odd cats in various types of crates on his sports field. His parade ground was jammed with the forty-two tractors or bulldozers, and his favorite fishing lake was being slowly polluted by the five seaplanes that periodically spouted dirty oil and gasoline into the usually clear water. Furthermore, the officer's club, though showing a huge increase in activity and bar profits, had taken on the appearance of a dirty, overcrowded waterfront dive. Now, to crown it all, his brand new medical officer, Captain Fox, who had only arrived two days ago, had requested an immediate transfer and, last but not least—and he shuddered at the thought-General Jansen was coming down to inspect the camp.

Damn it, somehow he must get those tractors cleaned up and exert his influence to get the air crews to look a little more military. It was at times like this that he longed for his mother to write to him. In this state of self-created gloom, he cast a furtive glance toward each of his office windows, then let his hand slide down to the lower drawer where he kept his bottle of Old Granddad Special and a glass.

Slate finished his second drink before he felt he was ready to approach the officer in charge of the pilots. But as he picked up his hat he was not sure of what he should say. Maybe, he thought, he should sit down again and plan how to tackle the problem and how to...well...

Colonel Slate went back to his desk and decided to get added consolation from Old Granddad.

CHAPTER XVIII

At the School of Military Engineering, a severe crisis had arisen. The commandant there, having complied with orders to ship all available cats to Camp Billings, had naturally requested, by cable to the Pentagon, urgent replacements for his Caterpillar tractors. Now to his utter surprise, he had just received a stinging message from the chief engineer. Why, demanded the chief, and on what authority, had every available tractor been sent to Camp Billings? And why hadn't the chief engineer been consulted? It was evident that the chief engineer was furious. All those tractors, he said, must be returned to the Engineering School at once. The Commandant's anger and blood pressure mounted. He called his adjutant, Captain Jenks, who had just returned from a fire-fighting course on the coast.

"Bob, I want you to get a message off to Billings demanding return of the forty-two cats at once. Someone has boo-booed and screwed this thing up," he said seriously. Yet, at the same time at the back of his mind, he was wondering whether there was any other courses to which he could send his adjutant. He must think of something to occupy his own free time when his wife Jennifer left the following week to attend a Girl Scouts' convention—and Marie Jenks was the best and most playful occupier of free time he could think of on short notice.

"Yes, sir," replied Captain Jenks. Right away, sir."

"And, Bob?"

"Yes, sir?"

"Make it most urgent. Just say, 'Essential you return forty-two Cats sent in error soonest.' That should do it, or I'm going to get my ass kicked from here to breakfast."

"Better still, sir, I'll phone Billings."

"Good God, no, you can't. This is PTS. Send a coded message."

"I will, sir," replied the adjutant.

"Thanks," said Colonel Platts. Then, as if in afterthought, he said, "Say, Bob, I was wondering, would you like me to send your name in for this guided missile course down at Fort Bloom? I've got to submit a candidate, and it's got to be someone I can really rely on. I'd appreciate it if you'll take it on—although I know you've only just returned from the fire-fighting course."

Bob Jenks looked back as he opened the door. "Where did you say it was, sir?"

"Fort Bloom."

"When, sir?"

"Oh, let's see," replied Platts, consulting the course instruction sheet on his desk. "It begins a week Monday and lasts for two weeks."

"Sure, sir, thanks. Put me in for it, I'd love it," said the adjutant as he made his exit. What could be better, thought Captain Jenks. Fort Bloom was not that far from El Paso and El Paso was where Jennifer Platts, the commandant's wife, would be staying for ten days attending her Girl Scouts' convention. Much nearer in fact that she had been last time while he was on his fire-fighting course at Pasadena.

At Edgewater Air Base, Mullins, the base supply officer, was feeling quite good.

He had rid himself and the Air Force of five hopelessly outdated Catalina flying boats that were used for training, and now he had just completed the details on the financial appropriations for new funds to pay for replacements. He read over the documents with an inner feeling of satisfaction. He was quite sure his superiors at Air Force Headquarters would be delighted. Just the same, he wondered idly whether he should leave the crews in Camp Billings until he got further orders or call them back to Edgewater now. He looked at his watch. It was five to five, it was Friday, and Monday was a national holiday—what was more, the golfing weather looked promising. In any case, the following Tuesday, when he returned to his desk refreshed, would be a much better time to make decisions. He locked his security cabinets, tidied his desk and went home.

Several thousand miles away in his small office in the basement of the Kremlin annex, Ivan Berialevski was a very worried man. Not only that, he was completely perplexed. The report in his hands just did not make any sense at all. As chief of his nation's intelligence services he had often dealt with some peculiar developments, but this latest issue was, he felt, quite the most insane in his entire experience.

His instructions were, however, clear enough. The memorandum attached to the top secret folio before him directed him to determine to what extent cats could be used in bacteriological warfare. He was to base his investigation on the report at hand.

Mr. Berialevski then read through the report submitted by Agent 66041.

This agent, who had a brother who was employed as a cleaner and maintenance man at a certain American military camp, stated that on the seventh of November he had been ordered to unload several vehicles carrying crates of large cats. He estimated the total number of cats at the camp would exceed several thousand. These animals were being assembled, the report continued, with a view to sending them by road to a nearby air base from whence they were to be flown to a destination as yet unknown. Several men who looked like doctors had arrived at the camp, and from one he learned that each animal was to receive several shots from a hypodermic needle. These, the agent calculated, consisted no doubt of a new bacteria. Agent 66041 further stated that his brother had overheard the following conversation:

First person with the insignia of two bars on his shoulder, possibly a captain: "Well, this will really shake the rats (an offensive imperialistic term usually applied to or denoting their enemies)."

Second person (a sergeant): "They will never know what hit them."

First person: "I wonder who thought of this, it's certainly cheaper than gas—the guy should get a medal."

Second person: "There will be a small job for the extermination squad after the cats have finished their work on the island."

First person: "Yes, indeed. After the cats have been at sea for a few days, it will be interesting to see how they react when they encounter the first rats they meet on the island."

Analysis of the problem was, according to the agent, quite simple. These animals carrying some dread disease were to be unleashed on some unknown island where they would attack anything or anyone they met.

In view of the recent summit agreement, during which the chiefs of the two great powers had told the world they would do all they could to eliminate any possibility of nuclear war, the agent concluded that this must be some new diabolic scheme to catch the valiant citizens of the Soviet Union unprepared while their minds were occupied with hopes of everlasting peace.

Intelligence Chief Berialevski was reading the report for the third time when the other two men entered. He waved them to sit. Against his own short and round five-feet-two inch frame, the newcomers seemed to tower over him—Janick, the head of Chemical Warfare, was over six feet tall and weighed at least two hundred and fifty pounds. Grutchev, the head of the Bacteria Department, was even taller and heavier. Both men seated themselves facing the intelligence chief.

Berialevski gazed at them for quite a while before he spoke. "What sort of deadly disease can a cat carry?"

"A cat?" asked Grutchev. "Did you say a cat?"

"Yes, a cat. What disease could it carry?"

"Well, rabies is common."

"I know that, but what else?"

"Well, they could be infected with a number of things, I suppose just the same as human beings."

"What, for instance?" inquired the chief.

"Well, cholera. Plague perhaps. But rabies is probably the best."

"Much the best," added Janick. "and much cheaper than gas or any other known chemical to use against an enemy."

"Ah ha!" said Berialveski, pointing his finger. "You too have said it. You see you said it too."

"What did I say?" asked the bewildered Janick.

"Cheaper than gas or any other chemical. That's what you said."

"Yes," said Janick, "I did, but."

"Now, what," said Berialevski, "Is the best possible defense against rabies?"

"Inoculate the cats, I suppose," said Grutchev. "That is the most common procedure."

"No, no," said Berialevski impatiently. "We don't want to inoculate the cats—what I want to know is, what would a person have to do to be absolutely safe against the bite of a rabid cat? What sort of injection against cats that had rabies?"

Grutchev and Janick cast each other a quick, uneasy glance.

Janick shook his head. "There is no defense against rabies—except to prevent the cat from biting."

"I see," said Berialevski, "I see. No defense, eh?"

"But," said Janick, "a man who wore special clothing—such as heavy leather gloves and outer garments—could be protected, no?"

"Oh, yes but they'd have to be extra heavy. Cats have very sharp teeth, and with rabies, they could be extremely fierce." Grutchev's words were slow and deliberate.

"Yes, I suppose so," said Berialevski quietly.

The intelligence chief pondered the matter for a few moments then raised his head. "Thanks," he said, "you have been a great help."

"Is that all?" Grutchev asked.

"Yes, except now we have to find out which island these cats will attack."

"Whose cats?" queried Janick. "Not the Chinese?"

"No. Theirs, the yankees," he said solemnly.

Grutchev was alarmed. "You mean—"

"Yes, said Berialevski, "we have just received the report that the Americans are assembling several thousand cats, that these animals are being given injections and that they are to be landed on a small island where they will attack and destroy the garrison."

"Amazing," said Grutchev.

"Diabolic," Janick added.

"Quite contrary to the Geneva Convention too," said Grutchev.

"Yes, but we don't know which island yet. We must find the island," said Berialevski. "We'll hand this to Bruisilloff. He'll find the island." Berialevski reached for the phone. "You two had better stay here because, when we have located the island, we shall need to come up with a defense plan for the premier. Oh, Comrade Bruisilloff, we must meet at once. We have a most important task for you and your staff."

Berialevski hung up. "He's coming. You know, you have to give these capitalist swine credit. They are very clever—very clever."

"And diabolic," said Janick.

"Amazing." Grutchev shook his head. "Absolutely amazing. What about the Geneva Convention? Does it mean nothing to them?"

CHAPTER XIX

Due to the tight security imposed on Operation Feline, General Jansen decided to visit Camp Billings incognito and without his usual entourage of staff officers, or even his aide.

He made the long drive from Washington in civilian clothes and in his own fire-engine red convertible, rather than risk the uncommon sight of an official chauffeur-driven flag car in the vicinity of the camp. To all outward appearances, the chunky, rosy-faced figure in sloppy porkpie hat, sunglasses, and a red and blue polka-dot scarf carelessly tucked into the neck of his yellow Viyella shirt, looked more like a movie talent scout than the efficient professional military man he really was.

Colonel Slate was waiting for the general at the camp gate and guided him to the camp's VIP quarters. Here the general shed his disguise and donned his bemedaled uniform that he had laid flat in the trunk of his car to avoid curious eyes.

When General Jansen emerged from his room, the sight rather upset Slate, for he counted fourteen ribbons above the general's left breast pocket and compared them bitterly to his own five home-service decorations. Hoping no one else would notice and wondering whether, in view of the unusually warm temperature, the general would follow his example if he removed his service jacket, Slate decided to try it.

"I find it a trifle warm, General, don't you?"

"Oh, I don't know," said Jansen.

"I think I'll travel in shirtsleeves today. How about you?" suggested the colonel.

"You go ahead, Colonel," replied Jansen. "If you like *I'll* keep my tunic on."

Slate got the message; he kept his jacket on. They had a cup of coffee in Slate's office, chatted awhile, then began a tour of the camp.

Actually, Colonel Slate had little about which he need have worried. His labor force had responded nobly to his staff sergeant's orders. They had worked hard and, in surprisingly short time, had cleaned up the entire camp almost to a point of beauty. Paint and whitewash had been splashed about liberally, and even the row of tractors on the parade ground sparkled. Besides all this, as if by some miracle, the ever efficient Staff Sergeant Jones had somehow persuaded the air crews to clean up the five flying boats and anchor them in a neat line by the edge of the lake and had convinced the flight leader and his crews to go to Billings, the small town adjacent to the camp, for the rest of the day. The single Air Force crewman who remained on guard made himself quite inconspicuous by sleeping inside one of the machines.

As far as the contingent of cats was concerned, Captains Gilly and Drewer had supervised the painting of all the cat crates in white, with the word "FELINE" stenciled in bold red letters on each box. The crates had then been placed along the perimeter of the sports field. With the normally overgrown tangle of grass mowed and rolled, the whole area had taken on the appearance of a well kept park; to Colonel Slate it was an inspiring sight and a complete surprise.

It was obvious to Slate that General Jansen became more delighted by the minute.

"By God, Slate, you've done a terrific job here, a terrific job! I'll see there's a commendation in this for you."

They were now standing in the middle of the sports field surveying the long lines of white cat crates from which there arose a continuous howl.

"Thank you, General, we try to keep a tidy camp. I have some good workers here. I'm happy you like it."

"I suppose you wonder what all this is about," said Jansen.

"Yes, General, I must say I'm curious," replied the unusually sober colonel.

"Well, all in good time, Slate, all in good time." The general sounded very enthusiastic. He turned toward the tractors. "Oh," he continued, walking toward the parade ground, "that's a nice line of well–kept tractors. What are they doing here?"

"Oh, they arrived a few days ago from the engineer school," said Slate.

Jansen tried to think why tractors were being assembled here, but amid the variety of cat noises, he found it hard to concentrate. He dismissed the problem—probably some hare-brained engineer scheme. In any case, he was not on speaking terms with the chief engineer right now. He said the only thing that came to his mind. "I would gather that there may be a big works program coming up, they're always either making lakes or drying or damning them up. Shouldn't be surprised if they don't do the same thing here. By the way, where is the lake?"

"Behind the water tower, sir. We'll go there now, if you like, sir," offered the colonel and led the way.

They were standing by the camp boathouse surveying the large lake.

"Yes," said Jansen thoughtfully, "I imagine this lake is what the engineers are interested in—probably going to dam up this area. By the way, how is the fishing here?"

"Well," replied Slate, "It was good, or I should say excellent, until those seaplanes arrived and started to oil up the water. That hasn't helped it."

"Seaplanes?" Jansen looked surprised. "What seaplanes—where?"

"Yes, General, five of them. They are just around the corner there in the inlet—they came from Edgewater Base. We can have a look at them if you wish."

"Well, okay."

Jansen was about to follow the colonel when the loudest and most ungodly medley of howls broke out from the sports field.

"What on earth is all that noise?"

"I think the cats are hungry," said Colonel Slate, "and they know it's feeding time."

"Oh, feeding time. Feeding time for the feline Battle Group." The general chuckled.

"Yes, sir," replied the colonel dryly.

Both men turned back toward the bedlam of yowls, screeches and other sounds normally associated with hungry cats.

Jansen's complete satisfaction with the camp, and particularly with Colonel Slate's efforts, became manifest two days later when certain unexpected rewards materialized.

The Chairman Joint Chiefs himself signed the letter of commendation to the worried and still sober colonel. Slate was thereby informed that henceforth he would be a one-star general and George Gilly and Tom Drewer would become majors. That evening in the officer's club, the memorable occasion was duly celebrated.

It was shortly after ten p.m. when Gilly was called to the camp headquarters office. The duty N.C.O. handed him an urgent message. It was from the Engineer School marked PTS, demanding the immediate return of forty-two cats sent in error.

Gilly and Drewer, still elated by their promotion to the rank of major, and both warmed to a state of extreme good nature, undertook the task themselves. They personally selected and crated the forty-two largest cats they could find and ordered the duty N.C.O. to requisition a truck without delay and return them to the Engineer School. The duty N.C.O. was at first somewhat reluctant to cooperate, but when George Gilly reminded him that this was a PTS matter, that did it. The cats were on their way within the hour.

Having attended to the dispatch of General Howell's letter of commendation with the announcements of the promotions for Gilly and Drewer and the Commandant of Camp Billings, Jansen was feeling very pleased when he received a rush call to report to the defense secretary's office.

He was in the anteroom waiting to be ushered into the secretary's presence when the Chairman Joint Chiefs entered. The two men exchanged questioning looks.

"He sent for you too, eh?" The chairman looked troubled. "Something up, Bob?"

"I guess so, General," replied Jansen.

"Wonder what this is all about." sighed Howell. "I thought he was satisfied to let you handle all this."

Jansen didn't get time to comment over the high-pitched excited voice that came from the inner office. "All right, let them in, let them in."

A rather sad-looking secretary stood by the open door and nodded to both generals with an apologetic yet somewhat exasperated smile.

They found the defense secretary in an agitated state pacing the length of his office much like an overfed, caged wart-hog, his mouth grim, his watery eyes set in an angry stare. The defense secretary was trying hard to look tough; somehow he was not successful.

"Come in, come in. Sit down." This last offer surprised the two generals.

"Trouble, sir?" ventured the Chairman, settling into a large chair and lighting a cigarette.

"Trouble? Huh." The secretary stopped in his tracks and merely glared at them. "Trouble—you ask if there's trouble? Maybe you two can tell me. What in hell is going on around here?"

The Chairman adopted his most charming pose. "Going on, sir? I'm afraid I don't quite follow you."

"Well, well, you fellows started this whole mess and now you don't quite follow me. Yes, it's trouble all right and with a capital T. Either that or sheer goddamned crazy stupidity." He waddled over to his desk and sat down, heavily, of course. "It's cats," he announced. "*Your* bloody cats, that's what it is. Do you know I've had to put off my fishing trip because of your cats?"

"Oh, the cats!" said Howell lightly. "You must mean Operation Feline, of course."

"Yes, by God, it is cats," said the defense secretary angrily, grabbing a sheaf of papers off the top of his desk and waving them in the air above his head.

"But, sir," said Jansen.

"Don't you but me, General. See these letters. Eight of them, all from citizens from all over the Midwest wanting to know why the Army is carrying out a cat extermination program. Not only that, several of these letters state that unless I provide answers, they are going to write to the patron of the SPCA—and I don't have to tell you in what a mess this will land me. So I hope you can explain."

"Uh-Oh!" exclaimed the now worried Jansen. "I see. Things do seem to have gotten a bit out of hand. But surely we can—"

"Out of hand?" screeched the defense secretary. "Christ, did we have to steal cats from private homes? Well, did we? You tell me, if you can."

"Sir, we merely asked the camps to provide some cats," said Jansen. "We did not, in the interests of good management, tell them how to do it. We try to allow, as usual—well—a little flexibility to—er—to our subordinates."

"But what in the devil's name are we doing with them?" said the red-faced defense secretary. *"What in hell is going on?"*

General Howell cleared his throat. "Operation Feline, sir."

"Feline?" The politician appeared baffled. "What's feline?"

"Yes, sir. Operation Feline," said Jansen.

"Operation Feline? Are you fellows nuts?" Kleffen's face was getting redder by the second.

"I beg to remind you, sir," said Jansen, "you may recall I mentioned it to you some days ago. "You remember, sir, surely—Operation Feline, a PTS operation."

"You did—when? A PTS operation? I don't recall it."

"Yes, I did, sir, but you, sir, told me that since it was a PTS you preferred not to get too involved unless we thought it necessary."

"I said that, did I?" The secretary seemed surprised. "Why would I say that?"

"I wouldn't know, sir." Jansen looked at the chairman, who shrugged.

The defense secretary rang the bell on his desk with an air of indignation. Almost immediately, the door opened to admit a long-faced, tall, heavily mustached major of artillery.

"And *where* have you been, Small?" demanded the defense secretary.

"You rang, sir? I was out buying those flowers for your wife." The major's voice was squeaky and of a rather high-pitched tone.

"Yes, I did ring, Small." The secretary's voice took on a threatening note. "Did I ask you to make a note to file on an operation called Feline? I don't quite recall it. Did I?"

"Yes, sir," replied the startled major, "you did."

"Oh. And what did the note say?"

The major took a deep breath before he voiced his answer. "Your note to file, sir, stated that Operation Feline was presidential top secret and was not to be mentioned. As a matter of fact, you—well, sir, you told me to put a bring forward tag on it for next January—in two months' time, sir."

"Oh, I did? I see. But why?"

"I don't know, sir," replied Small. "I thought you knew, sir."

"Don't be funny, Major. That's all," said the secretary with a sinister tone in his voice. The young officer retired hastily.

"I have an idea," the secretary said, "that Major Small needs a change of employment. I would like you to take care of it, would you, General?"

"As you wish, sir," General Howell said.

The secretary managed a wry smile of sorts. "You know, at least that's one good thing. I've been waiting for a good excuse to get him out of here. But you understand how it is, he's my niece's husband. Anyway, he's due for a move."

The chairman quite understood. His wife's younger brother, Rodney, was going to be his next aide as soon as he could get rid of the present incumbent.

"Now where were we?" Said secretary. "Oh, yes, you two had better tell me exactly what has happened on Feline to date. I fear that I lost track of it with all that other business I brought back from my trip to Korea. Quite a mess over *there.*"

"You go ahead, Bob," said Howell, "it's your baby. I mean, your project."

For the next hour, General Jansen explained it to him, this time in greater detail just how Feline had originated and how far it had progressed.

"I see," said the politician slowly as he drummed his fingers on the desktop. "Now I see it. Damn it, the secretary of state should have kept me informed. Now I do recall it, you did mention it to me, but damn it, Jansen, you only gave me the barest outline of the plan. Do you realize that, with a PTS tag on it, until this operation is completed, I cannot answer any one of these letters? Yet, I have to say something. My very position is at stake, or it will be if someone starts asking questions in the Congress. This could be very dangerous."

"We certainly understand, sir," said Jansen. "And believe me, I am sorry you were not put fully in the picture. It all came up so fast, and after all, being a PTS, well, open discussion is not easy. Not even under normal circumstances."

The defense secretary stood up and began to pace the floor again. It was clear to the other two men that his main worry was about his own position in the matter.

"Tell me, how many people actually know about all this?" he asked.

"What would you say, Bob?" Howell inquired. "Six, seven?"

"The details of the operation, sir, are known only to a very few people here. The president, the secretary of state, the national security advisor, you, the chairman here and me. That's on the American side. As I understand it, the British prime minister has put a prime ministerial top secret classification on it. So even in London the numbers of people in the know are very few. The foreign secretary, his liaison officer, Mr. Rollins, and the chiefs of the three services, and that's about it, sir—and of course the essential people at Camp Billings. Finally, there are a few others like Wilson, the U.S. ambassador at Paguda, and Admiral Lyman of SPCA, the U.S. commanders at Bulabar and Singabar. These last two, however, only have the barest of outlines, just enough to follow orders given them to cooperate. You must remember, sir, this is a presidential top secret matter. I am assured by the secretary of state that even the Pagudan ambassador in Washington will say nothing; even he does not know our detailed plans "Oh, all right, then," agreed the secretary. "But what about this one letter that these animals are being starved at Camp Billings?"

"I can only suggest, sir," said General Howell, "that this came from some discontented local worker at Billings. We're bound to run into this sort of thing. We can track it down and shut him up very quickly."

"Yes, I suppose so. Probably some disgruntled employee," the secretary said, not at all convinced. "But what about the SPCA, Jansen, can we rely on them?"

"I am sure we can, sir," said Jansen. "But if you think it best, I suggest that I go back to see their president, Admiral Lyman, sir. With your permission, I could explain the matter in fuller detail, stressing, of course, the security aspects. You see, sir, if the word bubonic is ever mentioned and gets to the press, we really will have trouble on our hands and we could be accused of withholding vital information from the WHO; the U.N. might get *very* upset. So far, a few camps and other service stations and the SPCA have been asked to provide as many cats as they can. We now have over sixteen hundred of them crated, and in three days or so these animals will be flown to Bulabar by the Royal Air Force." Jansen paused to check his notes.

"Go on General, go on."

"Then by the time the cats arrive in Singabar, Mitzu will be evacuated by the British ships and the evacuees deposited in Paguda until the island is clear of rats. The timings are all quite clear, sir. I'll give you my timetable, based on the fact that the cats go to Tenpost tonight, then by RAF to Bulabar. The ships at Singabar are ready. D-day is tomorrow, November seventeenth. The evacuation fleet leaves Singabar tomorrow evening. They take two days to reach Paguda, on nineteen November, tie up there for a day to make sure the cats arrive at Singabar and are put on board H.M.S. *Bulldog.* This means the ships arrive at Paguda on the nineteenth, the same day as the cat convoy leaves Singabar."

"I see," said the secretary, returning to his chair. "Is that all."

"Thus, on the nineteenth we have the evacuation ships at Paguda and the cats ready on their ship at Singabar. The British will then signal us so we can tell our ambassador at Paguda to pass on the order to the evacuation fleet to proceed to Mitzu. These ships will reach Mitzu in three days, on the twenty-third. The evacuation should not take more than a few hours. Meanwhile, the cats will have left Singabar on the same day as the evacuation ships leave Paguda. That is to say, on the twentieth of November. But as the ship with the cats will proceed to Mitzu direct, their trip from Singabar to Mitzu will only take three and a half days all told. So you see, sir, about half a day after the island has been evacuated, the cat convoy will be ready to land and destroy the rats. Actually, it's all quite simple and foolproof because the cats will not leave Singabar until we know the other ships have left Paguda. The Royal Navy has assured me of the actual mileage and times of arrival at Mitzu."

"What happens then?" As he asked, the secretary realized that he really did not understand anything that had been told him nor actually did he want to.

General Jansen cleared his throat. "The British want to give the cats three or four full days on Mitzu," he said, "during which time the two officers we loaned them to be in charge of the project will stand offshore, observe and report progress. When they are satisfied that the cats have done all they can—" At this point he turned to the Chairman, "Would you like to take it from there, General?"

"Yes," said General Howell. "General Topps, the British Army Chief of Staff, has already warned one of his special medical sanitation and engineer units to stand by at an airfield in Britain. On his order, they will be flown direct to Mitzu where they will proceed to decontaminate and cleanse the entire island, burn the dead rats, round up the remaining cats, returning them eventually to the British Tropical Research Center, where they are conducting research on plague."

"Hmmm." The secretary picked his teeth with a paper clip. "It sounds okay. Then you think that by the end of this month the whole thing will be finished, eh, General"

"Yes, I do, sir."

"And," said General Jansen, "the natives can then be returned to the island, and we can, if the president and the prime minister approve, then make a full release statement to the press. Actually, I think the British should reap a bonanza of publicity on this, and in the long run, so will we."

"You really think so?" said the secretary hopefully, and with more interest now. "Yes, it would be good for us."

"Why not?" Howell said. "When it's all over, you yourself can issue the statement at a press conference, sir. You can tell the world that we did not want to upset the chances for peace at the disarmament conference. We asked our allies to help us out. It will be considered a touch of brilliant diplomacy. We can arrange that. It will make very good reading, don't you think so, Jansen? It will place our country and you, sir, in particular, in a very good light. I'm quite sure the British will not mind us taking a bit of the spotlight on this occasion; in fact, I'm sure they will be quite happy, don't you agree, Bob?"

"Oh, I do, I do," said Jansen. "We can play up the idea of a small defenseless country asking for help, and us offering all our resources to the British in order to help these poor people and at the same time, maintaining the cloak of secrecy so that no one will panic."

"Yes, I see," said the now happier secretary, fingering his loose jowls, "now I do see it. Yes, it could turn out very well indeed. Yes, yes, it certainly could. What about the Vice President—does he know about this?"

"No, sir," replied Jansen, "he has not been given any hint about this. Besides, sir, he's been in Grenada and is not expected back for ten days."

"Ah, of course, of course. Just as well he's out of the way. Less chance of any leaks on this, much less, I think."

"So you see, Mr. Secretary, you are the next person to the president who has all the details of Feline." The chairman felt this would add to Kleffen's already apparent self-glorification.

"Yes, I see. I see it very clearly now, gentlemen. This could do us all a great deal of good."

"Yes, sir," agreed Jansen, "don't you think so?" He turned to the chairman.

"Absolutely," said Howell. "Especially for you, Mr. Secretary."

It was clear to the two generals that the secretary was at that moment thinking of himself as the central figure, organizing the entire operation, giving the orders, arranging everything. Actually, the secretary was wondering whether he might even be able to get the president's permission to arrange a trip to Paguda. It was surely worth consideration. He must think about it. His smile of almost angelic benevolence at his two generals did not make them any more comfortable.

"Good work, gentlemen, very good work. Now, I think I am fully in the picture now. Thank you. But, one other thing before you leave. General Howell, will you remember to arrange for Major Small's transfer and his replacement, please?"

"Do you have any preference, sir?" asked Howell. "I mean, have you anyone in mind? We do like to be sure you know something about the people we post to your office."

"Yes, as a matter of fact, I do—a Major John Loften. I'd like to have him here. Lofty is a good officer. Naturally, I expect him to be promoted."

Howell noted the name on his pad.

As soon as the officers had gone, the defense secretary made a mental review. That's that, he thought. Lofty was his wife's youngest and favorite nephew—that should keep her quiet for a while. Then the phone rang. "Hello? Oh, yes, Mr. President, fine, thank you. What, sir? Yes, I postponed the fishing trip. Oh, oh, the Arctic Training Center. Yes, sir. I've never been there, although I was hoping perhaps next year. Oh, I see, sir. And you want me to represent you? Yes, sir, very good. Mr. President. I'll leave tomorrow. What's that? No, sir, none of the assistant secretaries knows anything about the operation. Be assured, Mr. President, there will be no leaks—none. Thank you, Mr. President."

Horace Kleffen cursed and stared at the telephone for a few seconds before replacing it. He pressed the buzzer for his aide and cursed again. For once, Major Small appeared quickly, "Sir?"

"Look Small, I've just had a briefing from the chairman and Jansen on this Feline business. I told them I have to be informed on it step by step." As usual, Horace Kleffen was stretching the truth for he had no wish at all to become too involved in it.

"Yes, sir, step by step," echoed the aide.

"Unfortunately, this will not be possible, as the president has asked me to go to Alaska for a few days. I leave tomorrow night. So, I want you to keep in touch with Major Bonwell in the Chairman's office."

"Very good, sir, but does Major Bonwell know I am supposed to get this information from him?"

"I'll speak to him before I leave, but remember this is a PTS, so be careful."

Horace Kleffen began to look through the mass of loose papers that littered his desk. "Now, where the hell is that paper on transport? Damn it, it was here. Small, did you see it?"

The aide located the document and handed it to the defense secretary. "Here it is, sir, and you'll need the fuel statistics too."

"Fuel statistics? Oh, yes, here it is." Kleffen placed them in his briefcase. "Well, what else do I need?" He shuffled some of the other papers.

"What about this, sir?" Major Small was holding up a departmental notepad.

"Here, let me see it."

The defense secretary took the pad and looked at it as if he could not decipher what was on it. Then it came to him. Of course. There were three items on it. The first were the words *Feline Vaccine,* under which he had scrawled *PTS* and under that, the word *Alaska.*

He threw the notepad into the case and slammed the lid. "Alaska, he muttered, "of all the goddamn places."

"How long will you be away, sir?"

"Oh, maybe five days, if I don't freeze to death," he replied.

"Would you like me to cable the headquarters there and arrange for your cold weather clothing and things?"

"That won't be necessary. The president's office has already told them I'm coming, so they goddamn well better have things arranged for me."

Kleffen was about to open the door when Small decided to offer his chief some consolation. "Sir, I hear that Alaska can be quite pleasant at this time of the year."

The defense secretary turned and gave his aide a scornful glance. "Oh, for Christ's sake, Major, shut up."

With that caustic remark, he walked out. A few yards down the hall, he stopped at an office that bore a sign that read "RESEARCH OFFICER." He opened the door, entered, closed the door behind him and looked at the plump redhead behind the desk.

"Anything wrong?" she asked.

"Yes," he replied, "the Nova Scotia trip is off. I have to go to Alaska."

"Oh, honey, I'm so sorry. Can't I go with you?"

"Don't be silly, Liz. The fact that I'm going to freeze my balls is bad enough. No, you'll have to wait until I get back. Don't worry, we'll get together." Horace Kleffen leaned over and gave her a quick peck on the cheek. "Be a good girl till I get back."

She looked at him. "But who's going to keep me warm while you're away?"

At the door, he turned. "Liz, if I know you, you'll find somebody. Bye.

CHAPTER XX

The mid-November sun was just setting over the Kremlin as Dimitri Bruisilloff leaned back in his chair, removed his glasses and gave out a long sigh. His men had been working for four days, practically without sleep, trying to determine what island could possibly be a target of the attack, which, his chief had told him in almost a whisper, was to be carried out by several thousand germ-laden cats. It had to be a small island, of that he was sure. But where?

The ringing of the telephone interrupted his thoughts. "Yes, Bruisilloff speaking. Is that you Comrade Disleff?

"Yes, Comrade I think we have found the island," said Disleff, who added, "Our man at the camp overheard two officers talking about an island in the camp lavatory."

"Does it have a name and where is it?"

"It has no name but it is situated just outside the port of Talien." replied Disleff.

"In the People's Republic?"

"That's correct."

"Not one of ours? Are you sure?"

"I'm sure it's not one of ours."

"In that case, we must give it a name for reference purposes."

"Well, now, I don't know," replied Bruisilloff slowly. "It might serve them right—after all, they're not allies of ours. They have not showed us much friendship lately."

"I suppose that's so. Still, don't you think-"

"Leave it to me," said Bruisilloff, "I will discuss it with Berialewski and the premier."

Brusilloff's meeting with Berialewski and the premier took place just after lunch at the premier's home.

"So, Comrades, I hear we have a slight problem."

"Oh no, Comrade, not us, but apparently the People's Republic does," said Berialewski with a hollow laugh.

The premier shook his head, "Diabolic—that's what it is, absolutely diabolic. I would never have thought the American imperialists would go this far. They are going to terrorize the Chinese in order to blackmail us."

"Blackmail? You mean—" Brusilloff exclaimed.

"Ah, Brusilloff you do not know them as I do. They are like foxes, very clever. Yes, as I see it, they are going to try out this terrorist scheme on the Chinese, who are in no position to respond; then they will turn to us and say, 'Look what we have. See what we can do.' Oh, I tell you, Comrades they are clever devils—clever but stupid. But we are not stupid. There is still time to turn this situation to our advantage if we move fast. Now, our agent's last message this morning confirmed that the animals are still at the camp. They have not left yet, correct?"

"That's correct, Comrade. Our man will inform us the moment they leave. We estimate the attack will take place six or seven days after the cats leave the camp. Do you have a plan, Comrade?" Berialewski sounded nervous.

"Yes," the premier said, "we have a plan, and the general secretary agrees with it. As a matter of fact, after we have exposed this devilish Yankee plan to the world, the People's Republic will be indebted to us—and this could result in a change of attitude toward us. I tell you, we have a good plan, Comrade."

"Wonderful, Comrade," replied Bruisilloff.

"The aim of this plan is to bring this terrible scheme to the attention of the world and the American people before it can be put into effect. So that, even though all the preparations will have been activated, they will be caught in the act—exposed—and be forced to cancel it because of public outcry from their own people, the U.N. and the rest of the world. We must force cancellation no earlier than thirty-six hours and no later than twenty-four hours before implementation. Do you understand, Comrade?"

"Yes, we do. It is a brilliant plan, Comrade," said Bruisilloff eagerly.

"Brilliant, but we must act quickly." said Berialewski "Oh, we will." The premier leaned across his desk and pointed a finger at Berialewski. "I will explain how we will do it. First, I want you to contact Konilef at our embassy in Washington. He is very friendly with that newsman, Dan Samson, and Samson is a great favorite of Kleffen, their secretary of defense. Tell Konilef to have one of his French friends inform Samson that France is aware of the location of an island that is to be used at the end of this month for a special test of a new form of chemical warfare, a test in which some type of animals are to be employed in large numbers. That's all, no name. You understand? Don't mention cats."

"Yes, Comrade, I understand perfectly." Berialewski was grinning.

"And you Brusilloff, do you see what will happen?" asked the older statesman.

"I think I do. Yes, Comrade, I do."

"You know, this Samson has a nose like an anteater; if anyone can ferret out what is going on, he can, and what is even better, he and Kleffen are just like this." The premier held up two fingers. "I understand they even share the same mistress."

"But, Comrade," Brusilloff said uneasily. "this Samson surely is a loyal American. Would he break a story that would embarrass his own country?"

"Listen to me, both of you. I know his type. He would trade his whole family for a good story. These people are not restricted by an Official Secrets Act like the British. Believe me, this Samson will sniff out the bait we put out. He may be a loyal American in a sense, but you show me a Samson-type correspondent, and I'll show you a man for whom patriotism takes a bad second place to an opportunity to make world headlines. He is a headline hawker without scruples who believes God put him on earth to expose anyone or anything he thinks the public has a right to know about. This man would sell his soul to the devil if the latter promised him a scoop. Now, do you understand?"

"Yes, Comrade, if he is the sort of person you describe, he will not fail us." Berialewski agreed.

The premier gave a sly smile. "I'm sure he will not fail us. By the way, make sure our agent at the cat camp gets some sort of reward. What does he do for a living?"

"He's a peasant Comrade. Just a worker." Brusilloff replied.

"I see," said the premier. "Well, perhaps a hundred dollars will do."

It was just before ten p.m. when Ivan Konilef pulled into the parking lot behind Burger King in Fairfax. He turned off the ignition but made sure his doors were locked before he extracted the notebook from his overcoat pocket.

He was adding a note to the first page when he heard three taps on the passenger side window. Konilef flipped the automatic unlock switch, and Marcel Brun opened the door and settled himself beside him.

"You're late as usual, Marcel." Konilef sounded annoyed.

"For God's sake, Ivan, sure I'm late. Don't you know it takes time to get here from New York. Well, what is it this time?"

Konilef handed the Frenchman an envelope. "There's ten thousand dollars in there."

"So, there's ten thousand dollars. How far do I have to stick my neck out this time?"

"Not too far," replied the Russian. "Here are some notes for you to study." Konilef passed the notebook to the other man.

Brun produced a small flashlight and looked at the notes for a moment, then he switched off the light.

"Samson? Again?" he asked. "That son of a bitch?"

"Yes. I want you to contact him as soon as possible—before noon tomorrow. It's all there in the notes."

"Hell, Ivan," said the Frenchman, "before noon? I'm supposed to be back at my desk at the U.N. by ten-thirty."

"In that case, my friend, unless you want your nuts in the wringer, as the Yanks say, you'd better get moving." Konilef turned on the ignition. Marcel Brun took the hint, opened his door and got out.

Dan Samson was sound asleep when the doorbell rang. For a moment he thought he was dreaming, then it rang again. He looked at the clock. It was a quarter to three. He planted his feet in his slippers, reached for a robe and headed for the front door.

"Well, well. How's the great U.N., Brun? Fucking things up as usual?"

"Sorry about the hour, Dan, but this is important."

"Go on to the study, Marcel, I'll get us some coffee."

In minutes, he was back with the steaming mugs, then went to the bar where he poured two stiff brandies.

"Here you are, Marcel. You look as if you need it." Samson snickered as the Frenchman took the glass and downed it in one gulp.

"Thanks, Dan."

"Well, at least take off your coat and hat, you can't be in that much of a hurry." Dan sat down at his desk and picked up his mug.

"Yes, I think I will." Brun slipped out of his coat and let it fall to the floor with his alpine hat, then he sat down opposite Dan and took a short sip of coffee.

"I have a real hot one for you, Dan. Something really hot."

"I'm all ears, Marcel. Let's see if it knocks hell out of me, then I'll know how much it's worth. So, who's screwing whom in the diplomatic corps?"

"Nothing like that. My government has quite accidentally heard that your defense Department has selected an island, one that's inhabited too, as the test site for a very new form of chemical warfare. The chemical, possibly a bacteria, is to be conveyed there by hundreds of small animals, probably cats or rats. This test is to be carried out in ten or twelve days, and the island does not even belong to the States."

"What? Oh, for God's sake, Marcel, you must be kidding. No? I see you're not. Do you know the location of this island or who it belongs to now?"

"No, all I was able to learn is what I've told you. My God, Dan, isn't that enough? Look, can I have another brandy?"

"Sure. Over there. Help yourself." Dan took a slug of his own brandy. "I can't believe it. I'm in on practically everything Defense is doing, unless that Kleffen idiot is holding out on me. This is not on any of my lists. Look, Marcel, are you sure about this? Would it be a Soviet-owned island? No, I guess not—that would set off a goddamn world war."

Brun resumed his seat and gulped half of his second brandy. "Soviet-owned, no," Brun replied. "Maybe Chinese. All I could gather is that it is a small island, it might be a military outpost. Could it be the Middle East? One of Libya's? But I really don't know. I'm even afraid to look at a map in case."

"Have you mentioned this to anyone at the U.N.?"

"My God, no," said Brun. "Look, I've got to be back at the U.N. by ten-thirty, I'd better go. I'll miss my plane."

He rose, picked up his hat and coat, then reached for his glass and downed the rest of his brandy.

Dan Samson led him to the front door. "Did you leave your car near here?"

"No," replied the Frenchman, "a rented car. It's just around the corner. By the way, Dan, when do I get my money?"

Samson opened the door. "I'll get it off to you tomorrow."

Marcel Brun turned up his coat collar and walked out into the cold morning air.

As the correspondent pressed the oak door shut, he muttered, "Slimy little bastard. Why do we decent people have to deal with the likes of him?"

It might have given the newsman new insight into his own character had he known that, at that very moment, Marcel Brun was thinking the same thing about Dan Samson.

Later that morning, Dan Samson spent a full hour listening to the tape recording of his conversation with Marcel Brun. After listening to it for the fourth time, he switched off the recorder, reached for his diary and wrote three words—*Kleffen, Torrin, today*. Then, as an afterthought, he picked up a red pen and underlined the notation.

Dan Samson was halfway to the Pentagon when he picked up his car phone and called his editor-in-chief, Dave Boltin.

"Hello Dave, Dan here, look, I'm on to a real hot one."

"Yeah? How hot is real hot?" Dave asked.

"Capital letters. It involves Kleffen."

"Kleffen? What's that old goat done now? Is he screwing someone else besides the fat redhead in his office?"

"Nothing yet, but it's top secret." Dan heard a gasp. "You got that, Dave?"

"Sure, I got it. When can I expect the main dish?"

"That, I can't say. I'm off to see Torrin now and, hopefully, I can get a few minutes with the fat boy himself. I'll be in touch, Dave."

For the rest of the trip, Dan's mind toyed with the possibilities. A small inhabited island—Caribbean? No, too close to home ground. The Pacific? Diego Garcia? No, No. Maybe the Aleutians? Kleffen wasn't too good under careful questioning. Dan Samson made up his mind that today he'd have to give the defense secretary his best shot. And if that didn't produce results, he'd try one of his public information officer pals. At least two, Dan figured, owed him for past favors.

Military public information officers are usually an odd lot. A few are professional yes-men; a few can be placed in the yes-no category, but by far the majority fall into the slot reserved for maybe-men. They are, in fact, the professional verbal troubleshooters for their services. They excel in the presentation of the half-truth when it suits their purpose. The half-truth or well diluted fact is a favorite PR ploy. It is especially useful when a senior military official who is about to retire, and meeting a corporation president whom he wishes to impress (no doubt with a view to being offered a high-salaried position on retirement), leaks classified information. In such cases, the half-truth becomes a means of watering down any harm the leak may have caused, thus saving the culprit from losing his pension and the government from further embarrassment. Most military public relations officers are decent men dedicated to their profession. Torrin was certainly one of these, but Dan Samson was confident of his questioning ability. If he chose his words carefully he might learn something of value. After all, the chief information officer had himself been a newspaperman in his early years. However if Torrin proved uncooperative, a chat with one of Torrin's junior officers, one who owed him for past favors, might succeed.

Dan Samson was in the waiting room of the chief of public information when Brigadier General Wesley Torrin emerged from his office followed by the secretary of defense and Henry Westerman, the scientific advisor to the Pentagon.

All three men stopped in their tracks and seemed to exchange startled glances, as if the newsman had caught them while engaged in some unlawful act.

It was the secretary of defense who reacted first and broke the icy silence. "Ah, Dan, my friend, of course you know these gentlemen?"

"Hello, Dan." Torrin did not sound too friendly.

"Hi, Daniel." Even Westerman's greeting did not imply any pleasure at the encounter.

"Well, Daniel, what can we do for the media today?" asked the secretary.

"Good day, sir. I had hoped to take up a few minutes of your time, if you can spare them."

The secretary's reply was much more to Samson's liking. "By all means, Dan. Certainly, come along with me now. I have a few minutes before I leave for the Oval office." Mr. Kleffen opened the door.

Samson nodded to the other two men, smiled awkwardly and followed Kleffen out.

As the door closed behind the newsmen, Westerman cast a worried look at Torrin. "That son of a bitch, what's he trying to smell out now?" General Torrin never minced his words. "I don't trust that bastard. He'd sell his wife to a whorehouse if it made a good story."

"Amen," said Westerman. "You know, General, I think we had better call the chairman right away. I don't like the look of this. Whenever that useless bastard shows up at a time like this, I smell trouble and we have too much at stake now. He's clever enough to get Kleffen yapping his heart out."

"Let's do it now," said Torrin.

Both men turned back into Torrin's office and closed the door.

As it happened, neither Torrin nor Westerman need have worried. As the secretary of defense and Dan Samson approached the end of the corridor where they would normally turn to wait for the elevator, they were much too busy talking to see the sign with the warning "WET FLOOR AHEAD."

Both men were chuckling over some trivial matter as they made the turn. "You should have seen the look on Jansen's face. It really shook him, I'll tell you," said Kleffen lightheartedly.

"I'll bet it did, Mr. Secretary. I'll bet—" It was then that the floor under their feet seemed to have vanished.

Horace Kleffen was the first to tumble, then it was Samson's turn.

Half a dozen doors opened, and startled faces peered out to survey the scene. They saw two men, one of whom was easily recognizable, sitting on the floor cursing; they also saw the secretary's briefcase lying open on the floor and a dozen or so folders and assorted papers spread about soaking up the wetness. The light chuckles from the observers did not escape the secretary. He glared at the nearest door and shouted "What the hell is so goddamn funny? Get back to your jobs you stupid shits."

As if by signal all the doors closed.

Dan Samson was quickly back on his feet and helped the secretary to stand.

"Goddamn," exclaimed the pudgy Kleffen. "I've twisted my ankle."

"Don't try to move, Mr. Secretary. I'll collect your papers for you." Dan began to pick up the soggy documents.

"Hell, Dan, I've got to move," said the exasperated secretary. "I'm due at the Oval Office in thirty minutes, and I have to leave for Alaska tonight. What kind of idiot—".

Dan Samson looked up at Kleffen from his kneeling position. "Just stay put, sir, rest your ankle, I'll have all your papers in a minute. Then I'll help you back to your office."

As the secretary of defense was bending over inspecting his injured ankle, Dan Samson's eager eyes fixed on the small pad that he had just placed on top of the wet papers in the briefcase. On that pad the words "FELINE" and "VACCINE" glared at him in capital letters. Below it was the notation "NOW PTS," and under that was the one word "ALASKA."

With the help of two passing Air Force officers, Mr. Horace Kleffen limped to his office where his administrative assistant led him to the couch. Once there, the secretary removed his right shoe and sock. His foot was already badly swollen.

"It's just twisted, Marie, no harm done, I think."

“Mr. Secretary, shall I give these papers to Marie to dry out?” Dan asked.

“No, thanks, Dan,” replied Kleffen. She and I’ll do that later.” He looked at the clock. “Oh, my God, I’m due at the White House in fifteen minutes and I’ve got to get out of these clothes. Have I got a spare outfit here Marie?”

“I’ll get it for you, sir,” she replied.

“Good, I’ll have to hurry—and Marie, have my car ready in five minutes. Where the hell is that goddamn aide of mine?” With that, he picked up his shoe and sock and began to move toward his private bathroom.

“Well, Mr. Secretary, I’ll not take up any more of your time. Perhaps you can give me a few minutes next week?”

Kleffen turned at the bathroom door. “Can’t do it next week, Dan, but wait a minute, why don’t you come with me to Alaska? It’s going to be a short trip but it could be interesting for you because we’re doing several special tests. In fact, I can arrange for you to—well, I’ll explain to you later. If you’re interested, pack a bag and meet me at Andrews at nine tonight.”

Dan Samson was hoping his expression would not betray him. “I’ll be there, Mr. Secretary. I’ll be there at nine.”

On his way home, Samson stopped off at the Georgetown for a beer. As he sat there contemplating his good luck at Kleffen’s invitation to accompany him to Alaska, he heard a familiar voice.

“Hi there Dan old pal?” It was Robby. Dan had got to know him well. Robby was quite a skirt chaser.

“Hi Robby. Care to join me?”

“For a minute. I have a date. What’s up Dan?” He sat down.

Dan Samson was a quick thinker. He looked at Robby for a moment then produced a small pad and pen from an inside pocket. “I have something special for you.” and he began to write.

Slowly and with deliberate care, he wrote: *you can have a lot of pocket money, a lot, if you can give me any idea of what the word Feline means. Think it over and call me.* He folded the small sheet and handed it to the other man. "Don't open it until you are home, you understand?"

"OK. I get it." he got up. "Sorry, gotta go."

As Robby disappeared, Dan Samson felt very satisfied. The president's brother was a source he had not used lately. The newsman smiled to himself. No harm in trying it now. He knew Robby always needed pocket money.

The 747 took off from Andrews Air Force Base at twenty-one hundred hours and pointed its nose to the northwest.

At precisely twenty-one thirty-five hours, just as General Jason Howell was sipping his after-dinner liqueur, his phone rang. It was the Chief of Air Staff, General Rod Lohman.

"General? Lohman here. They took off at twenty-one thirty hours for Alaska; Samson is with him."

"Good. In fact better than good. It's wonderful," said the chairman. "Did you give the pilot our instructions?"

"Yes, sir, it's all set. On the return trip in three days, the plane will have to force land at one of the Canadian emergency airfields in the Northwest Territories. It will take roughly three or four days to carry out the necessary repairs because of a temporary breakdown in communication at the Canadian airfield. How is that, General? And it's all tied in with the Royal Canadian Air Force."

"Well done, Rod. Thanks, many thanks."

"My pleasure, General. Any time I get a chance to stick it to our flabby friend and get that bastard Samson at the same time, I tell you, it makes me feel like a new man."

"Me too, Rod. It must be catching," said the chairman joyfully and hung up. He decided to call his chief of public information.

Brigadier General Torrin and Westerman, the scientific advisor, had dinner together that same night at Torrin's Watergate apartment. It was over their coffee after Mrs. Torrin had left them that Westerman brought up the subject of the operation the chairman had described to them earlier.

"I read the Japanese report on their experience with cats; it went over very well. I hope we can say the same."

Torrin cupped his chin in his left hand and tapped his fingers against his cheek. "I don't know, it's all pretty tricky. I don't envy the British on this one, but you never know. I bet—" He was interrupted by the phone at his elbow. "Hello, Torrin here. Oh yes, General. What? You don't say. Kleffen and Samson? Both of them? We're certainly in luck today. Thanks, General. Good night." Torrin looked at the phone a moment before he replaced it. "Well, well!" he exclaimed with a chuckle. "I'll be damned. Can you guess what has happened?"

"Now what?" Henry Westerman asked. Torrin was grinning from ear to ear. "Horace Kleffen and our *bete noir* Dan Samson took off from Andrews about ten minutes ago bound for Alaska to attend the cold weather tests."

"That's not possible," said Westerman. "Those tests have been postponed for another five weeks. The president knows that. Good God, Wes, is this something to do with Feline too? I informed the president myself about the delay of those tests. He can't have forgotten surely."

"I know, old friend, you did indeed inform the president." Torrin clapped both hands together in joyful exuberance. "But Mr. Horace Kleffen was not so informed."

"You mean he didn't forget?" suggested Westerman, grinning.

"No, Wes." Torrin leaned toward him and slapped Westerman's shoulder. "I assure you the President did not forget—not this time."

"Oh boy. That's good. I must remember to congratulate him some time. By the way, how well do you know our president's ne'er-do-well sibling?" Westerman chuckled as he finished the question.

"Oh, you mean Robby. All I know is what I hear. Most of the women think he's a goddamn menace. Why do you ask?"

"Because one of my assistants complained to me that he made some pretty ugly gutter remarks to her at a party last week."

"I'm not surprised." said Torrin. "The little bastard is no asset to the office of the president. If I were you, I'd mention it to the man. Don't ever talk to Valerie about Robby. She thinks he's cute and refers to him as 'our baby brother.' I've already indicated to the president that his brother is a distinct security risk."

"You did? What was his reaction?"

"His reaction? Totally negative." Torrin replied.

"That's not good."

"No. I must say I was disappointed, but the man obviously thinks his little brother must have his fun. You know, of course that they both have a convenient common interest in—"

"Oh you must mean Helga and Laurie." Westerman laughed.

"And Jenny and Lora and…"

"We mustn't forget Marianne."

"My goodness, West." Torrin said gleefully. "You're well up on all our dark business. Maybe you should take over my job."

On that note both men burst into loud laughter.

Suddenly Westerman stopped. "Oh my God. It's well past my bedtime." He looked at his watch as he rose from his chair. "It's half after eleven. I must go. I have a lecture at American University at nine."

It was exactly eleven thirty when the president put down the phone. "Well Robby, there you are. It's all fixed. Our ambassador in Paris is going to be your host for the next three weeks. Harold Snell is an old friend. We were at Oxford together. He is arranging a complete tour of Paris and the surrounding area for you with the embassy's top VIP guide, Yvette. I can tell you that Yvette is really something. She'll be meeting you."

"Sounds interesting. When do I leave?" asked Robby.

"You leave at noon tomorrow. Get here by ten. Your tickets will be ready and I'll have a car to take you to Dulles."

As he reached the door, the younger man turned. "But what about Dan Samson's note asking about this Feline thing?"

"Oh, that?" The president laughed. "Dear old Dan must think he's on to something special. Well, he's not. Feline is the name we gave to a series of cold weather tests taking place at one of our Alaska bases. As a matter of fact, Secretary Kleffen and Dan are on their way there now. Don't you give it another thought. Just enjoy Paris. Now you better go home and get some sleep."

Robby nodded to his brother, waved a hand and closed the door.

For a full half minute, the president stared at the door then he produced a large pocket handkerchief. Finally he gave out with a long outward breath of relief and mopped his brow.

CHAPTER XXI

It took General Topps and Mr. Rollins some three hours to compose the message Topps was reading aloud.

TO: SINGABAR
PRIME MINISTERIAL TOPSEC - 218
FOR EYES OF COMMANDERS ONLY
OPERATION FELINE

PARA 1 - ROYAL NAVY ARRIVE SINGABAR 0800 HRS 15 NOV WITH FIVE SHIPS-FOUR FOR EVACUATION, ONE LANDING CRAFT CARRIER.

PARA 2 - D-DAY IS 17 NOV, EVACUATION SHIPS TO DEPART SINGABAR 17 NOV AND PROCEED PAGUDA TO ARRIVE BY NIGHT 19 NOV. CAPTAIN TO REPORT TO AMBASSADOR WILSON AT PAGUDA AND WAIT ORDER FROM SINGABAR TO PROCEED TO DESTINATION TO ARRIVE MITZU BY NIGHT 23/24 NOV AND COMPLETE EVACUATION ALL SPEED.

PARA 3 - FELINE CARGO. SIXTEEN HUNDRED PLUS CATS IN FOUR HUNDRED PLUS CRATES DEPART BILLINGS BY ROAD 17 NOV TO ARRIVE TENPOST 18 NOV. RAF DEPARTS TENPOST 18 NOV TO ARRIVE BULABAR 19 NOV AND TRANSFER TO ROYAL NAVY. TRANSFER OF CARGO TO RN MUST BE COMPLETED BY 2300 HRS 19 NOV.

PARA 4 - COMMANDER SINGABAR WILL ORDER EVACUATION SHIPS TO PROCEED FROM PAGUDA TO MITZU WHEN FELINE CARGO LEAVES SINGABAR DAWN 20 NOV.

PARA 5 - FELINE CARGO PROCEED FROM SINGABAR TO MITZU TO ARRIVE OFF MITZU FIRST LIGHT 24 NOV.

PARA 6 - SPECIAL FOR COMMANDERS TENPOST AND CAMP BURTON. MEDICAL - SANITATION UNIT WILL BE PREPARED TO PROCEED DIRECT TO MITZU BY AIR FROM TENPOST NOT BEFORE 25 NOV ON DEFENSE MINISTER ORDER ONLY.

PARA 7 - FELINE COMMANDER IS MAJOR GILLY. UNIT EXECUTIVE OFFICER IS MAJOR DREWER. TWO SERGEANTS ACCOMPANY. THEY WILL REPORT PROGRESS OF OPERATION VIA ASLT SHIP TO SINGABAR WHO WILL PASS TO DEFWASH FOR THIS HQ.

PARA 8 - SECURE PRIME MINISTERIAL TOPSEC.

"Sounds very good to me," said General Topps. "Don't you think so, Rollins?"

"Oh, yes, sir—very complete," replied Rollins. "Somehow I think that should do it. Don't you, General?"

"I bloody well hope so," Topps said, but without his usual confident tone.

Additional copies of this historic document were dispatched by special messenger to the foreign secretary, the defense minister and to the chiefs of the Navy and Air Force. Following this, and mainly out of reluctant courtesy, General Topps visited the commandant of the Royal Marines and briefed him on the operation. Major General "Soapy" Greenville was, to say the least, somewhat disturbed by the army general's account of the strange events to date. However, after Topps departed, the tough old marine made a mental, yet grateful note: He thanked God earnestly that his elite troops were not in any way mixed up in what seemed, on his limited knowledge of it, to be something that could easily become what he termed S-U-B-A-R, "screwed up beyond all recognition." He wondered vaguely how the Navy was taking its part of the assignment. Soapy Greenville and Hugo Stagg did not get along at all.

The American naval base at Singabar was always a busy place. The business and bustle of activities around the bases were never such, however, that the admiral and his more senior subordinates could not afford plenty of time for various forms of relaxation. It was known as a post where one could enjoy oneself either in quiet dignity or wild exuberance. But all this changed overnight.

When PMTS message number 218 arrived on the admiral's desk at Singabar U.S. Naval Base, he thought someone on his staff was having a huge joke.

The admiral was actually chuckling to himself when he phoned his first suspect, Captain Smithers, his chief of operations.

"Smithers?"

"Yes, Smithers here. Oh, yes, sir, Admiral—that you?"

"Smithers, you silly old bastard, when are all your bloody cats arriving?"

"Hello, this *is* Captain Smithers—who is this?"

"This is the admiral, John, I want to know when your cargo of cats is arriving."

"I'm sorry, Admiral, I don't get you."

"Oh, for God's sake, John, cut it out. Out with it—you thought you had me there, eh? You and your cats."

"Cats! Admiral, did you say cats?" Smithers sounded worried.

"Very amusing but I'm not your boy today. Try it on someone else."

"But Admiral, I don't know—you did say cats?"

The admiral paused. "You mean you didn't make up some damned message about the bloody cats? I mean, this message from the British."

"Hell no, Admiral—Admiral, are you okay?" Smithers sounded even more worried.

The admiral swore heartily and hung up. He looked at the wire. This, he realized, was no mere frolic of someone's imagination. There actually were some sixteen hundred cats coming by air to Bulabar and then to his base, and the Royal Navy ships coming in were to get the brutes to Mitzu. He called in his aide, Williams.

Lieutenant Williams, a strong, lean type of man with a freckled face, gave the message his usual frosty satire. He disliked cats intensely.

"Sixteen hundred cats, sir? Surely there must be some mistake, or is this tied in with the message about the British?"

"Sixteen hundred cats," confirmed the admiral, "and all bound for Mitzu. No mistake. It's a PMTS, same as our PTS, see? So that's it."

"But why, sir?"

"How the bloody hell can I tell? All I know is Operations can take it from here. I'm off to Pentang to Lady Lucy's house party at the plantation, and I don't want to get mixed up in this—no, sir, not me."

"But the Chief of Operations is due to go up there too, sir," said Williams, then added, "he's also invited to Lady Lucy' s."

The Admiral took no notice, he merely reached for the phone and grinned. He knew how to handle Captain Smithers, his operations officer.

"John, how's the boy? Look, John, I'm sorry but you'll have to call off your weekend—yes—I'm sorry, but you'll have to remain here over the weekend. It's this cat business. Can't talk about it now—it's that PMTS, just like our PTS. Come on over." He hung up and added, "You'd better stay, Lieutenant, and hear what I tell him. This may not be easy."

"Yes, sir," agreed the aide.

The admiral re-read the message. "Sixteen hundred cats. Oh, cripes!" He burst out laughing.

Some few minutes later, as Smithers, the chief of operations at Singabar, approached his admiral's door, he thought he heard rather loud and hearty laughter. Smithers wondered what sort of cats the admiral meant—just plain cats, or the other type, the kind one sometimes encountered at Lady Lucy's plantation parties. He wondered, too, whether the admiral had been really serious about his having to be at the base for the weekend. He soon found out.

At Bulabar General Bellows read his copy of message 218 shortly after lunch. He whispered every printed word; and as he progressed, his head ached with pangs of utter disbelief. Then, having summoned Colonel Mason, his chief of staff, he handed the message to him.

"No," he told his subordinate. "I don't want you to read it now. You do that after I've left. This is the reason why the Royal Air Force is in on this instead of us. It's all on file here." He tapped the folder on his desk.

The general stood up, put his braided cap on, picked up a packed overnight case from the floor and made for the doorway.

"But, sir," said the chief of staff, "supposing it's—"

"Supposing it's what?" the general said testily. "Read it, Dixie, it's all there clear as a bell. You can let me know how you make out when I get back."

"But I thought you—"

"Oh, yes, I forgot to tell you—I'm flying up to Singabar. The admiral just called me. It seems he now has an extra invitation for me for Lady Lucy's house party."

The chief of staff at Bulabar found it hard to speak. Even the slamming of the door behind his general had a carefree, debonair sound to it.

In accordance with the detailed instructions given out in PMTS message 218, the convoy of assorted cats left Camp Billings shortly after dark on the seventeenth. Majors Gilly and Drewer and two exasperated and depressed sergeants who had been assigned as assistants to Gilly and Drewer accompanied the heavy trucks carrying the furry creatures in wooden crates, four to a box.

The journey to Tenpost Air Base took a little over three hours. On arrival there, the crates were loaded into the belly of the huge RAF transport aircraft, together with an assorted supply of cat food that might be needed on the way. Gilly and Drewer were both surprised to find General Jansen and an odd-looking civilian named Rollins waiting for them on the runway.

Both men shook hands with Gilly and his assistants, and even made a hurried inspection of one aircraft to the tune of loud screeches, meows and other normal cat noises and smells.

It was not, as Jansen said later, a glorifying experience, but one of essential duty.

The evacuation fleet of four ships flying the white ensign of the Royal Navy left Singabar with the tide, as prescribed, on D-Day, the seventeenth of November. They reached Paguda three days later and moored in the outer harbor well away from the crowded shore area, which was, as usual, littered with junks, sampans and other small craft. The tardy arrival was mainly due to choppy seas and high winds, together with some engine difficulties on one ship. Because of this and the speculation that the visit of the ship's officers ashore might create, Ambassador Wilson decided it would be better not to have the ship's officers attend the grand chief's buffet party. He sent a confidential message to the captain of the convoy.

In it, the ambassador explained that as the British Government had no representation in Paguda, he had received extensive instructions from London and Washington. These instructions, he pointed out, had emerged from a top level conference between his own and the British governments. It was felt that the presence of the British crews might arouse too much interest and, in turn, suspicion.

So instead, Mr. Wilson and Mr. Heng, the Pagudan secretary of state, went out to the senior ship in a launch to bid a short welcome and godspeed. Mr. Wilson conferred with the Royal Navy convoy captain, who informed him he was in constant touch with Singabar. He hoped his orders to proceed would be given him within the next twenty-four hours. Meanwhile, the captain explained, he would carry out the few minor repairs to his over-sensitive engine. The ambassador and Mr. Heng were then piped off the quarterdeck in traditional style and returned to shore. So far, thought the ambassador as they neared the dock, so good.

In Paguda, all the reception arrangements had been completed. The neat rows of prefabricated houses were up in the state park. A tented hospital and medical reception center had also been newly established. It all presented a picture of high efficiency, with white-clad doctors and nurses who had been called in from various centers across the country standing at their posts.

Mr. Wilson and the Pagudan state secretary drove to the newly erected area. There they were met by Grand Chief Sultopan and his entourage and then carried out a tour of inspection of the new houses, the hospital and all the assembled personnel and medical equipment. It was an impressive array.

Then the grand chief's party, organized for him by Mr. Wilson's staff, started. The invitations sent out by His Highness' office had simply stated that the presence of those invited was required to mark the beginning of a Pagudan medical exercise and the goodwill visit of four ships of an ally. Except for the chosen few, not one other soul knew why the ships were really there or where they were going. Mitzu was not even mentioned. Thankfully, no one seemed to question it.

No doubt, the bands, the flags, the food and, of course, the flow of champagne—eighteen cases of which were contributed by Ambassador Wilson's household—did much to deaden any curiosity. It soon became a lively affair, due not only to an immense amount of food contributed to the cause by the ambassador but also to the grand chief's ability with the drums and the piano, which he thumped with increasing gusto as the hours passed.

State Secretary Heng was standing beside Ambassador Wilson. "Mr. Wilson," said Mr. Heng, "you have an aptitude for producing the best food and champagne in the world. Paguda will never be able to thank you enough, Excellency—never."

"My dear Mr. Heng," said Wilson, "please consider it our simple contribution towards humanity. Do not forget, it mustn't be known that my government is providing any of this. It might prejudice security. You do understand that?"

"Oh, yes, of course. I understand perfectly," said Mr. Heng.

"Ah, Mr. Wilson," Wilson turned to see Mr. Artovski, the Soviet ambassador, with extended hand and ever present smile.

"You know, Excellency," said the Russian, "one of the things I adore about Paguda is the way in which they have a party on the slightest excuse. Do you not agree? Such simple people, wonderful people, and such wonderful champagne, yes?"

"Yes," said Wilson, "wonderful."

"Do you also agree, Mr. Heng?"

"Yes, Excellency, surely, yes," said Heng, wondering idly how he could possibly arrange to get one of the beautiful bungalows erected at his beachside resort for Mrs. Heng.

On the following morning, Ambassador Wilson had his chauffeur divert from his usual route to the embassy and drive him along the quayside. Wilson had the car halt by the loading pier, and on the pretext of inspecting the rear tires, he managed to look out to sea. When he climbed back into his limousine, it was with a satisfied smile. The evacuation fleet had obviously departed—in any case it was nowhere in sight. He could now return to the embassy and try to sort out this fellow Stark.

Queer chap, this Stark, thought Wilson, as his car bumped over the pot-holed roads. What on earth could have prompted him to give the Pagudans these pianos, the outboard motors and, of all things, the two lawn mowers he had ordered for the residence grounds. Stark would no doubt have some explanation, but for the life of him, the ambassador couldn't think of what it might be.

As he alighted from his car, he felt the first rain drops. He cast a look at the sky, noting the black clouds. It looked like a severe storm coming up. The thunder started, distant at first, rolling noisily overhead as he entered the embassy. Then, as if to provide a crescendo for one of nature's overtures, the thunder increased, lightning lit up the mountains beyond the Lokong River and the clouds opened their floodgates to release torrents of warm rain.

The president had just finished reading PMTS number 218. "A very well organized message, I'd say."

"Yes, Mr. President," said General Howell. "The British produce excellent staff work. I wish some of our people could do as well."

"I must say, I'm really pleased at the way they're going about it," said the president. "It bodes well for success, I'd say."

"I agree, sir," said the national security advisor. "I have a feeling they'll pull this off, and no one else in the world will be any wiser. Is there anything else, sir?"

"No, that's it—oh, but wait, there is one more problem, and it could cause us trouble."

General Howell looked puzzled. "Something new, sir?"

"Yes, the agency, the spooks, they and our public information people may give us trouble."

"Yes, I see," murmured the general.

"You're quite right sir," the national security advisor added with some real concern in his voice.

The president rose from his desk and stood in front of the window. For a few seconds he gazed at the cluster of snow-covered buildings in the distance. Then, without turning, he said, "I'll have a word with the director. I won't give them the full picture at all, but I'll warn them that they have no part at all in this." He then turned to face the others.

"That's all very well, sir," said the national security advisor, "but what about their man in Paguda and the ones in Hong Kong, Bulabar and Singabar—and London, too."

"Good Lord, do we have them there too?" the president looked surprised. "I really must get to know these things."

"I'm afraid so, sir, and they may get nosy." the national security advisor had little use for the agency or its chief.

"They can't get nosy if they aren't there," said General Howell with a smile.

"Oh, you mean—I see." the president chuckled. "If they aren't there?"

"Exactly, sir," the general said. "All we do is get the director to recall his men from Paguda, Hong Kong, Bulabar and Singabar, and their men in London too. Get all of them back to Langley for, say, a special briefing or whatever—that should do it. At least I think it will."

He looked at the national security advisor, who was grinning and nodding his agreement.

"I think the general has hit the nail on the head, sir."

"Very good, gentlemen, very good. Just leave the rest to me. I'll have a quick word with Admiral Jenkins."

"It's Perkins," General Howell corrected him. "Jenkins was the last one, Mr. President. Remember, you didn't like him."

"Oh yes, I forgot. I'd better have a word with him."

"I'll go now, Mr. President," said the national security advisor, sensing he was no longer needed.

"Thanks, I think that's all for now."

As the door closed behind the advisor, the president rose and walked over to the window. He clasped his hands together as if uncertain of what to say next.

"Anything else, sir?"

The president turned and stood behind his desk. "Yes, there is. This visit of mine to the carrier on the West Coast…"

"Oh, of course. You mean the new carrier?"

"Yes. I was wondering what you think of this?" With that, the president produced from inside his jacket and put on a blue baseball-type cap emblazoned with gold braid on the front and five stars just above it.

The general stood there for a moment, not believing his eyes.

"Well, what do you think?"

The general gulped; he knew what he had to say, but it wasn't going to be easy. "Mr. President," he began.

"Yes?"

"Mr. President, where...?"

"Oh, my wife Valerie gave me this. She feels I should let the men know what I represent and wear it when I inspect the carrier."

"Mr. President, far be it from me to question your wife's good intentions, but the men on that carrier know quite well what you are and what you represent. Quite honestly, sir, I think it would be most unwise of you to wear that cap. You asked what I thought; I feel I have to be honest with you."

"But why? I *want* to wear it. Is it because I never served, is that why you think it unwise?"

"Well, sir, wear it if you insist, but if I were you, I wouldn't. I think you would find the media difficult and embarrassing. And don't forget public opinion, especially from the thousands of veterans from Vietnam, Korea and before that."

"You're really serious, aren't you, General?" he said, half laughing.

"Yes, sir, I am, I assure you."

"Thanks, General." The president turned abruptly to face the window.

The general wheeled about quickly and left. Whatever the president was muttering was obvious but inaudible.

It was just past seven p.m. when George Boothman, the deputy director of the CIA entered Admiral Perkins' office.

"Hope this won't take long, Admiral, I have a dinner at the Chilean Embassy."

"Not too long, George," Perkins replied. "Take a seat. I saw the man about an hour ago; we have to pull out our people in Paguda, Hong Kong, Bulabar, Singabar and London, and have them here by tomorrow night."

"What! Pull them out? What for?" Boothman was not pleased.

"How the hell do I know? All the president said was that he wanted those five men back here at headquarters for two weeks. So, you'd better move fast. I want you to meet them at Andrews Air Force Base."

"But, Admiral, what do we do with them for two weeks?" I have to give them some explanation when they arrive.

"Couldn't you arrange a special briefing or something?"

"Special briefing! Good God sir, they were here three weeks ago for the Far East Conference, and nothing has happened since.

George Boothman had had a run–in with the president some months ago and was still chafing over it. “Is this some sort of game our clever boy wants to play like he did before? He’s always fiddling with our people. Damn it Admiral, he knows sweet F A about our role and—Jesus, why can’t someone tell him to stay out of our hair and let us do our job.”

“All right, all right. I know they were here three weeks ago, but we have to get them back here again and arrange something for them. George—the man says they have to be pulled out and brought back.”

George Boothman shook his head sadly. “Pulling them out is no problem, but what’ll I tell them?”

Perkins was not too happy either; then he suddenly slapped his hand on the desk.

“Wait a minute, here’s an idea. The U.N. is having some sort of a special seminar starting two days from now. It’s about the emergency feeding operation in Africa, and it lasts, I believe, ten days. What about that?”

“But that has nothing to do with their jobs in the Far East. Or has it?”

“George, old friend, don’t worry about that. You just arrange it with our man at the U.N. Mission to look after them for ten to fourteen days—and tell him I want them to attend the seminar as observers so they’ll understand the sort of problems that arise, just in case we have a similar situation in their areas. I tell you, that should do it, unless you have any better idea?”

“No, sir, I don’t. But the whole idea stinks, I—”

“Look George, I don’t like this any more than you do, but it has to be done.”

“Okay, sir, I’ll get the cables off later tonight.”

“Good. Now you’d better hurry or you’ll be late for your dinner.”

At the door, George Boothman turned. “What’s going on, Admiral?” He sounded worried.

Perkins looked at him for a moment before he answered. “Even I’m not sure, George. The man was pretty elusive. All I can tell you is, it's a PTS between us and the Brits, a short-term humanitarian operation. He didn't offer me any more information, so I didn't press him for any more. I'll fill you in whenever I get the story, okay? Have a good evening."

"Thanks, Admiral," he said. "Are we getting to a point where no one trusts us?"

"No, George, it hasn't come to that yet—at least, I don't think so. You go on to your dinner. I'll try to contact the man later and see if I can learn what's going on."

When the president entered the private quarters later that evening, the president's wife, Valerie, could see that he was not in a good mood.

"What's wrong, Willy: Didn't they salute you enough today?" He could see that she was a bit wobbly after her usual third martini.

"Don't be funny. If you had to put up with the idiots like I do, you'd be climbing the walls." He dropped into the red leather chair. "Goddamn military people, they don't seem to realize."

"Don't tell me you forgot about the carrier," she interrupted as she began to pour herself another drink from the mixer. "You promised me that you'd tell the soldier boy general that they should name that carrier after you. I'll bet you forgot. Or did you get scared and cop out?"

She flopped into the other deep chair opposite her husband and waved a finger at him. "What's more, I bet anything you forgot to do something about the knighthood from the Brits. Damn it, they gave one to all those others who had your job. You're losing whatever guts you had. Don't they know how much we've done for them and all those others?"

"Look, Valerie—"

"'Look, Valerie,' it's always 'Look, Valerie.' You never think of me."

"Oh, for Pete's sake, woman, shut up and listen. Getting the British to give us a knighthood takes time. I've got people working on it. As for the carrier, Howell told me that Defense has already decided to name the ship after some admiral named Spruance. I've never heard of him. What's more, Howell doesn't think I should wear that cap because it might—"

"Howell? Who does he think he is telling you you can't wear it? Why don't you get rid of him and bring that man from back home who helped you with the draft. You owe him and, if I were you, I'd wear it."

"You don't understand, Val, I can't do that."

"You could if you had the guts." She walked out carrying her glass and the mixer.

As soon as she closed the door, he picked up his private phone and dialed. He looked at his watch; Helga or Laurie, one or the other was bound to be in.

CHAPTER XXII

The four lithe ships of the Royal Navy were plowing their way from Paguda through the heavy seas, in line, astern with the white ensign whipping in the wind. It was a wonderful sight, even for the proverbial landlubber. To the sailor, however, surveying the majestic scene from the bridge of the lead vessel, it was cause for the swelling of the chest.

On the convoy leader's bridge, however, the captain, a pipe clenched in his mouth, was beginning to feel somewhat apprehensive. The seas were getting much heavier and the clouds darker. It was his second day out from Paguda, and he was not pleased with his progress. He looked at his watch and realized the seas were slowing his convoy down to a crawl.

It was at about this time that Mother Nature, complete in her flowing storm-filled robes of darkest gray and purple, stepped onto the canvas of history.

The wind-swept rain descended in wild torrents. Huge waves heaped one upon the other and crashed onto the swaying decks. Swift orders were passed, and hatches were battened down to receive the full impact of the raging, storm-tossed waters. Hour by hour the storm worsened, and hour by hour the speed of the ships slackened. The four vessels suffered a terrific beating from the mountainous seas. There seemed to be no escape from the storm.

By the first light of morning on the twenty-fifth, with his flotilla still a hundred and fifty-odd miles northwest of Mitzu, the senior captain of the convoy realized he would have to reduce to less than quarter speed. By breakfast time, more bad news forced him to swing his craft about. He had just received a signal from two of the vessels following in his wake that they had collided and that the remaining ship had heaved to in order to attend to a dangerously buckling plate on the port bow.

The signal lamps began to flicker between the ships, and the first reports of the mishaps were sent on to Singabar. New orders were now flashed out and passed between the four ships. The captain in charge saw he had no course other than to report to Singabar that the evacuation of Mitzu would have to be delayed for at least three days or even more. He made it quite plain that his ships had suffered severely and asked in the same message that Bulabar inform the station in Mitzu to this effect. The Singabar Base was experiencing even worse communication difficulties, but they acknowledged the signals and agreed to pass this important information on to all concerned.

At Singabar the snarling wheels of the delicate procedures involved in handling such a top secret operation had already turned full cycle. As soon as the first four ships reported that they had reached the Port of Paguda, those in charge at Singabar ordered the ship that was now carrying Gilly, Drewer and the crates of cats to sail.

The captain of the cat-laden vessel, H.M.S. *Bulldog,* had been given sealed secret orders to be opened only after his ship was well outside the twelve-mile limit. He had just read them when the headquarters at singabar suddenly sent him the final orders to sail on to Mitzu. In those orders, the captain was instructed to maintain complete radio silence until he closed the shores of Mitzu. In this manner, so the chief intelligence officer at Singabar had advised the admiral, the secrecy could be maintained solidly without chance of further mishap.

When the troubled evacuation fleet informed the base at Singabar of its difficulties en route and of its probable delay in reaching Mitzu, there was naturally some concern. A message was passed to Bulabar asking that Mitzu be informed. Captain Smithers called in his signals and intelligence officers.

"Well," said Smithers, "we have a bit of a problem, fellows."

"Will we have to stop the cat ship?" said the signals officer.

"Yes, and as I see it there are two ways of doing this. One is to signal them direct, and the other is to send an aircraft after them. I mention these two because I realize this matter is a PTS and a signal may jeopardize security. What do you think?"

"It won't jeopardize security," said the signals officer.

"But are you sure?" said the intelligence officer.

"How could it? We merely say Feline is delayed so many days and wait till island has been evacuated, providing we can reach them, of course."

"What do you mean?" asked Smithers.

"Have you seen the weather report, sir?"

"No, I haven't," he replied. "Why?"

"We have a typhoon coming up within the hour."

"Oh, no. Oh, my God."

"Yes," said the intelligence officer. "It's true enough—same one that must have hit the evacuation ships."

"Then that cuts out any idea of an aircraft, doesn't it?" said Smithers.

"I'm afraid it does," said the signals officer. "I'll try to raise them on the air, but even that may not be possible; they've been ordered to maintain radio silence until they reach Mitzu."

"Yes, I know, but let's take a chance and hope they hear us."

The morning of the twenty-fifth of November found the four ships of the evacuation fleet floundering about in a suddenly becalmed sea, licking their wounds. Some sixty miles farther to the south, another vessel laden with howling cats and with single purpose ploughed through the blue green waters toward Mitzu at highest speed. Complete radio silence, as the sealed orders had instructed, was being maintained.

On Mitzu, the signal station, true to its tradition, had been silent, yet anxiously awaiting its final orders to evacuate.

Jackson was at the set when the signal came in telling them the evacuation would be delayed. He decoded it and was about to acknowledge it, when suddenly something inside the radio set let out a puff of smoke—and the set was silent. Mitzu was no longer able to receive or send signals, at least not for a while. The four signalmen, naturally anxious to learn whatever else

Bulabar may have had to say, tried every trick in the book to put life into their senseless radio—anything to get it into some semblance of working order—but to no avail. It was definitely dead.

Staff Sergeant Norton was not unduly alarmed. He explained to the others that the evacuation ships were obviously not going to appear for some days, so there seemed to be little point in wasting one's time on a radio that simply refused to be rejuvenated. Besides, as they all agreed, it was too darned hot to work; furthermore, they and the islanders were all packed anyway and ready to leave Mitzu as soon as the evacuation fleet arrived.

Back home at Mooneyville Junction, the exciting news of George Gilly's speedy promotion to the rank of major, which General Jansen had thoughtfully conveyed to Julie by letter, had been hailed as an event of historical importance. Mayor MacKay quietly saw to it that George's picture appeared in nearly all local stores, and the mayor even penned an elaborately worded letter of congratulations to Julie. He also gave the story a full page in his special two-page edition of the *Clarion.*

George's wife, Julie, was naturally pleased but a trifle bewildered by the new turn her life in the small town was taking. She now received a large number of daily telephone calls from people she hardly knew, all asking after the major. Some people even sent her cakes and pies, and she was being asked to attend local functions for no apparent reason. After all, she was, as Munro MacKay told her, the wife of a hero and, as such, must play her role. She tried but was not very happy.

The mayor and Mrs. MacKay called on her frequently, but for quite another reason. Mr. MacKay, his wife, his sisters at the post office and the telephone exchange, and his brother at the telegraph office had held a family conference. The subject under discussion had naturally been George Gilly. What, they asked each other, would happen when George Gilly returned? Would he be satisfied to go back to his garage? Or would he perhaps decide to take a turn toward greater things in Mooneyville Junction? Munro MacKay did not like this notion at all. It was a distinct threat to his position as mayor.

"A crisis may develop," he declared to his assembled family, "and we must be prepared to meet it—just in case George Gilly has some idea of—well—just in case."

Far away in Washington another crisis, a domestic one, was developing.

"Look here, Val. Enough is enough. You can't invite the new British ambassador and his wife for a week-end at Camp David, not this week-end. I'm having my Asian friends there. We need their money."

"Well then, Willy, that's too bad because I've already asked them. You'd better call and tell them they can't come. I can't see why you spend so much time with them. What can they do for you except give you money? I was only trying to make things easier for you to get that knighthood you're dying to get." She started toward the door.

"I told you I have someone working on that. This is the sort of thing you can't push."

"Where have I heard that one before? You don't seem to be able to push anything these days except your after-hours playmates. By the way, there's a message on your machine. Someone named Helga and she sounds a bit wacky."

She was opening the door when he stood up and pointed at her. "How many times have I told you to leave my private lines alone. You have no business to touch them and you have no business ever using my red phone. Don't do it again."

"Are you finished, you big important boy?"

"Yes, I am."

"Wonderful. I shall now leave your exalted presence." She slammed the door hard.

CHAPTER XXIII

In Paguda, Ambassador Wilson became aware that all was not well when Colonel Johnson, his military attaché, burst into his office unannounced. It was well after the attaché's normally set office hours. When Mr. Wilson saw Colonel Johnson's face, he sensed not a crisis, but a catastrophe. As the ambassador reached for the classified message clutched by the colonel, he thought Johnson was going to have a heart attack right then and there.

"From Singabar, sir." The attaché was actually trembling. "It's a hell of a mess—we're in deep trouble."

Mr. Wilson tried to assume an air of calm. "Oh? Something wrong?"

"I'll say, sir—the cats have left," said Johnson. "Do you know what that means?"

"The cats have what?" exclaimed the ambassador. "Already? They just can't—I mean—"

"They've left all right," said Johnson. "I'll read the wire to you, sir. *'Further to your A 4659 of 24 Nov. Regret to report delay of Mitzu Evac up to four days. All our efforts to contact catship failed due to typhoon which hit us early last night. No contact made and no aircraft can take off.* Have you aircraft to send and warn ship?"

Wilson glanced at it quickly, then leaned toward Johnson. "Do you realize what is going to happen, Colonel?"

"Yes, sir, I do," he replied unhappily.

"God damn it all, what's happened? We made it quite clear to Singabar about the trouble the evacuation ships had, didn't we?"

"Yes, sir, we did. What's worse, sir, is that the only way we can contact the cat ship, except via Singabar, is for us to send it an uncoded message—in clear, that is. Even than it may not work because Singabar told the cat ship to maintain radio silence until it got to Mitzu."

"No, no!" Wilson cried in despair. "And we certainly can't send anything that's PTS in clear. Have we any chance of contact at all with the weather station on Mitzu?"

"We tried over the relay here, sir, but we can't raise an answer from Mitzu. We can't blame them, sir, they aren't supposed to come on the air except in an emergency."

"Wait a minute." An idea struck the ambassador. "Why can't we send an aircraft to Mitzu as they suggest? What about the four aircraft we gave the Pagudans as aid? Couldn't we send one of them to Mitzu? I know they were all out of action a few days ago, but surely one can fly by this time. Not to land, of course, but just fly over the weather station and the ships and deliver the news, drop a message or something. Or better still, one of those aircraft to fly over the cat convoy and tell them to lay off Mitzu till the evacuation ships arrive?"

"We could, sir, but—"

"But what, man? Speak up Colonel." Ambassador Wilson was getting impatient.

"But I told you, sir, all four aircraft are out of action."

"Still out of action—all four? Why, we only presented them last month, and they were in excellent condition then—or were they?"

"Oh, yes," said the colonel, "they were in excellent condition, but—well, sir, you know the Pagudans."

"Yes, I'm afraid I do." The ambassador placed his head between his hands. My God, he thought, this is one hell of a situation. He had visions of being recalled home to explain all this before a Senate committee.

Suddenly Colonel Johnson had an idea. "There is the one chance, sir, that if the people of Mitzu are ready to evacuate when the ship with the cats arrives, they will leave the island first, and then once they're aboard, the cats will be landed—if the ship can take them all aboard."

"Do you honestly think anyone will think of that?" asked Mr. Wilson hopefully.

"It's possible, sir," Johnson said. "There's an Army officer in charge of the cats. It's possible that he might think of it."

There was an awkward moment of silence. The two men looked at each other.

"Yes, I suppose it is possible." Wilson sighed. "If only we had some way of contacting that damned ship. Anyway, I'd better get a wire off to State."

With his right hand he reached for the bell to call Miss Loffatt while his left hand sought the top desk drawer for some aspirin. He knew he didn't have a tranquilizer left.

Colonel Johnson stood back, saluted and hurried out, just in case Mr. Wilson changed his mind and asked him to do something else. In any case, the colonel was already late for the poker game at MAAG HQ.

A copy of Ambassador Wilson's cable from Paguda was brought into General Jansen's office by a very agitated Mr. Rollins, who had been instructed by the British prime minister to remain in Washington. It was as long and verbose as anyone might expect from the State Department.

> CONCERNS MITZU. ALL SHIPS SLATED FOR EVACUATION OF THE ISLAND HAVE ENCOUNTERED EXCEEDINGLY BAD WEATHER. TWO OF FOUR SHIPS ARE NOW OUT OF COMMISSION AND ARE BEING ASSISTED BY OTHER TWO SEAWORTHY SHIPS. EVACUATION IS DELAYED BY THREE TO FOUR DAYS.
>
> SINGABAR NAVAL HEADQUARTERS HAVE BEEN INFORMED BUT HAVE ALREADY SENT OUT SHIPS CARRYING CATS. CANNOT SEND AIRCRAFT AS NONE AVAILABLE HERE. FEAR THAT CAT CONVOY WILL REACH MITZU BEFORE EVACUATION SHIPS. THIS WILL CREATE NEW

PROBLEMS UNLESS LANDING OF CATS IS DELAYED TILL POPULATION IS OFF ISLAND. WE RECOMMEND DISPATCHING FURTHER MESSAGES TO NAVY SINGABAR ASKING THEM TO CONTACT CAT CONVOY AND ORDER CONVOY TO STAND OFFSHORE MITZU PENDING ARRIVAL EVACUATION SHIPS. ALL ARRANGEMENTS CONCERNING ACCOMMODATION AND MEDICAL TREATMENT EVACUEES COMPLETED AND READY HERE.

Slowly Jansen read out the message to the others who sat about the office. General Topps who had just flown in from London with Admiral Stagg and Air Marshal Burrows, leaned forward in his chair as if ready to leap onto the conference table. Mr. Rollins of the Foreign Office, sitting at the far end, doodled aimlessly on his notepad and waited for the outburst. It was not long in coming.

"Oh, my good God," gasped Topps. "This sounds as if it could be serious."

"Serious? Sounds like a real balls-up to me," added Burrows. "I'm sure glad my people didn't screw it up."

"I can't understand it," said Admiral Stagg. "What did I tell you—if you'd only have let us bombard the place, that would have settled it. I just can't understand it."

"Nor will the prime minister," said Rollins solemnly, "and I rather think he will want to know why our ships were not seaworthy and why it is that someone did not arrange foolproof communications to insure against this sort of thing happening."

"Dear God," said the admiral.

What Sir Hugo Stagg did not know was that the five ships sent out to Singabar by the flag officer at Royal Navy Headquarters in Hong Kong were the five oldest gunboats he had. Their keels had been laid in 1933 and had long been due for replacement. Yet, at the time he had dispatched them to Singabar, they were in fair condition.

“Well, sir,” Rollins said, determined to make his point, “The facts speak for themselves, don’t they?”

“Just a minute, Rollins,” said Admiral Stagg, determined to defend his service. “While I agree that the ships may have been old, they would certainly not have sailed if any of my captains considered that they were not seaworthy. What you don’t seem to realize is that a good storm can put any size ship out of commission and make communications almost impossible. Those ships ran into one hell of a big storm, and that’s what caused the delay. You just remember that.”

“Yes, I see,” said Rollins, “things do appear to have gone against us.”

“I believe,” said Topps as he paced the floor, “we have a crisis on our hands.”

Air Marshall Burrows was more to the point. “I think we’ve bought ourselves a real lulu; I thought so the minute we started this,” he said, pulling vigorously at his moustache.

The admiral sighed. “I’ll say. Hell, we’ve all put such a security rating on this operation that it’s a bloody wonder we can even discuss it among ourselves.”

“I don’t quite understand what you mean,” asked Rollins.

“I can see damn well what he means,” said the Air Marshal.

“I’m afraid I see it quite clearly now,” Topp said slowly.

“So can I,” added Jansen. “First of all, no one is supposed to know we even have an installation on Mitzu. Next, the signalers on Mitzu apparently have strict orders not to initiate any communication with anyone except in a matter of life and death, and then only so well coded that it takes hours to understand what it’s all about. All that the people at Bulabar and Singabar were told was they would arrange road transport and the matter was top secret. Now do you see? Gentlemen, I believe we have literally boxed ourselves in with security. No one is going to discuss anything that’s PTS if they can help it—with anyone. No American in his right mind will ever touch anything as hot as a PTS matter. As I see it, the four ships of the evacuation fleet were able to communicate with Singabar. Okay. But not with the cat ship because it was ordered to maintain radio silence until it reached Mitzu. Why Singabar has not been able to inform the cat ship of the delay, I don't know, unless the ship's radio has gone out too. It too may have run into bad weather. I hear that storm was one of the worst they've ever had in the area."

"And," said the air marshal, "because it's a PTS, you're not going to get any U.S. aircraft chasing after the cat ship—so we can forget about that one."

"What about some of the aircraft the Pagudans received from the Americans some time ago?" suggested Admiral Stagg. "You know, the ones we were considering training some navigators for—wonder where they are. I mean, you'd think your embassy in Paguda might have sent one of them to Mitzu, or after the cat ship anyway, or do the Pagudans themselves know your people are even on Mitzu—or even where Mitzu is?"

"I really don't know," said Jansen, "but there again, because it's a PTS for us, we can't have any aircraft flying around Mitzu. As you said, from a security standpoint, we're boxed in."

At this stage, Mr. Rollins was wishing to God he had never heard of Mitzu. In all probability, this mental attitude was shared by all the others.

"Anyway, gentlemen, let's not lose our heads," urged General Topps. "We appear to be the victims of rather odd circumstances. However, speaking for the prime minister and as acting chief of defense staff, I think, Hugo, you'd better initiate an inquiry as to the state of the ships sent by our people in Hong Kong. And you, Rollins, must ask the State Department to see if Singabar can contact the ship with the cats. After all, this is an emergency; they may be willing to break the rules this once."

"Indeed I will," replied Rollins. "Yes, I think that's a sound idea."

"Now," Topps continued in a calmer tone, "as I see it, the only thing we can hope for is that the chaps on Mitzu will have the sense to realize what has happened. It's really all we can do. Actually, I don't see too much here to worry about. I'm sure the men on Mitzu will sight the cat ship, and they may be able to signal it to explain the situation and probably arrange the evacuation without any trouble whatsoever. After all, these Army chaps are bound to be pretty sensible."

Admiral Hugo Stagg was sneering openly and was about to say something nasty, but he thought better of it; he merely shrugged his shoulders and shook his head.

"Look here," said General Topps, "no matter what has happened this far, hope of success is not lost by any means. Even if the cats get there first, surely the people on the island will be safe. Surely they will already have taken refuge from the rats. Don't you agree?" He looked around the room. It was clear that his listeners were not at all sure. "First thing is that not one hint must be given that all is not going according to plan—whatever happens. The rats will be exterminated, of that you can be sure."

"Yes, but what do we ask the State Department to tell Mr. Wilson in Paguda?" said Rollins. "We must tell him something."

"Tell him?" said Topps, arching his eyebrows. "You just ask State to tell him the operation has been a total success—just that, and leave the rest to me. Now, Jansen, we know you cannot afford, in view of that lease extension you must have on Mitzu airfield, to let anyone suspect there are any hitches to our plan. Normally, I'd clear this with your chairman joint chiefs but I say let's wait and see what happens. If your cat ship reports any real problems by tomorrow night, then we will fly the medical specialists into Mitzu, supported by some infantry, to shoot the rats and clean up the place. But only as a last resort. So, I say we wait till tomorrow. Meanwhile, you, Rollins, see to it that message gets off to the ambassador in Paguda. And remember, not one word of this to our foreign secretary till I say so. I'll go and see your General Howell now and sort it out with him."

As he left the office, General Topps had a feeling the others were not quite convinced. He was not far wrong. He wasn't convinced himself; neither was General Jansen.

It took Rollins some thirty minutes to follow General Topps' instructions and draft a message for the State Department to pass on to Mr. Wilson in Paguda. He was just about ready to take it in to the state secretary's office when he had second thoughts. He tore it up an started it again. This time it took him some ninety minutes before he was satisfied with the four closely typed pages he had carefully reworded to imply that whatever had gone wrong with the operation was not his fault or the fault of the Foreign Office or the State Department, but rather that the blame should be placed firmly on the defense departments of both nations.

"That's a really excellent message," said the secretary of state as he signed it. "You know, Rollins, these military people are more trouble than they're worth. We certainly didn't foul this one up; they did. Anyway, this should put Wilson straight on the matter and insure that if we have to find a scapegoat, we won't have to look any further than our respective defense departments. By the way, don't let them see a copy of this—at least not until after I've reported this mess to the president."

"By the way, Mr. Secretary, I'll be returning to London this evening with General Topps and his party. Is there any special message you want me to give the foreign secretary?"

"No," replied Secretary Bosk. "I'll see that a copy of this message reaches him in due course. I don't think he should see it before General Topps gets home, if that's all right with you. I'll send it off to our Embassy tomorrow and ask them not to deliver it until the following day. The general is well aware of the problem, and I don't think we want to get your foreign secretary or your defense minister too excited. In any case, when General Topps spoke with General Howell he suggested that we wait until tomorrow night and review the situation then."

"Very good, Mr. Secretary. It's been a real pleasure to be here. I hope we shall see you soon in London. Well, sir, I'll be off now."

The two men shook hands.

"Have a good flight," said Bosk.

When a copy of this same message reached Mr. Ryder's desk, he smiled. No doubt about it, he thought, this fellow Rollins was smart.

But Ryder himself was not dumb. He saw from the State Department's message that there was still a narrow, but distinct, probability that some of the blame might fall on him. So, he composed an equally long message to Mr. Wilson, suggesting in a rather ambiguous manner that the military experts had bungled the operation, that even Wilson had not made himself sufficiently aware of all the facts from the beginning, and that the colossal and costly blunder was bound to have drastic repercussions in certain quarters. That, thought Ryder, would scare the hell out of Wilson, and it would probably provide the secretary of state with a good future argument against assigning outsiders instead of career diplomats to ambassadorial posts. After all, Wilson wasn't even a career man, just a political appointee.

At the Mayflower Hotel, General Topps was about to get into bed when his phone rang. It was the chairman of the joint chiefs.

"Lucius, I'm sorry we couldn't touch base this afternoon, but your man Rollins has filled me in on the situation. Frankly, I'm baffled by the turn of events, but I do agree with you about waiting twenty-four hours."

"I'm glad you do, General. I feel we're bound to get a new reading on what course to take. The situation is going to become clearer by then."

"By the way, Lucius, I had a short session with our secretary of state, and from what he's said I gather your own Defense Minister Farr has somehow got into the picture, so you probably can expect some heavy crap from him when you get back."

"Thanks, General, I'm sure I will. Though I must say I'll be surprised if he gets involved; he's such a lazy bugger. Oh well, thanks anyway, see you tomorrow. Goodnight." He switched off the light.

CHAPTER XXIV

Mr. Wilson was giving his Rubik's Cube about the sixtieth turn when Miss Loffatt brought in the two cables from the secretary of state and Mr. Ryder.

"You know, this is the damnedest thing," he said without looking up. "How long does it take you to do it?"

"Usually about three minutes" she replied.

"Three minutes! You must be kidding. In that case, I'd better give up. Three minutes! I don't believe it."

"Yes Mr. Ambassador. Here, I'll show you." She reached across the desk and picked up the cube.

Wilson watched as she gave the pesky thing several turns to redistribute the colors, then looked at his watch.

"I'm ready," she announced.

"Go ahead," said the ambassador.

Miss Loffatt did not waste any time. She was as good as her word. In exactly two minutes and eighteen seconds she handed the plaything back to her boss.

"Well, I'll be." He looked first at the cube and then at his secretary. "How about that! Very good."

"Thank you," said Miss Loffatt. "Do you want me to stay while you read the cables?"

"Oh, yes, the cables. More of this Feline nonsense, I guess. Yes, you'd better stay. I wonder what State is going to say this time."

As Miss Loffatt took a seat opposite him, he picked up the first cable, the one from the state secretary. He read it aloud very slowly pausing every so often to shake his head in sheer disbelief. In it he was ordered to say absolutely nothing about anything concerning Mitzu to anyone, and certainly not to the Pagudan government, which would lead one to suspect that Operation Feline had not been completed according to the original plan. As far as the Pagudan government was concerned, the operation on Mitzu had been a success from start to finish. If any questions were raised by anyone, it was suggested that Mr. Wilson tell the Pagudan government that the actual evacuation of Mitzu had not been found necessary, that whatever rats had been there were now liquidated and that life on the little island would soon again be quite normal.

When he finally finished reading the lengthy cable, Mr. Wilson wondered vaguely if the end of his diplomatic career was at hand.

"Well, my dear, I'll be surprised if I don't get recalled home. This is the stupidest document I've ever seen. They must have gone mad. Oh, well, I'll draft a reply later. Now, for the second one."

The ambassador tossed the first cable aside in disgust and picked up the one from Ryder. He started to read it aloud, then suddenly stopped.

"Something wrong, sir?" Miss Loffatt asked.

"Huh? Something is wrong," he replied. "That idiot Ryder is implying in this one that I'm to blame for the mess we're in. Oh, my God, whatever induced them to put that ill-bred son of a—that fool in a position that he's allowed to send me this—the bastard is weaving the facts to save his own hide. Well, I'll fix that in due course, even if it means the end of my service."

During the afternoon, after numerous drafts and redrafts of telegrams to the State Department, Mr. Wilson paid an official call on State Secretary Heng and gave him the good news. Mr. Heng was, of course, overjoyed and quickly excused himself while he telephoned the grand chief. The Sultopan, having first showered his minister with verbal bouquets, then suggested that Mr. Heng call the minister of trade so the latter could proceed with the sale of half of the prefabricated houses, tents and supplies that Mr. Stark had so kindly donated to meet the crisis envisaged by the evacuation of Mitzu. The remaining half of the bungalows were, His Highness decided, to be dismantled at once and stored. He would decide on their disposal at a later date, but he promised his state secretary that the latter's urgent hope for a suitable summer beach residence would be forgotten. Mr. Heng beamed with gratitude.

In short order, Mr. Heng summoned the other cabinet ministers of Paguda and broke the news to them. They were a very happy group; they shook Mr. Wilson's hand; some even embraced him. Finally, they all insisted he stay to celebrate.

Food and drink appeared miraculously, and a joyful occasion began with champagne toasts to the United States of America, to the president, to Mr. Wilson, to the grand chief and, of course, to the brave people of Mitzu. Curiously enough, no one mentioned the British.

As the revelry progressed into the late afternoon, Wilson suddenly realized that whatever errors may have been committed by his colleagues at home, in relation to Mitzu, and compounded by passing it to the British, the whole matter could, if handled skillfully, (providing, of course, the rats were really cleared off Mitzu) be turned into a personal diplomatic triumph. He was not far wrong. The local newspaper next morning bore the largest picture of her husband that Mrs. Wilson had ever seen. The photo's caption, in guarded terms, hailed him as the brilliant negotiator of a new aid and trade agreement. It gave no details other than to report that the American ambassador had passed to the government of Paguda a lengthy list of the items of farm machinery, road repair equipment and a fleet of twenty trucks that had been authorized as aid to Paguda. Exactly what the Grand Chef's regime was to respond with in the form of trade was not defined, and no one was interested enough to ask.

Mr. Wilson's popularity rating with the local population at once took a bright turn. This was no doubt due to the Pagudan propaganda machine, which exhorted the populace to shout and cheer whenever the ambassadorial limousine appeared. The fact that it was often unoccupied made little difference. But this was not all. The Sultopan cabled the president directly, requesting he allow Mr. Wilson to be honored for his services. The president signaled his agreement, and Ambassador Wilson was informed that, in due course, he would be accorded entry into the Sublime Order of the Sacred Pagodas and made a member of the Grand Temple of the Golden Star. These were high honors indeed for a foreigner, the last of which carried with it a rather peculiar privilege. In this case, the American representative to Paguda would be obliged to spend one day a month doing manual labor in the gardens of the Grand Temple alongside some thirty other luminaries, including the grand chief, Mr. Heng, and the French, Russian and Chinese ambassadors.

On the following morning when the colorful investiture took place in the sunken gardens of the grand chief's palace, Mr. Wilson was accorded the place of highest honor, being seated on the grand chief's right, between him and State Secretary Heng. After an hour-long speech by the grand chief, in which he used every complimentary adjective in his limited English vocabulary, he beckoned to the ambassador to rise and come forward to receive his accolade. The military band played the Pagudan Chant of Freedom, then swung into what was supposed to be the guest of honor's national anthem; although, to the better–tuned ear of Mrs. Wilson, it sounded very much like "On Top of Old Smokey." Drums began to beat, the honor guard presented arms for the fourth time, the crowd cheered, all the invited guests stood erect, and Mr. Wilson suddenly felt himself being weighted down with a series of gold chains and assorted ornaments. Two of Sultopan's aides came forward to assist the ambassador in remaining upright during the ceremony and then to help him back to his seat, but not before the grand chief had risen on tiptoe to put his arms about the American diplomat's neck and planted a rather flabby wet kiss on each of the trembling ambassador's cheeks.

Proceedings came to a close after Mr. Heng read a letter of commendation from the people of Paguda, expressing gratitude and thanking the United States government profusely. Ambassador Wilson, though weary, felt pleased, but as he rode back toward his official residence through the streets crowded with cheering, flag-waving natives, he wondered whether he would fare as well when he eventually returned home to Washington.

Amidst all this atmosphere of serenity and happiness, however, there was in Paguda one very troubled individual. When he received the royal summons to attend the ceremony for Ambassador Wilson, the Soviet ambassador was extremely puzzled. Now, after watching the investiture from his place of honor on the main stand, he was no longer just puzzled, he was completely bewildered. Even a side glance at his Chinese colleague a few seats away had brought from the latter only a shrug of the shoulders and an utterly blank expression.

Mr. Artovski lost no time returning to his office, where he called a conference of his own embassy officials. His first, second, and third secretaries, his two political advisors, his three service attachés, and his four economic and trade counselors all gathered in the embassy ballroom. Mr. Artovski greeted each one with a rather sulky and suspicious look. Motioning to the Russian servant to close the door, he began to pace to and fro before his startled, though silent, audience.

"What's going on?" he said angrily. "Surely one of you must know. Why does the American ambassador have his picture in the paper? Why is he decorated? What is all this about the aid and trade treaty?" He looked at his audience like an irate bull.

Alas, none of his comrades was able to shed any light on the matter. Each of them in turn avowed complete lack of knowledge. Mr. Artovski raved, he ranted, he even threatened them, but all to no avail. Finally, after an hour and a half—during which he told each of his associates in turn that he was stupid and a disgrace to the Party—he dismissed them.

During the ensuing evening hours, Ambassador Artovski brooded. Should he send a cable to Moscow about this? But, what should he send? He poured himself a stiff drink. What could he tell his superiors? None of his staff knew anything.

Yet, if he did not warn them at home that something strange was happening, those stupid Czechs or Poles or Yugoslavs might beat him to it, and he would be in real trouble. He poured himself another drink. What sort of idiots did he have for colleagues who did not even have a clue about this aid and trade treaty? He had to think of something to tell his superiors at home. As he thought about it, he brooded still more and got quite drunk.

When Madam Artovski, his bulky spouse, returned to the residence later that night after attending a meeting of the Asian wives' association, she found her disconsolate spouse asleep on the drawing room floor under the large tiger rug. He was not alone; his two mongrel dogs also lay under the rug, one on each side of his snoring master.

CHAPTER XXV

Everyone on Mitzu was enjoying their usual mid-afternoon siesta when the ship carrying George Gilly and the cats approached the long white beaches of the island. It was hot and humid, and even the four signalmen, one of whom should normally have stayed awake on duty by the radio, had fallen into a deep, contented slumber. They were beat. After sixteen steady hours of work, Morton and Jackson had finally adjusted the damaged radio to a point at least where they could hear static. But, to receive or send a message was another matter. The set would not respond; nothing came in or went out—except static. The men were not unduly worried; after all, they had been told earlier by coded message that the evacuation of the island was to be delayed three or four days. So, having reached that condition of heat exhaustion so easily acquired in the tropics, they had packed in to rest.

Like the four hundred-odd inhabitants of Mitzu who had for the past two days been packing all their belongings in preparation for the move to Paguda, neither Morton, nor Jackson, nor Pope, nor Watowski felt there was much point in exerting himself. Later, in the cool of the day, perhaps they would have another try at fixing the radio receiver. Right now, there was no hurry. And in the tropics when you have nothing to do, you sleep.

With everyone securely enfolded in the arms of Morpheus, no one in Mitzu was aware that from the bridge of HMS *Bulldog,* five pairs of eyes were aimed at the glistening sands of Mitzu. At this point, the *Bulldog,* with four hundred and twenty crates of hungry cats in the assault boats, swinging from the davits, was six miles offshore. She was on true course, moving quite slowly as her crew stood by the davits waiting to lower the small craft onto the calm blue water. Gilly had arranged for his two sergeants and six of the sailors to take on the job of releasing the cats from their crates. Thus, each landing craft had two men who, as soon as the ramps were lowered, would open each crate and allow the animals to move inland.

As the order to lower away was shouted by the young British skipper, George put aside his binoculars and looked over the side. The landing craft all seemed to hit the water together; they were unhooked, and, like ducklings, they swung away from the mother ship and out into the open calm water.

"See anything?" asked George. "I can't see a move."

"Not a thing," replied Drewer. "Place looks empty to me."

"Nothing moving that I can see," added the ship's number one. "They've all gone, all right."

"We're still too far out," said the skipper. "I'm going to take her in slowly while the landing craft get lined up for the run in. I'll give them the go-ahead when we're about two miles off. Then we can still follow them in and see what goes on."

"What about Tom and me?" asked George, raising his glasses again.

"I'll put you both into the small motorboat when we close in, and you can follow them ashore."

The freckle-faced Royal Navy lieutenant on watch swung his glasses across the line of vision as the ship headed inshore. "That looks better," he smiled. "I can see a rise in ground that must be the plateau, I guess. The airstrip must run along the top or on the other side. And if you look far to the left, you'll see a metal shack gleaming in the sun. That's the signal station. Yes, it is. I can see the radio mast beside it. Do you see it?"

"Yes," said Drewer as Gilly raised his own glasses.

"Doesn't seem to be a soul around," said Gilly.

"No, of course not; they were all taken off yesterday," said the skipper of the *Bulldog.* "You two may as well get into the small boat. As soon as the assault craft and your boat are in position, you can make for the shore. Give me a shout on the blower when you're ready."

Gilly lowered his binoculars and made for the companionway, followed by Drewer. "Okay," he called back to the skipper, "We're off. Wait till we're formed up, then give the small craft the signal to get on with putting the cats ashore. As soon as the four LCAs are empty, you may as well put three of the craft back and swing them aboard. But leave one afloat just in case, will you?"

"Wilco, Gilly," said the skipper. "Good luck."

Gilly, Drewer and the skipper had agreed upon the general plan earlier. The first and second landing craft would each have one of the Army sergeants and two sailors available to open the crates. The last two craft would have three sailors each. Their job was to get the cats ashore as quickly as possible. The four assault craft laden with the cats would make for the beaches, followed by Gilly and Drewer in the smaller boat some distance behind. The ramps of the landing craft would be lowered as soon as the vessels touched down on the beach; the cats would be released and urged to leave the craft as quickly as possible. As the cats headed inland, Gilly and Drewer would land, if possible, and follow the feline hordes as they went about the business of killing rats. Gilly and Drewer had walkie-talkie radios tuned into another set aboard the *Bulldog* through which they would converse if separated, and also communicate with the ship. One landing craft would be left near the shore for emergency use if required.

Aboard the Royal Navy ship, the communications officer was becoming frantic. He had been trying for the last hour to raise the base at Singabar after the long period of imposed radio silence that was to end only when the ship was moored off Mitzu. Singabar, however, did not seem inclined to answer the signals. The radio operator did manage to catch some garbled words intermingled with heavy static, but could not make contact with the naval base.

"Oh, hell!" cried the radio operator.

"Just keep trying," ordered the communications officer, "it must be the bloody storm that's screwed things up."

Suddenly a voice blared from the radio. "Hello, Matador Pooch, message, over."

"Hey, there's our call sign. Quick, answer them."

"Hello, Matador Pooch, send your message. I think we're got them," the operator said happily. "Matador Pooch, I hear you only strength one, over."

There was only static.

The communications officer shouted at his operator, "For God's sake, man, what's wrong?"

"Matador Pooch, repeat your message, over.

It was no use. The sounds from the radio became screeches and high-toned whines interspersed with barely audible half syllables that disappeared amongst the ear-piercing sounds of nature's interference. The chain of events toward chaos was about to progress one step further.

Alfred George Washington Watowski awoke to find his gaze fixed on the other side of the room. He realized the other men were asleep in their bunks, and it did occur to him that he should have stayed awake on the duty watch. Oh well, no harm done, he thought, raising himself on one elbow to draw the bamboo curtain across the window. It was then that he heard the strangest sound. He sat up slowly, drew aside the curtain, and peered out toward the stretch of beach to the south.

At first Watowski thought he was still asleep. He shook his head quickly and then took a second look. "Ye Gods!" he exclaimed, scrambling to his feet. He went over to the water bucket and splashed several handfuls of cold water on his face. Then he looked at himself in the mirror, stuck his tongue out and even felt this own pulse; it must, he decided, have been that third helping of spaghetti and meatballs. Finally, he turned again to the window and parted the curtains cautiously. Then he fell with a thud to the floor in a dead faint.

"Alfie, what's the matter?" Morton had heard the noise from the fall and sat up shakily. He was off his bunk in a flash and saw Watowski on the floor. He went over to kneel by his prostrate friend.

Watowski opened his eyes and gasped. He tried to roll over and muttered, "Cats."

Morton grabbed him and tried to raise his head.

"Cats," murmured Watowski.

"Cats? Alfie, what cats? Where?"

"On the beach. Hundreds of them."

"Aw, come off it, Alfie, you were dreaming. There aren't any cats here."

"Hundreds of cats," whispered Watowski and fell back. This was serious. Morton had seen men go this way before, in the desert. Come to think of it, he'd just read about it in that book about the Foreign Legion—*cafard,* they called it. This sure looked like *cafard* to him. He called to the others for help.

"Jackson, Pope, give me a hand. Alfie's passed out."

"What's that?" Jackson was sitting up. "Christ." He flung his legs to the floor and stood up in one motion.

Pope was awake now. "What the hell's going on? What's up?"

"Come on over here, it's Alfie. He's passed out."

Alfie opened his eyes slowly and fixed them on the staff sergeant's face.

"It's all right, pal, it's all right," Morton assured him. "Take it easy; you'll be okay in a minute. Just take it easy. You just got too much heat."

"Sorry, fellers," said Alfie, "it was the cats."

"Cats?" The word had barely left their lips when the noise began. Alfie's head was dropped to the floor unceremoniously as the three signalmen rushed to the windows.

"Cats!" yelled Morton incredulously. "By God, he's right—look! But where the hell—quick, Jackson, get on the air. This is an emergency. Send an SOS."

"SOS?" Jackson was shaking as he reached for the radio set. "What'll I say?"

"Say? Oh, for God's sake, man, just send the SOS. Send it and keep sending it," said Morton. "You, Pope, barricade the door. I'll get the rifles."

"Okay," yelled Pope, "but I still don't believe—where did—"

Jackson needed no further exhortation; he became a whirlwind of action, twirling dials on the radio set and shouting into the microphone. He just hoped the set would come alive.

'Hello, Zulu Echo Hotel. Sierra Oscar Sierra. Over."

While Pope pushed the table in front of the door, Morton was unlocking the corner cupboard in which the carbines and ammunition were kept. Surprisingly enough, despite what he had just witnessed, Morton remained quite cool and collected. As he undid the security chain that held the weapons to their rack, he cursed.

There was no doubt about it, he had looked out the window and had actually seen several hundred cats advancing across the rocky ground toward the hut. Of course, had he been able to see beyond the rise in the terrain between the hut and the beach, he would have spotted the Royal Navy ship at its anchorage, but the beach was hidden from his view. As far as Staff Sergeant Morton was concerned, the island was being invaded by hundreds, probably thousands, of cats. God alone knew where they had come from or what they might do to a man if they caught him in the open. All this ran through his mind as he laid the weapons and boxes of cartridges out on the lower bunk.

In the background, Jackson was still at the radio. "Hello, Zulu Echo Hotel. Sierra Oscar Sierra, Sierra Oscar Sierra, over."

"The door is barricaded," said Pope, reaching for a carbine and spilling the cartridge boxes out on the blanket. "Now what?"

"Damned if I know. Just load up and watch the windows," replied Morton, cramming shells into an extra magazine. "I wonder if they'll try to get in here?"

Pope's answer did not help to raise his hopes. "They will if they're hungry enough."

Jackson, at the radio, had raised one hand to call Morton's attention.

"What's up?" Morton said.

"I'm getting through," said Jackson. "They're acknowledging my signal. We're through—we're—"

At that precise moment, the air resounded with an unearthly howl from the horde of cats; and as if by the touch of a magic hand, the felines changed course and streaked in one furry mass toward the eastern end of the island where the islanders' fish-drying sheds were located.

"Tell them the cats are on the way to the fish-drying sheds," said Morton, "but keep sending."

"Okay, okay," replied the frantic Jackson. "Hello, Zulu Echo Hotel. Cats now on way to island fish supply. Sierra Oscar Sierra. Over." There was a moment of anxious silence until Jackson yelled, "They got it." He was about to shout some other expression of joy when they heard a human voice outside the shack, and the radio went dead again.

Gilly and Drewer had watched the landing from their small motorboat that followed the four assault landing craft to shore. They saw the ramps of the craft being lowered and experienced the sight of one thousand six hundred forty-nine cats springing out onto dry land. It was clear that the animals were a trifle mystified. At first they moved toward the higher ground cautiously, with much sniffing of the air and considerable meowing. When George saw they were about a hundred yards inland, he ordered his own boat close to the shore, then, jumping into the shallow water, he motioned Drewer to follow.

Both men felt hot and sticky under their rubberized overalls and long rubber boots they had been advised to wear for the trip ashore. Gilly had a loaded carbine in case an encountered any live rats, while Drewer carried two cameras to photograph any live or dead rodents for the record. The two men moved slowly, scanning each yard of the ground ahead. Then, as the cats began to spread out on the run uphill, they halted. Gilly was puzzled;

where in the hell were the rats? Raising his binoculars, he focused them on the shack on top of the western rise.

"Holy cow!" he exclaimed. "It's not possible."

"What is it?" asked Tom Drewer.

"I think I see something. It's moving—in the window. Yes, it is—oh, shit. Its a man."

"What?"

"It's a man," cried Gilly. "Someone's in the hut."

"A man? You've gone nuts, George. It can't be. They were all evacuated. Let me see." Drewer focused on the hut. "By all that's holy, it is a man."

"Stop a minute, Tom. There's something wrong here."

"Sure is," replied Drewer. "I don't see a single rat."

"Nor do I. But there's someone in that shack."

"I saw a face at the window too."

"Do you suppose it's someone who got left behind?" asked Gilly. "I think I'll give them a yell."

At just the same time as Gilly took a deep breath, the cats stopped their advance, raised their noses once to sniff the air, gave another deep-throated howl and bounded away from the shack toward the eastern portion of Mitzu. Both men stood there wide-eyed as the entire mass of screeching fur disappeared over the crest of the hill.

"Rats?" said Drewer with a look of utter bewilderment.

The light sea breeze coming in from the northeast provided the answer. Gilly sniffed the air, then smiled. "No," he replied. "Fish. A bit stale, but it's fish."

Major Gilly then gave out his loudest yell, and both men moved forward with quickened pace toward the signalmen's shack.

Within minutes of getting the SOS message from Mitzu, Bulabar had passed it onto the State Department in Washington.

The secretary of state appeared stupefied by the message. He couldn't believe his eyes. He reached for the phone.

"Yes?" General Howell sounded very far away.

"General, have you got the Mitzu message?"

"Which one?" asked the general.

"Which one? For God's sake, the one about the cats."

"Surely, Mr. Secretary, you mean the rats."

"No General, I mean this damned SOS from Mitzu, telling us the bloody island is being overrun with cats."

"Good God! What's happened?" asked Howell with alarm in his voice.

"How the hell do I know? I thought you people and the Brits had all this under control. By the way, have you informed the defense secretary?"

"No, sir. He should be back from Alaska soon. I'll brief him as soon as he gets back, or would you prefer to tell him yourself?"

"No, General, that's up to you, and the sooner the better. I have an idea he's not going to like this at all."

The secretary of state hung up.

CHAPTER XXVI

General Topps, together with Admiral Stagg, Air Marshall Burrows, and Mr. Rollins, had just arrived back in London from Washington. All four men were tired, but at Topps' insistence they followed him to his office to read the latest reports on Operation Feline. The general's orderly brought in a pot of tea, and they had just had a second cup when the telephone rang. General Topps snapped up the receiver in his usual debonair manner.

"Hello, this is Topps. Yes?" The three others were on their feet and on their way to the door, and the admiral had just opened it when the general yelled, "Wait." They turned to face him and saw General Topps' face undergo a series of color changes as he listened to the easily recognized high-pitched wailing of the British defense minister's voice.

"What the devil could have happened?" the admiral asked Rollins quietly. "Surely no one has told the defense minister about the foul-up on Mitzu?"

Rollins hoped not, as he had himself abided by General Topps' direction and had not even mentioned it to the foreign secretary. After all, Topps had said to wait till tomorrow night; that was tonight. Mr. Rollins was uttering a silent prayer of hope that neither the admiral nor the air marshall had tried to beat the gun when the general's cry of anguish interrupted his distressed thoughts.

"What?" General Topps, tone was one of distinct disbelief. "Oh, no—no, sir, there must be some mistake. There must be, sir. Are you sure, sir—are you? You are. But, sir, we got the request directly from the U.S. government through the Foreign office from Washington. Yes of course, through the foreign Office. Yes, we most certainly did." The General's voice had begun to take on a note of despair.

As Topps listened, the others could see the perspiration begin to gather on General Topps' face. General Topps glanced at each of the men in turn. His usual smile had vanished. Air Marshall Burrows was lighting a cigar with a shaking hand. The admiral was counting his pocket change and trying to hum a few bars of "Anchors Away" under his breath. Rollins was pulling at his nose, obviously in deep thought.

As he leaned against the wall with his eyes closed, Rollins looked quite ill.

"Look, sir," Topps said, shaking his head, "This whole thing smells to high heaven. I am sure there must be a mistake—it just can't be right. There must be a mistake, sir, of course. They must be referring to the rats. Yes, rats. Yes, sir, oh, I will."

When he replaced the phone, the general's face bore the look of a beaten man. Topps produced a large blue silk handkerchief from his well–cut sleeve and mopped his face, while the gaze of the other men focused on him.

The air marshal spoke first. "Something else wrong?" he asked glumly.

"Now what's the newest crisis?" The admiral's tone was suspicious.

"That," said Topps, "was Mr. Nicholas Farr, our ever wandering minister of defense. Yes, my friends, something is very, very wrong. Mitzu has just come on the air with an SOS."

"Good Lord, the poor fellows." The admiral sounded sympathetic. "I guess the cats didn't make it."

"But that's impossible," cried Rollins. "Didn't the rescue force get there at all?"

"I'm not so sure. The SOS said cats," replied Topps.

"Cats?" said Rollins. "Oh, surely not; it couldn't be."

"Well, I'll be damned," said the admiral with a forced laugh.

"Look, gentlemen, this is no laughing matter," said Topps. "Here it is: Mitzu has just sent out an SOS. They report that hundreds of cats have landed on the island and are overrunning it. The cats are attacking everything in sight and when last seen, were gobbling up the entire island's dried fish supply. Now do you understand?"

Mr. Rollins appeared as if he were going to faint. He found a chair and fell into it. Burrows was chewing hard on his cigar while the admiral merely shook his head woefully.

"But what about the rats?" asked Rollins in a faraway voice. "I was told there were rats there—the report said rats."

"So was I, Rollins. Your guess is as good as mine," offered the general, "But it seems to me someone has boo-booed."

Admiral Stagg looked angry. "Don't look at me," he said. "I only gave the orders to land the cats, I—oh, hell, what's the use?"

"Do you mean to say," said the air marshal, "there were not any rats there at all—that we've all been acting like a bunch of—oh, my God."

"Good Lord, is that it?" yelled Admiral Stagg.

"That's what it looks like," said Topps. "I'm damned if I know what to make of it, but someone has buggered the whole thing up."

Silence fell over the room, but it did not last long. Suddenly the door was almost taken off its hinges as Nicholas Farr, the minister of defense rushed in, his red face at least two shades redder than usual. The others started to rise as he practically ran to the head of the table.

"Oh, for God's sake, sit down. Sit down, all of you," said the frantic Mr. Farr. He placed his hands on the table and glared at the rest of them. "Who the devil is responsible for this—this—this fiasco? Who? I want to know, and I want his resignation within the hour."

The room was strangely silent.

"Well," he said, "who did it? I demand to be told."

Topps took the lead. "I do not know just what you mean, sir," he said very quietly. "Please, sir, if you will calm yourself, we can try to sort this out."

"Calm myself? Calm myself. General, all you can say is, 'Calm yourself?'" The fat man's voice almost reached D above high C. "The whole of creation is falling about my ears, and you—you say, 'Calm yourself.' My God, talk about a fuck-up."

"Sir," said Topps with slow, sarcastic politeness, "All we know is that we got a proper request from the Foreign Office for urgent help because this island of Mitzu was being overrun by rats. All we have done is take the necessary action within the scope of the prime minister's directive, and that is it. Whatever we have done was done at the prime minister's direction, of course."

Mr. Farr was obviously not impressed; he went to the window and stood with his back toward them and muttered to himself for a few seconds. Then he turned angrily on his audience. Like a raging bull, he sniffed the air. "What's that awful smell?" His gaze settled on Air Marshall Burrows, who started to butt his cigar hastily.

"Now," said Farr, "do any of you quite realize the vast amount of money this government has spent in getting Operation Feline underway? Have you forgotten that first our Air Force flew to the States to pick up a huge force of cats-and flew them to the other side of the world, and we sent our Navy a few thousand miles from their base to take the crates from Singabar to Mitzu and ordered hundreds of boxes of cat food? We laid on an evacuation fleet to move the natives and force of assault boats to land the cats. We practically planned another Normandy invasion. And what do we get? I'll tell you, my fine high-ranking colleagues, what we get. We get an SOS from Mitzu, and here it is—I'll read it to you.

He held up the message as if to provide the final proof. "SOS, island invaded by horde of savage cats," he read. "That's only the first one. Here's the second one. Listen to this: SOS, cats now devouring entire island's fish supply. We will hold out as long as we can. SOS."

He looked around the table at the men, all of whom studiously avoided eye contact. "These came an hour ago. God only knows what has happened since. Now I ask you, what in God's name have you fellows done?"

He returned to the conference table and paused as he rested his hands on the glossy surface. "Now, it's too late to worry or argue about how all this happened. What you must do is undo it all and as soon as possible. And, of course, in complete secrecy. There must be no fuss at all. Then, and this is important, we must get the two American officers sent out to Mitzu, back home—back home and back to civilian life or wherever they came from. You, Burrows, had better arrange with the Yanks to get a plane to Mitzu without delay to get those two officers off the island. You, Admiral—you return those ships back to Hong Kong, all of them. And, please, not one move other than these will be made without telling me. Oh, God." He shut his eyes and massaged his temples. "Now I'm off to the Prime Minister. He'll have a bloody stroke when he hears about this."

"But what about the cats?" asked Topps. "What do we do about them?"

"Surely I don't have to bring the damned things back, too?" said Admiral Stagg. Burrows also hoped not.

"Oh, yes, the cats," said Farr. "Get in touch with whoever is in charge on Mitzu. Just tell him to dispose of them. By the way, who is it? The prime minister will want to know."

"A Major Gilly, he's an American," said Topps. "He's on loan to us."

"All right, all right," said Farr testily. "Tell Gilly to give us whatever plan he has for the disposal of the cats. No, better still, tell *him* to dispose of them as he sees fit—humanely, of course. But for God's sake, don't let one word of this get out, or the SPCA will be on our necks." He made for the door and, as he opened it, he turned. "And let's get on with it. Good day." Then he muttered, "I hope you realize this bugger-up will probably cost me my job." He slammed the door.

For a full twenty seconds after the defense minister's departure, there was a complete silence. Then General Topps rose, and he, too, made for the door. The others followed without a word—at least, not one word was audible.

Back on Mitzu, George Gilly and Tom Drewer were going over the events to date with Morton and his three companions—or at least two of them. Alfred Watowski, still in a state of semishock, had decided to take a long walk by the sea to ease his shaky nerves.

To the men on Mitzu, it was now obvious that someone had made a ghastly error.

After a short meeting, George returned to the *Bulldog* to discuss the matter with the skipper. He requested the skipper to wait at his mooring, signal his base at Singabar, explain what was happening and ask them to relay the news to British Defense Headquarters and to the Pentagon.

It was some twenty-five minutes later that the HMS *Bulldog* captain replied that he had Singabar on the air and had passed George's message on for transmission to the two capitals. Now there only remained to hear what Jansen's instructions would be.

The cats were certainly causing no trouble. In one sense at least, they were quite happy; they had found their way to the island's supply of dried fish, eaten their fill, and now most of them were contentedly sleeping off their first good meal in days.

Mitzu's inhabitants, however, did not take lightly to the invasion of their island home. The drying sheds had held their food supply for the coming months of the rainy season, and in short order a delegation of the older islanders presented themselves at the weather hut to appeal their case to Staff Sergeant Morton.

Led by Yung Bhop, the little group of islanders approached the weather station slowly. It was Morton who met them, spoke to them a while and then asked George Gilly to step outside. The result of the introduction was surprising—to Morton, anyway.

"Gilly-san!" cried Yung Bhop with a bow.

George looked surprised, then he ran toward the headman and hugged him. He then circulated happily among the rest of the delegates, shaking each by the hand warmly and greeting each one in Pagudan.

"You mean you know these fellows, Major?" said the surprised staff sergeant.

"Sure do," replied Gilly. "I was here for five years. They're old friends."

"Well, I'll be damned," said Morton. "Well, in that case, you'd better tell them the story—or what you can of it. I sure as hell can't explain it."

"Suppose we hear what they have to say first," said George, turning to the headman.

Despite his elation at seeing Gilly, Yung Bhop was not a very happy man. Their reserve of food was gone, and all the islanders were wondering what would happen now.

George raised his hand to break the chatter of the others. He spoke to them in broken Pagudan and tried as best as he could to explain the story of what had happened. George started in by relating that a report of a plague of rats had reached the mainland, that he had been given the job of bringing the cats to Mitzu to destroy the rats, and that boats had also been sent to remove the people to safety. As George unfolded the story, Yung Bhop relayed the information, translating with frequent gestures to the other natives. Gradually, the glum and bewildered faces again took on a look of understanding and trust; they became quite calm. No doubt about it, thought Morton, this fellow Gilly has a way—with the natives here anyway.

"Then," said Yung, "Does it mean we do not have to leave our homes and move to the mainland?"

"That's right," said Gilly, "you do not have to move. You can go back and tell your people to start unpacking. All is well, it was all a mistake. You will all stay here."

"But our food supply, what about that, Gilly-san?" asked another of the delegation.

Gilly broke into Pagudan to reply. "Don't worry, any of you. Please go back and tell your people to settle down again and not to worry. The food will be replaced; you can be sure of that." George hoped he had said the right thing.

After a few minutes of further questions and answers, the natives shook hands all around again, bowed deeply and filed back toward their settlement in their usual easy-going style. Morton breathed a sign of relief.

It was a little after seven when George and Drewer decided to walk down towards the beach.

"You'll not see a sunset like this anywhere else in the world," said George as they stood facing the western horizon.

"Curious isn't it. Here we are watching this wonderful sight but somewhere at home someone must be going nuts wondering how this mess got started and who started it."

"No use worrying about it Tom. By the time we get back someone will have it all figured out."

"Damn it George, I was there when General Jansen got his orders form the Chairman of the Joint Chiefs and the State Department. The message General Jansen got most certainly said that there were rats here." The two men turned back toward the shack.

Forget it, it's over Tom," said Gilly. "In any case, Jansen knows the story by now. We'll get our new orders before long, I'll bet you. It'll be good to go home."

Just then Pope's head appeared at the door of the shack. "Hey, fellows," he cried to the others. "I think I have it."

"Oh?" said Gilly, raising his eyebrows. "What?"

"Yeah, what have you got?" said Morton.

"It's the condenser and leads," said Pope. "They're worn out—kaput."

"And the tube," Jackson added from within the shack.

"Oh, yeah, and the tube," said Pope.

"How long will it take to fix?" asked Morton.

"Don't know. One hour, maybe two." Pope disappeared inside again.

"We've got communication to Singabar, if that's what's worrying you," said Drewer. "From HMS *Bulldog* I mean."

"That won't help them much," said George. "Bulabar is on the restricted frequency we are not allowed to use. By the way, how far is it?"

"Bulabar? That's about four hundred miles southwest of the naval base," said Morton.

"Look, did you manage to get any signals off before we got here?" asked Gilly.

"Sure did, Major. Jackson got off two SOSs," said Watowski.

"SOSs?" George was alarmed. "What do you mean?"

"Yes," Morton said. "You see, when we looked out and saw all those bloody cats—well, you can imagine what we thought."

"Christ, I've never had such a fright," said young Watowski, who had just returned to the shack. "I thought I was dreaming or drunk."

"I guess so," said Drewer, "We know these SOS signals are going to scare a few people and cause some trouble."

"Why?" said Morton. "Hell, we thought we were in trouble."

"We sure did," said Watowski. "How will it cause trouble?"

"It will," said George. "Think it over. The first messages that are supposed to have come from here said the whole place was being overrun with rats. Now you fellows have sent SOSs out saying the place was overrun with cats. My God, that'll give the Pentagon and the British Defense Department something to think about. I guess Drewer and I had better get back to the ship. Come on, Tom, we'll try to relay the information to Singabar for them to pass on to Bulabar and try to sort this thing out."

"Yeah," said Drewer, rising, "I guess so."

Next morning aboard the *Bulldog,* Gilly and Drewer had just finished composing a series of lengthy signals to Singabar when the young skipper entered the wardroom.

"Got one here for you, Major." He handed it to Gilly.

"Well, fellows," said George after reading it. "It looks as if Operation Feline is over. This is from General Jansen via Singabar. It tells us to dispose of the cats in a humane manner and that a plane will be here in three days to pick us up and to take us home. The evacuation ships have been recalled." He paused for a moment. "Well, that's it. Drewer and I are to wait here. Skipper, you can leave any time." He passed the signal to Drewer.

"Looks as if someone really has screwed up, wouldn't you say?" said Drewer with a loud chuckle.

"Looks like it," said the skipper. "What are you going to do about the cats? It says here to dispose of them."

George wrinkled his nose in disgust. "I'm not going to worry about it now. I'm tired and I'm going to hit the sack."

"How does one dispose of nearly seventeen hundred cats in a humane manner?" said Drewer. "Holy cow, I wonder who dreamed up this one."

"Let's all hit the sack," said George. "I'm pooped."

This problem of how to dispose of the cats, however, stayed with George far into the night. He lay on his bunk staring at the ceiling wondering how to dispose of over sixteen hundred cats. He was too tired; surely tomorrow he'd think of something. He fell asleep.

George Gilly slept fitfully for about two hours, then opened his eyes to find Drewer sitting on the edge of his bunk. He sat up with some alarm in his eyes. "What's wrong Tom?"

"Nothing, just couldn't sleep. I kept thinking of how we're going to get rid of the cats. Damned if I know. Any ideas?"

"Oh, Tom, I'm too damn tired. We can't shoot them or drown them. We have to get rid of them in some way. Hell, for all I know, we may have to just leave them here."

"Leave them here?" Drewer was puzzled.

"Yes, leave them here and just tell Jansen they've been disposed of safely and humanely. After all, who's going to know the difference? No one's going to come to this place to check, and there's plenty of fish for them to eat. I don't know. I just don't know. God, Tom, go to bed. I'm pooped."

Drewer rose form the side of the bunk. "Okay, George. Anyway, we can settle it in the morning. Good night."

"Good night, Tom. Don't worry, we'll think of something."

CHAPTER XXVII

On Mitzu, the following day, it was nearly siesta time, HMS *Bulldog* had departed some hours earlier and was sweeping its foamy path back to Singabar. George Gilly was sitting on a blanket in the hot sun just outside the weather station shack, writing to Julie. Inside the shack, Morton and the others were unpacking the boxes they had so hastily prepared for the evacuation. Drewer, who claimed some slight knowledge of the working of radios, was with Jackson trying to help in the repair of the long-silent set.

George Gilly looked up as a shadow fell across him. "Oh, hello, Yung." He smiled at his old friend. "I'm glad you came."

"Good day, Gilly-san," said the old man. "May I speak with you?"

"Sure," replied George, "and you may as well sit down." He moved his hand in a broad gesture to indicate a seat on the blanket on the ground beside him.

"Thank you, Gilly-san, but no, I will stand."

Yung Bhop then began a dramatically gestured speech; in it he explained that the islanders were no longer angry about the arrival of the cats nor about the loss of their supply of fish. He and the islanders hoped, in fact, trusted, that the good Major Gilly, whose friendship he and the other Pagudans valued greatly, would see that their food supply was replaced. Besides that, he and the elders of the settlement wished Gilly-san would honor them with a visit, as many old friends were waiting to greet him.

"That's very kind of you, Yung," said George. "We really appreciate your attitude about all this. Don't worry, it will all end well, and I promise you your food supply will be restored. And yes, I will gladly visit the settlement."

Yung grinned happily. "It is you who are kind, Gilly-san. You are indeed our benefactor. My people are now very happy. They think your arrival is a good sign."

"Your benefactor?" George was puzzled. "How come? I mean, why do you say that? I thought this idea of moving would be very upsetting for them."

"No, Gilly-san, I have just come from a meeting of my people, and they wish me to thank you and to ask if it is possible to keep the small fur animals here on Mitzu."

"What?" George was more than surprised. "You really mean that?"

"Yes, we mean it," said the old man. "We would like to keep them."

"Hey, Morton, Drewer, all of you, come out here," George shouted.

As soon as the other five men were gathered about him, he asked Yung to repeat the question. He did so.

"Wait a minute," said Morton warily. "You actually mean you want to keep all the cats here on Mitzu? But why?"

Gilly and Drewer exchanged apprehensive glances.

"Why not?" Drewer said.

"It's one way of disposing of them." Morton agreed.

"Wait a minute, Tom," said Gilly, then looked at Morton. "Staff Sergeant, what do you think?"

Morton nodded to Gilly, then addressed the old man. "Tell me, Yung, why do your people want to keep the animals here? Do you like them—is that it?

"Yes, we all like them, Mr. Morton," replied Yung Bhop. "We think they are very nice for the children, and the women think they are beautiful. We would like to keep them."

"Well, what do you know," Morton said, shaking his head. "This would be a quick answer to our problem, Major."

Gilly stood up and shot a quick look at Drewer, whose facial expression was almost one of joyful anticipation.

"Well, now," George said, "I really don't know what to say. What I mean is—I'll have to think about it."

Gilly beckoned to Drewer and pulled him to one side. "Any ideas, Tom?" he asked. "What do you think?"

"Well, I don't know," Drewer said. "It's a possibility, isn't it? What I mean is, we've been ordered to dispose of them, haven't we? And we would be doing it humanely."

"Yes, we have, but we'll see." George Gilly stroked his unshaven chin. It was evident he wasn't at all sure about this. "I'll just have to think a bit more about it."

"Yung, the officers will consider your request," said Morton quietly. "We all understand your interest. After all, these little animals are very friendly—very valuable too—and they have young ones many times a year, and that would assure you of a supply of them for many years. They could be very useful in case you are troubled by rodents, and they do make good pets, too, for your children."

Gilly suddenly realized that Morton was fast becoming a salesman.

"Yes, we would like that, Mr. Morton. It would make all of us here on Mitzu very happy."

"Yes, I'm sure it would. Well, it might be possible," said Morton, then added, "especially if—well—if we could come to some sort of an agreement."

"Oh, you mean a bargain perhaps, Mr. Morton? My people would be most willing, if you wish."

"Well..." Morton looked at George again. "Well, yes. Yes, a bargain, perhaps. We'll talk about it and call on you later."

The six men had just finished their dinner and were sitting around the table.

"Damn it," said George, "but I can't—I just can't sell or trade government property. Damn it all, it's illegal. It's just not right."

"But why not, Major?" said Watowski. "You've been ordered to dispose of them, haven't you? How else can you do it? This is an easy way to do it and come out on top—if you know what I mean."

Gilly looked at him. "Yes, I do, but—well, it just doesn't seem right."

"Why? Besides," said Pope, "you're not really selling them; you're obeying orders. You're disposing of them."

"And," said Jackson, "who in hell is going to set about shooting sixteen hundred cats? That wouldn't be right now, would it?"

"Hell, we don't have to shoot them," said Drewer. "we could, but—well, we don't necessarily have to shoot them. This looks like a good way out for us."

"Look, Major." Morton stood up to stretch his lean frame. "I don't think you quite realize it, but you do have a good thing here. You have over sixteen hundred cats and you have orders to dispose of them. Those are your orders from headquarters, and the islanders have said they want them. As I told you, I saw Yung again this afternoon, and he's willing to make a damned good trade. We can make a real deal. He'll give you—I mean, us—two good sized pearls for each cat. Now, as I see it, we give them sixteen hundred odd cats, and they'll give us thirty-two hundred odd pearls, and we split them. It's as simple as that. An even trade."

"And," said Watowski, "that's over five hundred pearls each." An awkward silence followed.

"Come on, Major, have a heart," said Pope. "Just think of it. You'll never get a chance like this again."

"Pearls?" said Drewer. "Its's not a bad idea, George. We should give it a thought."

Pope grinned. "I'll say it's not a bad idea.

"That's right—big shiny, white pearls," said Jackson. "They get them from the lagoon. That's what they do in their spare time here. And I'll bet they keep plenty hidden away."

"I know," said George, "but—well, I'm not so sure, but don't they use them to pay taxes?"

"Yes, but in any case, Major," Morton said, trying to press the point home, "let's look at their side of this. There is one thing you do know: Your cats have devoured their entire supply of food, now haven't they? It's only fair to help them out. Besides, if I know the government in Paguda, now that they think rats have been here, you won't see any tax collectors coming here for years."

"That may be true. But, hell, look, men, I don't know what to think. My god, it could mean a court martial for all of us if—I just don't know what to say."

"Well, Major, it's all pretty clear cut to me," said Morton. "We have been ordered to dispose of all the cats. We weren't told how. Just to dispose of them. So we dispose of them; we obey orders."

If George could see Morton's point, his expression did not show it.

"That's right, sir," said Watowski eagerly. "Come on, Major, be a sport."

"Look, Major." Morton seated himself again. "Let's be sensible about this. Just leave it to me. I'll go and do all the work on it. I'll look after it, okay? All you have to do is agree. Just say that we deal."

Gilly looked at Drewer and the other three signalmen. He shrugged. "Oh, what the hell. Go ahead and make the deal."

The next morning Yung Bhop arrived at the weather station earlier than usual. He reported that all the cats had been rounded up and were now safely locked in the fish drying sheds and guarded by admiring young Pagudans. At the same time, he invited the two majors and the four signalers to his home that evening to celebrate the occasion and seal the bargain.

It was an occasion that neither Gilly nor Drewer would likely ever forget. As soon as each of the guests arrived, and there must have been forty, each received a garland of flowers from a bevy of pretty native girls clad in colorful sarongs. They were then treated to a succession of glasses of native wine, after which they seated themselves on low cushions around the multi-colored mat on the floor. The mat was decorated with flowers and laden with more kinds of fruit and varieties of food than either Gilly or Drewer, or any of the others, had ever seen. The meal was both long and enjoyable. Then, after the meal, Yung led them aside, and the negotiations for the proposed bargain began.

The entire process proved rather less painful or embarrassing than Gilly or Drewer had anticipated. Yung Bhop's philosophy was really quite simple: one cat for two pearls. By midnight, after a great many toasts with native wine, bowing and handshakes, the deal was completed. All the islanders were extremely happy. But the evening did not end there. They all returned to the table and enjoyed a special treat. The girls put on a series of native dances. It was a memorable occasion, and George had to admit the food was better than he recalled ever having tasted on Mitzu during his previous tour.

Some hours later, as the first signs of dawn appeared over Mitzu, Staff Sergeant Morton was leading the way home with the lantern. The others followed either singly or in pairs, all a bit wobbly and stumbling as a result of the quantities of heavy native wine they had imbibed.

George Gilly was not quite sure whether he was supporting Drewer, or vice versa. It was Drewer, however who raised the one distasteful point that, had they been completely sober, would not have been passed over so easily.

"Say, that was a damned good meal," exclaimed Drewer. "Damned good meal. Boy, can these guys cook."

"Sure was," mumbled Gilly. "Best damned meal I ever tasted."

Drewer smiled amiably. "Say, I thought you said they only ate fish here. That was the best damned fried chicken I ever tasted, and I've had some good fried chicken in my time."

George stopped on the narrow path. "Wait a minute. I thought that—say, Staff, do you think that really was fried chicken?"

"Come on Major," said Morton warily, "let's hit the hay. It's late and I feel like hell. We can talk about it tomorrow."

"Yes, sir," mumbled the drunken Drewer. "Best damned chicken, best damned wine, best damned girls. Jeez, I'm tired. Let's all hit the damned hay."

"Sure, let's all hit the hay," said Watowski.

"Good idea," said Pope. "Don't you think that's a good idea, Jackson?"

"Yeah, it's a good idea. Ain't it a good idea, Major?"

"Yes," George said quietly. "It's a good idea."

The six men continued on to the shack in silence.

The following morning, during a late breakfast, there was little chatter; it was obvious that each man had only one thought in his mind: that sixteen hundred forty-nine times two divided by six was about five hundred and fifty.

"Seems to me we've done pretty well," said Drewer. "Don't you think so, George?"

"Well, in one way, yes. But I'm still not sure we did the right thing," said George absentmindedly as he sipped his coffee.

"Well, the way I see it," said Drewer, "sixteen hundred forty-nine times two divided by six is—"

The four weathermen chorused the answer happily in unison: "Five hundred and forty nine."

George Gilly suddenly laughed. "Okay," he said, "let's not dwell on it. You do it, Staff Sergeant, you count them out."

"Suits me," said Watowski gleefully. "Oh, boy."

"Me too," said Jackson with equal enthusiasm.

The first count was soon over, but the end of it was marked by an uncomfortable silence. Each man merely stared with wide open eyes at the plate full of glistening pearls resting on the blanketed table in front of him.

"Real beauts, eh?" said Pope. "Here comes my new Chevy."

"Yeah, did you ever see anything like these?" said Morton.

"Wait a minute," Drewer said with an air of authority, "something's wrong. We're short."

"Short?" Staff Sergeant Morton sounded annoyed. "Don't be silly. Who says so?"

"I say so," said Drewer. "I say we're short on the count."

"Wait a minute, Tom," said Gilly. "I don't quite follow you. As far as I'm concerned, we've all got a fair share."

"Sure," said Drewer, "a fair share of what there is here."

"I sure don't get you, Major," Jackson said, shaking his head.

"You heard me," said Drewer. "We're short. We landed sixteen hundred forty-nine cats. We're twenty-two short, see? Look, we landed sixteen hundred and forty-nine. I know, I counted them. So, that figure multiplied by two is three thousand two hundred and ninety-eight. Divide that by six and we each get five hundred and forty-nine pearls with four left over. We only got five hundred and forty-two each with two left over because there were only sixteen hundred and twenty-seven cats. Where did the other twenty-two go?"

"Oh, for Pete's sake, who cares?" Pope said. "Maybe some died on the trip. Who gives a damn?"

"Some may have died. Morton sounded hopeful.

"Yes, but how come?" Drewer said. "If they had died we would have found them. If they didn't, where'd they go?"

"Look, Major, so what? What's a few cats or pearls one way or the other?" Watowski was getting impatient. "Let's just count what we've got."

"Go on, Morton," said Jackson. "Let's count what we've got."

"Hey, wait a minute," said Drewer. "Do you suppose—do you think we—I mean they—no." He rose and made for the door.

The four signalers watched in indifferent silence as he disappeared. George Gilly rose form the table. He had suddenly realized what was bothering Drewer. It was the fried chicken of the night before—fried chicken on an island where there were no chickens. He decided to say nothing and remain standing.

"Yeah, go ahead," Jackson said slowly. "I guess Major Drewer don't feel so good."

They all looked at George.

"You go ahead," he said. "My count is okay. I have my share." George did not feel well. He tried hard not to show it as he made for the door. He needed some fresh air.

"Right," said Morton. "we all count together—get it?"

Once out in the sunlight George looked around and saw Tom Drewer sitting on the sand looking out to sea. He walked over and sat down beside him.

"What's wrong, Tom?"

"Don't you know?" said Drewer.

"Well, I can guess, but there's not a damned thing we can do about it."

"I know, but I thought it was chicken, didn't you?"

"Yes, I did," said George quietly. "What the hell, Tom, we all thought it was chicken."

For a few minutes the two officers sat there silently staring out to sea.

"You know, Tom, things could be worse. At least we're going to get home sooner than we expected."

"I know, George, but damn it, it tasted like chicken. I'd have sworn it was chicken."

"Oh, Tom, quit harping on it. You're going home with a bagful of pearls. Think of that."

"Yeah, I guess so." Drewer rose and started to amble toward the water's edge. He shook his head slowly. "I'd have bet on it, that it was chicken."

CHAPTER XXVIII

Defense secretary Kleffen's aircraft was supposed to touch down at half-past seven at Fairbanks, but Fairbanks reported a severe blizzard and ordered the pilot to go straight on to the test-site area some forty miles to the north, where the weather was defined as clear with good visibility.

The first hint that anything might be wrong came to Horace Kleffen when the pilot informed him that the air controller at the test-site airfield had asked him who his passengers were.

"For Christ's sake, doesn't the fool know I'm expected? Did you tell him I was on board?"

"Yes, sir, I told him, but—"

"Good, well, I just hope they have things properly organized for my visit."

The airport reception area turned out to be one of a dozen or so Quonset huts from the chimneys of which the smoke spiralled slowly straight up to the sky, an indicator of a still atmosphere, but very cold temperature.

"Who the hell is in charge here?" said the secretary as he entered the reception hut.

"I'll be down in a moment," came a hoarse voice from above them. The figure who descended the steps from the control tower was a staff sergeant clad in a long parka. "Hi, gentlemen, what's up?" he said. "Welcome to Test-site fourteen. I'm Staff Sergeant Bender."

Dan Samson looked at the defense secretary, who seemed about to burst a blood vessel.

"Are you in charge here, soldier?" Kleffen asked suspiciously.

"Sure am, mister. Who are you and what—"

"Who am I?" said Kleffen. "You mean you don't know? Didn't Fairbanks tell you we were coming?"

"Well, they started to tell me to expect an aircraft with two passengers, but then the line went dead and I can't raise them on the air. Must be a blizzard. I couldn't even hear your pilot when I asked him who was coming."

"Oh, my God," Kleffen moaned. "What kind of organization am I in?"

"Sergeant, this is the secretary of defense," said Dan Samson. "My name is Dan Samson, I'm a correspondent."

The warrant officer's eyes looked as though they might pop out. "Jesus, the secretary—gee, sir, I'm sorry, I certainly wasn't told to expect you."

"You weren't? I don't understand it. We're here for the tests."

"The tests? Oh, the tests. Yes, sir, but they've been put off for five weeks. Weren't you notified? I thought everyone knew that."

Kleffen looked at Dan. "You hear that Dan? They postpone the goddamn tests and the secretary of defense doesn't even know about it."

"I'm real sorry, sir."

"Oh, don't you worry sergeant, it's not your fault, but I'll sure as hell have somebody's ass for this mess."

At that moment, the pilot appeared with his four crew members. "Everything okay, sir?" he asked.

"No, major, everything is not all right. The sergeant in charge here tells me we were not expected and the tests have been put off for weeks."

"Five weeks, sir," the sergeant offered.

"Whatever. So, I guess the only thing to do is to put up here tonight and then start back tomorrow. Can we do that? I mean, they do have fuel here?"

"Oh, yes, sir, we have fuel and we can kick off tomorrow early," replied the pilot.

"Sir, our accommodation is not too good, but I can put all of you up, okay? Do you mind sharing a hut—you, sir, and Mr. Samson." The sergeant looked apologetic.

After a plain but hearty supper in the simple mess hall with the sergeant and eight enlisted men of various ranks, Kleffen and Samson were shown to their sleeping quarters.

Within a half hour, Dan Samson was fast asleep, snoring like a maniac. Kleffen was not so lucky; Samson's snores and periodic snorts kept him awake most of the chilly night.

Next morning, they were about an hour into the flight homeward, when the pilot gave him more bad news. The port engines were acting up. He would have to force land as quickly as possible, and force land they did.

The emergency airfield belonged to the Royal Canadian Air Force. It was one of a series of such emergency landing areas in Canada's Northwest Territories and was run by an R.C.A.F. staff sergeant and a bunch of Eskimos. For the next four days, a ferocious blizzard engulfed the entire area, and while the sixty-mile-per hour winds whined outside, there seemed to be only one thing to do.

Horace Kleffen and Dan Samson drank up all the whiskey they had brought for the trip. He had never before been so cold. Even the pilot's announcement that they would take off the next day did not help his mood.

"Dan, this is the biggest snafu I've ever experienced. I'm going to have someone's head for this, you mark my words."

"But you'll come back for the tests?"

"The hell with the tests. I'm going home and raise bloody hell about this," he replied. "I'll have that goddamned Howell's balls for this."

"I can't understand how that message about the postponement didn't reach you."

"You can't, eh? Well, I can. It's that damned idiot of a chairman. As I said, I'll have his balls for this one. I'll fix him but good."

Dave Boltin had not been home for more than ten minutes. He was making himself a cup of coffee when his security buzzer sounded. It was Dan Samson.

"Dave, I've got to see you."

"Okay, Dan, come on up."

Boltin was waiting at the door when Samson got off the elevator. Dapper Dan Samson looked like hell; he was unshaven, his clothes were rumpled, and his eyes clearly indicated that he was angry. He tossed his coat and hat carelessly on a chair.

"Of all the goddamn stupid assholes," he blurted out as he dropped himself on the couch.

"Who?" asked Boltin.

"Who? That SOB of a defense secretary, that's who. I'm going to fix him good."

"All right, take it easy, Dan." Dave Boltin sat beside him. "Tell me what's up." Then he rose again. "Coffee or a drink?"

"Drink—I'll take a brandy."

When Boltin returned, he found Samson with his face buried in his hands. He was surprised to see Dan in this unhappy state. "Here, take this. You look as if you need it."

Samson took the glass and downed it in one gulp as Boltin resettled himself beside him.

Over the next hour and over three more brandies, Samson related his experiences. He told Boltin about his contact at the UN, the tumble in the Pentagon hallway and the clues he had gotten from the defense secretary's scattered papers.

"I tell you, Dave, we're on to something big."

"Didn't Kleffen give you anything to go on?"

"Not a thing, damn the old goat."

"That's not like Kleffen—not at all like him." Boltin tried to sound sympathetic.

"I don't know for sure, Dave, but I suspect that bastard invited me to Alaska deliberately to get me out of Washington. I'll bet he's grinning from ear to ear, thinking he's put one over on me."

"Hold it a minute, Dan. If this thing is as big as you say, why don't you let me try my contacts? Tell you what—give me about ten days—looks as if you need a rest right now anyway. That should give me enough time to dig around, and whatever I find, I'll pass it on to you, and you can take it from there. That's a promise."

"You think so, eh?" Dan did not sound convinced. "Well, I suppose we can try it."

"Yes," said Boltin. "I do. Why don't you just take off and have a damned good holiday? You can have my place down at La Romana in the Dominican Republic for a couple of weeks. Lots of food and booze. The housekeeper can look after you, and if you feel like company, I know a couple of real beauties down there. I'll give you their numbers."

Dan Samson suddenly became interested. "You know, Dave, that's not a bad idea. But who handles the costs, airfare, etc?"

"Don't worry, Dan. It's all on the network. I'll have your tickets ready for you by noon tomorrow. Now, you get home and rest. Just trust me."

No sooner had the front door closed behind Dan Samson than Boltin dialed Henry Westerman's number.

"Hello, Henry, sorry to call you at this hour, but Dan Samson just left here."

"That's okay Dave, I'm still up. What's this about Samson? How much does the nosy bastard know?"

"Not a thing, Henry. He's mad as hell at being dragged off to Alaska, but so far, he hasn't a clue. And what's more, tomorrow he leaves for ten days at my place at La Romana. Is that enough time? If it isn't…"

"Ten days? Oh, yes, that's fine, Dave. That's really good—and thanks. I won't forget this favor. By the way, give my love to Jill. Good night."

As Dave hung up, Jill, who had been reading in bed, appeared at the living room entrance.

"Who was that?" she asked with a yawn.

"Hi, honey. Just Uncle Henry."

"And how is Uncle Henry? Nothing wrong, I hope."

"Oh, he's fine, just fine, said to give you his love. You go back to bed. I'll be there in a minute."

The thought occurred to Dave Boltin as he turned off the lights that it was really great to have Henry Westerman in the family. Four years ago, Henry had made sure that Dave Boltin would become editor-in-chief of the network. He also reminded himself that it takes much longer than four years for blood to become thinner than water.

The chairman of the joint chiefs was just about to call General Jansen when the defense secretary burst into his office, followed by the stubby general.

"What in hell is going on?" the defense secretary said.

"I beg your pardon, sir?" General Howell tried to sound unworried. Kleffen was in a highly agitated state.

"You heard me, General. I just got back from Alaska and find we have a real mess on our hands—a real screwup."

The general shook his head. "Sir, I understand something has gone wrong with the Mitzu Operation."

"Wrong? Did you hear that, Jansen? He thinks there's something wrong. Damn right there's something wrong, General. We just got an SOS from Mitzu that the island is being overrun by cats. Didn't the British know the island had to be evacuated first? Didn't they understand that the cats had to be landed *after* the evacuation? Good Lord, gentlemen, what have we got ourselves into? This is a bloody disaster—and that's not all."

He delved into his jacket pocket and produced an assortment of other papers. These two he waved aloft. "I have here two letters. Look at this one, it's from the Game and Fisheries Office, and they say that seaplanes have landed on Billings Lake, which, in case you don't happen to know it, is a government fish preserve. The oil from these aircraft is killing all the fish for miles around. Now, would someone mind telling me what in God's name seaplanes are doing on Billings Lake? If you can tell me, that is. And, I've got another one here—a member from the Billings area has brought up a question in the House as to why so many Caterpillar tractors are sitting idle on the parade square at Camp Billings. I called your chief of Army Engineers, General, and he tells me the commandant of the Engineers School was ordered by *me*—by *me,* mind you—to send all his tractors to Billings, and that when the return of the machines was demanded, the school received some seven crates of your bloody cats. My heavens, gentlemen, what have you been doing? Do you know what's going to happen to all of us if any of this ever hits the papers? I ask you, what in hell is going on, who is responsible for this chaos?"

Howell looked at Jansen. "Can you shed any light on this? You did send the message requesting cats, didn't you?"

"Yes, I did, said Jansen, "and I have a copy of it here. As you can see, it's a perfectly straightforward message and quite clear." Jansen handed the copy to the defense secretary.

"Yes, it does appear to be quite clear," Kleffen said, suddenly calm. He was obviously thinking of his own future. "Well, General, you'd better find out what the British are doing about this and let me know. I gather you are in touch with their people?"

"Yes, sir, we are, and I'll contact them right away."

"Do that, please." Having said that, the defense secretary began to walk out, but at the door he turned. "Oh, yes, one other thing, General, why wasn't I informed that the cold weather tests in Alaska had been postponed for five weeks? Do you realize the president sent me off on a wild goose chase? Why didn't you tell him about the postponement? Here I wasted nearly ten days just because your people don't keep me or the president informed. I shall certainly make sure the president is aware of this lack of communication."

Howell held up his hand, "Mr. Secretary, I regret all the inconveniences, believe me, sir, and if you will allow me a few minutes later today, I will try to explain what has happened. Most certainly, I accept full blame for this and I—"

"Very well, General, I'll see you later this afternoon, but make no mistake about it, I will want a full explanation. I hope to God you can provide it." With that, Horace Kleffen slammed the door behind him.

"Oh, boy," said Howell. "It looks as if either we or the British have boo-booed on this. Let me know what they say, will you?"

Back in his own office, a weary General Jansen sat down to reflect on the day's events. Yes, now that he thought of it, he did remember seeing quite a few tractors, and Colonel Slate had told him about the seaplanes at Camp Billings. He even recalled that he had asked Colonel Slate why they were there, but he could not for the life of him remember the colonel's answer at that time. Anyway, it was too late to worry about it. Now he had to disentangle the whole mess. He wondered if the State Department could be relied upon to keep quiet.

Needless to say, over at the State Department, Mr. Ryder was at that very moment wondering the same thing about the military services.

The president sighed heavily and shook his head in exasperation as he listened to his defense secretary's voice over the phone. He placed one hand cautiously over the mouthpiece and glanced up at General Howell, Brigadier General Torrin and the national security advisor. "Boy, is he mad," he whispered, then his tone changed drastically. "Oh, yes, Horace, I can certainly understand what you've gone through, and you say the tests have been postponed for several weeks? Well, I'm really sorry about this. What's that? You weren't informed about the delay of the tests? Oh, yes, I agree with you. Oh, yes, yes, by all means, arrange an inquiry into it and let me know what you find out. We cannot afford to have this sort of inefficiency. No, sir, I'll not tolerate it. Good, good, Horace, and don't you worry, I'll make sure the chairman hears from me about this. Goodnight."

As he replaced the phone, the president winked at the three other men, then he clapped his hands and chuckled. "I'm afraid, General, you are in for a bit of a rocket from our friend, Horace."

"I'm expecting it, sir," replied Howell.

"By the way, have our British friends got this thing under control yet?"

Howell smiled confidently. "It looks that way, Mr. President. I think they've done very well, all things considered."

"Great. And, General, don't take whatever our friend Horace says too seriously."

"Don't worry, Mr. President, I won't. I've been insulted by experts."

After the three others had left, the president called the vice president, who had just returned from Grenada.

"Hello, Stan, I thought I better fill you in. It's about the point you raised with me yesterday. Yes, Feline. What? Oh, yes, I'm sorry about it, but I couldn't take the chance of compromising security by a cable to you. It's really nothing to worry about. I tell you what, come over for a drink this evening, and I'll tell you the whole story. What's that? Oh, no—no good reason. We deliberately put a PTS classification on it at the start. Yes, on a need-to-know basis strictly. Well, it was one operation we had to make sure of before we said anything to the media. By the way, Stan, how did it go on Grenada? Ah, yes, they do appreciate what we did for them. Good. And I take it you had a pleasant time? Wonderful. Okay, see you this evening."

As he replaced the phone, it occurred to him how fortunate it was to have a running mate who loved to travel.

Back in London, the prime minister was reading the message he had just received from the American president when his secretary announced that Nicholas Farr, the secretary of defense, had arrived.

The prime minister did not even look up. "Show him in."

"Good evening, sir," said Farr. "Looks like snow."

The prime minister looked up and placed both hands on his desktop. "Don't sit down, Nick, you haven't got time."

"Oh," Nick Farr said, surprised. "You wish me to get on to something right away?"

"No, Nick, I don't want you to do anything now—at least not here. I want you to go on an extended tour of inspection of our military bases in NATO, Hong Kong, Belize, and on your way home you can stop off in Ottawa on a liaison visit. And I don't want one word—not one—of Operation Feline mentioned to anyone anywhere, at any time, understand?"

"Good Lord, Prime Minister." Farr's voice took on an angry tone. "Am I to be the scapegoat for this mess?"

"No, Nick, you are not the scapegoat in this matter, but the chief of defense staff and the chiefs of the Navy, Army, and Air Force are hopping mad at you. Apparently your latest verbal lambastings at them had quite an effect. I'm afraid, Nick, old chap, that they are not too fond of you, and I can't afford to have them resign. Your absence will give them time to cool off." He paused and looked away. "If there is any scapegoat in this affair, it's me. I agreed to help the Americans; I agreed to the use of cats. The three services did exactly what I asked of them. From what I know now, someone at the Pentagon started it all. They handed the ball to their State Department, and they ran away with it. We went along without question. Of course, if Parliament gets wind of this, I may have to go myself. But, for the present time, let's not worry about it. You just go on your trip."

"Very well, sir," Farr said quietly. "I'll leave at once. Would you like for me to resign?"

"No, Nick. Maybe later, but not now."

"But I will resign if you want me to."

"No, Nick, just bugger off and do as I say. I'm a busy man."

As soon as Nick Farr had left, the prime minister picked up the red and white phone, intending to call the president and thank him for the message.

"Hello, Mr. President? I want to speak to the president. No, madame, I know you are the president's wife, but this is not a matter I can—please, let me—what? I'm sorry madame, I realize you are quite capable of conveying my message, but I still cannot discuss this with you. I beg your pardon? I regret, madame, I wish only to speak to your husband. Thank you, and goodbye."

As the prime minister replaced the phone, his private secretary entered and laid some papers before him. Seeing his master was gazing thoughtfully down at his cupped hands, he asked. "Sir, is anything wrong?"

"No, Albert," the prime minister replied, "not here, there isn't anything wrong here. But somehow, it appears that the powers of the president are about to be usurped by his overly ambitious, over-educated and—"

"Oh, you mean his vice president, sir?"

"No, Albert, not *that* poor chap. The wench, old boy, the wench. I think she wants his job."

Seated at her desk at the White House the president's wife gazed at the phone in her hand. "What a rude bastard," she said and slammed the instrument down.

"Who, Madame? said Daisy, her secretary.

"That silly prime minister, that's who. Daisy, what do you think of the British who visit us here?"

"Some of them talk funny. Sometimes I can't understand what they say. A friend of mine says they're all snobs. I don't know. Are they?"

"Who cares if they are or not? They still think they own the whole damn world. Just wait until we start telling them and the rest of Europe how to handle their problems."

"Do you think they'll listen?"

"They better listen." She rose and went over to her bar trolley. "They better listen, and the French and the others we've saved over the past years. That stupid man. Who does he think he is?"

"You mean—"

"I mean that damned prime minister, that's who." She reached for the silver martini mixer and began to shake it.

CHAPTER XXIX

The two majors were flown out of Mitzu late that afternoon. George Gilly was naturally happy at being recalled, and especially at the prospect of a speedy reunion with Julie. Tom Drewer, however, was not in good shape. He was suffering from the effects of the previous evening; he had a distinct hangover and was snoring in his seat even before the aircraft left the ground.

It was a quiet journey, with only two stops—Manila and Honolulu—after which the aircraft headed into the rising sun, and George Gilly went to sleep.

At Andrews Air Force Base, they were met by a tall and elegantly attired colonel who announced he was from General Jansen's office, and a motorcycle escort of two outriders. This rather worried the two majors, but within half an hour they were shaking General Jansen's hand.

General Jansen appeared in an extraordinarily good mood. "By God, gentlemen, welcome home. I'm really glad to see you. You've certainly had quite an adventure. Sit down, please. In due course you must tell me all about it.

Jansen was obviously in top form today. "Well, now," he said, after the two officers had seated themselves. "I trust you're not suffering any ill effects from your experience. You probably have a great deal to tell me."

"To tell you, General?" asked George. "Don't you know about—well, sir, about what happened—on Mitzu?"

"Oh, that." Jansen's smile faded somewhat.

"Yes," said Drewer, "There weren't any rats there. Someone must have—"

The general appeared slightly uneasy as he seated himself. "Of course, of course," he said, "a regrettable error, gentlemen, a most regrettable error. But, as you know, one can't go through life without making the odd mistake. The main thing is to profit by it—but it's all over now. And, what is more important, you are both back home safe and sound. That is the main thing, of course. Yes, it certainly is the main thing, isn't it?"

"Yes, thank you, sir," said Drewer, although he couldn't quite figure out why he said it.

"Now," Jansen went on, "do I take it that your—well, your charges have been disposed of in a satisfactory manner, as we ordered? You know what I mean, of course?"

"Oh, yes, General, you mean the cats," replied George slowly. "Yes, sir, very satisfactorily."

"And, of course," said the smiling Jansen, "in such a manner that we shall not hear of them again, I hope. Am I correct in that assumption?"

"Absolutely, sir," said Drewer.

George sincerely hoped so.

"Well now, that's fine, fine!" General Jansen stood and began to pace the room. "But now, I have very good news for both of you. You, Major Gilly, are to be released from active duty at once and returned to your civilian status, but with the rank of lieutenant colonel. You, my boy, are going home. You, Drewer, are also promoted and will go on leave as of today, and then you are getting a new assignment—a very good one too—out of the country. As a matter of fact, over in NATO, as a liaison officer with the Turkish Army.

"Did you say the Turkish Army, sir?" Drewer did not sound at all elated.

"Yes, in Turkey. With NATO. You'll enjoy Istanbul, I'm sure. Well, anyway, we're all very pleased with both of you. You two officers carried out a most delicate mission and made us all very proud of you. Certainly I know of no other two men who could have done it so well. But, all in all, I need hardly tell you, gentlemen, that for obvious reasons the matter must remain presidential top secret. Is that quite clear? I hope you both understand that."

Both men nodded.

"Good, good." General Jansen rose, faced them, and held out his hand. "It really was nice work, very well executed, and we all owe you a great deal."

Jansen's phone rang. As he listened, Jansen's face lit up. "Yes, sir?" He placed his hand over the receiver and turned to George. "Don't go yet, it's the defense secretary. Oh, very surely, sir. Yes, sir, yes, I know they'll be pleased. Three? Yes, sir. I'll have them there."

As soon as he replaced the phone, General Jansen rubbed his fat hands together. "Well, well, gentlemen, this certainly is a day full of surprises. That was the defense secretary speaking from the president's office, and he tells me you are both to be awarded a decoration. My, my, do you realize this hasn't happened in a long time? Gentlemen, this is great. Now, both of you, you're expected at the administration unit to get all your discharge and leave and other documents fixed up, but be at the secretary's office at three. I'll see you there." He fairly bounded forward to shake their hands.

Elsewhere in the Pentagon, however, especially in the defense secretary's office, things were not going too well.

"But, sir, you do not seem to quite understand," said Major Loften, the secretary's new aide. "This is a PTS matter."

"Oh, what don't I understand, major?"

"Sir, I do not think we have any suitable decorations for this sort of operation. The British have them. They have them for practically everything, but we don't unless you are prepared to write up a proper citation for them, and since this is a PTS matter, that might prove unwise. We cannot afford any publicity on this—we can't."

"I don't care, I tell you," Kleffen bellowed. "I asked the president if we could award them a medal, and he agreed to it. As a matter of fact, he said it was a good idea. Damn it, Major, there must be something we can give them."

"But, sir, I repeat, this is a PTS matter."

"I'm not interested in any of your arguments, Major. I tell you, I want two commendation medals of some sort here by three o'clock this afternoon to award to these two officers, and that's all there is to it. Who makes these damn things, anyway?"

"The government does, sir but—"

"There you go again, Major. Look, I'm not interested in your blasted excuses. You go to wherever these things are available. Tell them the president has to have two suitable medals of some kind. Tell them anything, but get me those damned medals here by three o'clock, and that's my last word. Now get going, and let's get this thing over."

Under normal circumstances, Major Loften's task of getting two commendation medals by three o'clock that afternoon should not have been too difficult. There was a department that handled this sort of thing, and the mere hint that they were required by the defense secretary would be enough argument to get them. Apart from this, the major had a close friend in that department, Captain Joe Kenton, his brother-in-law. He called him.

"Hello, Joe. Johnny here."

"Hi, Johnny, how's the boy?"

"Fine, thanks. Look, Joe, the secretary wants two commendation medals by three this afternoon. Any problem?"

"Uh-oh. Yes, there is. We haven't got any now, but there's a batch due next week. Can't it wait?"

"No, Joe, it can't. By the way, where are they made?" asked Loften. "Damn it Joe, I can hardly hear you. Where? Oh, some small shop in Georgetown. Some Italian has the contract. Listen, I don't want to get into this on the phone, how about if we meet for a cup of coffee in the cafeteria, say in ten minutes, okay?"

Ten minutes later Loften looked across the table at his brother-in-law.

"Did you call him up?" he said.

"Who?"

"The Italian who makes these things."

"Yes, I did. His brother said he's on holiday in Italy."

"Oh, God," Loften mumbled. "There must be some way to get the damn things."

"Well," said Kenton, "we have plenty of the higher awards, but we just don't have any of the ordinary ones on hand."

"I've just got to find them somewhere. Look, Joe, can you let me have the address of this Italian? Perhaps if I go there, he might have something. Oh, hell, look at this." Loften had scribbled the letters PTS on one of the paper table napkins and pushed it across to his brother-in-law.

Kenton took one look and whistled. "Hot damn, you're kidding."

"No, I'm not, Joe. This is for real," said Loften, retrieving the napkin and putting it in his pocket.

"Ye Gods."

"For God's sake, Joe, take it easy. We could both end up in trouble."

Joe Kenton gulped his coffee, looked at Loften for a few seconds and then produced a small piece of paper.

"Here's the address in Georgetown, but you'll have to cover for me if anyone starts asking questions."

"Thanks, Joe. Can you call him again so he won't be surprised when I turn up?"

"Okay, I'll call him, but you'd better take proper requisition forms with you."

"Don't worry, I will, and thanks."

It was a small, grubby looking stone building near the river. Loften pressed the bell and looked at his watch. He saw it was just after two o'clock.

When the door opened, a short and dirty, bearded man of about fifty greeted him with a frown. "What you want? My brother in Italy."

"Is this the place where I get the medals?"

"Oh, you fellow from Army office."

"Yes, I am."

"Okay, this place make medals. You come in."

As Loften stepped inside, the man secured the lock on the front door.

"Why the lock?" said Loften.

"Lock? Oh, my brother in Italy. He say to me, keep place safe all the time."

"You make the medals here?"

"Sure, me and my brother. We got contract with Army. You want medals?"

"Yes, that's why I'm here. I need two commendation medals today."

"That's too bad."

"Too bad? Why? Don't you have any?"

"Commendation medal, no got. Good conduct medal I got. You take good conduct, is okay."

"I guess so," Loften said exasperated.

"Okay, you come to shop."

The bearded man nodded toward the back room, and Loften followed him into what was obviously a workshop. There was a long counter along one side.

"You see, all new today," explained the grubby Italian, pointing to the rows of shiny objects.

Loften was about to pick one up when the bearded Italian cried out a warning.

"No, no, not yet pick up. Too damn hot, finish not dry. Have to wait."

"Is this all you have, good conduct medals? I mean, can't you find any of the others I can have?"

"What you mean, others?" said the Italian with obvious annoyance. "You want or you no want?"

Good God, thought Loften. "Yes, yes, I want. I want two."

"You got paper for taking medals?"

"What?"

"My brother, he say you gotta have paper."

"Oh, yes, you mean the requisition form, I have it here." Loften produced the form and handed it to the other, who inspected it.

"What is name here?" the man asked, pointing to the place where Loften had made an attempt to fake the secretary's signature.

"That is the secretary's signature."

"Who? Secretary? My brother say lady's name no good on paper, must be boss. Boss name okay."

"Look, that is the boss's name, the secretary of defense."

"Okay. Okay, boss sign paper. You wait, I make package. But you careful, metal still hot—glue on box wet."

By two forty-five, Loften was back in Kleffen's office with two red velvet covered boxes. As he placed them on the secretary's desk, he noted that the glue on the boxes wasn't quite dry. He was sure he could feel the heat from the recently molded medallions. He hoped the recipients might be late; these things took time to cool.

Gilly, Drewer, and General Jansen arrived promptly at ten to three, and Loften asked them to wait in the secretary's anteroom.

The secretary was late, as usual, arriving at quarter after the appointed hour, and he was not in a good mood. As he passed the three waiting men, he did not even glance at them but just as the door closed to the secretary's office, Jansen heard the secretary's voice.

"Who the hell are they, and what the hell are they doing here, Major?"

"Sir, don't you remember? Those are the two officers from Mitzu. You asked them to be here, and I have the medals."

"The medals? What medals? Oh, yes, the medals. Well, let's see them."

The major opened the top red velvet box and exposed the bright disc with the red and green ribbon. "There you are, sir."

"What kind of medals are these?" asked the secretary.

"They are good conduct medals, sir," Loften replied.

"Good conduct? Couldn't we get anything better than that? I mean, a secretary of defense doesn't hand out good conduct medals. Any officer can give those out. Is that all we could get?"

"They were fresh out, sir. These are the new batch. I'm sorry, sir, it's all they had available, unless you're prepared to make out proper citations for a more important decoration—and in view of the PTS classification, I would not recommend it, sir."

"And what about the photographers? Why aren't they here to record this event? What's the matter with our public relations people? And why didn't you call Dan Samson? He'd give us a good write-up of all this."

"Sir, we can't have Samson or the PR people here. When General Howell found out from the president that you planned to decorate these officers, he called me and asked me to remind you this is still PTS—no publicity, sir."

"Well, in that case, let Jansen give them the medals. How about that?"

"I do not think that would be wise, sir," Loften said. "After all, you, sir, are the one who suggested these awards to the president."

"Yes," said the disgruntled secretary. "I suppose so. Well, get them in here, and let's get it over with. I have other things to do."

The ceremony, if it could be called that, did not take long. As George Gilly and Tom Drewer stood at attention, the secretary pinned the medals on their chests. He shook hands with each of the majors, and it appeared that he was about to walk away from them when General Jansen gave out a loud cough. The secretary looked at him.

"Oh, yes," he blurted out, "of course. Those awards are—er—are for your devotion to—er—duty, gentlemen, Yes, that's right. Isn't it, Jansen?"

"Right, sir," said General Jansen.

"Yes, very definitely, devotion to duty. Thank you, gentlemen. Thank you. Now, if you'll excuse me, I'm late for a meeting." Kleffen picked up a sheet of paper from his desk and left the room.

"I'm sorry, sir," said Major Loften to General Jansen, "but the chairman made it quite clear there was to be no publicity. I hope you agree, sir."

"Don't worry about it," Jansen said quietly. "I understand your problems. Thanks anyway."

George Gilly was glad it didn't last long. All he wanted to do was get his travel tickets from Jansen's administrative officer and be on his way home. He also had to phone Julie to warn her of his arrival.

General Jansen had wanted to take the two majors to meet the Chairman of the Joint Chiefs and asked Gilly and Drewer to wait in his office while he called for an appointment.

The general had no luck at all. The chairman had suddenly decided to visit certain units in Hawaii. When he called the office of the national security advisor, he was informed the advisor was just leaving for a conference in Barbados.

Undaunted by these disappointments, Jansen decided to try the secretary of state's office, only to be told that he had already departed for NATO headquarters in Brussels.

Of all the main players in the Mitzu operation, only the president, General Jansen, Majors Gilly and Drewer, and Horace Kleffen remained in Washington. Only these five had any knowledge of operation Feline or of the strange circumstances associated with its termination. Oh well, thought Jansen, perhaps it's best that way. With all the principals involved away in widely separated parts of the world, there was little chance of the matter being brought up in the immediate future.

The secretary of defense was tired. He felt he'd had enough for one day. He scribbled a note to his aide and departed for home much earlier than usual.

At six-twenty-five, clad in his red smoking jacket and matching velvet slippers, with a large martini in hand, he settled himself to watch Dan Samson on the international news. He rarely missed Samson's half hour and was wondering what might come out of the latest sex scandal involving his old friend Senator Wylie, when an unknown voice interrupted his thoughts.

"Good evening, America, this is the international news, and this is Peter Flint, standing in for Dan Samson, who is on vacation prior to his transfer as network station chief in Istanbul. Kleffen leaned forward, turned down the sound, picked up the phone and dialed Dave Boltin's number. It rang once, then Boltin's familiar voice came through.

"Hello, Boltin here."

"Hello, Dave, Horace Kleffen. What's happened to Dan?"

"Oh, Dan? Sad business, Mr. Secretary," Dave replied.

"Sad? I don't understand. He's not dead, is he?"

"No, sir. He's okay, but we had to move him. He's been on vacation in the Dominican Republic. He needed a rest. But he's been calling the president of our network in New York repeatedly and babbling about some crazy idea he has that the government is developing some new system of chemical warfare using small animals as carriers. Our president is fed up. He thinks Dan is going mad. I think so too, so we decided to extend his vacation and then move him to Istanbul next month. We didn't mind his nutty ideas too much, but when he actually threatened our network president and accused him of covering up for the Oval Office—well, we all felt that was a bit too much. Overwork, that's probably what's wrong with him."

"I see, Dave, but does he have anyone on the hill who will listen to him?" Kleffen asked worriedly.

"Not a soul, Mr. Secretary. They all hate his guts. He hasn't a single friend in the House."

"Is that good or bad, Dave? For you, I mean."

"For us, sir, it's too bad, really. Yet for the country as a whole, I'd say it's good."

"Yes," Kleffen said quietly, "I suppose it is."

"Anything else, Mr. Secretary?"

"No, thanks, Dave, just wanted to know about Dan. Good night." Horace Kleffen hung up, reached forward again and turned up the volume.

Further afield, down in the Special Locations Section of the Pentagon, Horatio Bixon was feeling rather pleased with himself. He stood back and surveyed his secret map with pride, then stepped forward to place a small green flag on the island of Mitzu. This now indicated that the airstrip on the island was again in operation. The last few weeks had been something of a harrowing experience for Horatio. He recalled receiving an inquiry about Mitzu from the Air Force, and he had answered it. Then for some reason he had not yet been able to discover, he had been ordered to close Mitzu and place it on the inactive list till further notice and to inform Mr. Ryder of the State Department to this effect. Today he had received another order, this time to reactivate the airfield on Mitzu and to effect an immediate resupply of the emergency stores there with fourteen thousand cans of assorted cat food. This was now being done. He decided to call Mr. Ryder and report this fact. The conversation, as it turned out, was short.

"Hello, Ryder here."

"Hello, Mr. Ryder?" said Bixon eagerly.

"Yes, go on, this is Ryder."

"Oh, sir, this is Major Bixon, Special Locations Section."

"Yes, Bixon?"

"It's about Mitzu, sir. I—"

"Go to hell, Bixon."

"Sir?"

"I said go to hell."

"Yes, sir."

"And, Bixon?"

"Yes, sir?"

"Oh, nothing. Just go to hell, and while you're there, screw yourself."

After Ryder replaced the phone, he studied the posting instructions he had just received from Personnel. They informed him he was to be the new U.S. chargé in Kinshasha in the Congo, and he was required to report for duty within ten days.

In contrast, in certain Pagudan government circles, everyone was elated at the outcome of the operation to aid the little island. The hundreds of thousands of dollars worth of accommodations and medical supplies the U.S. government and Mr. Charles Quentin Stark had so generously provided were going up for immediate but cautious sale.

Notice of this bonanza was speedily circulated to a select group of ministers, who then approached their favorite local firms. Within a few hours of the announcement, one firm made a particularly lucrative bid, one the Pagudan minister of trade lost no time in authorizing. He explained to the Sultopan and other colleagues that the firm that had won the bid was going to be nationalized anyway within the next three months.

Some of the prefabricated bungalows originally designated for the prospective evacuees from Mitzu had also been put to good use. These were wisely and speedily erected near a variety of foreign embassies, and arrangements were in progress to rent them out to the foreigners at excellent rates.

Mr. Wilson, despite his elation with his personal local success, still wondered whether he might be recalled home. In the meantime, however, he was pursuing his normal ambassadorial duties, reviewing the latest demand for aid from the Pagudans. The request was indeed a strange one. They now wanted two hundred tons of cat food. According to the Pagudan secretary of state, Mr. Heng, it was to be sent to Mitzu to reward the cats that had so valiantly battled and eliminated the rats on the island. The ambassador could not see any fair way to refuse this request, for, as Mr. Heng so politely reminded him, had not Mr. Wilson's own government arranged to place the cats on the island in the first place? Mr. Wilson was regretfully obliged to admit the truth of this statement.

He therefore called in Miss Loffatt and drafted a message, recommending that the cat food be provided with all possible speed. After all, he thought, the sooner this whole damned affair was pushed into the background, the better. But being a man with an eye for the future, he also dispatched a letter to his broker with an order to buy a thousand shares in Continental Pet Foods. If he remembered correctly, that was the main firm the government purchaser dealt with back home.

A week later at the Far East Air Headquarters at Bulabar, test flight number 255 had been reinstated on the planning board and was given the all-clear to proceed to Hong Kong. The long cable from Major Bixon contained some pleasing information; it reported that the crisis on Mitzu was over, that fresh stores and supplies were to be flown in to replenish the Hush-Hush, and that the airstrip was in excellent condition. Flight 255 could proceed.

On Mitzu, it was a busy day for the signalers. The resupply plane had arrived and off-loaded its cargo. Earlier that day, Staff Sergeant Morton had entered the Hush-Hush and brought outside twenty-two boxes of stores and rations on which the expiration dates had long passed. These boxes were now stacked to one side, while the recently arrived new boxes were being handed by Pope and Jackson to Morton, who in turn placed them in neat rows inside the Hush-Hush.

"Well," said Morton after he had set the last box inside. "That about does it." He gave the list on the clipboard a final check, placed it on the hook beside the door and stepped outside.

He walked over to the pilot, who was seated on the ground nearby, enjoying a cold beer. The airman looked up.

"All checked out?" he asked.

"Yep," Morton replied. "All checked out. So, whenever you're ready, you can get your crew to load up these outdated boxes and return them to Bulabar."

The pilot rose and came over to inspect the stack of boxes. "You mean these boxes?"

"Yes, sure. That's the idea," said Morton. "These go back with you."

"I'm sure as hell not taking those boxes back," he said. "Not after the damned rats have been all over the stuff. As a matter of fact, the chief at Bulabar said you'll have to either burn it or take it out to sea and dump it and send him confirmation later."

"Okay, if you say so." said Morton.

"Hey, you fellers," the pilot yelled at the four crewmen standing by the shack. "Okay, guys, we're ready to go. See you the next time, Staff."

"Sure, see you next time," Morton replied.

With the new boxes of supplies safely in the Hush-Hush, Morton signed and dated the inventory sheet by the door, which he closed and locked. He and Jackson then retraced their steps towards the shack.

"Those guys must be nuts," said Jackson. "There's probably lots of good stuff still in those boxes."

Morton stopped. "Hey, wait a minute. Are you thinking what I'm thinking?"

"I'm thinking about all those outdated boxes we're supposed to burn or dump into the sea, and what's in there besides rations?"

"There's the old inventory list still inside the Hush-Hush, I'll check it out," said Morton.

Morton only had to glance at the list. "Well, well, well," he muttered. "Soap of all kinds, clothing, towels, blankets, kitchen equipment, medical supplies and rations." He put the list of date-expired items in his pocket, relocked the huge door and made his way to join the others.

"Hi, Staff," Pope hailed him as he entered. "What's up?"

"What do you know, Santa Claus is here," announced Morton.

"Was I right?" asked Jackson. "Are we back in business?"

"We sure are," replied Morton gleefully. "Tomorrow we move all the old boxes up here, open them and check the contents, then we go into the retail business."

"We what?" asked Pope.

"You heard me," said Morton. "We call Yung Bhop, he's our middleman."

The four signal corpsmen grinned at each other. Life on Mitzu was really not so bad after all.

Yet, amidst the backwash of this unfortunate miscalculation, one bright spot did appear. The world situation, that variable so often tilted by a fiery speech from a world capital, regained a certain aspect of calm. This was probably due, so a reliable diplomatic source reported, to the Soviet dictator's stomach ulcer that, for some inexplicable reason, had suddenly ceased to bother him. For the past week, it was reported, Mr. Kutchevksi had attended a series of celebration dinners, and during the course of each, he had indulged himself in large quantities of both caviar and vodka, all without the slightest twinge of discomfort. He was, to put it clearly, a well and happy man.

Consequently, when, on that cold, bright December day, he made his monthly appearance on Moscow television, he was in the highest of spirits. Mr. Kutchevski waved the palm leaf of peace and goodwill in all directions. He did not even remove his shoes. He offered to meet all heads of all governments anywhere. He agreed to halt all tests of nuclear devices, and to allow the entire U.N. organization to inspect one of his nuclear test sites some five hundred miles north of Ostrov Rudolpha in the Arctic. It was a good omen, so good in fact, that both the

American president and the British prime minister were inclined to agree that the prospects of everlasting peace might not be too far over the horizon.

By coincidence, in Mooneyville Junction the announcement of the highlights of the Soviet premier's speech came on the local radio, and mayor Munro MacKay heard it. About the same time, Julie Gilly got George's phone call from Washington, telling her he was coming home.

Naturally, Julie lost no time in spreading the news of George's return to all her friends; and within a few hours the mayor was at her door. Julie gave him the time of arrival of George's train, and she told him George had been promoted. That was all the mayor wanted to hear.

After all, had not George been called away when the world situation looked its blackest? And now with the world tension eased and the oil spreading on the turbulent waters, George Gilly was coming back. The mayor and undertaker saw it clearly, and Mrs. MacKay agreed; the Defense Department had called upon George for a good reason, probably something very special and very secret. Munro wondered if he might get George to tell him about it later. Perhaps if he made him an alderman or a school board trustee?

When Julie and the mayor's wife arrived at the station, the high school band was, as usual, playing its loudest. A huge crowd had gathered; due to Mr. MacKay's foresight, a school holiday had permitted all the children of Mooneyville Junction to be there. There was an air of excitement as dozens of little flags clutched in tiny hands waved in the light breeze. A platform had been erected with a row of chairs on it behind the public address system, and when the train appeared, the band struck up "Hail, the Conquering Hero," the mayor lit a cigar, and Julie began to weep.

George Gilly looked rather frightened as he stepped down to the platform. He had not bargained for this at all. He wanted only to find Julie and go home. Besides, during his train journey he had fortified himself somewhat with several belts of the excellent whiskey Tom Drewer had given him as a farewell gift.

Mr. MacKay, however, had other plans. After a hasty kiss from Julie, a few handshakes and slaps on the back, George was led to the stand.

Munro MacKay was at his best that day. The mayor told the good people of Mooneyville Junction how, in the darkest hour of the world crisis, one of the town's sons had been called to his country's service. Now, explained the mayor, the crisis was over, the forces of evil had been halted at the very gates of freedom, and George Gilly, the heroic colonel, had been returned to his home and family. There was loud cheering.

During the speech, however, despite Julie's gentle nudging, George successively yawned, twiddled his thumbs and sighed audibly. Mrs. MacKay was evidently displeased, and she even cast the odd glance of benevolent reprimand at Julie. But Julie Gilly was much too happy and excited to care; she merely smiled and held on tighter to her husband's hand. George had almost dozed off when a burst of applause and a heave from the mayor's hand brought him to his senses and to his feet. Before he knew it, George was gazing at the microphone and trying to find words.

Neither George nor Julie will ever remember exactly what it was that George said. He recalled thanking the mayor, the people, the children and the band, and that he was about to tell a joke when from the darkness under the platform came the long, forlorn wailing of a tomcat in search of a mate. George Gilly fainted.

CHAPTER XXX

In the late fall of 1980, John Bosk, now the dean of an eastern school of diplomacy, was enjoying a reunion with two old friends; General Jason Howell, who had recently stepped down from the chair of a West Coast think tank, and Field Marshal Lord Lucius Topps, who had been on a Canadian lecture tour.

After a superb dinner, the three men were in Bosk's panelled study with their coffee and brandy. Eve Bosk had wisely decided to retreat and leave them to their recollections of times long past.

It was Topps who first brought up the subject. "By the way, does anyone have any idea what happened to all the main players in our glorious screw up?"

"You mean Feline?" said Howell with a chuckle.

"Of course he means Feline," Bosk said, shaking his head wistfully. "Well, Lucius, if you really want to know, you certainly came to the right place. What do you think, Jason, should we tell him?"

"Why not?" replied Howell.

John Bosk rose and went to the bar, where he proceeded to open another bottle of brandy. "If we're going to talk about Feline, I reckon we'll need added stimulant." Having popped the cork he returned to his chair but before he settled himself he turned and raised his glass. "Gentlemen, we drink to Feline. After tonight, may it be forgotten forever. To Feline."

The other men raised their snifters.

Bosk looked at his companions for a few seconds and stroked his chin. "Okay, suppose the best place to start is with the president, because it was his dear lady's greed that sparked the investigation that Jason and I were called back into service to handle. Anyway, we all know about the girlie trouble he had during his last year. After he was defeated he retired to his Southern mansion, maintaining to the last that he never received his draft notice for service. Well, one morning he was found, gone to his reward, wearing a Harvard sweat shirt, jogging socks and a condom. It was revealed later that he had spent several nights with a Mrs. Towers, an old friend, in relaxing sexual frolic. One could say, I suppose, that the noble fellow died in the saddle."

At that all three burst out laughing.

"Hold it a minute, there's more." Bosk said. "When his wife lost the power of his office, she abandoned him. It was then that her rich West Coast friends, ever eager to create new business for themselves, introduced her to the heir to a Middle Eastern kingdom. The prince bedded her and wooed her and, in the firm belief she'd become a queen, silly woman, she married him. Alas, no such fortune awaited her. After a very short time of her attending to the prince in the royal bedchamber, he decided he needed a fresh and younger crew of playmates. The entire harem were paid off handsomely and put out to pasture. Our lady settled in Cairo, where she has become famous as a reader of palms and tea leaves for tourists, mainly Americans."

Bosk took a sip of brandy. "It was in Cairo that she met a person who shall be nameless because he once was a member of our spook gang at Langley. This man was not there by accident. He had spent some time at the national archives during which, quite by accident, he came across a dossier about Feline. He quickly realized that here was something worth looking into with a view to making a lot of money. Then he made one hell of a big mistake. He knew that the late president's ex-wife was settled in Cairo. He went there and suggested that with her knowledge of what might have gone on at that time, they should join forces, produce a book and become very rich. She agreed, but when she demanded seventy-five percent of the earnings as her share, he said "no dice," and walked out. She in turn got mad and reported him to the agency."

"And you two had the job of reporting on all this?" Topps said, trying to control his amusement.

"Yes," Bosk replied. "And it damn near drove the boys at Langley up the wall. Now, I'll rest awhile and let Jason take over."

"Fine with me," Howell said. "Let's start with George Gilly. He and his family are still in Mooneyville Junction, where he now owns two garages, a general store, the movie theater and a lumber yard. He told me he was thinking of running for mayor of the place. Tom Drewer, who went to Mitzu with Gilly, retired in Istanbul, married a Turkish beauty and became a muslim. My old pal, Fireball Jansen, made four-star general and took over the SPCA from Admiral Lyman. Bixon, the idiot whose garbled message started this whole mess, left the Air Force. The last we heard, he was somewhere in Malaysia with IBM. One of these days we'll hear he's screwed up all their systems."

"Tell him about the enlisted crew on Mitzu." Bosk suggested.

"Oh, yes." Howell continued.

"The enlisted men on Mitzu all returned to civvy life when this fiasco ended. Staff Sergeant Morton went to Florida, met and married a rich widow with a forty-foot yacht. At last report he was on his way to Rio. The other three pooled their resources and now operate the largest Cadillac dealership in Las Vegas."

Topps furrowed a brow. "What about the chap Kleffen? Didn't he go somewhere in Africa, or was that Wilson?"

"No." Bosk shook his head. "That was Kleffen. We sent him to Brazzaville but he didn't last long there. We had to move him out after he made insulting remarks about their president's wife. Silly asshole. The lady in question had a habit of adorning herself with a cosmetic fragrance that Kleffen described as being similar to the odor of a rat long dead. That he said it at all is bad enough but that he said it at a diplomatic function to a man who was the lady's brother, well, that did him in for good. Frankly, I don't think anyone shed any tears over his departure. Did you, Jason?"

"Not me. By the way, John, we must not forget our troublesome boys, Dan Samson and Charles Quentin Stark. Or, for that matter, the great Sultopan."

"Certainly not," Bosk was at the bar refilling his snifter. "Dan Samson was pulled out of Istanbul by his network. Apparently he had become the most despised member of the foreign press corps in the entire Middle East. He disappeared for a while, then people reported seeing him in Washington wandering about talking to himself. One day he was stopped by a cop for jaywalking, whereupon Dan proclaimed in a loud voice that the government was producing a new type of chemical warfare item to be carried by small animals And used against the Soviets."

"I'll bet something hit the fan then," chuckled Topps.

"Oh, you bet it did. The police called the FBI and the CIA. Dan was hustled off for a few days of solitary confinement. As you can imagine, all this caused one hell of a stir at the Oval Office, at the UN, and the Kremlin. In due course, Dan was given a secluded place where he could spend his last days under strict medical supervision. The infamous Mr. Stark, the man who first mentioned the use of cats to Wilson, he spent several years in Laos. While there he wrote a rather brilliant but erotic report on the annual Laotian fertility festival. That report, so I hear, is still being passed around the department from one desk to another. Not so much for its factual or cultural value but for its entertainment.

"You know, gentlemen, this is absolutely fabulous," Topps said, wiping the laughter tears from his face. "It's like a comic opera."

"Last of all we have the Sultopan, who still rules supreme. He has threatened to throw out our embassy at least a dozen times, but as soon as he sees the speed with which our people start to pack, he recants the order. His withdrawals from the Western camp on Monday and his re-entry on the following Wednesday never fail to give diplomats plenty of confusing and amusing material for their reports back home."

"Quite a story, eh, Lucius?" said Howell.

"Absolutely fabulous, like a—" Topps began to laugh.

Howell began to laugh. John Bosk joined him and in seconds all three were laughing themselves silly.

The noise of the door opening caused them to stop laughing and turn. They saw Eve Bosk standing there, shaking her head.

"Don't worry dear, we're not drunk," said Bosk. "We're just recounting our various associations with the biggest screwup ever."

"Not Feline?"

"What else?" her husband answered.

"In that case, boys, have your fun." Eve Bosk barely made a sound closing the door.

EPILOGUE

The soothing sound of the autumn rain against the window of the foreign secretary's office had provided an undisturbed background for the task which the ministers of defense and agriculture had just completed.

Aston Williams and George Barker had finished their examination of the files on Operation Feline. They retied the green cords on the red folders carefully and replaced them on the foreign secretary's desk. In the manner characteristic of true professionals, each man had read through the account of the operation without so much as a word exchanged between them.

For these two robust gentlemen, it called for a pouring of two glasses of ice water and a frantic search of their pockets. It was Barker who first succeeded in locating his small silver pill box and who offered it to his colleague seated beside him on the couch.

"Here," said Barker, "better have one of mine. You look as if you need it."

"Thanks, George" Williams replied. "Mind if I take two?"

"Go ahead. After that mess, I'll take a couple myself."

"By the way, Aston, what did you think about the prime minister's report on his little run-ins with the president's wife on some of his phone calls to Washington. One would gather that she was a bit ambitious.

Williams nodded. "I know two people who knew her. One was an ambassador, the other an assistant secretary of state. My ambassador friend referred to her as a highly educated egotist who overestimated her ability." "What about the other chap?"

"Oh," Williams replied. "He was a bit more cold blooded about it. He said that she was a pain in the arse. Pity, really because she was a clever woman and a good looker too."

"Yes, she was," Barker said. "but I heard that he didn't pay much attention to her. It was well known that he had some popsies brought in for him up the back stairs of the great white palace. Funny when you think of it."

They were having a good laugh when Ruall, the foreign secretary, entered. "I take you find all this amusing," he said as he settled himself at his desk.

"Do I take it that you are now both well acquainted with our Feline venture? Because if you are, I had better give you the coup de grace."

Barker and Williams stared at him. "Good God, is there more?" Williams said.

"Alas, yes. But only a little." Ruall produced a small piece of paper. It bore the prime minister's familiar scrawl. He placed it on the desk as the two ministers rose from the couch and drew up chairs to face him.

"Bloody awful mess," said George Barker.

"And costly too," added Williams.

"Costly? Oh, yes. But I can assure you of one thing." said Ruall. "This is a mistake of which even the former administration is not proud. At the same time our own party dare not capitalize on their foolishness. No matter which party was in power, the prime minister fears, and well she might, that our national prestige will suffer, and the whole nation could become the butt of international ridicule. This is the one thing we do not want to dig up and had no intention of digging it up until last week."

"What's all this stuff about awards?" asked Barker.

Robert Ruall placed both hands flat on the desk as he leaned forward. "Last week the prime minister received notice from the Pagudan ambassador that the Sultopan wants to celebrate the twentieth anniversary of the Mitzu affair by presenting the Most Exalted Order of the Golden Elephants to six people who were responsible for saving Mitzu. Naturally she was a bit shaken, and so was I. We were vaguely aware about the operation but really knew none of the details. We do now."

"Great scot, what a mess," Williams murmured.

"As you can understand," Ruall said, "under the present political conditions and especially with the continual pressure being exerted by the Soviets on Paguda, neither we nor the Americans can afford to offend the Sultopan, Besides, we must not forget, the Americans have the agreement on the lease renewal for Mitzu coming up in the next three months."

George Barker released a deep sigh. "Certainly I agree, but I can't dig up any of the service chaps involved. The two field marshals, Ronnis Jones and Lucius Topps, are dead. Hugo Stagg has been bedridden in a veterans home for the last two years. Douglas Burrows is retired somewhere but quite doddery, so I hear, and the defense secretary of that time, Nick Farr, I don't know where he is."

"He's dead," Ruall said.

"Well, in that case, I know where the old bastard is. Who can we nominate for these awards? I'm going to have a hell of a time convincing any of my people in Defense to accept them."

"Don't worry," Ruall said, "they won't have to. The prime minister has made her decision on this matter and I agree with her." He leaned back in his chair and grinned sheepishly. "You, Aston, you, George, and I, and the chiefs of Army, Navy and Air Staffs will receive these awards from Mr. Loon, their ambassador at the Pagudan Embassy in Washington next Sunday week, twelve days from today."

"You're not serious," said Barker.

"Yes, gentlemen, I am." Ruall smiled. "This is what's going to happen. The awards will be publicized in accordance with a press release prepared by the prime minister's public information officer, in agreement, of course, with the Pagudan government. As far as the public is concerned, these awards are being made for special services in aid rendered to Paguda. So, apart from the brief press release and the usual photographs, that will end the matter."

"Thank God for that," said Williams, wiping his face with his over-sized handkerchief.

"Not so fast," said Ruall. "It will end the matter except for one thing."

"I knew there would be a catch in it," said Barker.

"Well, you're quite right. You may recall that just before the opposition was voted out, aid to Paguda was cut solely for the purpose of hiding the deficit caused by the extra amounts the operation cost us. While we have increased aid slightly over the years, it is still meager."

"If I had my way," said Barker, "I'd cut them to nothing."

"Same here," Williams agreed.

"I know, gentlemen, but as the prime minister sees it, when news of these awards hits the papers, some damn fools in parliament are going to ask questions. They may want to know what these special services are. So, my friends, Paguda is going to get some aid it never expected, and it's going to get it within the next eight days to justify these awards. Here are the prime minister's orders. Very soon a mission of economic aid to Paguda will be set up in Paguda. Not a full office, just on a token scale; about four people, a chargé, a junior officer and two clerks. Something like that, no more. Aston, your ministry will provide three or perhaps four metric tons of grain of some sort to get the whole thing started. Also, a few tons of powdered milk, eggs and cheese. I understand you also have about twenty-eight thousand boxes of outdated emergency rations in our reserve warehouses which we have to replace anyway with a fresh batch. You can have those as well.

"What? Did you say outdated rations?" asked Williams.

"Yes, but I am sure they are still quite edible. I was told they are still good for another few months. If I know the Pagudans, they'll finish them off long before that. I'm sure they won't complain.

To the other two men Ruall did not sound completely sure.

"I'll get on this right away," said Williams.

"Now, George, for your part in this, your task is to provide Paguda with some defense materials from our surplus stocks.

You told me the Navy could get some PT boats out of mothballs. Give them six of those. What else do you have to spare?"

George Barker scratched his head as he glanced through his lists. "How about some barbed wire? I can give them four thousand rolls of that, also eighteen jeeps with trailers, about five hundred each of the World War II steel helmets and gas masks and, let's see...oh, yes, six hundred Lee Enfield bolt action rifles. I can throw them in. Mind you, I don't think we have any 303 ammunition for them. We don't make it anymore. Does that matter?"

"Never mind about the ammunition. Leave that to the Americans. I'm pretty sure the Americans will find some way of getting it for them. They're pretty generous about that sort of thing, especially now with the lease agreement for the Mitzu airstrip coming up."

"What about the RAF?" said Barker.

"The RAF will provide them with any six light aircraft it can scrape up, and if you have a few old choppers, give them those too, plus a small amount of spare parts. Now, I want all these items in Pagudan hands before the investiture, is that clear? Oh, one more thing, we will give the Pagudan armed forces one vacancy at the Staff College starting next year, and that's it." Ruall gave a deep breath of relief.

"Well, we'd better get going on this," said Barker, rising to his feet.

"Yes, no time to lose." said Williams.

"All right then, let me know when the items are on the way. Let's hope that will be the end of it."

"By the way," Barker said. "How are the Americans handling their part of this business?"

"Strange you should ask," replied Ruall. "They're not involved in any of this. The prime minister phoned their president yesterday just to check how they were going to participate in the so-called anniversary. Their president denied any knowledge of it. At that point, our dear lady called their secretary of state fearing that she was on touchy ground. She obviously was. The secretary of state, on being told of the pagudan offer, reacted very strangely. He said he'd never heard of Mitzu. So she dropped the matter. It seems that no one in the U.S. wants to be reminded of Mitzu. So be it."

"Perhaps they haven't been offered any of these gorgeous awards. Who knows?" Barker chuckled.

"Strange fellows, these cousins of ours across the pond." Williams said. "What do you make of it? We do them one hell of a big favor, they bugger it up and now they won't talk to us. The chap was was president then is dead, isn't he? What about his wife, is she gone too?"

He died, bit of a scandal about it. Apparently he had been carrying on with this one lady for years but as far as I know the wife is still around. I read somewhere that her desert prince cleaned out his harem when he decided he needed younger stock. He paid them all off and she settled in Cairo—maybe it was Damascus or Baghdad. Anyway, why worry? You two have work to do."

As there was not much else the two ministers could say to that, they made their exit.

Outside in the corridor Aston Williams took his colleague's arm gently as they stepped off together toward their own offices.

"You know, George," said Williams quietly.

"What, Aston?"

"I was thinking," said Williams.

"So was I, Aston," said George Barker. "So was I."

They continued down the long carpeted corridor in what might well be termed as confused silence.

FINIS

Printed in the United States
4051

9 780759 662667